A PROMISE IN BLOOD

The braves began to cut Count Sergei free . . .

The young nobleman smiled cunningly as he asked the general, "Is it over, then? Am I truly free and under the protection of the United States Army?"

"Of course you are, Count Sergei."

The Russian nodded slyly as he shot a sidelong glance at Satangkai, leaning forward to accept the notes from the paymaster. Then he swung a length of rawhide he'd been saving for the chance and caught the chief right across the eyes with a vicious slash!

Satangkai reeled from the blow and almost fell as his pony shied and danced back from another attempted blow. A red streak across his face half-blinded Satangkai with blood as one of his braves screamed out, "Ah-ta-nag-hree!" and threw his lance almost without thought!

The lance tip took Count Sergei over the heart and passed on through, leaving him transfixed and dead even before he could slide from his saddle pad with a bewildered expression on his haughty face.

Satangkai, raging with pain and anger, flung the money in a great green cloud at the white men and roared out, "So be it! Hear me, White Eagle! Tell your people this is war and that I think this is a good day to die!"

METRO-GOLDWYN-MAYER TELEVISION

presents

HOW THE WEST WAS WON

starring The Family Macahan

JAMES ARNESS
as
Zeb

BRUCE BOXLEITNER
as
Luke

FIONNULA FLANAGAN
as
Molly Culhane

KATHRYN HOLCOMB
as
Laura

WILLIAM KIRBY CULLEN
as
Josh

VICKI SCHRECK
as
Jessie

Executive Producer: John Mantley

Producer: John G. Stephens

Novelization by Lou Cameron

Based on stories and teleplays by:

Calvin Clements	John Mantley
Colley Cibber	Katharyn Michaelian
Howard Fast	Jack Miller
William Kelley	Earl W. Wallace

Directed by Bernard McEveety
Vincent McEveety

How the West Was Won

LOU CAMERON

Based on stories and teleplays by
Calvin Clements
Colley Cibber
Howard Fast
William Kelley
John Mantley
Katharyn Michaelian
Jack Miller
Earl W. Wallace

BALLANTINE BOOKS · NEW YORK

Library of Congress Catalog Card Number: 77-25159

ISBN 0-345-27401-6

Manufactured in the United States of America

First Edition: January 1978

CHAPTER 1

A trail-weary Zeb Macahan rode slumped in the saddle as he led his pack pony into Fort Sully, the sun at his back. Yet he seemed taller than most men in any saddle as the sentry in the lookout tower spotted his distant outline and called down, "Scout coming in from the west!"

There was nothing wrong with the soldier's eyesight. Zeb Macahan was *big*. Had he been in the habit of standing straight, he'd have stood nearly seven feet tall in his boots. He seldom bothered to try. Thirty-odd years of survival west of the Big Muddy had left Zeb sort of bent out of shape, and too many men, red and white, had taken a shot at that massive gray head for Zeb to be all that interested in carrying it any higher than he had to.

Not many of the men who'd tried to kill him were still around these days. The big man moved, when he had to, with the deceptive clumsy grace of a grizzly. When he didn't have to, Zeb moved slow, and this seemed one of those rare happy times. He didn't really have anything all that important to report, and he intended, after reassuring the soldier boys about their hair, to have a drink, a bath, and a good night's sleep, in that order. The gate was swinging open and faces were peering over the stockade at him now. He supposed he was a mite late reporting in, and Fort Sully was on the prod.

Zeb supposed the army had a right to feel uneasy this summer. The treaty signed after the Fetterman Massacre had been the army's reason for building the little outpost. Opinion in Washington seemed divided on whether the soldiers were sent here to keep whites out of the Black Hills or to keep the Dakota in. The treaty guaranteed the remnants of the once-mighty Sioux Nation full title to the Black Hills, and both sides had promised not to cross the invisible line Fort Sully guarded, rather weakly. The trouble was that some ornery jaspers, red as well as white, hadn't thought so much of the treaty. Renegades on both side had sure made things interesting hereabouts of late.

Zeb noticed there were two flags fluttering from the parade ground staff this afternoon, and wondered idly what that meant. A strange, mostly white-and-blue banner had been hoisted just below the Stars and Stripes. It wasn't British. It wasn't Mexican. What in thunder was it? Nobody else had troops west of the Missouri.

As Zeb reached the gate, another surprise stared down at him from the parapet. He reined in and touched the brim of his battered hat to an extraordinarily beautiful young woman in an expensive, low-cut dress. The girl returned Zeb's salute with a raised thin-stemmed glass. In her other hand she seemed to be holding a bottle of . . . champagne?

By thunder, it purely looked like some sort of fancy Frenchified liquor, and that dress belonged on a window dummy no farther west than St. Louis. Zeb's gunmetal-gray eyes were bemused, but he betrayed no obvious surprise on his lived-in features. He'd seen too much in his time and powwowed with too many Indians to let much show on his face, but, next to the Grand Canyon and the Great Salt Lake, he couldn't remember seeing anything as out of place out here in recent memory.

With a friendly nod to the outlandish beauty on the parapet, Zeb rode on in and turned his ponies over to the hostler, who told him the C.O. wanted to see him on the double. That at least was no surprise.

Major Drake was a pure caution for wanting to see folks on the double.

On foot, Zeb Macahan moved with an odd sideways swiftness. He'd healed a few broken bones in the saddle in his time, and while he could cover ground afoot with surprising speed, he never seemed comfortable doing it.

As he limped toward the orderly room the adjutant, Captain MacAllister, intercepted him to blurt, "Good Lord, Zeb, where have you been?"

Zeb shrugged and said, "Doin' what I was sent out to do. Ain't that a Russian flag up there?"

"Yes, it is. I'm surprised you recognized it."

"Didn't, right off. Then I remembered the time I fooled around with the Russians up at Fort Ross, afore we run 'em out of California. Must have been back in the forties. What are they doin' here in the Dakota Territories?"

"The major will explain it to you. He wants to talk to you right away."

"That's what they keep tellin' me. What's goin' on here, Mac? When I rode in there was this hell of a good-lookin' gal smilin' down at me with a bottle of champagne and a dress she oughtta be ashamed of. What in thunder are you boys runnin' here, a bawdy-house?"

MacAllister sighed and waved a hand toward the parade ground. "Look for yourself, Zeb. It's a little confusing to me, too."

Zeb stepped out from the angle formed by the postern and stables to get a fuller view of the parade ground, and this time he allowed his surprise to show as he came to a dead halt and simply stared in wonder.

The interior of the compound had been transformed into a grotesque setting for some Russian opera. An enormous striped canopy had been set up on the parade ground. Under it stretched a long table draped in damask linen and laden with delicacies. There were brass samovars, bowls of fruit, buckets of iced champagne, silver tureens of caviar, bowls of sour cream, and piles of pastries that looked too pretty to eat. A chef in full uniform presided over the edibles, and a corporal's squad of Cossacks just as tall as Zeb lounged on their sword hilts in flamboyant full regalia. Liveried servants puttered back and forth with refreshments, and on a sort of improvised throne at the head of the table sat an imposing figure flanked by courtesans and lackies.

Zeb shook his head and muttered, "I'll bite. Who is it, the Czar of Russia or just the Pope?"

MacAllistar explained, "It's the Royal Hunting Expedition of His Highness, the Grand Duke Dimitri Romanov. The big kazoo himself is the one getting all the attention. The younger hairpin in the gorgeous uniform in his nephew, Count Sergei of Kiev. Watch out for him, he's a mean son of a bitch."

Almost as if he'd heard them, Count Sergei looked up suddenly from the glass he was sipping and fixed Zeb and the American officer with a look of bored contempt. Zeb nodded to the young man, but the count turned away with a faint sneer, as if he'd just noticed a crack in the plaster of a second-rate hotel he'd been forced to spend a tedious night in. He was obviously not a young man who bothered with peasants.

Zeb grinned and swept his eyes over the rest of the outfit, which filled in more than half of the compound. The heavyset grand duke seemed to travel in style. He had a small city of silk tents set up for his servants and followers. Zeb pointed with his chin at a train of what looked like gilded circus wagons, dominated by a decorated coach inlaid with ivory and onyx panels, and marveled, "Good God, did they come all the way out here in that gypsy caravan?"

MacAllister said, "They built a road along the way. We're having a time getting used to this outfit, too. The major's still waiting."

But Zeb didn't move, for he'd spotted the expensively gowned young woman who'd nodded to him from the parapet as he was riding in. As she joined the men at the head of the table she nodded once again in Zeb's direction. Count Sergei got gallantly to his feet as she waved to Zeb. She said to the count, in French, "Do you see that big American over there? I'll bet he's the scout we've been waiting for all this time."

Sergei shot Zeb another bored look and said, "I suppose you're right. I must say, he looks as if he was raised in a hollow tree."

"I think he's magnificent. Under that wool and buckskin he is all man!" Again she raised her glass in a half-mocking toast to Zeb.

Zeb nodded back with a bemused smile. He asked MacAllister, "Why are they jawin' in French instead of Russian?" The adjutant explained, "The Russian court speaks French because they're too grand to speak anything else. Let's go."

"Hold on a minute. I savvy French, some. Likely they don't know that."

Count Sergei, oblivious of the tall scout, was saying, "Valerie, my dear, your basic instincts are most fatiguing, and, shall we say, base indeed?"

The girl flushed, but recovered with a smile to quip, "Why, Your Highness, I thought it was my baser instincts you found so appealing!"

Sergei laughed and said to the others, "The more we try to polish Valerie the more her peasant background shows through, *non?*"

The girl's smile remained in place, although strained, and Zeb sighed and muttered, "I think I've got just time enough to hit that dude one good lick afore reportin' in, Mac."

But the adjutant insisted, "Sorry to spoil your fun, but the major's waiting. That's an *order*, Zeb."

The scout shook his head, muttered, "Shucks, that's a pity, ain't it?" and followed the younger officer.

At the table, Count Sergei turned from the girl he'd insulted and smiled fawningly on his uncle, the grand duke, observing, "Well, Your Highness, since they seem to have found their unwashed scout for us, our wait appears about over."

The duke grunted. "It's about time. This American

wilderness does have a certain visual grandeur, but I'm perishing from the heat and beginning to feel a certain ennui."

He reached for a bowl of out-of-season strawberries, crushed a single berry between his fingers, and licked them before shooting a sardonic glance at Valerie's retreating back. "By the way, dear nephew, if you will persist in keeping yourself amused with that little slum girl, I do so wish you'd do your bickering in private. Some few of my cossacks speak French, and we must set an example for the lower classes, *hein?*"

Meanwhile, Zeb and the adjutant had reached the orderly room, where Major Drake stood up to shake Zeb's hand and exclaim, "Zeb! I can't tell you how glad I am to see you, but we expected you last week. What on earth kept you out there so long this time?"

Zeb shrugged and said, "Well, you asked me to find out what the Indians was up to. I sort of poked around a mite. I needed some new moccasins, and there's this little Cheyenne gal I know who does real neat work. I talked to her folks some, and none of the Sioux allies seem to be on the prod right now. To make sure, I went on a hunt with some Crooked Lances I know, and all they seemed interested in killin' was buffalo, so I moseyed on back. You never said I was to hurry."

"There wasn't any hurry when you left. But you hadn't been gone more than two days before I got a message from Washington about those Russians out there."

"Yeah, I saw 'em just now. I thought at first they was a traveling circus."

"Well, they're not. The big gun, Grand Duke Dimitri, is the kid brother to the Czar of All the Russias, no less. When they told me he was coming out here on a royal hunting expedition, I expected three or four people. He seems to have brought his whole court with him. You know about the Russian claims on Alaska don't you?"

"Sure. But I thought we bought Alaska offen the

Czar fair and square. They ain't asking for it back, are they?"

"Not if Washington can help it. My instructions are to make Grand Duke Dimitri feel at home. Washington's given him carte blanche, and I've orders to furnish him with the best available guide."

"Guide?"

"That's you, Zeb. My other orders are to see to their safety, and I don't know another man out here who knows more about keeping a white man's hair in place than yourself. I've had one hell of a time making them wait for you. I gather the grand duke's not used to waiting all that much. But you're here now, so we can get the show on the road at last."

Zeb's face was blank, but his tone was cautious as he asked, "Just where am I supposed to take these folks, Major?"

Drake shot a worried glance at MacAllister, who managed to be looking somewhere else at the moment. Major Drake had been treated kindly by the fortunes of a military career—up to now. He'd graduated from the Point just early enough to be given a company command during the Civil War and just late enough to keep from getting killed in the bloody holocaust back east. He'd hung on to his rank after the war and been as lucky with the Indians as he'd been with Johnny Reb. Until just now, he'd sort of gotten used to having things his own way. There was something in the set of the big civilian scout's jaw that told Drake his luck was about to run out.

He said, "Look, Zeb, I know you don't take these blue-blooded dudes too serious, but this is really important. Our orders are to send His Highness home a happy man."

"I got that part. You said it was a hunting expedition. Where are they headed and what do they aim to hunt?"

"They, ah, want to hunt buffalo."

Zeb scowled darkly.

Drake insisted, "That's what the State Department

invited them to hunt, Zeb. They don't have buffalo in Russia, and—"

"They don't have Dakota in Russia, either. Don't them jaspers in the State Department know the free herds have been shot to bits? There ain't enough buffalo left outside the Black Hills to bother lookin' for, and . . . Judas Priest! You'd best not be thinkin' what I think you're thinkin'!"

"Listen, Zeb. This man's army's been bled dry by the Civil War and the economies since. The goddamned Czar's been rattling his saber over a second reading of the deed to Alaska, and we just can't afford trouble with Russia or anybody else right now."

"You let them damn-fool dudes cross the treaty lines into Dakota hunting grounds and you'll have trouble all right. You'll have the Dakota Confederacy boiling outten them Black Hills in bonnets and paint!"

"Look, nobody said anything about breaking the treaty with the Sioux Nation."

"The hell they didn't! The south herd's been shot away by the hide skinners. Damn near every buffalo north of the U.P. tracks will be up in the Black Hills at this time of the big dry. If those dudes mean to kill buffalo one, they'll have to do it on Indian land. What in thunder's wrong with them fools in Washington? Don't you remember the big flap they got into when Red Cloud wiped out Fetterman's whole command just a few summers back?"

"Of course I remember. We've been keeping peace between the Sioux and the settlers ever since, and I know—"

"You don't know beans, Major! In the first place, the folks you keep calling Sioux are really Dakotas. In the second place, your so-called Sioux Nation ain't just the Oglala, Yankton, Santee, and such. The Dakota Confederacy includes the Cheyenne, Arapaho, Blackfoot, and just about ever' other fed-up Indian in these parts!"

"Come on, Zeb. I don't need another of your lectures on Indian lore. I've heard you call them Sioux, more than once."

"That's 'cause I get tired tryin' to explain things to tenderfoot cavalry, Major. It don't make me no never mind if Washington calls 'em Sioux or Dakota or Zulus. I'm just tired as hell of seein' folks stretched out with their hair peeled off!"

"Zeb, for God's sake, I agree with you! I'm not aking you to lead the grand duke's party into the Black Hills. I just want you to ride out a few miles to the south, or east, or somewheres, and help them gather a few trophies."

"What does a grand duke call a few trophies?"

"I don't know. Not more than a hundred head or so."

"A couple of hundred? A couple of hundred *buffalo?* Major, I don't know a damned thing about international relations, but if Uncle Sam wants a war, he don't have to worry about having one with Russia! I don't know if the Czar can whup us or not, but what I do know is that a lot of Indians we've diddled out of their hunting grounds are starving right now because the rations and supplies the government keeps promising 'em never seem to show up. We've got the finest mounted soldiers on this continent penned up in the black Hills with the last scattered herds of what we've left of the buffalo, and now you want me to lead a party of dudes in to shoot up the little meat they just might get through next winter on. You must have been drinkin' a lot of that French champagne of the old duke's!"

"I've been assured by the Indian Agency that supplies are on the way, Zeb. In the meanwhile, for heaven's sake, be practical!"

Zeb's eyes narrowed as he snapped, "All right, Major. Practical! In the past few years since the war every market hunter in America and a lot of dudes who never fired a gun afore have been out killin' buffalo for hides, tongues, and the hell of it! I've seen dudes shoot buffalo from the platforms of a moving railroad train as they left the meat to the buzzards. I've heard men boast of killin' three or four hundred in a day without they gave me reason why they done it. There ain't enough of the poor critters left for market hunters like Bill Cody to bother with, but ever' time one of your soldier boys rides off post for a look-see he shoots anything and ever'thing he sees out there. I'll allow they ain't shot many buffalo of late. I'll bet you my last bean there ain't a buffalo within fifty miles of this fort."

MacAllister, unable to restrain himself, cut in with "You mean this side of the treaty line."

It was a statement, not a question, so there it was, like a raw gobbet of spit between Zeb and the major, quivering wetly on his desk. Drake shot his junior officer a murderous look as he tried to think of a nicer way of putting it. But there wasn't. All three of them knew it.

Drake cleared his throat and said softly, "I have my orders. The grand duke's not to return east without his trophy heads."

Zeb's voice was soft too, but it was the softness of a distant thunderstorm as he said flatly, "Major, in the April of *this year* the U.S. Government signed a ratification of their treaty with Red Cloud and the Dakota Confederacy. Your so-called Sioux *won* the last round when they wiped out Fetterman's whole command. Red Cloud agreed to retreat into the Black Hills for only two reasons. One is that his medicine man, Sitting Bull, told him the Black Hills are the sacred home of Wakan Tonka—"

"Wakan Tonka?"

"The Great Spirit. The Dakotas say Wakan Tonka made the Black Hills afore he got around to makin' the rest of the world. But let's not jaw about religion. That part's only half of it. Aside from bein' the sacred huntin' grounds of the Dakotas, the Black Hills have been guaranteed forever to 'em by the Great White Father. The Dakotas and their allies have been promised no white man will ever set foot in their Black

Hills. It's been promised in black-and-white. I've read the treaty myself."

"Come on, Zeb, I'm not suggesting we break any treaty. But the Black Hills aren't fenced. I'm sure no buffalo ever read any treaty. Maybe if you took them sort of, well, along the treaty line, you might find a herd that had wandered out onto open range or . . . Damn it, Zeb, this hunting trip is the State Department's number-one priority!"

The big scout shook his head and snapped, "To hell with your priorities. Send them Russians home and tell 'em if they want a fight over Alaska or anything else we'll kick their hindquarters from here to breakfast. If you want me to fight Russians for you, I'll be pleased as punch to start this very afternoon, but I'll be double damned if I'll declare war on any Indian just to please a fancied-up dude who eats fish aigs for lunch!"

"Zeb, you're an employee of the War Department, too."

"I just quit. I don't aim to shoot no buffalo just for the hell of it, and I don't aim to watch nobody gettin' his hair lifted just for bein' stupid as well as furrin."

As he turned on his heel, Drake rasped, "Where do you think you're going, damn it!"

Zeb said, "I'm off to the high country, Major. And I'm going' to do the best I can to keep my hair. If I can, I aim to forget all about what's goin' on down here, but you'll likely have you a war we'll feel all the way over the front ranges."

He went out and slammed the door behind him as Drake leaped to his feet. MacAllister tried to say, "It's no use, Harry." But Drake ran after the mutinous scout and yelled after him from the orderly-room porch as Zeb reached the parade ground.

The assembled Russians and every soldier within earshot turned to stare as Drake thundered, "Macahan, I order you to come back here this instant!"

By this time Zeb had reached his tethered pony and

was unhitching it. He turned toward the red-faced officer warily and shook his head as he called back, "I'm not one of your soldier boys, Drake. You can't order me to do anything, and if you could, I'd still tell you to go to blazes afore I'd commit suicide."

"Damn you, Macahan! You're still on the army payroll as a scout!"

"Nope. Like I told you, I just went off."

Zeb started to mount, but the dapper Count Sergei had approached him unnoticed, and the Russian put a hand on Zeb's arm as he said, "One moment, my good fellow. You are the guide we have been waiting for these five long days?"

Zeb frowned down at the count, trying to decide whether to just brush him off like a fly or maybe spit in his eye and drown him. Sergei was oblivious of the American's size and scowl as he insisted, "You're being very tiresome, my good fellow. If it's a matter of more money, name your price."

Zeb stared silently, wondering how any dude in such a fancy shirt had made it this far west. The count smiled contemptuously as he continued, "Not money? Well, every man has his price. Join us for a moment at the banquet. I'm sure you'll find something to your liking there."

Zeb's voice was curiously gentle as he said, "Sonny, take your hand off my arm afore you lose it. I got me a long ride ahead of me."

"Ah! I know how it is with you mountain men after long days and nights on the trail. What are you looking for? Something to drink, a woman? We have both in ample supply. Come, join the party like a good fellow."

Zeb glanced down at the pale white hand on his buckskin sleeve. Then he repeated, "Let go my arm, I don't aim to say it again."

Count Sergei was more puzzled than afraid as he slowly released his grip on the scout's sleeve. He frowned after Zeb's retreating form as the big scout led his pony toward the gate. Then he shrugged and turned back to rejoin the other Russians. The grand duke asked, "What was that all about?" and Sergei said, "I'm sure I don't know. These American peasants are amazingly obtuse."

Major Drake came over to the table, flushed and flustered, to blurt, "I'm desperately sorry, Your Highnesses. Macahan's an excellent scout but, as you see, a bit mad. I give you my word, I'll find another just as good."

The grand duke didn't look at Drake. Sergei turned enough to favor the major with about as much recognition as he might have offered a toad as he asked sullenly, "Indeed? And how long shall we have to wait this time?"

"A few days at the most, Your Higness. Fortunately we have a telegraph line tied in with Regimental Command, and I'll send the request at once."

"I see, and can you tell me, then, why we were kept waiting for this madman Macahan all this time?"

"Well, he is a very good scout, Your Highness."

"No doubt. Very well, send for another guide and make certain he gets here quickly. While you're at it, wire for some more champagne. This whole thirsty business is most fatiguing."

Drake blinked in surprise and asked, "Champagne, Your Highness? I doubt if there's so much as a bottle this side of St. Louis, or maybe Denver."

"Then order it from either place and remember we drink nothing but Mumm's, *sec*. How far is this St. Louis village?"

"About eight hundred miles, Your Highness."

"Indeed? This does present a problem, doesn't it?"

Turning to his uncle, Count Sergei explained in French, "This lout tells me there may be a problem with the refreshments after all. With your permission, I'll order the chef not to serve our finer stocks to your bodyguard. If worst comes to worst, we may have to serve the girls we brought along mere sherry, but they are no doubt used to roughing it."

The grand duke shook his head and said, "My Cossacks eat and drink as well as I, Sergei. By the time you reach my age you may know the value of loyal retainers. How low are our supplies, anyway?"

"Oh, heavens, there's enough champagne and caviar for another month if we restrict it to those among us of noble birth."

"All right. Noblemen and Cossacks eat like gentlemen for another two weeks. By then we should have shot our silly buffalo and returned to civilization. Did you tell that American officer I'm fatigued with waiting?"

"But of course, Your Highness. He says he has another scout on the way from some other fort."

"Eh, *bien,* in that case we shall wait another day. If these fools keep us waiting longer I intend to push on without a guide. Do you know the way to these Black Hills they keep talking about, Sergei?"

"But of course, Your Highness. They lie just to the north. Valerie and I were going to ride over to them the other day, but there's some tedious business with an Indian boundary of some sort."

"Bah! Since when is the House of Romanov bound by a treaty some American made with some unwashed savage? We shall have our hunt this weekend, with or without an American guide."

CHAPTER 2

Luke Macahan was the grizzled Zeb Macahan's nephew. He was looking for his uncle that afternoon as he rode the high country. But finding Uncle Zeb could be a problem at the best of times. The older Macahan moved like spit on a hot stove, and everywhere Luke asked his uncle had been seen headed somewhere else. Luke's presence in the high country was occasioned more by knowing Uncle Zeb wasn't in any town in the territory and that his nephew knew he liked to range near timberline when he had a worry to chew on. Luke didn't see how Uncle Zeb could have learned the bad news from home, but if he had, it'd have him feeling poorly. Uncle Zeb had always cottoned to Mom as strong as a Christian brother-in-law was allowed to, and her death had been an ugly one. Yep, if Uncle Zeb knew, he'd be up here in the high country, working off the hurt in his heart against the granite rocks and doing his crying where nobody but the mountain hawks could see him.

Luke rode alone on a tired pony. The air was thin and the grazing was dry, and Luke was trying to remember the last square meal he'd had his ownself. Luke was young and half the hunter his uncle was, but hunger has a way of sharpening even a boy's senses. So when Luke spotted the flash in the brush, downslope, he reined in and slid out of the saddle slick as a cat, drawing his saddle gun from its boot and silently slipping a round into its firing chamber. It had only been a blur of pale movement, but Luke knew the flash of a mule deer's rump when he saw it. The critter had flashed and moved off down the mountain at a slow trot. Luke knew old muley deer didn't trot when he really had his wind up. Likely the deer had half sensed him and the pony and moseyed off a mite to stop and test the wind.

Luke remained frozen in place near his pony. The pony was trained to remain motionless with its reins on the ground, and the smell of horse flesh wouldn't spook the deer. Luke wet a finger and held it up. The slight breeze was moving upslope, toward him. The deer could snort and sniff all it liked. So long as it stayed put.

Luke stepped away from the pony, carbine at port, searching the brush with his eyes. The slope was steep and a boot heel slipped on the talus, sending a pebble rolling with a terrible clatter.

And there it was! The deer had raised its head to look for the source of the sound. It saw Luke as Luke saw it, swung the carbine up, and fired.

He missed. He knew he'd missed as soon as he saw the way the deer took off down the slope. Angry with himself, Luke ran a few steps after his quarry, hoping against hope to have at least a distant shot as it topped the next rise.

And then his boot heel betrayed him a second time and Luke fell backward, starting to slide down the mountain on the seat of his pants. He cursed and grabbed for a branch as it whizzed past, missing that, too. Swearing more in disgust than out of fright, Luke slid on down the ever-steepening slope and crashed through a wall of aspen seedlings. He saw he'd reached the bottom of the little ravine, and dug his heels in to check his undignified progress. His booted feet slammed against the sandy bottom, something snapped with a metallic finality, and Luke screamed in agony. He slid to the bottom of the slope in an awkward sprawl. Without looking, he knew that a bone in his right leg was broken.

He tried to move, felt another sharp pang, and gritted his teeth so as not to cry out again as he gingerly raised his head from the dust and leaf litter to identify what had him by the leg.

It was a bear trap. A huge single-spring grizzly getter with steel jaws as wide, and as sharp, as a man-eating shark. Some silly son of a bitch had set the trap down here in the ravine, and another silly son of a bitch named Macahan had stuck his fool foot in it!

Carefully, Luke sat up and reached for the jaws holding his shattered shin by the bleeding bones. He took a jaw in each hand and tried to pry them open. They wouldn't budge. It would take a strong man and a lever to wedge those jaws apart.

Trying not to move his leg in the trap's deadly grip, Luke reached across it for the chain it was attached to. Maybe if he could drag himself back up to the trail . . . Then he pulled the last slack out of the heavy chain and saw, with a groan, that it was spiked solidly to a tree trunk. The man who'd set this trap had been purely out for grizzly, and no human hands were about to draw a spike meant to hold a half-ton bear.

Grimacing in pain and growing desperation, young Luke looked around for his carbine. By great good luck, the saddle gun had followed him down the slope and was resting nearby. It cost him another pang of agony to reach that far, but he managed after what seemed a million years to get the gun and sit back up.

Taking careful aim at the spike holding the chain to the tree, Luke fired. He didn't fire at the spike, of course. He fired at the gnarled wood holding it. The first bullet tore some splinters away near the spike, but the trapper had chosen well. The damned spike was driven into the iron hard knot of a fallen limb. Luke knew it was nearly useless to try to dig the spike out with the limited ammunition he had, but he couldn't think of another blessed thing to try, so he fired again.

By the time he'd emptied his carbine into the tree, he'd gouged out a handful of hardwood. He still had his sidearm, so, drawing the old Colt, he started pecking at the tree with its smaller bullets. He didn't seem to be getting anywhere, but he fired until the pistol, too, was empty.

It wasn't until he slumped back, exhausted with pain and frustration, that Luke considered just how foolish he'd been. He was caught in a bear trap, which meant there were bears, and he looked to be spending the next few nights here, bleeding, alone, and unarmed.

Wait a minute. He still had some cartridges in his gun belt, didn't he? It was hard to think straight with a right leg half torn off, and there were pretty little stars swimming around in front of his eyes.

Luke lay back and closed his eyes, trying to think

what Uncle Zeb would have done. That wasn't much
help, he told himself wryly. Uncle Zeb hardly figured
to go sticking his foot in no bear trap!

As the hurt, frightened boy fought to remain conscious, he seemed to be hearing voices. Luke groaned
and muttered, "Oh no, first stars in front of my eyes
and now voices! I'm in real good shape, ain't I?"

"Hey!" the mysterious voice repeated. "You done
shootin' down there, friend?"

"Help!" called Luke. "I'm caught in a trap down
here, and I think my leg's broke!"

"Well, you just don't shoot no more and I'll have
me a look-see."

Another million years went by before Luke spied
a gnomelike figure moving gingerly down the wall of
the ravine. He seemed to be a white man, but he was
about the most busted-up and tattered white man
Luke had ever seen. As he reached bottom, Luke
saw he walked like a crab and something like a
man with a godawful limp. The outlandish little man
peered uncertainly at the trapped boy and asked, "All
right, who are ye?"

"I'm Luke Macahan. I'm caught in a bear trap!"

"Well, hell, of course you are. I already knowed
that. I asked who you was, is all. No need to be long-
winded with a man."

"Could you hurry it up, mister. I'm hurt bad!"

"Well, maybe you are and maybe you ain't. You
try any tricks on me, boy, and you won't be hurt,
you'll be daid!"

The old trapper came a few paces nearer, holding
his shotgun on Luke as he sized the situation up.
Then he cackled madly and said, "You purely stepped
in it for sure, boy. Next time look where you're going'!"

"It's not funny. I told you, I think my leg's broke!"

"'Course it's broke. What did you expect? That's
a b'ar trap, son!"

Putting his gun aside, the old man came over to
hunker down by Luke's side. "That's one ornery trap,
son. Biggest damn trap I ever seen. Don't know as I

can help or not. This chile ain't as husky as he was in the shinin' days. Come to think on it, I don't know as I ever was strong enough for a trap like this'n. Looks like a job for the two of us."

He stood up, stepped over to a fallen tree, and snapped off a limb with some effort. He came back and handed it to Luke. "You'll have to do your share, boy. Do I git her open a mite, you shove that stick in hard as you can, savvy?"

Luke nodded weakly, and the old man dropped to a seat, placing the heel of his boot against one jaw of the trap as he grasped the other in both callused hands. He tugged hard, and as Luke felt an agonizing movement, he shoved the limb between the jaws near the hinge. The old man paused to catch his breath as he gasped, "We'll have to do better'n that, boy, or you're here for the winter!"

Luke's would-be rescuer tried a second time, gritting his teeth as he mused, "It was that McQuiston gang put this hyar, or widder women ain't willin'!"

Luke gasped, "What?" and the old man snapped, "Never mind! Shove the damn stick!"

This time there was a lessening of the pressure, but Luke screamed in pain as his boot filled with blood. The old man said soothingly, "Good sign, boy. When it hurts like that it means you still got blood runnin'."

"Are you sure it's broke?"

"Course it's broke. An' hold still or you'll have nothin' to show for it but a bootful of laig!"

He set himself again and added, "This chile's got the leverage on the son of a bitch now. I mind I can part her a few more inches. When I give the word, you pull your fool laig out. Mind you pull her out by the boot top, savvy?"

Luke nodded weakly and grasped the top of his boot in both hands. As the old man snapped, "Now!" he pulled his injured leg free. The old man let go. The jaws snapped shut and severed the wedging stick as if it had been a candlestick. Luke's rescuer cackled, "Hahh! Tried to take this chile's fingers, didn't you,

you old bastard? You see the way he chewed that poor stick, boy? Do Jesus, you're lucky you still got a laig at all!"

Luke didn't answer. The old man stared down at his unconscious form for a time, gingerly examined the leg, and muttered, "This here younger generation ain't got much sand in its craw, has it. I'd best git you to the cabin, boy, 'fore you git both feet in the grave!"

Standing up, he whistled loudly and called out, "Horse? Where in hell are you? Come on down hyar, old son, we need some help with this fool kid!"

A few hours later Luke began to wonder where he was and who in thunder was singing so loud and so badly. He seemed to be tied to something that moved, and after a while he decided it might be a saddle. Some damned way he'd gotten out of that trap and aboard a bronc. This day had purely turned out confusing.

The cracked reedy voice tormented Luke with another chorus:

> Bringing in the sheaves!
> Bringing in the sheaves!
> We shall come rejoicing!
> Bringing in the sheaves!

Luke groaned. "Don't you know any other songs?"

The gnomish little man leading the pony Luke was lashed aboard threw back his head to roar, to the tune of "Rock of Ages":

> Christ's the Savior.
> I'm His lamb.
> Jesus Christ, how glad I am!

"I don't believe this," Luke muttered. "I must have died and gone to hell. Nobody but an imp of Satan could sing so godawful, and I wouldn't be able to stand the way my leg's feelin' if I was alive and in my right senses!"

Luke's eyes were open now, but his vision was blurred from the loss of blood, and he couldn't see much, tied down over the swells and horn like this. Luke experimented and discovered his hands weren't bound. The old lunatic who'd freed him from the trap had lashed him to the saddle horn by his gun belt and wrapped leather latigos around his knees and the stirrup straps. Luke's left leg was braced in the stirrup on that side. His right leg had been doubled back at the knee and seemed to be slung some way. Luke looked back and down, leaning out a mite for a better view, and saw that the broken leg had been splinted between two slabs of bark and slung at the ankle to the concho of the old man's saddle skirt. The boy grunted in approval and called out, "You seem to know a mite of doctoring. You learn it in the war?"

"Shoot, I was settin' busted laigs afore the *Mexican* War, boy! Out here in the shining days of the great beaver hunt us mountain men didn't have no sawbones worth mention, and the Injun medicine men never done much good shakin' rattles at ussen, so we larnt our own doctorin', the hard way. I reckon iffen I'd known as much the first time I got busted up as I know now, I wouldn't walk so funny."

"My uncle was a mountain man back in the gold-rush days. I was lookin' for him when I fell into that durned old trap."

"Well, you ain't in shape to look for nobody now, boy. You better keep your haid down, too. You lost a lot of blood, and the little brains you got need what's left. You just lay your haid on the saddle swells and let me look where we're goin'. I promise not to lead you into another b'ar trap."

"I purely hope so. Where are you taking me?"

"My hidey-hole. Got me a cabin tucked away in a holler nobody knows about. Leastways, I hope nobody knows about it! That McQuiston gang's been out to cut my trail since I don't know when. But I reckon this chile knows these mountains better'n any murderous Irish owlhoots like McQuiston's bunch."

Luke stared at the passing scenery from his awkward head-down position as he tried to get his bearings.
It didn't seem all that easy. They were on a narrow
twisting trail in dense timber, and Luke couldn't see
enough of the sky to get a fix on the sun. He noticed
most of the trees around them were tall young aspen,
their green-and-silver leaves quivering in the almost
dead calm air and the smooth green columns of their
trunks packed close enough to bar a man on horseback from leaving the narrow trail. He spied a larger
trunk of dead charred spruce and asked, "What is this,
an old burn?"

His rescuer, or captor, said, "Yep. Whole mountain-
side burnt out mebbe six, seven years ago. Aint this
second growth pretty, though? I purely like aspen. It
grows too thick to spit through in an old burned-out
tract like this'n. Look down at the trail and tell me
what else I like about aspen, seein' as you reckon
you're so all-fired smart!"

Luke stared dully at the forest duff they were passing over, and after a time he nodded thoughtfully and
said, "The trail looks old and deserted, like nobody's
been by for months or maybe years. It's the way aspen
keep droppin' leaves all the time, right?"

"Well, by gum, you may not be as green a horn as
I reckoned, son. Most trees either keep their leaves,
like pine, or drop 'em all at once, like oak or maple.
These quick-growth aspen shed leaves like a hound
sheds hair on a sofa, and they dry out fast in this
mountain air. Day or so from now there won't be a
sign ahint us to show we passed this way. I'll bet Mc-
Quiston ain't never hunted a man in aspen woods
afore."

"Who in blazes is this McQuiston you're so worried
about?"

"Shoot, I ain't worried about McQuiston. Mc-
Quiston's worried about me! You see, he sort of thinks
I'm a *ghost!*"

"That sounds reasonable. You are sort of spooky.

You still haven't told me why these men are hunting you."

"I know I ain't. I never was a man for blabbin' all that much."

"Do you have a name? When I told you mine, you didn't seem to get around to introducing yourself."

"I know I didn't. Like I said, I ain't one for blabbin'."

"Well, what in thunder am I supposed to call you, then?"

"Hell, boy, I been called all sorts of things. You can call this chile anything but late for breakfast. Mebbe after I make up my mind about you I'll tell you my handle. You see, McQuiston knows he wants to kill me, but he don't know my name or what I rightly look like."

"All right, but what's that got to do with me? I don't even know who this durned McQuiston *is!*"

The old man cackled wildly and said, "Mebbe you don't, and mebbe you're one of his men! I'll allow stickin' your foot in a b'ar trap just to git on the good side of me may be goin' a bit far, but them McQuistons is tricky sons of bitches, and they purely want this chile bad!"

"If you don't trust me, why'd you save me from that trap then?"

"Well, that purely has me stumped If I'd'a had a lick of sense I'd'a left you back there shootin' at your toes. But, I dunno, somethin' sort of come over me. I feed squirrels, too."

CHAPTER 3

Luke Macahan didn't remember passing out again, but he knew he must have when he found himself lying on his back, staring up at the crooked beams of a rustic ceiling. He was under a greasy blanket on a leather-strap bedstead built into the log wall of the small one-room cabin he'd come to inside of. He propped himself up on one elbow, winced in pain as his leg flared up at the motion, and managed with an effort not to moan aloud.

He saw the gnomish little man squatting on the floor across the cabin. As he rummaged in an open crate he seemed to be muttering to himself, or perhaps praying to the Lord. He found a shriveled turnip, held it critically to the light, and groaned. "Now see what you've done to me, Lord. No beaver in the creeks, and the deer is full of worms with winter comin' on, and you saddle me with a busted-up young pilgrim to feed. He's got a big mouth and no possibles in his pack, 'cause he ain't got pack one, an—"

"What happened to my pony?" Luke asked from the bunk.

The old man turned with a scowl. "Pony? I ain't seed your cussed pony. I thought you was traipsin' through the high country on foot. You like turnips?"

"Not much. Do you reckon my pony's run off with my saddle and pack?"

"Seems likely. Did you have anythin' worth lookin' for in your possibles?"

"Just my bedroll and such. I was out of grub and huntin' a deer when I fell into that damn trap."

The old-timer snorted and said, "It ain't worth my lookin' for it, then. Lay back down and I'll see kin I bile some of this jerked venison soft enough to chaw."

"Mister?"

"Name's Billy. What do you want from me now, damn it?"

"Mr. Billy, how do you think I'm doing? I mean, me leg bein' broke an' all."

"Shoot, you're alive, ain't you? I'd say you was hoverin' 'tween poor and worse. We'll know in a day or so if the laig has a chance. I hope it's still hurtin' like hell."

"It is. Feels like a swarm of red ants are chewing their way outten my shin and spittin' out bones!"

"That's good. Long as it hurts, it's alive. I never cut no laig off as long as it's still alive."

"Good God, do you think I really might lose it?"

"Now don't you go blamin' God. It was your own self went and stuck the fool laig in that b'ar trap. What in tarnation was you doin' up here in the high country at this time of the year? Don't you know the winter's comin' on?"

"I know. I was looking for my uncle. He was at Fort Sully a few days ago. The blue bellies told me he said somethin' about headin' up for timberline, and if he's heard the bad news from home . . ."

"Never mind your damned uncle. Whilst you was asleep I went through your pockets. You tolt me true about your handle, so I reckon I'll tell you mine. I'm Billy Fargo. Name mean anythin' to you?"

"I'm afraid not, Mr. Fargo. I don't think I ever heard of you."

"Well, do Jesus, you're an ignorant pilgrim, then, and that's a fact. Ever'body worth their salt in these parts knows Billy Fargo. This chile crossed the Big Muddy ahead of Lewis and Clark. This chile's half hoss an' half alligator, an' it's gener'ly knowed he dug the Grand Canyon an' lit the fires under Yellowstone! This chile trapped the fust beaver an' whupped the first Injun! He's old an' mean and full of beans, an' he's forgot more'n most men ever know."

Luke grinned wanly and said, "I'll go along with the Grand Canyon, but Lewis and Clark come west back in 1804!"

"Well, hell, of course they did. Who do you reckon showed them the way? Why, when old John Jacob Astor come over from Germany to start the fur trade, the fust chile he hired was Billy Fargo! Didn't you read about me in your history books?"

"I must have skimmed over you. You don't *look* a hundred years old."

The old man cackled and began to sing:

I was borned a hundred thousand years ago,
There ain't nothin' in this world that I don't know,
I seed Peter, Paul, and Moses, playin' ring
     around the roses,
And I'll whup the man who says it isn't so!

Luke nodded in agreement but cut in to ask, "Do you reckon you could set my broken leg, Billy Fargo?"

The old man stopped singing and squatted there, head cocked to one side like a curious monkey as he considered the request. Then he patted his own twisted leg with a callused palm and snorted. "Shoot, when I bust a laig I jest let her grow back any durned old way she aims to."

"Yeah, but I'd sort of like to have both my legs the same length some day. You reckon we could sort of pull her straight and bind some splints around her?"

"If you want to. It'll hurt like hell, though, boy."

"It hurts like hell right now. I reckon we'd best start by cuttin' me outten this boot, don't you?"

"Shoot, I'll pull her till she snaps and we'll bind her boot an' all. You want a drink first?"

Luke considered, licked his lips, and said, "No. I'll have to feel it when the bones snap in place, won't I?"

The old man nodded. Then he said, in a gentler

tone. "You're all right, son. You ain't got much sense, but, by gum, you do have hair on your chest. If it's all the same to you, though, I aim to have my own self a good smart belt of corn afore we give her a try."

"What the hell for? You ain't the one who figures to be hurtin'!"

"I know. I reckon I'm jest a softhearted son of a bitch."

CHAPTER 4

Half a day's ride away, Luke's uncle, Zeb Macahan, rode his pony at a cautious walk under a darkening sky. He was well below timberline and it was Arapaho range. Zeb generally got along with Arapaho well enough, but the outline of a white man could draw an arrow long before a spooked Arapaho got around to asking questions. Like the Dakota, the Algonquin-speaking Arapaho were nominally at peace this summer, but while peace on paper was one thing, the chance to pick off a lone white intruder might be another. Zeb knew the Indians had been disappointed by the way the Indian Agency had lived up to the terms given that spring. The Arapaho hadn't signed it, either. Like their Algonquinoid cousins, the Cheyenne, the Arapaho were assumed to be part of the Sioux Nation by Washington's fuzzy thinkers. Zeb was one of the few white men who bothered to keep tribal distinctions in mind. Unlike his erstwhile army buddies, the well-versed Zeb Macahan didn't delude himself that he knew just what any Indian would do. He wore his hair because he was cheerfully willing to admit his own ignorance of just what any frightened and be-wildered Indian might or might not do.

Hence, when he spotted the glow of a campfire over the next rise Zeb reined in to consider his next move in detail. From the glow it seemed there was either an Indian council fire up ahead or a white man's camp. No small Indian band would have built such a large fire.

He ran a thumbnail through the stubble of his jaw and muttered, "All right. If it's an Indian powwow this chile can likely ride right in. No young buck figures to take a potshot without reason with his elders looking on. Yep, I'll top the rise and yell out in Algonquin as they spot me. That ought to get me to the fire in one piece, and after that this chile'll play by ear."

He started to spur his mount forward. Then he reined in once more to reconsider. If that big blaze hadn't been set by Indians, it meant a party of white men. A *large* party of white men if they were acting so brazenly in Indian country. All right, that meant soldiers, or hunters, or . . . Hmmm.

Zeb slid from his saddle with surprising grace for his size and tethered his pony to a sapling as he drew his saddle gun from its boot. Knowing that if anything was being guarded it would be the trail, Zeb crabbed sideways into the underbrush between the trees and moved forward on the balls of his feet. He moved as silently as a ghost, for thirty years on the frontier separated men who crashed through brush from those who knew better.

He found a vantage point between two boulders and peered over into the next hollow. The fire was foolishly large, but there were only two men in view. They were white. They looked to be a pair of hide hunters. One was small and badly needed a bath and a change of buckskins. He sat on a log near the fire, holding a jug in one hand and poking a stick aimlessly at the fire as he hummed an old Civil War song.

His companion was a buckskin-clad giant with a full piratical beard.

Zeb ran his eyes over the rest of their gear and relaxed. Aside from their tethered pack animals, the two men had scattered bundles of hides and the gear of a professional market hunter and his skinner. From the way the big man helped himself to the smaller man's jug without so much as a nod, it was easy to see who was the hunter and who was his skinner and wrangler.

Neither man looked like wholesome company, but there was a pot on the fire, and the vagrant breeze carried the scent of pretty fair coffee up to Zeb's nostrils. He decided he'd hunker down with them a spell and compare notes.

He went back and got his pony. Then he led it on in without trying to be suspiciously silent about it. As he expected, one of the men by the fire heard the sound of a horseshoe on a stone and called out, "Who's there? Speak up, god damn your eyes!"

Zeb called out, "Rest easy," as he led his pony into view, adding, "Just smelled your coffee, and I'm lookin' for a place to set a spell.

The smaller man got to his feet. His larger companion remained seated as he stared sullenly at the stranger and growled, "We ain't askin' for no company, pilgrim. You'd best be movin' on."

Zeb shrugged and said, "Be glad to. I ain't lookin' for trouble."

"You'll get trouble anyways, iffen you don't do as I say, mister."

"The names's Macahan, Zeb Macahan, and like I said, I'll be glad to leave you be."

But as Zeb started to turn away he heard a low moan from a dark mass just beyond the firelight. The others heard it too, and the smaller man suddenly bent for the rifle near the fire pit.

He didn't make it. He froze in place as he suddenly found himself staring into the unwinking eye of Zeb Macahan's Colt. Zeb's voice was still friendly as he said, "I wouldn't do that, friend."

The bigger man smiled crookedly and said, "Take

it easy, Horn. There's nothin' to get all riled about."

Zeb asked, "What is going on, here? You got somebody hurt?"

The bearded man nodded and explained, "The kid's down with the mountain fever. He'll be right come mornin'."

Zeb didn't move. He'd probably have bought the story if it hadn't been for that nonsense with the rifle there. Not lowering the muzzle of his drawn revolver, Zeb nodded and said, "I know a thing or two about mountain fever. Maybe I'll just have a look at your friend."

"Hey, he's all right, I tell you. You got no call to act so suspicious, Mr. Macahan. I'm sorry I was sort of unneighborly just now, but you see, we was afeared you'd catch the fever, too."

"Now that's right friendly of you, friend. You got a name?"

"Name? Sure I got a name. I'm Jack Krater. This here nervous nelly is Old Frank. Frank Horn. We ain't wanted nowheres, iffen you're the law."

Leaving his horse where it was, Zeb moved sideways around the fire, gun still trained on the two men as he got the moaning figure under the pile of furs between him and the fire. He knew he was only a blur to the suspiciously unfriendly hunters now. Unfortunately for them, they forgot he could see them clearly by the firelight.

Zeb dropped to one knee and lifted a flap of the uppermost hide. The mysterious someone under it cried gutturally, and a filthy claw shot out to rake Zeb's face with its nails.

Zeb flinched back in surprise and pain as, in the same split second, Frank Horn dropped for his gun and Krater rose with a bowie knife in throwing position.

Zeb fired at the rifleman as Horn's gun went off. The skinner jackknifed around the .44 slug in his middle as the bowie knife missed Zeb's head by a whisker. But the giant Krater hadn't thrown the knife.

He was still attached to the wicked blade's hilt after a head-first dive across the fire.

The shoulder of the giant's knife arm slammed into Zeb's face, and the two of them rolled end over end beyond the fire's glow. Parting in the semi-darkness, Krater reached his feet first and once more dove at Zeb with a triumphant cry. But Zeb had remained on his back for a reason. He'd lost his gun in the unexpected crash of bodies. As Krater loomed over him, Zeb kicked up with both feet and catapulted the burly knife wielder backward into the blazing campfire. Krater roared in pain and surprise as he did a backward somersault through the coals to land on hands and knees next to the fallen Frank Horn's rifle.

Krater snatched the rifle up to aim it at the blurred form of the still-sprawled Zeb. But Zeb had a bowie of his own tucked in his boot leg and, not taking time to search for his gun in the leaf litter, threw it hard with a whip-crack snap of his big thick wrist.

Krater rose with the rifle in his hands and Zeb's bowie buried to the hilt in his chest. His eyes were glazed, and his bearded jaw fell slack as he swayed for a moment, dead on his feet, before pitching head first into the fire, where he lay without twitching, face buried in the glowing coals.

Zeb rolled up to one knee, found his pistol, and got his breath back before he gingerly reached for the mysterious bundle of furs a second time.

This time he snatched the hides away and kept his face out of range, but the fingernail attack failed to materialize. The woman under the furs was only half conscious. Her eyes were half closed as she groaned, "Dear God, please leave me alone!"

Zeb said, "It's all right. You don't have to be afraid. How long have them two been holdin' you?"

But the woman didn't answer. At the sound of his reassuring words she'd fainted, or perhaps fallen back into an exhausted nightmare-filled sleep.

Zeb stared down at the impassive face for a silent moment in the dim light. It was a handsome face, give or take a few hard times and maybe forty-odd years in a rough frontier world. Zeb brushed a strand of matted gray-streaked hair away from the still-beautiful features. A name formed on his lips. Then he shook his head and said, "It can't be you. You're dead."

The clearing was filling with a very unpleasant smell. Zeb got to his feet, holstered his Colt, and walked over to the campfire. He bent to grasp the dead Krater by the booted ankles and pulled his smoldering form from the fire.

It took him about an hour to bury the two owlhoots. When he went back for another look at the woman they'd been holding, she was still asleep. Zeb nodded and said, "You purely look like someone drug you through the keyhole backwards, don't you? Well, a good night's sleep never hurt nobody."

He unsaddled and rubbed his own mount down before unrolling his bedroll near the fur pallet of the sleeping woman. But he wasn't able to sleep. She kept moaning in her sleep, and he had to comfort her with words, although the first few times he tried to soothe her with a friendly pat she flinched and screamed aloud in her sleep.

By morning he'd gotten her to where she'd allow a hand on her shoulder without flinching, and Zeb had managed to catch a wink or two by the time the sun ball rose.

In daylight there was less chance of being wrong about that handsome face, although she was still covered with smoke and grease. Zeb went down to the nearby creek and wet his kerchief. He wiped her face clean and swore in wonder. It was her all right.

The cool damp cloth seemed to comfort the unconscious woman, but she didn't wake up. Zeb's nose wrinkled as he thought of what she'd been through and at the smell of filth and scorched hair and flesh that still lingered around the scene of her captivity.

Picking her up gently, Zeb carried her perhaps a quarter mile downstream in the morning sunlight be-

fore choosing a place spangled with wildflowers and
framed in dawn-pink mountain peaks. He lowered the
unconscious woman to the flowery meadow, took out
his knife, and cut balsam boughs for a soft, clean bed.

The woman's body was barely covered by a torn
shift; he could see the filth and bruises of her captivity.
Dampening the cloth again, he washed as much of her
as he could reach without shaming her. Then he threw
his buckskin jacket over her and left her for a moment
or two to fetch his pony and pack.

She'd turned over and was huddled comfortably with
her naked legs drawn up under the jacket by the time
he returned. He muttered, "How long do you figure to
sleep, gal?" as he retethered his pony and hunkered
down to build a breakfast fire.

The coffeepot was just coming to a boil when a female voice gasped, "Zeb? Zeb Macahan? Is it really
you?"

Zeb turned to see her sitting up, tears running down
her face as she repeated, "Oh my God, it *is* you, Zeb!"

Zeb nodded, trying to hide the pain in his heart,
as he said numbly, "Yeah, it's me. I reckon it's you,
too. Last night, when I first saw you, I thought I was
looking at a ghost. Beth Harrison's been dead for years.
She died with her husband in the massacre at Fort
Nills!"

The woman sighed and said, "Beth Harrison is dead,
Zeb. I wanted it that way."

"Yeah? Well, you likely had your own way, then.
For you purely fooled me. I reckon you had a reason,
huh?"

"I did, Zeb, but it's so hard to explain."

"Well, there's no need to explain, then. You need
rest more'n anything else I can think of."

She nodded as if in silent thanks. Then she put a
hand to her bruised forehead and winced. Zeb said,
"You look like they roughed you up a mite."

"I tried to escape when they . . . when they caught
me. The big one hit me with his fist. How did I get

here, Zeb? Where am I, and what happened to those brutes?"

"It's all right, Beth. They're dead. Both of 'em. Try to forget what . . . what they might have done."

The woman looked startled and gasped, "Both of them, you say? There were three of them, Zeb!"

Zeb considered a moment before he nodded and said, "That explains the extra gear at their camp, then. Likely the third jasper lit out afore I stumbled on to 'em. Headed for parts unknown, most likely. If we ever meet up with him . . . Well, never mind that now. How do you feel? You got anything busted up?"

"I don't think they broke any bones. I'll know in a week or so if I'm in a family way."

Zeb flushed and said, "Hell, Beth, that ain't what I meant."

Her voice was level as she forced a wry smile and insisted, "I know about your delicate feelings, Zeb. But when a woman's been raped she does sort of worry about some things nice people shouldn't mention."

"Well, damn it, let's not mention 'em, then. We'll cross that bridge when and if we come to it. If the one got away ever crosses your path again, just point him out and I'll kill him slow for you. You want some coffee?"

"Zeb, I can't believe it's really you after all these years. We have so much to talk about!"

"No we don't. Not now, least ways. Right now you need a square meal and some more rest. We'll talk about . . . other things later on."

But there was no use trying to shut the past away, no matter how Zeb tried. Beth slept some more after breakfast as her big rescuer lounged beside her, occasionally brushing a fly or a tendril of hair from her sleeping face. It didn't hurt none to let his feeling show whilst the fool gal was asleep, and, damn it, he still felt more than he wanted to. He'd shut Beth out of his heart a long time ago, and once he'd heard she'd been killed by Indians, he'd been sure the hurt was gone for good. Hell, there'd been other gals since. A heap of other gals, and some had been good-lookin'. A lot of water had flowed under both their bridges since the last time he'd seen Beth. He could see the years had left their marks on her, too. Fool gal had to be over forty iffen she was a day, and . . . Damn it, she was still pretty as a picture. Time's cruel shark hadn't robbed her fine-boned features of the inner beauty that was there. If anything, the lines of character etched in the sleeping woman's face showed some improvement over the somewhat flighty young thing he remembered. Do Jesus, hadn't he ever made a fool of hisself over her, once upon a time when the world was younger and he'd thought it was run on the level.

Zeb managed a nap of his own by late afternoon and awoke near sundown, famished. He got some vittles from his pack and started fixing supper. The smell of cooking, or perhaps sleeping nearly round the clock, awoke Beth Harrison once again. This time she sat up wide awake and bursting with curiosity.

As Zeb greeted her with a curt "Supper's almost ready" she shook her head and said, "I don't want to eat. I want to talk. Do you realize it's been over twenty years, Zeb? We have so much to talk about!"

"Yeah, you always was one who wanted her own way, Beth, but I don't want to talk. I want to eat, and you're to eat, too. Since knowin' you, I've gotten a mite set in my own ways, too."

Grudgingly, Beth allowed him to feed her two helpings of everything. By then the first stars were out, and she pushed a last pan of food away, insisting, "I've been a good girl and eaten my supper. Now can I talk?"

"Is there any way of stopping you?"

"No, damn it. You know what I want to ask, Zeb. Why didn't you come back to me that time? You promised to come back, remember?"

Zeb stared away for a time. Then he shrugged and said, "I tried to, Beth. Maybe I tried too hard. The world was younger then, and I knowed how your father felt about you and me."

"Oh, Zeb, you know I could have handled Father!"

"I know. Knew it then. Knew that if we'd really gone through with it he'd have fumed and fussed some, but in the end he'd have given us his blessings."

"Then what made you so stubborn? What were you trying to prove to my father?"

"That he was wrong about me. Maybe that *I* was wrong about me, too. You see, Beth, it wasn't just that your folks looked down on me like the dirt farm boy I was in them days. I reckon I sort of looked down on me my own self. Your folks was proud. Too proud to have a no-account like me for a son-in-law."

"You never said you were leaving for good, Zeb. You said you were coming back with a fortune to make me feel proud of you. But I was already proud, and you never—"

"I just told you I *tried*, Beth. I went off that summer aiming to bring back the the biggest fur pack any white man had ever seed, and I meant it, too, only, well, I got hung up."

Her voice held a slight edge as she asked, "Oh? What was it, a poker game or a pretty squaw?"

"Neither one. It was a grizzly. Biggest, meanest brute of a bear I ever met, and since that time I've met my share. Anyway, the world was young and I was a fool and too proud to back off when he raided my camp. You see, I *had* me one hell of a fur pack by then, and it riled me beyond common sense to see that fool bear tearing up my hides for the salt in 'em."

"Good heavens, what did you do, kill it?"

"Yep, in the end I killed it. Got tore up some doin' it, though. A neighborly Blackfoot medicine man nursed me back from the edge of the big dark, but it took a spell. Time I was on my feet again the summer was gone and we was snowed in. I'd sent word by another trapper about my accident. But by the time I come down off the mountain . . . you wasn't there no more."

"Zeb, we never received your message. I swear, no

trapper never came back with so much as a word about you."

"I know. Few years later I learned what happened to the poor cuss. He was drowned trying to run white water in an overloaded canoe."

"Zeb, I swear we thought you were dead. I waited nearly a year, and nobody'd heard a thing about you. Every trapper who'd ever been up in the high country with you said you were likely dead."

The big scout's voice was bleak as he nodded and asked, "That's why you run off with Captain Harrison, right?"

"Zeb, that's not fair. I didn't run off with anyone. I thought you were dead, or, worse, that you no longer cared for me. I thought you'd have come back long before I married Captain Harrison if you were alive, or still wanted me."

Zeb didn't answer.

Beth looked into the embers of the fire as she said, half to herself, "Robert Harrison was young, terribly handsome, and very much in love with me. He was first in his class at West Point, and young for a captain. He had a brilliant future ahead of him."

"I know. When I heard you'd married up I sort of asked around about the cuss. It might have made forgettin' you easier iffen he'd been a scoundrel or a coward. The word I got was that he was a good man. I reckon you might have done worse. You may have noticed my future ain't been all that brilliant."

"Zeb, I hardly knew what I was doing. I was heartbroken over you, and I had so much preying on my mind. My father was very ill, and the folks kept pressing me to get married before he died, and . . . I don't see why I'm explaining all this to you, damn it. *I* never did anything wrong!"

"Beth, nobody never did anything wrong. Life just turns out that way sometimes. You don't owe me no explanations for marryin' up with a nice young feller. I am a mite confused about what happened afterwards, though. I mean, they told me you was dead, too! They told me your husband and you and ever'body else was wiped out by the Indians that time."

"Robert and all the other men were killed. The Indians took the adjutant's wife and me captive."

"I see, but you haven't been with no Indians all these years, and . . ."

"The other white woman went mad and killed herself. I hung on. The squaws made a slave out of me. The braves . . . well, I got away a month or so later. I got the brave they'd given me to drunk and lit out on his pony."

"You got away within a month? I don't understand you at all, girl!"

Beth got to her feet and turned away, arms folded across her chest as she stared into the darkness and softly explained, "Everyone thought I was dead. My father died shortly after I married Robert, and my mother followed him a few months later."

"All right, so you had no family, but you still had your friends."

"Friends, Zeb? After being held a love slave by the Indians for a month? I knew the looks I'd get. I knew the badgering the newspaper reporters would put me through, and, damn it, I was *ashamed,* Zeb!"

"Hell, what was there to be ashamed of? You didn't run off with no Indian brave of your own free will, did you?"

"No, but I could have killed myself, like the other girl did. You know what they say about a fate worse than death, Zeb?"

"Shoot, there ain't no fate worse than death."

"That's the way I saw it. That's why I let those savages use me as their love toy, smiling and flattering and pretending I liked it till I could get away. I guess you could call me a survivor, Zeb, but I've done things I'm not proud of just to stay alive."

"Yeah, well, things happen. The Pawnee say never judge another jasper till you've hunted a summer in his moccasins. What happened after you got away from the Indians, Beth. You ever marry up again?"

"No. What about you?"

Zeb shrugged and said, "I got married once. Cherokee girl. Lost her in a fire one time."

"Oh, I'm sorry. Did you . . . love her?"

"Must have, some. It was a long time ago."

"You're not going to try to tell me you've never been in love since . . . us, are you, Zeb?"

He shook his head with a wry grin and allowed, "I know you're too smart to buy such a yarn, Beth. Hell, I'm a man, ain't I?"

"I'm not talking about sex. I'm talking about real love."

"Well, you got me betwixt the hard place and a rock, Beth. I'd be lying' if I said I ever got over you, and I'd be lying' if I said I ain't never hankered after another gal. What passed betwixt us happened twenty years ago, honey."

"Then there have been other women in your life."

"Hell, I just got through sayin' I was a man, didn't I? Sure there's been women in my life. Lots of women. Some was just a warm place to lay my head, and others . . . others left some holes burnt in the rug of this ornery old heart. I guess a man's always in love with a gal a mite, at the time. Lookin' back from a safe distance, though, a man can count all the gals who ever meant anythin' on the fingers of his hands."

"Am I a finger on your hand, Zeb?"

"You know you are, damn it, but, like I said, it was a long time ago."

"I never stopped loving you, Zeb."

She turned around to face him again, her eyes moist in the light from the little fire. Zeb met her level gaze with an odd lump in his own throat as he stammered, "I guess if it comes to that I'd have to say the same."

Beth put her hands on Zeb's sleeves and asked softly, "Could a lady get a kiss for old times' sake, darling?"

Wordlessly, the big man took her in his arms and pressed his lips to hers, and twenty years vanished as if by magic as the world was suddenly young again.

Beth's lips were warm and responsive to his, and Zeb's hand slid down her spine, until he suddenly realized what he was doing and stiffened, drawing his lips from hers to mutter, "God, I'm sorry, gal."

She hugged him to her and said, "Don't stop. We're not the children we once were, darling!"

"Jesus, you mean that, Beth? I mean, what you just went through and all . . ."

"Don't be silly. We've both been married, and, well, by now we know the difference between rape and wanting! Don't you want me, Zeb?"

"Hell yes, I want you so bad I can taste it!"

"What's stopping you, then? I'm hardly a blushing virgin any more, and . . ." and then there was no further time for talk. Nothing existed on that night except their need and the long bittersweet desires thwarted a full generation ago!

Zeb carried her to his bedroll, and their clothes vanished by some magic only eager lovers are capable of, and then their flesh was one and, yes, dear Lord, it was just as good as they'd hoped for all those years and through countless lonely nights, and then . . . then . . . Zeb lay staring up at the stars, Beth's tousled head on his naked shoulder, as they shared a smoke he'd rolled and some still small voice inside of him was marveling, "I don't believe it. It couldn't have really happened after all these years. This can't be *Beth* beside me on these blankets! In a minute I'll wake up and remember it was just a fool notion I had down in Denver. You remember how that gal reminded you of Beth, old son?"

Beth took a drag on his smoke and murmured against his moist shoulder, "Now that we've found each other again, promise never, never to let me go?"

Zeb didn't answer.

It was something he had to study on a mite.

CHAPTER 5

Billy Fargo hadn't told Luke Macahan the whole truth about the so-called McQuiston gang. In truth, they were not a gang. They were a band of mountain men who'd ridden up to the high country in search of animal pelts to sell. The price of beaver was down, and fox, this time of the year, sold for less than the thicker furs of winter. McQuiston and the other hunters with him had every bit as much right to the furs near Billy Fargo's cabin as any other white man. They'd have been quite surprised, as well as outraged, to hear themselves described as outlaws.

On the other hand, Billy Fargo was dead right about one thing. The McQuiston bunch had every intention of killing the old-timer on sight. Catching sight of Billy Fargo, however, presented a problem. Opinion in the McQuiston camp was divided on whether the gnomish figure raiding their traps and stealing their supplies was a human enemy, a terribly cunning bear, or some twisted mountain spirit.

They'd found the trap they'd set for whoever or whatever haunted them. The blood on the jaws had been encouraging. The fact that whatever they'd caught in it had sprung a trap too strong for man or bear had not. The bullets in the tree made simply no sense at all. Bears didn't shoot bullets at a trap spike. On the other hand, men didn't step in bear traps all that often, and when they did they had more sense than to try to shoot their way out like a cowpoke caught with his pants down in a bawdy house!

Trapper Rackley, a large, scruffy-looking citizen

distinguished for neither looks nor brains, was pondering these points as he took his turn at guarding the camp that day. The others were out running the trap lines and scouting for sign as Rackley squatted by the campfire, cutting another slice of venison from the haunch roasting over the coals. He ate without enthusiasm, lonely and feeling sort of cold at the back of his hairy neck. Rackley had no idea why the hairs on his neck were spooked, but there was something wrong hereabouts. Rackley looked around at the wall of trees around the clearing as he tried to figure out what it was. At times like these he purely wished he were smart like McQuiston. There didn't seem to be a durned thing wrong. The wind had died and not a leaf was stirring. It was so quiet a man could hear his own heart thumping in his chest, and . . . "Birds," Rackley muttered. Then he grinned, pleased at his own surprising wisdom. He was all alone in the camp. He wasn't doing nothing or making noise one. Yet the birds that had been chirping at him from the trees all morning had plumb stopped! It wasn't only the hairs ahint his haid that were spooked. The birds were spooked, too!

Rackley hummed a snatch of "Blue-Tailed Fly" as he idly reached for the butt of his revolver. From behind him a nasal voice twanged. "One twitch and I'll blow your brains all over that there fire pit, son!"

Rackley stiffened, but he didn't twitch. A good old boy born short on brains learns to do as he's told.

Billy Fargo stepped into view. He held his shotgun trained on the moronic trapper as he said, "Belly down, pilgrim."

"Huh?"

"Lay down flat on your belly with both hands out to the sides. I don't aim to say it twice!"

"Old man, whoever you are, don't do 'er. Not *agin!*"

"You jest belly down and I'll do as I've a mind to, son. Come on, *move it!*"

Rackley got to his hands and knees and lowered his trunk to the pine needles, protesting, "McQuiston'll skin you alive for this, old-timer! This time he'll catch you sure!"

"No he won't. McQuiston's down to Parson's Gap!"

"Like hell he is! Him an' the others is up on High Creek!"

Billy Fargo cackled with glee and said, "That's all I wanted to know. Thank's for tellin' me, jackass"

He stepped over to the prone trapper and nudged his spine with the gun muzzle. "All right, put your hands ahint your back."

"Old man?"

"Shet your face."

"Old man, I'm jest tryin' to warn you friendly. Mc-Quiston says do you rob us agin he'll track you to the ground does it take all winter!"

Billy bent to lash the trapper's wrists with a length of rawhide latigo as he laughed again and snorted, "You can tell McQuiston he couldn't track his own hog through the slop house, son!"

"I'm tellin' you true, old man. McQuiston's a borned tracker, and meaner than a Dodge City madam. What's the matter with you, anyways? You cain't go runnin' about stealin' from other folks like this!"

"Cain't hear you, son."

"I said you cain't—" and then Billy Fargo had Rackley by the hair and was yanking his head back muttering, "Hold on, I ain't out to scalp you, son. Jest aim to put a gag in your big mouth. But you'd best open it or I might change my mind and scalp you for the hell of it. You think McQuiston's meaner than a Dodge City madam? Hell, who do you reckon *made* them gals so mean?"

Bound and gagged, Rackley pretended not to be looking at the camp raider, but he risked a peek now and then and, yep, the old son of a bitch was a human being, sort of. Rackley knew the boss would be madder than hell when he come back, but at least this time they'd know what the jasper they was after *looked* like!

Billy tucked the gun under one arm and began to

rummage for supplies tucking what he needed into a gunnysack he'd brought along for just that purpose. He helped himself to salt, a sack of flour, a side of bacon, and a can of waterproof matches. Before leaving camp he helped himself to a half dozen beaver pelts the trappers had stretched to dry between two tents. Rackley saw him do it, but turned his head away as the old man passed. What Billy had just done went beyond swiping vittles. Pelt stealing was a killing offense, and Rackley knew his word in court was good for a long stiff prison sentence if the old man ever got lucky and fell into the hands of the law before some vigilante caught up with him.

Rackley lay there, quiet as a church mouse, as the sounds of the old man's putterings faded away. Rackley was uncomfortable, and now he knew the boys were gonna purely hoorah him for letting the old buzzard get the drop on him like that. But Rackley was pleased, at the cunning he'd shown. It was nice to think at least one man on this mountain was dumber than he was. Had the old camp raider a lick of sense he'd have never left a witness alive to tell the folks what he looked like. Rackley knew it was important to remember every detail. The thief was maybe eight years older than God and wearing raggedy buckskins. He walked sideways like a crab and cackled like a canyon jay about to rob a frying skillet. His face was scarred and . . . Jesus, nobody was ever gonna believe him. Nothin' human could look that ugly and still be alive.

CHAPTER 6

Despite what he'd told Luke the day he freed him from the bear trap, Billy Fargo hadn't given up on the boy's pony. A day or so after setting Luke's leg the hermit had gone back to where he'd found him, searched for sign, and tracked the still-saddled-and-bridled horse to a mountain pasture.

The pony was in Billy's lean-to stable with his own mount now, rubbed down and fattening on summer hay. When old Billy returned from his latest raid he carried his stolen skins directly to the stable, not to show them to the ponies, but to hide them with the others he'd stolen over the past few months.

He had a bale and a half of beaver pelts, or plews, as old mountain men prefered to call them. There weren't as many mountain men as Billy could remember, and them rascals in St. Louis hardly paid for beaver no more. But what was a feller to do? Billy Fargo knew no other trade, and since his strength and skills had faded, even getting beaver plews was dangerous hard work.

Billy removed the tarp he'd put over the furs and added the plews he'd just stolen to the half-completed bale, muttering, "Got 'most two bales, McQuiston. You and your boys keep up the good work an' I'll be able to git me another grubstake."

Billy limped over to the cabin, still muttering to himself. He didn't like the things he'd been forced to do, but fair was fair, and he'd found this mountain first.

He stomped inside, snorting, "Folks crowdin' in on

me from ever' side, Lord, I don't know what this durned country's comin' to. Keeps up this way, the next thing they'll be wantin' to do is build them a post office on my mountain!"

From the built-in bunk bed, Luke Macahan called out, "Mr. Fargo?"

"What? You still here? I thought you died."

"I reckon I might have done, had not you come along. I'm pure obliged to you for setting my leg."

Billy Fargo shrugged and said, "It ain't fixed. It's set. You could still come down with gangrene or blood pizen, boy. At least we got her pointed in the right direction. The rest is up to God or the devil. Does it still hurt?"

"Not half as bad as my head."

"Well, you drunk enough of my busthead whiskey to give a bear sore head. Did the job, though. Didn't holler when I cracked the bone back in place."

"Mr. Fargo, you drank the whiskey, remember?"

"Well, sure I remember. Like I said, it did the job for both of us. I mind you had a snort or two your own self, afterwards."

"I guess I needed it. It's hard as hell to sleep with a drunk old man singin' 'Bringin' in the Sheaves' all night!"

"Don't you sass me, boy. You sass me an' I'll likely bust your other laig!"

"I'm just funnin'. How long's it likely to take afore I can walk?"

"On a busted laig? Six weeks, Lord willin' and the cricks don't rise. What's your hurry? You in a hurry to git somewheres?"

"I told you, I'm looking for my Uncle Zeb."

Billy Fargo suddenly cocked his head to one side and ran the name Zeb through the cobwebs of his mind. He nodded and asked, "Didn't you tell me your name was Macahan, son?"

"That's right. I'm Luke Macahan. You knew that."

"I just connected the handles up. Your uncle wouldn't jist happen to be old Zeb Macahan, the mountain man the Injuns call White Eagle, would he, boy?"

"That's Uncle Zeb! Don't tell me you know him!"

"Know him? Hellfire an' damnation, boy, old Zeb an me go back thirty-nine . . . nope, thirty-seven or so, to the Green River rendezvous, where I showed Kit Carson how to Injun-wrestle and . . . Lord of Mercy, that was a long time ago and we was green as grass. Greener'n grass, by jumpers!"

Billy slapped his knee and added, "Why didn't you tell me you was kin to Zeb Macahan? I'da given you my *good* whiskey!"

"Lord, no! No more whiskey!"

"How 'bout some salt pork? I just fetched it from my, uh, other camp."

"Salt pork'd sit real nice, Mr. Fargo."

"Shoot, if you're Zeb Macahan's kin I'm jist plain Billy!"

The old man went to the fireplace with the side of salt pork he'd stolen and began to putter with the half-dead coals. He muttered, "Sorry I cain't do better by you, son, but I don't git around as spry as I used to. Old age and hard livin's caught up with my old bones."

Luke felt uncomfortable as he said soothingly, "Shucks, everybody gets old. You can't help that."

"Boy, I *got* to help it! Ain't nobody else to row my hoe but me, and that's a thing ever' man larns, does he manage to live long enough."

Then he shrugged and added, "Hell, don't pay me no mind, boy, we'll make out. Ever'body makes out all right iffen he's got the hair on his chest an' the sand in his craw to keep tryin'. That's all a man kin do, boy. Keep tryin'."

"I guess so, Billy, but just what is it we're trying so blamed hard to do? I mean, what the *goal* we're tryin' for?"

Billy Fargo laughed wryly and said, "There ain't no goal, son. Life is jest a greased pole the Good Lord puts us on with orders to claw up or slide down. I been climbin' this damned greased pole all my days, and lately I seem to slidin' a mite, but as long as I'm breathin' . . ."

"I don't follow you, Billy. What's *up* there, at the top of life's pole?"

"Hell, boy there ain't no top. No matter how high in life a man climbs, there's always somethin' higher to reach for. No matter how much money a man gits, there's some other jasper with more. No matter how many gals you kiss, there's always millions more you've missed. You cain't trap all the beavers. You cain't drink all the whiskey. You cain't never stop and say, there, I've done it all."

"Then what's point of climbing?"

"The point of climbin', boy? The point of climbin' is to keep from slidin' down, of course. God's big greased pole of life runs up to the stars and down, down to dead an' buried an' forgot."

"I see. You figure the only real aim in life is to simply fight like hell to stay alive."

"Now you're larnin', son. The whole point to God's big joke on us is that in the end, we all gits tired, or lose our grip, and . . . Zoooey. Forever and ever in the big dark. Ain't that a bitch?"

"You've cheered me up somethin' fierce. Meanwhile, what are you doin' out there in the woods all day? You still doin' some trapping?"

Billy Fargo shrugged and said, "Got me a few sets out. I'm too old and busted-up to run a full line."

"Much fur out there?"

"Some. Nothin' like it was afore that McQuiston gang came over the pass. Them rascals has nigh trapped my mountain out."

Luke frowned and said, "McQuiston's a trapper? I thought you said he was an outlaw!"

"Well, 'course he's an outlaw, damn it! Him and his gang has been trappin' on my mountain since they come in here last fall. Things was tolerable till they come in an ruint my range. *They* was the ones as set the b'ar trap you got caught in, sure as God made farkleberries! Don't tell *me* about no outlaws!"

Luke considered before he said, "I dunno, Billy. Seems to me anyone has a right to set traps in unclaimed country."

"What unclaimed country, damn it! I was here fust, by gum! Don't you go talkin' about what's fair and what ain't, boy. Them jaspers come to my territory and trapped me damn near out of business! If you aim to be fair-spoken, you'll have to admit I got ever' right to hang the whole damn bunch of 'em!"

"I'm sorry if I'm, uh, fair-spoken, Billy. Have you had it out with this McQuiston feller?"

"Hell no, I ain't had it out. I'm outnumbered ten to one. You jist let that laig heal, though, and mebbe when you're up an' about the two of us kin take them dudes on."

Luke gasped, "Are you serious? Two against ten?"

"Hell, that beats one agin ten, don't it? Let's eat, son. We'll figure the odds when you're fit to side me agin them varmints."

CHAPTER 7

The rain had let up, but the forest floor was a spongy mass of muddy duff as trapper Harley Gordon limped back to McQuiston's camp in waterlogged boots.

Rackley and another trapper named Potter were drying by the fire as Gordon came into view. Gordon was the best tracker in the band, but the others knew, even before they asked, what Gordon had found.

Rackley asked, "No sign?" and the disgusted Gordon said, "Rain washed away any track he may have left."

Potter shook his head and said, "Ghosts don't leave no tracks."

Rackley protested, "Damn it, he wasn't no ghost, I tell you. I seen him in broad daylight, and he was an old busted-up crazy man!"

Gordon stood over the fire, trying to dry his soaked pants, as he observed, "Ghosts don't eat salt pork or bacon, either. Rackley's right. The thief's a man, wild-lookin' as he sounds."

Potter insisted, "I think Rackley's tetched in the haid." But before the argument could continue, their leader walked into the clearing from the other side.

McQuiston was a lean, hard-looking man with the cold gray eyes of a professional executioner. Like Gordon, he was cold and wet, and utterly disgusted with himself as well as his men.

McQuiston hunkered down by the fire to warm his bloodless-looking long-fingered hands as he stared soberly into the coals for a silent moment. Then he muttered, "Rackley, you say he's an old man. Just how old is old?"

Rackley shrugged and answered. "Older than most folks, Boss. He had white hair and was wrinkled up like a dried-out apple."

"You say he walked with a right bad limp?"

"That's right, Boss."

"All right. How come he outruns us every time?"

"I don't know, Boss. Likely he's a tough old man."

Potter insisted, "It ain't no man, it's a ghost. I tell you."

McQuiston shook his head and said, "Never heard of a ghost stealin' beaver plews and salt. He's hit us, what . . . ten . . . twelve times since we come over the pass, and nobody here has the brains to catch him!"

Rackley offered, "Mebbe he's a smart old man, too, Boss. Nobody knows when he's comin' in on us. He don't come often enough for us to lay for him all the time."

Gordon defended Rackley by cutting in with "We couldn't do much trappin' if we laid for the old goat ever' day, Boss. You remember the time we staked out for a full week, waitin' to git hit?"

McQuiston's voice was bitter as he nodded curtly and said, "Yeah, and he hit us two days after we gave up on the idea. You boys know what I think? I think he's hiding somewhere near. I think he scouts us a full day or so afore he moves in."

Gordon shrugged and said, "We've searched high and low for a hideout, Boss."

McQuiston shook his head and said, "Not every square inch of the mountains all around. I figure what we're up agin is some sort of crazy old hermit. He knows this country better'n we do, but, God damn it, we're supposed to be mountain men! He's been hitting us more often of late, too. Twice in the last ten days means he's likely stockin' up for the winter. The bastard's doin' it with our supplies, and I want him *caught*. You boys got that?"

Potter said, "Sure, Boss, but what do we do when we catch him, turn him over to the law?"

McQuiston reached for a nearby coil of rope and began to braid a hangman's noose as he muttered, "Nope. We'll take care of the son of a bitch our own selves!"

Gordon frowned and said, "Jesus, Boss, ain't that likely to git us in trouble?"

McQuiston shrugged and went on braiding his noose. "We're already in trouble. He's skimmed half the profits from a long hard year of trapping. You boys just bring him in, and I'll see that he hangs by the neck until he's dead, dead, dead."

"Is that legal, Boss?"

"Who the hell cares if it's legal? Who's gonna turn us in to the law, the damned old thief?"

Potter giggled and said, "Do Jesus, McQuiston, you purely have a mighty fine sense of humor. You know he cain't complain once he's daid, don't you?"

The hatchet-faced McQuiston shot Potter a disgusted look and muttered, "Jesus, I'm so surrounded by brains I'm fixin' to puke. Gordon?"

"Yeah, Boss?"

"You know how to read a map, don't you?"

"Sure, Boss."

"All right. Here's what we're gonna do. I've got a government survey map of this territory in my possibles. It's out of scale and a mite rough as to details, but at least it's something to work with. Instead of wastin' time trying to cut this jasper's trail, we're gonna cut the map into penciled squares and search the whole damned area for . . . How far do you reckon he'd be likely to be hiding out?"

"Hard to say, Boss. Rackley here says he was afoot, but he might have had a pony tethered somewhere off in the trees."

"He's scouting us from less than a good hard lope through timber. How do you feel about less than ten country miles, Gordon?"

"Sounds about right, Boss."

"All right. We divide the map into quarter sections and search each section inch by inch, spiraling out from here."

"What if he just keeps movin', Boss?"

"He can't. He's stolen too much to carry it on his back or even on a bronc. The bastard's got a hidey-hole less than an hour's ride or run from here. I'll fetch the map and you boys can get cracking."

CHAPTER 8

Beth swam nude in the cool clean waters of the mountain tarn. The sun stood high in the Indian-summer sky, and as she opened her eyes underwater she smiled down at the diamond glitter of the coarse mica sands of the sunlit bottom. As she came up for air, Beth saw

Zeb Macahan seated on a log near the bank, fully dressed and wearing a bemused smile on his battered but still handsome face.

Beth smiled back and waved to him. Zeb's voice was laconic as he said, "You're naked as a jaybird, ain't you?"

Beth laughed and called back, "Silly, jaybirds wear feathers. I haven't got a stitch on my old frame!"

"Ain't you ashamed to be carryin' on like that at your age, Grandma?"

"Nope. The sun is shining, you're here, and I'm here, and I'm alive and in love and feeling so wonderful I have no scruples whatsoever!"

"They got a name for loose women like you, gal."

"Is that so? Why don't you shuck your clothes, dive in here, and whisper it in my ear?"

Zeb smiled regretfully and shook his head as he said, "I took a dip at daybreak. 'Fore you woke up. 'Sides, I got me some chores to do."

"What chores, darling?"

"Well, for one thing, I got to shoot us some game or we don't figure to eat tonight. You may have noticed I ain't been doin' much huntin' the last few days."

Beth grinned roguishly. "You've been hunting pretty well under your blankets, of late, and I must say I approve. And, speaking of country matters . . ." She came toward him, rising from the water like a latter-day Venus as the sunlight painted her wet nude curves with a light worthy of Botticelli.

As Zeb rose from his log seat she put her wet arms around his waist, pressed against him, and purred, "Do you really have to go hunting? Right now? Right this *minute?*"

Zeb laughed boyishly, kissed her, and grinned. "Well, I reckon there ain't all that much of a hurry. The critters'll still be there an hour from now, and if they ain't, I'd as soon skip supper as *this!*"

He kissed her again, scooped her up, and carried her, laughing, back to their unmade bedroll by the fire.

But as he put her back on her feet Beth blinked in surprised dismay, and would have fallen had not Zeb steadied her with a lightning grab. He frowned down at her glazed expression and asked, "What's wrong, honey? You look like someone just hit you a lick with a length of stove wood!"

Beth shook her head as if to clear it as she murmured, "I don't know. I've always been moved and knocked a little dizzy by your kisses, darling, but this is . . . oh dear . . . I feel so . . ."

And then her eyes rolled upward in her head and her knees buckled as she collapsed completely in Zeb's arms.

Zeb carried her to the bedroll and wrapped her in a blanket. He felt her pulse and found it strong. He placed the back of his wrist gently to her forehead and felt no fever, but the clear skin near her hairline was still mottled by the bruise she'd received at the hands of the ruffians he'd killed and buried.

Zeb rolled a smoke and thought about the past day or so, and this time he kept his mind chess-master clear. They'd been skylarking like a couple of naughty kids who'd just found out why boys and girls were different. But, getting down to cases, hadn't Beth been acting a mite odd, for her?

Sure, she was twenty years older, she'd been married, raped, and likely had her share of lovers since the last time he'd seen her as a blushing-virgin army brat. There was love, real love, and there was the human body's natural needs. Most civilized folks prefered a tablecloth with candles lit and silver service, if it was there. If it wasn't, a hungry man or woman could be talked into eating cold beans from a tin can. And Beth was a healthy, lusty gal. Lusty, anyways. Just how healthy might be something else entirely.

Zeb nodded to himself, snubbed out his smoke, and gently dressed the unconscious woman in the patched and mended clothes he'd retrieved from the hide hunters' camp. She didn't so much as flicker an eyelid as he finished dressing her, wrapped her in two blankets, and cut two aspen saplings with his bowie. He got a ball of rawhide twine from his possibles bag and quickly lashed an Indian travois together as he hunkered on his heels near Beth. His big hands moved with practiced skill. He'd spent enough time with Indians to lash a travois in his sleep. It was Beth he was interested in right now. He cast glance after anxious glance at her sleeping face as he worked, trying to figure what was wrong.

He pulled a knot tight with an angry oath at his own big rawboned hands. What in thunder had got into him? Why hadn't he seen that she was still shaken and spooked by her ordeal? The fool gal had been beaten clean out of her head!

Zeb took the narrow point of the big A-frame travois and dragged it to his tethered pony. He placed the end of the travois over the pony's rump, lashing it to the saddle skirt. Then he led the pony, dragging the spread ends of the big A, to where Beth still lay unconscious. He rolled her, still wrapped in his blankets, onto the laced rawhide sling he'd woven above the lower crossbar and began to lash her gently but firmly in place, head up and bundled feet just above the ground, between the drags. He was almost finished when Beth opened her eyes and murmured, "What happened, dear? What are you doing?"

Zeb tied a knot and grunted, "Takin' you to a doctor."

"Doctor? What are you talking about? I'm fine, Zeb. I just had a chill from my swimming in that melt-water and—"

"Hell, girl, you're in great shape. Them dizzy spells yesterday and a dead faint just now. I swear to God, somebody ought to horsewhip me for a fool. You been sleepin' too much and carryin' on too wild when you ain't. We need us a doctor to tell us what's busted loose inside that pretty head of yours!"

She struggled to free herself as she protested, "Zeb, I'm all right I tell you. I've been banged around a bit, and the shock and joy of getting you back has sort of knocked my senses loose, but I'm not sick. Right now my head is clear as a bell!"

"Yeah, I've seen this sort of thing afore. Knowed a Cheyenne Dog Soldier, once, who caught a good lick on the head from a Crow raider's war club. He said he felt just fine, too. It won't wash, honey. You still got a bad bruise on your temple. I'm draggin' you to the nearest town and the best doctor we can find, and I'll hear no more about it."

She started to protest. Then she relaxed and sighed. "All right, I know better than to argue with you once your mind's made up. What happened to your Cheyenne friend? Did he start fainting on you, too?"

Zeb hesitated. He didn't want to worry her, and they were a good day's travois from the nearest settlement. Beth caught the hesitancy and nodded, saying, "He died, didn't he?"

"That's the trouble with womenfolk. Even when you don't say a thing, they answer their own questions!"

Beth dimpled and murmured, "It only works on the ones we love, dear. If I promise to be good, will you promise *me* something?"

"Sure, what is it?"

"Uh, when we get to town, I, uh, don't want anyone to know who I am. I'm going under the name of Elizabeth Smith. Can we keep it that way, Zeb?"

He finished a last knot, nodded, and said, " 'Smith' ain't a hard name to remember. We'll call you anythin' you want."

"I suppose you think I owe you some explanations?"

"Beth, friends don't owe each other anything. I may not look all that smart, but I've suspicioned you're hiding more'n the way you was made a widder woman twenty years ago."

She looked away as she said, "I am. I've been trying to think how to put it into words you'd understand, Zeb. I'm afraid my life hasn't been all that pretty since I was the girl you left behind and—"

"Hey, we've got to get a move on," he cut in, with

a crooked smile, and added, "You can tell me when you're ready, in any words you have, or you can just stay pretty as a picture and we'll leave things lay."

"You haven't changed, Zeb. The hair's gone gray and the sun and wind have had their way with you, but under that rough façade you're still the most delicate, gentle man I've ever known."

He stood up, brushed some dust from one knee with his hand, and snorted, "Yeah, and now this gentle old fool aims to drag you like a sick squaw to the town of Three Rivers."

"Why can't I ride with you? I feel fine now."

"Don't care how you feel. I won't let you walk or ride until the doctor says it's safe."

She stuck her tongue at him, and they both laughed like children. Then Zeb got another pony and mounted it to lead the one pulling the travois. He set a steady mile-eating pace, and distance as well as the grating song of the travois drags cut off further conversation. Beth was surprised at how gentle the ride aboard the dragging springy poles was, once she got used to the grating vibration.

She snuggled into a more comfortable position, feeling drowsy again and oddly disconnected from reality. It seemed such a shame that their childlike return to the Garden of Eden had to end so soon, but everything ended, and the days of a Rocky Mountain Indian summer were only one of the many sweeter things in life that slipped through one's fingers like grains of diamond sand, or the years of one's youth.

She knew, despite her protestations, that she was suffering from concussion. Dear God, let her spells of unconsciousness not betray her secret! She wondered what she might have murmured aloud in her sleep in Zeb's safe arms. Would he have said anything if he knew?

Of course he wouldn't, but what must he be thinking of her? Even with her secret safe, she'd been acting the part of a shameless hussy, and she still couldn't understand it. Perhaps it was because she'd found her long-lost love in the Garden of Eden, where the common sordid sins of mankind didn't seem important?

But there was a price to pay for Eden. Adam and Eve had paid it for their sins, and next to the things *she'd* done to keep alive these past few years, poor Mother Eve's apple thievery seemed pretty innocent!

CHAPTER 9

The trail town of Three Rivers was within a half day's ride of Fort Sully, and part of its business came from serving the soldiers on leave. Market hunters, cattle drovers, and teamsters comprised most of the other visitors in need of supplies, a drink, a game of cards, or a few minutes of tawdry soiled sex in one of the cribs off Market and Third.

Like the fort itself, the town was built as close to the Dakota-white treaty line as the law allowed. Whether common sense allowed it or not was up for grabs.

It was a sleepy-looking little town, but Three Rivers slept light in the shadow of the Black Hills, and to say that the appearance of Zeb Macahan pulling Beth on an Indian travois caused a small sensation would be to put it mildly. Yet, despite the turned heads and moving lace curtains in the windows along Main Street, there was little overt curiosity. Those townies who knew Zeb knew better than to question him before he'd indicated a willingness to jaw. Those who'd never seen him before were put off by his size and the worn grips of his holstered Colt and saddle carbine. Doubtless the giant stranger would get around to telling folks where he'd found the pretty gal on the travois, and why he was dragging her in that way, in his own good time.

They were right. Zeb looked neither right nor left as he dragged Beth to the false-fronted hotel near the center of town. She in turn was mortified to be seen in such a weird position, and now after having dozed on the trail, she thought Zeb was being silly about the whole thing.

Zeb reined in at the hotel, dismounted, and came back to unlash Beth. She sat up, protesting, "Darling, I really feel all right now."

Zeb grunted. "Uh-huh, well, I'm taking you upstairs and putting you to bed."

"Now that makes sense, dear. Do we register as man and wife or what?"

"We register you as Elizabeth Smith and put you in a private room."

"Does this mean the honeymoon is over?"

"Stop joshing, girl. I'm putting you to bed, and you're not to move, that way or any other, till the doctor I fetch says you're able."

He picked her up and carried her up the steps, glaring hard at a grinning cowhand who suddenly looked away, the remark he'd been about to pass forgotten.

The room clerk inside knew Zeb. He knew him well enough to hand over two room keys without asking any fool questions. Zeb growled, "I'll register us later," as he carried Beth to the second floor. Behind them the room clerk grinned and said, "Any way you like it, Mr. Macahan!"

Beth snuggled in his arms as he climbed the steps, and murmured, "I think we've caused a few raised eyebrows. I've never checked into a hotel just like this before."

Zeb didn't answer. He kicked open the door, carried Beth to the brass bedstead, and lowered her to it, still wrapped in the blankets. He straightened up and said, "You stay like that till I come back with the doctor, hear?"

"Zeb, I have to go to the toilet!"

"There's a thunder mug under the bed. You can use

it once I light out, but you're not to leave this room and you're to stay in bed. You got that, girl?"

"Yes, Master, just rub the lamp three times and your every wish shall be my command."

He laughed and went outside. He closed the door gently behind him, and Beth sat up as she heard the final, no-nonsense click of a key turning in the door lock.

"Come back here and unlock that damned door!" she called, but there was no answer. She hadn't really expected there would be.

"Oh, well," she thought, throwing aside the blankets, "at least, if I'm locked in, nobody can pester me with damn-fool questions. I didn't recognize any of the crowd out front. Maybe this time nobody from my past will catch up with me."

CHAPTER 10

That night, as Zeb lounged against the bar of the hotel's attached saloon, a pleasant-enough-looking cuss wearing tie-down holsters came through the swinging doors and headed in Zeb's direction. Tie-down holsters made a man in Zeb's line of work thoughtful, but he studied the approaching stranger blank-faced, in the mirror behind the bar. It was an old trick, but tricks got old because they often worked. Zeb's back was to the approaching stranger, but he could see every move, and sometimes it paid to give a man an inch or two of rope. The stranger eased his way around a card game and kept coming. The piano player and a bar gal were behind him in Zeb's possible line of fire now, so the stranger either didn't care all that much about piano players and bar gals or, just as likely, didn't have a war in mind.

The stranger bellied up to the bar next to Zeb and, catching his eye in the mirror, asked, "You Zeb Macahan?"

"That's me. What are you drinkin'?"

"I'm Clay Logan. Deputy U.S. Marshal, and Uncle Sam says I have to pay for my own drinks, but I'll shake to show I don't aim to be disrespectful."

The two tall men shook hands and, ceremony out of the way, turned back to carry on their conversation by way of the mirror. The Federal lawman smiled thinly as he said, "I noticed you had me under your gun with that pier glass, Zeb. Doesn't surprise me. I've heard a lot about you, Macahan."

"Nothin' you can prove, I hope."

"Wouldn't try. You want another? I'm allowed by Uncle Sam to *buy*."

Zeb nodded and said, "When the company's right a man's a fool to refuse."

Logan caught the bartender's eyes and called out, "Bottle and another glass, Charlie."

The deputy marshal waited until the bartender supplied them with his order. Then he poured two drinks as he asked Zeb quietly, "That woman you got the doctor tending to up in the hotel—you mind if I ask what happened to her?"

Zeb shrugged and said, "As long as you're the law, I'll tell you. Some trashy hide hunters caught her and, uh, sort of mistreated her. Doc says she's got a concussion from bein' walloped about a mite."

"My God, you mean they . . . Where are the bastards now?"

"Just keep on drinkin', Deputy. You don't have to worry about arrestin' nobody."

"I don't? Oh, she's too ashamed to press charges, huh? Lots of times it happens that way, but, damn it, I hate to see animals like that get away with it!"

"They didn't. Not the two I run on to, least ways. They're both in the ground. The other—don't know.

She says there was three. I never laid eyes on the third, and he's likely gone for good."

Logan nodded and said, "What about the woman? Who is she and where does she hail from?"

"She says her name is Smith. I never got around to askin' where she hailed from."

The deputy sighed and said, "Look here, I'm not bein' nosy to rawhide folks, Zeb. It's my job."

"Hell, I know that. But it's over. What happened happened, and them as done it is dead and buried and forgot."

"Dead and buried, mebbe. Not forgot. I've been gettin' a lot of fuss and feathers from the circuit judge on the killing in this territory. Since the Indian troubles have died down folks are clucking their tongues a mite back east about the way you old boys do things out here. I mean, you likely had a right good reason for blowing two growed men away, but there's papers to fill out and such. The judge likes to ask questions and see the corpus delicti once in a while."

Zeb took a sip of his drink, shrugged, and said, "Well, I don't know how delicti them two corpuses is, they been in the ground a few days. If he's all that interested in seein' 'em he has a smart ride an' some diggin' up to do."

"Zeb, 'corpus delicti' means the body of the crime, not a real body, lessen a crime's been committed."

"I know that. I was only funning. Only, there wasn't no crime in my gunning them two rascals down, Deputy. Leaving out what they done to the gal, they was trying to do me in when I finished 'em in self-defense."

"If it was up to me I'd take your word for it and we'd be quits, Macahan. I know your rep, and your word would be good with me. The judge is due into Three Rivers the first of the week, though, and he's a funny bird. It'd be better if he was to hear the story from you instead of secondhand from me, savvy?"

"Am I under arrest?"

"Do I look like an idiot? I ain't got charge one agin you, Zeb. I'd just take it sort of kindly if you could see your way clear to stay over here in town a few more days."

"Well, my ponies deserve a rest, and I wasn't headed no place special."

Logan heaved a sigh of relief and said, "Thanks, Zeb. You'll never know what a favor you've done me by being so reasonable."

Zeb laughed and said, "I reckon I know. Your orders was to hold me here for a hearing, one way or another, wasn't they?"

The deputy smiled sheepishly and nodded. "Yeah. I was sort of wondering if I had a chance agin you, too. Like I said, I know your rep."

Zeb shrugged. "I'd say it would have been fifty-fifty, but I've never been a man for gunnin' down reasonable folks, and, what the hell, I ain't got nothin' to hide from judge or Jesus."

CHAPTER 11

Upstairs in the hotel room Beth was with the doctor Zeb had fetched her. Dr. Cox was a handsome man in his thirties and Beth had been working on his manly feelings, not to seduce him, but to get him on her side. With the fine honed instincts of an experienced woman of the world, she knew he was at least a little charmed, but the young doctor was trying to remain professional as he asked her sternly, "Have you been seeing double, Miss Smith?"

Beth dimpled and said, "Only when I don't get my own way."

"I can see you're a woman who's used to having her own way, ma'am. You haven't lost your sense of humor, either. I'm sure your skull wasn't fractured, but—"

"I was about to say I'll be seeing double, triple, and fire engine *red* if you dare tell Zeb Macahan I'm to remain in bed a whole damned week!"

The doctor shook his head and said, "I'm going to tell *you* something, Miss Smith, and batting those pretty lashes at me won't make a bit of difference. You've had a concussion of the brain. A bad one. Concussions are tricky affairs. I've seen riders thrown on their heads and sorry as hell they climbed back aboard a bronc instead of going to bed like I told them. Try to think of it as a bruise *inside* your head, ma'am. It swells, subsides, then maybe swells again. The less you move your head, the quicker it'll heal."

"But I feel fine right now, Doctor!"

"I'm sure you do. A year ago I signed the death certificate for a drover who caught a bottle with his head in a barroom brawl. He said he felt fine about an hour before he suddenly pitched from his wagon seat, dead as a mackerel."

"You're just trying to frighten me."

"I wish I could. You don't seem to grasp a thing I'm saying. That idea you have about riding out of here in the morning is madness. You follow my advice and stay the hell away from horses. If you won't stay in bed, at least promise me not to ride!"

"I'll think about it. For how long, Doctor?"

"At least two or three weeks. A month would be better. I wouldn't lay odds on some clot inside that pretty head being jogged loose by a fall, or even a hard ride."

"Oh hell, I promise not to ride off any cliffs on horseback."

The doctor began to close his bag. Not looking at her, and trying not to blush, he said, "Uh, there's something else, Miss Smith. You, um, asked me about the way those men treated you."

"Oh, I'm not worried about that, now that I know I'm not pregnant."

"Miss Smith, I'm, um, a *doctor,* and it was your idea to have me examine you . . . thoroughly."

"For heaven's sake, stop hemming and hawing young man. You're not talking to some blushing schoolgirl now."

"I . . . uh . . . gathered as much. It's none of my business, and I'm not making a moral judgment, but . . . well . . ."

"You're trying to say I've been getting screwed regular, right"

Dr. Cox turned beet red, but he managed not to lose his dignity as he sniffed and said, "Thinking only of the danger to your brain, I have to advise you strongly against, well, hand-holding in the moonlight."

"My God, how delicate you put things, Doctor. Your words of caution have been duly noted. But I'll personally poison you if you relay a word of that to Zeb Macahan!"

"I'd just as soon the two of you worked it out between you, ma'am. Warning you of the clinical dangers is my duty as your physician. As I said, your morals are your own business."

"For that I thank you, Doctor. Don't worry about Zeb and me. We'll be careful."

But Dr. Cox was worried as he rose to leave. The patient was a beautiful woman for her age, and the body was that of a firm girl half her admitted age. Cox didn't know what Macahan was made of, but he knew *he'd* have a hard time leaving her alone for three weeks!

CHAPTER 12

Back near Billy Fargo's hidden cabin, a rabbit nibbled a camas bulb atop a small sunspangled rise between two trees. Young Luke Macahan spotted it as he hobbled out onto the porch with his improvised crutches. Standing on his good leg, Luke leaned the crutches against the cabin wall and reached for the rifle hanging on the rail.

Before he could draw a good bead, however, Billy Fargo burst out with a roar of "Hold on there, boy! Have you gone loco?"

Luke turned, still holding the rifle, to ask, "What's wrong? It's a chance for fresh meat on the table, damn it!"

"Yeah, and the sound of the shot will carry for miles. I ain't anxious to 'nounce my whereabouts for no rabbit, boy."

Abashed as the meaning of his words sank in, Luke said, "I forgot the McQuiston gang. I'm sorry, Billy. I just aimed to help. We're low on grub, and it's time I pulled my weight hereabouts!"

"Gimme that goddamn gun and set, boy. I'll tell you when it's time to worry about such. I knows it's time to fetch more grub. I'll be back directly, Lord willin' and the cricks don't rise."

Luke leaned against the rail to steady himself as he persisted. "You're not going to raid those trappers again, are you?"

Billy hefted the rifle with a crooked grin and said, "Hell, they git lonely 'lessen I come out to play with 'em once in a while."

"Damn it, Billy. You're gonna purely get your fool self killed!"

"Shucks, I been kilt by Arapaho and kilt by avalanche, but I always got over it. You jist set a spell, and I'll see do they have some chocolate."

Ignoring the youth's shouted warnings, Billy vanished into the trees and scampered through the thickest brush in a zigzag course forming part of a great circle. Despite his crippled legs, Billy Fargo moved, without conscious thought, like an Indian brave on a medicine raid.

The second growth and downed rotten logs of the old burn were a jackstraw tangle that would have made it almost impossible to walk on the soft forest floor even if he had not been covering his tracks, or, rather, not leaving many.

Billy ran along a long charred log in a crablike scuttle, leaped to the flat expanse of a granite outcropping, and followed the hard rock a good four hundred yards without leaving so much as a scuff mark in the mossy lichen. He leaped from the last half-buried boulder to a patch of sun-dried mud. Ran along another log in a doubled-back but goal-oriented course, then came to the little running brook he could wade up for a mile or so without leaving footprints. The place he left the brook had been cunningly chosen, and missed more than once by the keen-eyed tracker, Gordon. Most men leaving a stream searched for a rock or fallen log, to avoid leaving footprints in the streamside mud. Billy knew this as well as Gordon. Gordon and the others would be going over every hard surface near any stream near their camp with a fine-tooth comb. Billy left the stream by way of a lily-pad-covered frog swamp, being careful not to tear or displace so much as a leaf.

The wily old man stopped in the center of the little boggy pond, slung the rifle across his back, and reached up to grasp a low-hanging branch of crackwillow. He pulled himself up into the tree and swung through its wide crown hand over hand, like a crip-

pled but still spry little ape. He slid out along another
branch, yards from the muddy edge of the frog pond,
and dropped lightly to the flat top of a big tree stump.
His next leap landed him in the dead center of a
huge ant pile.

Astonished and enraged harvester ants boiled out of
their mound of twigs and pebbles as Billy jumped
away to another rocky ledge, cackling with glee. Within an hour, he knew, the ants would have repaired
the damage to their mound and his unavoidable footprints would be filled in.

He worked his way along the safe side of the mass
of boulders ridged between him and the trappers'
camp. There was no way over the rimrock, and both
ends lay in open soft sand. The trappers had considered their raider's coming from this direction more
than once, but they'd never found a way over, and
Gordon had pronounced the pathways around it free
of recent footprints.

Billy knew a better way. He came to a cavelike
crevice in the massive wall of rock and, dropping to
his hands and knees, moved through it. The low rock
tunnel led through the rimrock. The trappers didn't
know this. They'd found the entrance on the other
side as soon as they'd thought to look for it, months
before. But after a long uncomfortable crawl from the
far side, Gordon had pronounced it a blind tunnel. It
seemed to end in a mass of tangled dead roots and
fist-size pebbles.

It did. A colony of pack rats had walled the narrows
of the natural tunnel in with their huge communal
nest of gathered twigs and stones.

Billy Fargo reached the pack-rat nest, pulled a
crowbar from his belt, and smashed his way through
on hands and knees as pack rats chittered and ran
over and around him in the darkness. Billy paid them
no mind. Pack rats were kind of cute and seldom bit.
The little cusses were his friends. He'd likely have to
bull his way through a half-rebuilt nest coming back.
The rats were regular little beavers for building nests.

They'd repair it ahint him and block pursuit if those damn-fool trappers even bothered to have another look down the narrow hole.

When he reached McQuiston's camp this time he found it seemingly deserted. Two newly constructed canvas-covered lean-tos caught his eye. It was hard to say what might or might not be in either one. Billy moved in, cautious, keeping to the shadows of the trees, and reached the first one. He slid the skin door aside, peered in, and saw that it was filled with furs. The boys had made a right nice haul since he'd visited them last.

The second lean-to door was built more solidly, of saplings tied with rawhide. Billy whipped out his bowie, cut a lashing, and opened it.

The lean-to was full of food—fresh supplies they'd likely just packed in. Billy took the wadded gunnysack from under his jacket and shook it out, stepping inside to help himself.

A gruff voice suddenly called out, "That you, Potter?"

Billy Fargo froze in the shadowy interior, a ham half stuffed in his gunny sack. The voice belonged to that big oaf, Rackley. Who in hell was Potter? Oh, yeah, the halfwitted wrangler they all made fun of. Billy relaxed. Neither one of them old boys had a lick of sense.

Billy filled his sack, and was getting ready to slip away when Rackley called out, "Damn it, Potter, the boss tolt you to stay outten them vittles!"

Billy Fargo nearly jumped out of his skin when a voice right in his ear yelled out, "I ain't in the vitttles, Rackley! I just done *catched* the one who *is!*"

Billy whirled to face the halfwit, Potter, who had him covered with the rifle trained on his belt buckle.

Potter grinned agreeably at the man he had the drop on and said, "Haw, you ain't no ghost after all, are you? I reckon you didn't think I seed you pussy-footin' in outten the treeline, huh?"

Billy didn't answer. Moving as if his life depended

on it, and knowing it did, Billy threw himself under the muzzle of Potter's rifle and pushed it up as it went off. Crabbing along in an impossibly low squatting run, he kicked Potter's shins out from under him and dove through the wall of the flimsey lean-to, bringing half the roof down on the surprised and suddenly seated Potter.

He ran for his life, all thought of caution abandoned, as, behind him, Potter and the aroused Rackley followed at an angry lope, gaining on the old cripple with every bound.

Billy Fargo vanished from their sight a moment as he tore between a boulder and a massive tree. Rackley and the halfwit followed at a dead run. They slowed to a puzzled walk on the other side as they faced an open expanse of mountain meadow with no sign of the old thief.

A rifle round snickered into the firing chamber, and both men turned to face Billy Fargo, holding his Hawkins on them. He'd ducked to one side and suckered them like greenhorns!

"You both git back afore I blows you both off your bootheels!" Billy warned.

Potter's voice sounded reasonable, considering, as the halfwit grinned and said, "Hey, you're crazy, ain't you, old man?"

Rackley added, "He'll kill you, Pop. McQuiston'll kill you deader'n hell, this time!"

Billy snapped, "He'll have to catch me fust. You both git along an' leave me be. I'll kill you both, lessen you move out fast!"

Rackley pleaded, "You can't go on this way, old man. You can't jest come in and take our food like we'uns was some general store! Why don't you jest go 'way and leave us be? We don't *aim* to kill you, but—"

"I said *git* and I *means* git. You varmints is on my mountain, and if anybody dies, you'll have brung it on your own selves."

Rackley shook his head, turned to his sidekick, and

said, "Come on, Potter. Let's go on back afore the old fool pulls that durned old trigger. The boss ain't gonna like this, old man."

Potter followed his slightly brighter comrade, asking, "Cain't we take him, Rackley? It frets me to let him go after I was so foxy in catchin' him."

Rackley turned to see Billy Fargo slipping away around a rise and shook his head again, saying, "He won't git away so far, old son. There's no use takin' chances agin a man who's already daid."

"What does you mean he's daid? He jest got the drop on us and cussed us out, Rackley. I used to think he was a ghost, but—"

"That's my point, Potter. He *used* to git away clean as a whistle. He had us flummoxed, and none of us knew who or what he was lookin' fur. But I've seen him twice. You jest saw him, too. The crazy old coot's takin' chances and gettin' bold as a wolverine full of trade likker."

Potter nodded and said, "That's how you know we'll catch him, huh?"

"Yeah. That's how I know he's a dead man, too. Let's find the others and see if we can cut his trail afore sundown."

CHAPTER 13

Once recovered from his fright, Billy Fargo started thinking clearly again. He deliberately left footprints leading safely away from his hideout before heading home with his loot in a wide, safe circle. It took time, though, and by late afternoon young Luke Macahan was worried.

He'd learned to get around with one crutch, leaving one hand free for action. Outside the cabin, Luke was searching without success for Billy's sign when the old man suddenly appeared behind him and snapped, "What are you doin' out here away from the cabin, boy? Spyin' on me, was you?"

Luke turned with a relieved smile to say, "Spying? What are you jawing on about now?"

"Well, what else does you call it . . . sneakin' around out here on that sly crutch of your'n!"

"Why, you crazy old fool, I was worried about you!"

"Why why'n hell cain't you stay put, 'stead of pussyfootin' up on a man an' scarin' him outten a year's growth! Your worry about your own self, boy. You'll fall and bust that laig agin, tryin' to follow a growed man on that crutch!"

Luke hobbled after Billy awkwardly, as the old man made no effort to set a comfortable pace for the boy. Luke called after him angrily, "I told you I come after you because I was worried about you. It's almost sundown and you've never been gone this long. I figured you maybe got drowned, or clawed by a bear, or . . . Hell, anything can happen to a crazy old coot like you!"

Billy Fargo stopped and whirled about to shout, "Old coot, am I? Well, I'll allow this chile walked these mountains afore you was a gleam in your daddy's eye, but, old as I may be, I got more sense'n to go stickin' my fool foot in a b'ar trap! This chile ain't the fool in these parts, sonny. The only fool hereabouts is you!"

"Hey, you have no right to call me no fool, Billy!"

"I got ever' right! I'm the one puttin' grub in your fool mouth, ain't I?

Luke flushed. As he hobbled back to the cabin he snapped, "Well, if that's the way it is, then I'll be sayin' thank you for ever'thing and I'll be lightin' out right now!"

"Ha! I'd like to see how far you'll git on one laig and a stick!"

Luke swore under his breath and hobbled over to the lean-to stable and pole corral. He braced his crutch against the lean-to and hopped on one leg to get his saddle. His pony flinched at its master's unfamiliar motions, but Luke soothed the nervous mount with his voice and, awkwardly, managed to get the saddle in place.

As he was cinching up, Billy joined him with Luke's holstered sidearm and saddle gun. His voice was like that of a pouting child as he snapped, "Here. Don't want you to leave nothin' of your'n ahint!"

Luke was pouting, too, as he muttered, "Much obliged."

The old man swallowed, then said, "Boy, you're a-gonna wish you wasn't so choosy of your company, come an hour from now. I mean, even if you do manage to mount that fool hoss . . . Do you hear me, boy?"

"I hear you!" snapped Luke, not looking at the old man. He grasped the horn and cantle, kicked off with his good left leg, and swung the splinted broken limb around and over.

Luke almost made it. But the enormity of his mistake was obvious as he felt the world spinning round and saw the sky go dark for some blamed reason. He swayed atop the pony, fighting to hold his thoughts together, as a wave of fire lanced up his right side and numbed his fingers. Then he was falling from some great height, wondering who he was and where he'd fallen from.

Billy Fargo moved fast and caught Luke by the shoulders as he slid out of the saddle in a dead faint. The old man got an arm under the boy's legs and started carrying him back to the cabin, muttering, "You must be a Macahan, right enough. Your whole damn tribe is stubborn as army mules, and twice as ornery!"

CHAPTER 14

By guess and by God, Zeb bought Beth a new dress at the general store. It didn't fit all that well, but she looked respectable at least, and once he had her fit to be seen on the streets of Three Rivers he took her back to the store in person to pick out some more new duds. She needed a whole new wardrobe, and despite her protests, Zeb allowed as he had enough to outfit her. He pointed out how much he'd saved by not marrying up with her twenty years before.

The store was gloomy and inhabited by two old townies playing checkers near the cold potbellied stove and a pair of clucking old hens who sniffed but pretended not to notice Beth and her tall escort as Beth rummaged through the racks for something less tasteless. She was beginning to forgive Zeb's first choice in dresses. Apparently he'd picked the best one in the store at that!

Holding up a gingham print, Beth muttered, "Somehow doesn't flatter, does it?"

Zeb grinned and asked, "Who are we out to flatter? You or me?"

"I'm trying to look like a *lady,* dear. I'll bet there's some delicious gossip going on behind our backs, Zeb."

"I don't mind. You're the best-lookin' thing that's ever hit this town."

"Yes, and I'll bet everyone knows you've been paying all my bills at the hotel. You know what they'll be making of that, don't you?"

"Sure. That's why I take it as flattery. Old goats

74

like me don't git to have a scandal with a goddess very often."

"Oh, dear, that does deserve a kiss, but let's not add fuel to the talk that's already going around about us."

Zeb nodded wryly and murmured, "The hell of it is that the gossip's not true. I've been afraid to touch you since we come down off the high country."

"I told you it was safe, silly."

"I know what you told me. I asked the doctor, and he sort of looked off into space without giving me a straight answer. What did you threaten him with, scalping or burning at the stake?"

Beth selected another dress. Holding it against her, she looked in a mirror as she muttered, "I said I'd poison him if he told you about my concussion, but I see I wasted my time. That's the trouble with being in love with a mind reader. I don't think any of these store-bought town dresses are worth having. Do you mind if I select some riding togs, dear?"

"Sure, go ahead. I told you to buy anything you want. I've been savin' the money the army paid me, and next to clean livin' there's nothin' like spending hard-earned coin on a pretty gal."

She picked up a split riding skirt from a counter, looked at it through eyes suddenly blurred with tears, and murmured, "Oh, Zeb, if only you'd come back to me that summer. Or if only I'd had enough faith in you to wait a little longer . . ."

He looked away and muttered, "Yeah, likely both our lives'd been a mite different, Beth."

"We'd have had grown children by now. Maybe even grandchildren!"

"Mebbe. I ain't so sure that'd been such a great idea, though."

"Why not? I'd have been proud to . . . to bear your children, darling."

"I dunno, Beth. What if the boys had looked like you and the girls had taken after me? Likely we got off easy, once you think on it!"

"Oh, you big goof!"

She turned to him, putting her arms on his sleeves, as Zeb nodded at two old biddies watching them from near the cash register and warned, "We'd best make our purchases and light out, honey. Afore we cause the local pillars of the church more palpitations!"

Beth laughed and quickly chose a trail-worthy riding outfit from the rough stock on hand. Zeb paid and they went out. It was early, so, after dropping her new clothes off at the hotel, Zeb hired a coach and took Beth for a drive out to the lakeside picnic grounds near town.

The grounds by the lake were deserted at this hour and day of the week. Zeb helped her down, and as they strolled hand in hand along the lake shore, Beth suddenly laughed out loud and said, "Oh God, I feel like singing! I haven't felt so . . . so satisfied and comfortable about myself in years. I think I feel truly alive for the first time in, damn it, twenty years! We wasted twenty years, you wonderful brute!"

Zeb kicked a stone from the path into the water and nodded with a frown before he answered, "You know, I said I wasn't one for explanations betwixt friends, Beth. I mean, I could live with a twenty-year gap in your life betwixt your husband dying in an Indian attack and me gettin' you back from them hide skinners. But we was together when we made that signed statement for the Deputy U.S. Marshal, and, well, some of what you said won't wash, Beth."

She snuggled against him and said, "I don't want to think about the past, Zeb. We're together again after all those awful empty years, and what does anything else really matter?"

"It ain't me, Beth. It's what you told Deputy Logan."

"All right, I lied when I said my name was Smith. But I've used it for years, dear. There's nothing terribly complicated about my past. After running away from the Indians who captured me I took a new name and started a new life. It wasn't a terribly exciting life.

Just teaching school as plain old Spinster Smith, down near White River."

"You've been teaching school near White River, Beth?"

"I said so, didn't I? Does that surprise you? My teaching school?"

"No. You always was smart enough to do most anything, Beth, but are you sayin' them hide skinners captured you down near White River?"

"Yes, of course. You heard me tell the deputy marshal how they kidnapped me as I was on my way home from the schoolhouse."

"Yeah, I heard."

"What's the matter, dear? Why don't you believe me?"

"I don't know what I believe or don't. You see, Beth, the south herd's been shot off for a good two or three years. Yet them hiders had you hid under prime buffalo robes. It sort of makes a man wonder some."

"I have no idea where they got their hides, darling. After they kidnapped me they weren't interested in, um, hunting."

She looked away and added bitterly, "Do we have to keep talking about that nightmare, Zeb?"

"I don't like to think how high is up or how long is forever, Beth. Thoughts on dyin' can keep a man awake at three o'clock in the mornin', too. But I've found facin' unpleasant facts can sometimes solve 'em."

"Darling, there's nothing to solve. What's done is done, and it's time to start thinking of our future. We've years ahead of us to rake over the little that's interesting about my past."

"Beth, when that judge gets here, he's not gonna ask about no future. Two men have been killed over you, and another one's wanted for rape, kidnapping, and who knows what else."

"I gave the deputy the best description of him I could, Zeb."

"Yeah, and you told him your name was Smith and that you're a schoolmarm."

"You don't believe me, Zeb?"

"Don't matter what I believe, Beth. Don't matter to me why you lied to the deputy, neither. But, be-twixt old friends, we're gonna purely have to come up with a more likely story for that damned old judge!"

CHAPTER 15

For whatever reason she had, Beth stuck to her story in the face of Zeb's skeptical questioning. But Zeb was righter than he knew, for as they returned to town and went to eat at the hotel restaurant more than one pair of eyes were watching them.

Deputy Marshal Logan was lounging in the doorway of his Federal office as Beth and Zeb vanished for the moment from his view. Dr. Cox had noted them alight-ing from the carriage as he walked along the board sidewalk across Main Street. His eyes met those of the bemused deputy as he approached the Federal office. Cox and Logan were drinking associates and occa-sional confederates in a criminal investigation, as Cox was the nearest thing to a forensic surgeon in the terri-tory and had helped Logan more than once after a shootout.

Cox slowed his pace as he spotted the deputy. Fol-lowing Logan's gaze across the street, the doctor nodded and grinned. "The town's got a nice little ro-mance to talk about, hasn't it?"

Logan shrugged and said, "Don't give a hang one way or the other who's been sleepin' with whomsoever.

I've been lied to, Doc. It riles me when folks lie to me on the job."

"Who are you talking about, Macahan and Miss Smith?"

"Yeah, ain't that name, Smith, a bitch? I wonder what her real name is. She didn't tell you, did she, Doc?"

Cox shook his head and said, "Medical ethics aside, I haven't anything on her you could use, Logan. All I'm prepared to swear to is that she's a forty-odd-year-old white woman. She told me her name was Smith, and the two of 'em have made no secret about their being, well, sort of friendly."

"I don't care what she's doing here in Three Rivers, Doc. It's the story she tells about being kidnapped down near White River by them hide hunters."

"I can tell you she's been beaten and abused. That part seems to be true enough."

"Mebbe. But I just got me a telegram from Johnson City. U.S. Marshal's office. That's headquarters for the White River district, Doc."

"All right, so?"

"So neither the sheriff of White River County, the U.S. Marshal in Johnson City, nor anyone else down there has word about a schoolteacher being kidnapped, missing, or Smithed."

"You mean there's no schoolteacher named Smith, abducted or otherwise, from White River?"

"That's about the size of it, Doc."

"But, damn it, the woman *had* been abused, and Macahan said he had to kill two men to free her!"

"I know. Sort of makes you wonder, don't it?"

"Come on. Macahan's known in the territory as a tolerably honest man!"

"I know his rep, Doc. Know more'n one good old boy to make a fool over hisself over a good-lookin' filly, too. You mind what the Good Book says about Samson and Delilah?"

The doctor shook his head and insisted, "I've heard

a lot about Macahan, and Kit Carson and Jedediah Smith and Joe Walker. The mountain men are rough and live by a fierce code of their own, but they hate a quitter and they hate a liar. Besides, you've missed one thing."

"What's that, Doc?"

"Let's say Zeb Macahan *has* turned bad for the sake of a beautiful woman. Let's say after a lifetime of living by the rough but honest code of his breed he's suddenly changed. It still won't wash!"

"You already said that, Doc. Git to the point."

"The point is simply this. Zeb and the woman had no reason to come to you with a made-up story!"

"Huh? Sure they did. You can't jest gun down two growed men without you say *somethin'* about it!"

"You're dead wrong, Logan. Who else but Zeb and the woman told you word one about the killings? How would you have heard of the kidnapping or the rescue if they'd just kept their mouths shut? Think about it. Has anybody filed a missing-persons report? Has anybody filed a murder charge? Hell's bells. If Zeb's not telling it like it is, how do you know any-body's *dead?*"

Logan pursed his lips as he digested the doctor's words. Then he nodded and said, "All right. Suppose we try it thisaway. Suppose we go along with ever'thing happening jest the way Zeb Macahan says it did, from the time he came upon them hide skinners and the gal? That still leaves *her* with a mighty spooky story, Doc."

"Keep talking, I think I follow what you're getting at, Logan."

"It ain't all that hard to follow. Like I told you, there never was no schoolteacher named Smith near White River. There never was a kidnap near White River, and what in hell would hide hunters be doin' down that way if they aimed to kidnap schoolteacher one?"

"I see. You think Zeb's telling the truth as he sees it, but the woman's story is a lie. Wouldn't that mean she's been trying to pull the wool over old Zeb's eyes?"

Logan spit and asked, "Why not? She's purely been trying to pull the wool over ever'body else's, ain't she?"

CHAPTER 16

At Billy Fargo's cabin, young Luke Macahan opened his eyes, groaned, and muttered, "Double damn! Did I bust the fool leg again, Billy?"

The old man looked up from the beaver trap he was fixing by the light of the fireplace and said, "Nope. You put a fright in both of us, boy, but when I mends a laig I mends it right. Your foot'll stay on short of earthquake or Injuns, but you ain't got enough blood in you yet for sudden moves."

"I guess I should say thanks for hauling me back inside."

"Shoot, I'm gettin' used to it. Comes from takin' up with green kids, I reckon."

Luke sat up, swung his legs to the floor, and, finding his crutch nearby, hobbled over to join the old man by the fire. As Luke sank to a seat in a barrel chair, Billy Fargo snorted, "All rested up and full of beans agin, are you? Why don't you go out and wrestle a b'ar while you're about it?"

Luke smiled sheepishly and said, "It's feeling better. What's that?"

"What does it look like? It's a beaver trap."

"I mean that big brown jug beside your tool kit."

"Oh, that's my medicine. Good for what ails a man. Want some?"

Luke nodded, and Billy pulled the cork and handed

him the jug with a sly expectant grin. Luke sniffed at the contents, expecting whiskey, and gasped, "Jehovah's whiskers! What in hell *is* it?"

Billy cackled and said, "I sure was hopin' you'd take at least a sip, but this ain't my night, I reckon. You may not cotton to it, boy, but to a beaver it smells like true love!"

"Kee-rist! It smells like a dead skunk buried under chickenshit!"

"It's the oil from a she-beaver's privates, son. Put a dab on a trap stake and the he-beavers come a-runnin' and a-courtin'. I know it don't smell like perfume to ussen, but, then, we'd have to be right hard up to want to kiss a she-beaver in the fust place. Likely there's jest no accountin' for taste in sech matters. It's jest as well. How'd ugly wimmen ever git married iffen ever'body had the same idears on beauty?"

Luke handed back the trap oil with a laugh and said, "My Uncle Zeb used to tell us about the old days in these mountains. I'd forgotten about beaver glands and such. I reckon there was a lot to learn, back then."

Billy Fargo nodded and said, "We larned. Those of us who stayed alive did, least ways. I remember your Uncle Zeb larnt faster than most. Yep, he larnt fast and he larnt good. Good as any chile ever et fat cow."

"Fat cow?"

"Injun buffalo talk, boy. Fat cow was good times. Tough bull was bad. Mostly we et buffalo cow an' beaver tail. Chile can live forever on meat like that. Only . . . well, them days didn't last forever. Seems they was gone almost soon as they got started, but, do Jesus, them was days to remember. There was never a time like that afore, and there'll never be a time like that again, but while it lasted them days did shine."

"Uncle Zeb used to talk about the shining days, Billy. Why were they called that?"

"Shining? 'Cause they shone, of course. Like the sun catchin' the sights of your rifle as you drawed a bead at dawn, or the shine of sun on the ice froze to a lodge pole on a winter's mornin' when your squaw lay warm in your arms under a buffalo robe. Ever'thing seemed to shine more then, boy. The Injuns knowed shinin'. They taught us 'bout it when we fust come west followin' the beaver."

"I guess you old-timers got to know the Injun gals right well, huh?"

"Yep. The shinin' times was friendlier times, and the Injuns was eatin' fat cow. Sometimes they'd git riled and kill some old boy who'd wronged 'em, but it wasn't red agin white in the shinin' times. It was good agin' evil, neighborly agin' mean. Lord, Lord, it was jest too good to last."

The old man's fingers caressed the battered beaver trap as if it was the head of an old and faithful hound as he went on, half to himself.

"Shinin' times they was for shore. Back when nobody had no idea what lay beyond the headwaters of the Platte or north of Taos. The best days was afore Jim Bridger rode his bull boat down Bear River and come to the Great Salt Lake. That must have been a sight to see, boy. Old Jim Bridger stompin' about in the shallows of the Great Salt Lake, throwin' his hat in the air after tastin' the waters, and yellin', 'By God, boys, we've reached the Pacific Ocean!' "

Luke laughed and asked, "How long did it take them to know Salt Lake was still miles from the west coast, Billy?"

"Year or so. Then Jed Smith crossed the salt deserts, rode down the Colorado, and took him a walk to Californee. Mexico owned Californee then, so they arrested Jed Smith fur trespassin'. That's why we had a war with Mexico and took the best parts of the country away from 'em."

"Come on. No mountain man declared war on Mexico. That war was over the Texas border or something."

"Likely you're right, boy. Nobody knowed or cared about us in them shinin' days, but it didn't matter. We

was young an' we had the whole of the Rocky Mountains to our own selves then. Yep, from the Wind River
Ranges to the Wasatch and south through the park-
lands to the Sangre de Cristos and the canyon lands
past the painted desert. An' damn near ever' stream
was alive with beaver. Men wore beaver hats in them
days, you see, and a chile could git rich in a summer."

He stared down dully at his old trap and sighed.
"The fashions changed. These days a beaver plew's
hardly worth the cost of harvestin' it. Time has got
hard on us, boy. But in the shinin' times there was no
stoppin' what a chile with a Hawkins rifle and a bowie
could do! No preachers or lawmen to tell a chile he
was doin' wrong. No government to tax him outten his
profits or run him offen his claimed-for-his-own-self
valley."

"What about women? Didn't you miss having white
women, Billy?"

"White women? Hell, that's the worse kind of
wimmenfolk there is! Chile says how do to a white
gal and the next thing he knows she's got him hog tied
to a steady job in some fool farm or town. White gals
is mean as hell about nacheral fun, too. They allatime
frets over shavin' and baths and sech, and dast a chile
look at a well-turnt ankle they throw the Good Book
and a fit at him!"

He stopped to light his pipe, and his eyes dreamed
through the smoke as he rambled on. "Squaws was
better. Did a chile feel the need of a woman's nekked
flesh in the shinin' times, he'd jest take him a pretty
squaw an' do what come nacheral. I mind I took me
three, one winter. Three was one more than I could
rightly service, even in my shinin times, but it was
one cold winter, and . . . Yeah, them was shinin'
times."

"What happened to your squaws, Billy?"

"Don't rightly remember. One run off with another
trapper. The Blackfeet kilt another. The Blackfeet
come ornery, for Injuns. Us an' the Crow took a lot of
Blackfoot hair betwixt us. I mostly hunted with Crow,

you see. Crow gals is pretty, and the men was lik-
able cusses."

"Then there were Indian troubles even in those
days?"

"Well, hell, it helped make life interestin', boy! We
never had no wars with Injuns, like the army does
these days. You might say the game we played
amongst our own selves was sort of a blood sport. Nobody cried, and nobody took it personal when some
old boy went under. Ever'thin' we did was *fun!* Jesus,
it's all like a sweet kid dream now. A sweet, bitter-
sweet dream."

CHAPTER 17

The next time Luke tried his luck at mounting up, his
leg was much better. He'd graduated to a homemade
cane by now, and as he saddled up again it was without
bitterness. Luke was as anxious to find his Uncle Zeb
as ever, and he'd wasted weeks up here with the old
recluse.

He asked Billy to join him in a ride to the nearest
town, Parson's Gap. But Billy refused, saying, "I got
enemies in Parson's Gap, son."

"My God, is there any place you don't have enemies,
Billy Fargo? Who's after you in Parson's Gap?"

"Damn-fool Deputy U.S. Marshal, for one. His
headquarters is in Three Rivers, but he does poke by
Parson's Gap now an' again."

"Why's he mad at you, Billy?"

"He ain't mad. He wants to arrest me. There was
this funny jasper shot a hole through my hat for fun, so
I shot one through his in return."

"The law's after you for shooting a hole in a man's hat?"

"Well, sort of. You see, I aimed a mite low. Took the son of a bitch right betwixt the eyebrows, but I still say he had it comin'.""

Luke shook his head and said, "I know the feeling. The law's sort of after me, too. That's one reason I have to find my Uncle Zeb."

"*You're* on the run, son? What for?"

"I sort of shot a lawman."

"A lawman? Do tell! Did you kill the bastard?"

"No, but the law took it kind of serious just the same."

"That'll larn you never to bother shootin' nobody lessen you aim to kill him right. I ain't partial to badges. Allus poking their noses into folk's business. What'd you shoot this lawman for?"

"It's too long a story, Billy. I don't reckon any lawman will know my face in these parts. It's more important that I find my uncle. Need his help, and there's bad news from home he may not know about."

Billy Fargo looked down at his scuffed boots and muttered, "Well, if you have to, you have to, but this chile was sort of gittin' in the habit of havin' company."

Luke nodded and limped over to a shapeless bundle under a tarp. As Billy suddenly recognized the bundle, he scowled and said, "Them's *my* goods, boy! You aim to steal a bundle of my plews in front of me an' God an' ever'body?"

"Hey, I'm taking them down to Parson's Gap for you. If you can't come along, I'll just have to sell them for you."

"Sell em for *me?* That mean you're comin' back, son?"

"Sure. I'll be headed back this way as soon as I catch up with Uncle Zeb. Don't worry. You know you can trust me with your money."

"The hell you say, boy. This chile don't never trust nobody!"

"You trust me, you old goat."

Billy Fargo grinned slyly and said, "Yeah, I reckon I do. But how long do you aim to stay, once you're back?"

"I don't know. How long do you think you'll need me?"

"Need you? Why, you young pup, Billy Fargo don't need nobody. Besides, you got no call to be needed. What have I ever done for you?"

Well, you saved my life and nursed me back to health. I reckon that puts me sort of in your debt."

"Hell, son, let's not go blubberin' up all over one another over a little Christian charity. I tolt you, I feed squirrels, too."

"I know. I'll be back, Billy. Promise me one thing while I'm gone?"

"What's that, damn it?"

"Promise you'll stay away from McQuiston's camp? You've got enough food and supplies to last you months, and I'll be bringing back more when I come from Parson's Gap."

Billy Fargo shrugged and nodded without saying anything. It wasn't as if he aimed to lie to the boy. Doubtless the fool kid meant well. But couldn't he see how much fun it was to run them ornery rascals ragged?

CHAPTER 18

Zeb Macahan was crossing the street when a rider hailed him with a glad cry of "Uncle Zeb! Zeb Macahan!"

Zeb turned to see his nephew, Luke, reining in a few paces away. Zeb grinned and said, "I'll be damned f it ain't little Luke Macahan, only you've growed some, boy! What in thunder are you doin' here in Three Rivers?"

"They told me in Parson's Gap that you'd been seen here, Uncle Zeb. I've been looking all over creation for you!"

"Well, son, you purely found me. What happened to your leg there?"

"Busted it in a bear trap. It's almost better, and it ain't important."

"You look skinny as hell, too. Get down off that pony and let's put some grub in you. I was headed for the restaurant anyways. Me and a friend is stayin' over there at the hotel."

Luke waited until they were seated in a booth inside and his uncle had ordered before he took a deep breath and said, "I got bad news for you, Uncle Zeb. It'll likely spoil your appetite, but I can't hold it in."

"What's wrong, boy? You in trouble?"

"That ain't important, neither. Uncle Zeb . . . Ma . . . My ma's *dead!*"

Zeb's jaw dropped as he stared at his nephew in numb dismay. Luke nodded and said, "I know how you feel, Uncle Zeb. I can't believe it either. None of us kids can!"

Zeb stared blank-faced at his nephew as he tried to take the news in. Kate Macahan dead? Pretty little Kate of the golden hair and laugh-wrinkled eyes. Zeb licked his lips and asked quietly, "How, Luke?"

Luke said, "Freak accident. Back home at the ranch. She and my brother Josh was out lookin' for a strayed mule when a sudden thunder squall caught 'em in the timber. Before they could ride out of the trees, well, lightin' hit an', Jesus, Uncle Zeb . . ."

"What about Josh?"

"Josh got burned some. He's all right, though. It was Josh carried Ma down from the hills. He was startin' to sleep without dreamin' too much when I left home."

"You poor kids! How did the girls, Laura and Jessie, take it?"

"Bad. Not as bad as they might have, though. Josh thought fast for a kid. He, uh, wrapped Ma's body in a saddle blanket, and us boys never let the girls see what the lightnin' done to her face."

"Oh, Jesus! You're right about one thing, son—I just lost my appetite entire. Your brother and sisters are alone at the ranch now, huh?"

"We'll make out all right, Uncle Zeb. We just thought you ought to be told."

Zeb tossed a silver dollar on the table to pay the waiter for his trouble and got to his feet, saying, "I've got to tell a few folks where I'm headed. I'll meet you at the livery stable, Luke."

"You'll be heading for our spread, then?"

"Of course. Won't you?"

"I can't go home with you, Uncle Zeb. A least, not for a while."

"Why not?"

"I got to go back to the high country. I got some money belonging to an old friend of yours. I sold some pelts for him in Parson's Gap, and, well, he's in trouble and he needs me more'n the kids back home do."

Zeb frowned and asked, "An old friend of *mine,* you say?"

"Yep, the feller who pulled me outten the bear trap and patched me up. Name's Billy Fargo."

"Billy Fargo? Is that old pack rat still alive?"

"Sort of. He's old and beat and tuckered out. He's got a cabin up in the watershed of the Parson. I got to stay with him at least a month or two. With winter coming, I have to make sure he's got a few cords of firewood cut, few haunches of elk hung, some possibles I aim to pack up there with me."

Zeb shook his head and said, "Don't leave without me, then. As I remember, Parson Creek is on my way to your ma's . . . I mean, to your spread. I'd be proud to see old Billy again. I ain't seen Billy Fargo since rendezvous days. Hear later he got in a fight with Liver-Eatin' Johnson and dang nigh lost his liver.

Ever'body figured he'd crawled off to die from the cuttin' Johnson gave him."

Zeb took some coins and a folded paper from his pockets and handed them to Luke, saying, "Might save us some time lighting out if we doubled on some chores, Luke. Like I said, I've got to talk to some folks. This is a bill I run up at the general store. Why don't you pay up as you buy Billy Fargo some possibles and, like I said, we'll meet at the livery stable?"

Luke agreed and Zeb left him to attend the errands. Zeb went first to the marshal's office. He found an old swamper called Bumper mopping Logan's floor. Zeb asked for the deputy, and when Bumper said he'd gone for the afternoon, Zeb explained he had family business to attend to and would be back in about ten days.

He had it easy at the marshal's office, next to the awkwardness of telling Beth about it. She was combing her hair as he explained how his sister-in-law had been killed by lightning and how he was needed for the moment by his orphaned nieces and nephews.

Beth studied him in her mirror as she asked, "Wasn't Kate Macahan that pretty little blonde thing who married your brother before they came west?"

"You know about Kate, Beth. I told you how I sort of fell into my brother's shoes when he went and got himself killed in the war."

"Yes. I was just sort of wondering if his shoes were all you . . . stepped into."

"For God's sake, Beth, the woman's dead!"

"I know. But she was very pretty, and not much older than me, when she was alive."

"All right, have it your own way. I'm riding back to the ranch to make love to my dead brother's dead wife. I'll be back in about ten days."

"Ten days? Oh . . . Zeb!"

He came up behind her and took her in his arms. "Hey, it's no big thing, honey. You'll still be here when I get back, won't you?"

Beth didn't answer. She kissed him. With the

hungry yearning of a woman who knew that when he returned he'd find her once more gone. Back to the limbo, or the hell, of her fugitive life!

He returned her kiss and insisted once more, "I really have to go. The kids need me."

She nodded bravely and asked, "Will you tell me something, honest Injun?"

"What's that, honey?"

"Kate Macahan and you. You did think I was dead. Both of you were free, and she was very pretty. You see, I saw her once, passing through."

That remark raised more new questions than it answered, but Zeb was in a hurry. Passing on the chance to ask how a schoolteacher in White River could have seen his dead sister-in-law at any time, Zeb said, "There was nothing between us, Beth. I liked Kate a lot, but we was never more than friends."

He told himself, as he left, that one white lie deserved another.

CHAPTER 19

Deputy Marshal Logan hadn't told old Bumper where he was going for a very good reason. A lawman staked out likes to stake out private.

Less than an hour after Zeb and Luke Macahan rode out of Three Rivers, Beth "Smith" entered the livery stable in riding clothes and a heavy coat. She'd paid up front and told the stableboy she'd do her own selecting and saddling. The lazy youth had warned her about the walleyed mare named Ribbonbow and gone back to the penny dreadful he'd been reading.

Beth selected a placid gelding with the lines of a good walking horse and began to saddle him. Deputy Logan stepped out from the shadows of the stall he'd been waiting in and opined, sardonic-like, "Well, well, seems like ever'body's in a hurry to git outten town afore Judge Resnick gits here, don't it?"

Beth stammered, "I—thought I'd ride for an hour or so, Marshal."

"I'm a deputy, not the marshal. Ma'am. You do seem to have trouble keepin' life's little details straight, don't you?"

"I don't know what you're talking about. I'm just going for a canter around the lake and back."

"Do tell? That's why you're wearin' that winter coat with the pockets stuffed with vittles, huh? Forgive me for noticin', ma'am, but I see you have a pistol under your coat, too. You reckon there's ducks out by the lake?"

"Listen, after what I've been through I'm not about to ride alone and unarmed any more. Besides, there's been talk about the Sioux getting restless and—"

"Ma'am, I purely hate to call a pretty lady a liar, so mebbe you'd best keep quiet afore you screw yourself in deeper."

"Listen," Beth began, but Logan snapped. "No, *you* listen, Miss Smith or whomsoever! Dr. Cox is a drinkin' buddy of mine, so I know you've been forbid to ride for fun. It's a warm dry afternoon, so that coat means *night* riding, and from the way it's stuffed you're fixed to ride a week."

"I'm very tired of arguing with you," said Beth loftily. She added, "I don't care what you think. I'm going for a ride, and where I ride or when is no concern of yours. It's a free country, isn't it?"

Logan shook his head and said, "Not for a material witness to a double homicide."

"Homicide?"

"That's a fancy word for killing folks. We can do this two ways, Miss Smith. You can go back to your hotel and stay there till Judge Resnick gits here for the hearing, or I can throw you in protective custody. That's a fancy word for jail!"

"Jail? Are you trying to tell me I'm under arrest?"

"Not tryin', ma'am. Tellin'. I'm holdin' you as a material witness under house arrest. That is, I am lessen you make more foolish sudden moves."

"That's insane, sir! *I* haven't done anything! *I* was the *victim!*"

"So you say, ma'am, but, beggin' your pardon, you and old Zeb Macahan have been shadin' the truth a mite. You see, I've been in touch with White River, and, leavin' whether you was ever kidnapped or not, two men have been gunned. It'll be up to Judge Resnick to say if Zeb done it legal or not."

Beth hated herself for what she had to say, but her position was desperate. She smiled wanly and said, "Look, have it your own way. Say I'm a liar, a whore, whatever. I'm *still* not the one who shot it out with those buffalo hunters. Zeb shot them! I was naked and unconscious!"

"Well, I know that, ma'am. That's another good reason for having you hereabouts for the hearing. Don't you want to testify for Zeb Macahan? I mean, without your witnessin' for him, he stands accused by his own words of shootin' down two good old boys just for the hell of it!"

"Oh dear, I hadn't thought of that!"

"I know, ma'am. Likely that was why you figured to light out on us."

"Listen, I really didn't see the shootout. I'd like to help, but . . ."

"Ma'am, you'll help a heap just by staying here for the hearing. You see, I was hunkered down in that there stall when Zeb and that boy rode out."

"I don't follow you. If you didn't want any of us to leave town—"

"Hell, woman, do I look like a greenhorn fool? Of course I didn't want none of you to leave afore the hearing afore the judge. For one foolish minute there, I thought fool thoughts about tryin' to stop a notorious gunfighter sided by his own armed kinsman, but stupid thoughts like that can put a man in Boot Hill pronto."

"Surely you're not afraid of Zeb Macahan?"

"You're damned A I am, ma'am. Hunkered down there, tryin' to git up the nerve to draw on two growed men, it come to me there was a better way. You're it, Miss Smith. I know Zeb Macahan'll never leave you to face the music and the judge alone. As long as I have you, I have Zeb whenever I need him."

"I see, and if you don't have me . . . ?"

"Hell, Miss Smith, you're talkin' foolish. I'm gonna forget this here little talk and you're goin' back to your hotel to await the judge."

"And if I refuse?"

"I told you, jail house for at least ten days. That's when Zeb says he's comin' back. But you won't run agin, Miss Smith. You ain't that stupid. You know you're bein' watched, and even if you should slip out of town on a stolen pony, it's a full day's ride to the next settlement, and should you git there, I'll have wired ahead and they'll be waitin' for you. No, Miss Smith, I reckon you'll be here when the judge wants to question you. One way or t'other."

CHAPTER 20

McQuiston, Gordon, and Potter dismounted as they spotted Rackley's signal from the aspen grove, and tethered their mounts before joining him. As McQuiston reached the gleeful Rackley, Rackley pointed down the slope to a plume of smoke rising above the treetops and said, "There she be, Boss. It's his cabin and spread. I been down and scouted her already. The old spook's alone!"

McQuiston shook his head in disbelief and marveled, "You mean that cabin's been here all this time and in eight months of hunting we've never found it before?"

Rackley shrugged and said, "Could have been there fifty years afore anyone found it, save for the smoke and this rise."

Gordon nodded and observed, "It's ten miles from our nearest trap line, Boss. I don't know how the devil's been covering his tracks, but I'll tell you one thing. He never left track one leading in this direction! Your idea of searching blind, a section at a time, paid off."

McQuiston nodded, snubbed out the corn husk smoke he'd been enjoying and hefted his carbine, saying, "All right. Let's take him!"

The trappers moved down through the trees with a certain woodcraft of their own, for despite his contempt for the newcomers, the overconfident Billy Fargo had misjudged McQuiston and his friends. They were hardly greenhorns. They were hard-bitten mountain men who'd had enough of his harassment.

Billy Fargo was poking at the fire, cursing the green aspen wood for burning with more smoke than heat for his coffeepot, when suddenly the door burst inward, kicked off its leather hinges by the triumphant angry Mike McQuiston.

McQuiston had the old man covered with the carbine he held at hip level. He said, "So this is our ghost! On your feet, old man. You're fixin' to meet your Maker!"

Behind McQuiston, Rackley crowded in, laughing. "That be him, Boss!"

McQuiston said, "The trial's over. Fetch me my rope!"

Billy remained hunkered on his heels, staring up at the men covering him, as he asked, "You aim to hang me?"

"You got it right, old man. I'm gonna fix you so's you'll never steal nothin' agin!"

Billy Fargo shrugged as if in resignation. Then, quite suddenly, he wasn't where he should have been. Crashing over and behind the chair near the fire, Billy rolled along the floor and snatched his old Hawkins gun from where he'd leaned it against the cabin wall. McQuiston and the old man fired at the same time, filling the room with noise and clouds of dense gun smoke. By some miracle, both men remained unscathed. McQuiston fired again and again into the rolling gun smoke, unable to see three feet in front of him in the shadowy confines of the cluttered little cabin.

He realized his mistake almost as he committed it, and snapped, "Take cover, boys!" as he slid his own back along the logs, out of line with the doorway.

McQuiston and his comrades waited tensely, gun muzzles trained on the smoke, as it slowly cleared. When they could see again, the cabin was empty.

Potter moaned. "Oh Jesus, he *was* a ghost!"

But McQuiston pointed his chin at a door ajar in the far wall and snapped, "He slipped out the back way. Follow him, you idiots!"

As McQuiston ran out Billy's back door he met Gordon coming around a corner of the log cabin. The skilled tracker of the outfit pointed at the nearby lean-to shed and said, "He's in there! Look at them heel marks in the dust!"

A mile or so away, Zeb and Luke Macahan reined in at the sound of the distant shots. Luke moaned, "Oh hell! Them shots are comin' from old Billy's spread, Uncle Zeb!"

Zeb nodded and unlimbered his saddle gun, saying, "Let's go!"

Meanwhile, back at Billy's, the old man had reloaded as the trappers started battering in the shed door with a length of log and angry curses. The trouble with a Hawkins was that it fired single shot. The good thing about it was that it fired damn near anything.

Billy loaded it with double ball and a handful of gravel, aimed it at the door, and fired, sending the trappers howling back unharmed but spattered with splinters and dust. Billy laughed. "That'll larn you!" He quickly reloaded.

The old man slipped out another small entrance they didn't know about. Like a prairie dog, Billy Fargo believed in having more than one exit to every chamber. He still carried some scars from the time he'd been trapped in a bawdyhouse crib by an outraged pimp with a broken bottle.

As Billy ran for cover, doubling back to his cabin, he almost ran full tilt into Gordon, who fired from the hip, missed the zigzagging little cripple, and shouted, "Thar he goes! Sweet Jesus, look at him scoot!"

In another part of the forest Zeb Macahan frowned and said, "One of them guns sounded like a Hawkins. T'other was a Spencer repeater. Has Billy picked a feud with anybody you know, Luke?"

Luke said, "Ever hear of Mike McQuiston's bunch?"

"Mike McQuiston? Trapper?"

"That's him. He's been after Billy for months."

"What for?"

"I'm not sure. Billy never said. I think he's been stealin' from McQuiston's outfit."

Zeb groaned and muttered, "Hell, what's the old fool been stealin'?"

"Food, maybe. Maybe beaver plews."

Zeb sighed and said, "Wish you'd told me sooner, boy. It's gonna take us over an hour to work our way up this mountain. Let's go."

But Billy was no longer at his cabin. He was running for his life along a ridge covered with second-growth timber. His bad leg was numb, and his lungs were filled with fire, but he kept running. He had to. McQuiston and his men were right behind him—and gaining!

Billy ran out of cover, but kept running, out in the open across a grassy expanse to who knew where. He wasn't lost. He just hadn't been too concerened with where he was, up to now. Then he saw the cliff ahead, and moaned a curse between gasps for air.

"Look what you've done, you damn fool!" he cursed himself aloud, "You've run clean to the Parson River Gorge, and they've got you hemmed in on a spur!"

Billy limped over to the edge and peered over.

Parson River was a ribbon of white water nearly a thousand feet straight down.

Billy turned, wondering where in thunder his rifle was. Had he dropped it in the woods? What was he gonna do? It was so blamed hard to *think* with lungs full of fire and a heart full of fear!

McQuiston and the others came out of the treeline less than a hundred yards away. They moved out slowly but confidently. McQuiston had nearly tripped over Billy's Hawkins in the woods, so he knew their quarry was unarmed as well as trapped.

McQuiston walked toward Billy Fargo with his carbine cradled in his elbow, a quizzical smile on his hatchet face. He called, "What do you aim to do, old man, jump?"

Billy whipped his bowie from his boot and yelled, "No, I ain't gonna jump. I come out here so's none of you egg-suckin' coyotes kin git ahint me! You're brave as hell, ain't you? Four of you agin an old crippled-up chile? Well, come on then! Who aims to git cut fust? How 'bout you, McQuiston? You want this blade in your gizzard clean up to Green River?"

McQuiston laughed. The halfwit, Potter, asked, "Don't you aim to shoot him, Boss?"

McQuiston shook his head and said, "Hell, that'd spoil half the fun!"

He lowered the muzzle of his loaded gun and moved toward Billy with the slow and confident steps of a house cat moving in on a mouse trapped in a pantry corner.

Behind him, the others grinned and followed, fanning out to take Billy from both sides.

The old man faced them, no trace of fear on his battered features, as he danced back and forth in a crablike shuffle, daring them. "Come on! Come one and all! I've sung my death song to Wakan Tonka, and my blade's honed sharp! What are you all waitin' for? Ain't this a lovely day to die?"

CHAPTER 21

When Zeb and Luke Macahan rode into Billy Fargo's clearing they found the halfwit, Potter, patting down a mound of earth with one of Billy's shovels. As the two Macahans rode down on him, Potter grinned up at them and said, "How do! You boys come to see the ghost? You're a mite late."

Luke gasped and asked, "Who you burying there, friend?"

Potter laughed and said, "Old man. Old man lived hereabouts. It's all right. He was daid."

Zeb silenced Luke with a warning look and asked Potter quietly, "How'd the old man die, friend?"

"McQuiston hung him. Had to knock him down a mite, fust. He was a *fightin'* son of a bitch!"

Luke gagged and gasped. "My God, you killed Billy Fargo?"

"That his name? I didn't kill him. Mike McQuiston did. Mike had to. The old man kept stealin' from ussen, he did. I seed him with my own two eyeballs, stealin' vittles and plews and thangs. He cut Rackley bad, and dang near took my hand off at the end. Lookee here!"

Potter held his bandaged wrist up and added, "Had him a bowie knife, he did. Never seed an old man with so much mean in him!"

Luke put a hand on his holstered Colt, but Zeb grabbed his wrist and muttered, "Easy now."

"Damn it, they *hanged* him, Uncle Zeb!"

Zeb nodded and said, "I know. Let's talk on it afore we make sudden moves. You there, sonny. You say he was caught stealin' plews?"

Potter nodded and said, "That's right. Only way to treat a camp robber."

Zeb turned back to Luke with a questioning eyebrow raised. Luke's face was a mask of misery as he nodded and said, "I was afraid of it. I sold those beaver plews for him in Parson's Gap. He wouldn't tell me where he got 'em."

Luke suddenly turned on Potter and snapped, "Which way is McQuiston's camp?"

"Up to the west. Right by them big rocks as looks like they was pitchforked in a pile."

Luke nodded curtly and spurred his mount around Potter. Zeb caught up with him and called out, "Luke, where do you think you're headed?"

"I'm payin' that murdering McQuiston a visit."

"Might be he's with friends, Luke."

"I'll handle it, Uncle Zeb."

"Luke, listen to me. I knew Billy Fargo afore you was born, and I liked him. But it's startin' to look like he sort of got what was comin'."

"Damn it, Uncle Zeb, he was a harmless old cripple!"

"Son, Billy Fargo was about as harmless as a sack of sidewinders drunk on white lightning! We know now that he was a camp robber."

"Come on, what's stealin' a side of venison or a beaver plew now and again, Uncle Zeb?"

"A beaver plew now and again, son? In this country you'd be safer stealin' a man's woman, or even his horse! Billy was a mountain man, Luke. He knowed the chances he was takin'."

"I don't care! There was no need to murder him!"

"It don't seem like they murdered Billy, Luke. That boy back there says they hung him. Hangin' camp thieves goes with the territory. If Billy was here, he'd tell you the same. If Billy'd caught anyone robbin' him, he'd have done the same. Let it be, Luke."

Luke rode on, saying, "Uncle Zeb, I know you're kin and I respect you, but don't try to stop me. I've made up my mind to search McQuiston out."

"All right. Then what?"

"I'm takin' them in for murderin' Billy Fargo!"

"Takin' 'em in, huh? What if they don't see fit to be took peaceful?"

"I reckon I'll just have to bury them where they drop!"

"You've grown mighty sure of your gun hand, Luke."

"I've had to, Uncle Zeb. I'd take it kind did you wait for me here."

Zeb let him ride off alone for a cooling spell. He trotted his pony back to where Potter was putting a flower on Billy's grave and asked, "How many men with McQuiston, son?"

Potter thought and said, "There's me an' Gordon and Rackley and Mike hisself an', lessee, that's the whole bunch, mister."

"Four, huh? Thanks for buryin' the old man proper like."

"Oh, that's all right. I likes to bury folks. I buried a dog one time. But folks is more fun."

Zeb nodded, checked the chambers of his six-gun, and rode after his nephew, Luke.

Before he could catch up with the boy, Luke had reached the trapper's camp and dismounted behind the screen of the treeline. Luke slipped his pistol from its holster and stepped out into the sunlight, covering the trappers before they'd spotted him.

Mike McQuiston was shaving, feeling pleased with his own reflection in the cracked mirror nailed to a tree. Rackley nursed his injured arm near the fire with Gordon, who was brewing coffee for them.

As McQuiston saw Luke moving in on them with his six-gun leveled, he shot a wistful glance at his own holstered gun, hanging from a branch too far for a sensible man to try for, and, keeping his voice cool, called out to the men at the fire, "Stay put and hang easy, boys. Some young jasper's got the drop on ussen!"

Luke gestured with his muzzle at the men by the fire, snapping out, "I want those rifles chucked into the brush and your pistol belts about your ankles! Move!"

As the trappers hesitated, frozen with surprise more than fear, Luke fired once into the fire, scattering coals and flaming embers over their booted feet. Rackley and Gordon came unstuck, leaped to their feet, and threw their weapons out of sight.

Luke nodded and said, "That's better. Now your knives and pistol belts. On the ground and kicked my way, pronto!"

He waited until they'd disarmed themselves before he turned to their leader and said, "I see your pistol. Where's your rifle?"

"In the tent yonder. What's this all about, sonny?"

"Wipe them suds offen your face and put your shirt back on. I'm takin' you in for the murder of Billy Fargo."

"Was that the old coot's name?"

"It was, and he was a friend of mine. Do you deny killing him?"

"Shoot, boy, the old fool kilt his own self. We'uns only helped him over the Great Divide a mite early. He was dead the day he decided to start stealin' furs."

"You had no right to hang him. You're not the law!"

"Mebbe I ain't, but I live by the code of the mountains. What about your own self, sonny? I don't see no badge on your shirt front!"

"We'll find someone with a badge in Three Rivers, and when we do I'll turn you over to him. You're going to trial for what you done, mister!"

McQuiston shook his head and said, "You're talkin' foolish, sonny. Three Rivers is a long hard ride from here. That's why we made our own rough justice when we caught the old scamp. We hung him 'cause what he done was a hangin' offense. Your friend knowed that. To give him his due, he expected us to do him, and he went down fightin' like a man. Spit in my face just afore I strung him up, an' never said word one 'bout bein' sorry!"

"Get your shirt on. You can tell it to the judge."

"Sonny, I ain't goin' nowheres. I got chores to do."

McQuiston turned his back to Luke and calmly started shaving once again.

Luke fired a shot past McQuiston's ear, shattering the mirror. But as Luke turned his attention from the men by the fire, Rackley snatched a burning brand and threw it, knocking the pistol from Luke's hand as all three rushed him.

Luke was a fair scrapper, but it was three to one and these were mountain men. They had him flat and pinned before he could get in more than a couple of good licks. But before it could go further, Zeb Macahan stepped out from the tree line and shouted, "That's enough, boys!"

McQuiston said, "Hold it, fellers. Seems we got more company." He climbed off Luke to ask Zeb, "Who the hell are you, pilgrim?"

"Name's Macahan. That's my kin you boys are beatin' the stuffin's out of."

McQuiston blinked and asked, "Macahan? Zeb Macahan?"

"The same. Get off my nephew. I reckon he's had enough for now."

As the trappers quickly moved away from the downed youth with anxious grins, McQuiston explained, "We tried to tell him he was crazy, Zeb! He's all riled over nothin'."

Zeb nodded as Luke rose unsteadily to his feet, and told the boy, "That's what I tried to tell you, Luke. I know how you feel, but, damn it, boy, you're purely in the wrong right now!"

"But they killed him, Uncle Zeb, and the law—"

"The law of the mountains is in their favor, Luke. Up here the only law is survival, which you're losin' sight of. Up here when a man robs another's camp he's broke what law there is. When you steal a trapper's pelts you may as well bury an ax in your own fool skull and save ever'body the chore of killin' you!"

Luke sighed, shook his head, and said, "It don't seem right. You mean we just ride off and forget about Billy? Just like that?"

"You ride on, son. I have mebbe a few words to say about what went down. Get goin', boy. I'll catch up in a minute."

Luke hesitated. Then he said, "I'll meet you at the cabin. I aim to leave a marker on Billy's grave."

"You do that, Luke. Have you forgot about them plews you sold in Parson's Gap?"

Luke frowned thoughtfuly at McQuiston for a long hard moment. Then he reached into his jeans and took out a roll of bills. He handed it to the trapper, explaining, "I reckon this is rightly yours, but it don't seem fair!"

McQuiston grinned and said, "By gum, that's white of you, boy. I admire an honest man!"

As Luke walked away without another word, McQuiston turned to Zeb and said, "Your nephew's all man, Zeb. Give him time to grow a mite more bark an' he'll be a real Macahan!"

"Macahans pay their just debts," said Zeb.

Then he swung hard, and knocked McQuiston to the earth with a bone breaking blow.

McQuiston struggled to rise as his two comrades moved toward Zeb. Zeb drew his bowie and kicked McQuiston unconscious in one motion as he purred, dangerously, "Don't mix in it, boys. I don't aim to kill him. Like I said, we Macahans pay our debts, and he's off easy with a busted jaw and a mouth full of loose teeth!"

Rackley and Gordon stepped back uncertainly as Zeb explained quietly, "The code of the mountains gave you the right to kill Billy Fargo. A white man, like you call yourselves, might have offered a worn-out hungry old-timer a hand instead of a rope, but I ain't passin' judgments. I likely had no right to bust anybody's face like that, but I done it, and iffen anybody aims to make anythin' of it, you know my name an' where I can be found."

He waited, saw there were no takers, and nodded curtly. "I'll be on my way, then. When that skunk comes to, remind him what I said about us Macahans never forgettin' our just debts. I'm lettin' Billy's murder slide, knowin' McQuiston didn't know he was a friend of mine. You tell him next time to ask. If anyone else I've ever had a drink with dies at his hands . . . Well, you likely get my meanin', so I'll be sayin' adios, you sons o' bitches!"

CHAPTER 22

In the small trial town of Elk Creek, Zeb's other nephew, Josh Macahan, lounged against a pillar of the stagecoach stop, staring down at one dusty street. Nearby, seated on a bench despondently, were his sisters, Laura and Jessie.

Laura was a willowy blonde in her late teens. Jessie was a younger brunette who normally wore a smile on her gamin face. None of the three Macahan kids had all that much to smile about this afternoon.

Josh turned to the station swamper, sweeping the porch, and sighed. "They coulda busted an axle, I reckon."

The swamper shrugged and said, "Yep, could have."

"Could have been held up by bandits."

"It's possible."

"You reckon maybe the Sioux jumped the stage?"

"Could be. Sioux're ornery Injuns."

"Well, dang it, how long do you wait for that overdue stage afore you do somethin' about it?"

"Till somebody comes along and tells me what to do."

"What if the stage never comes at all?"

"It'll come, son. Always has an' always will."

Josh turned to the girls on the bench with a wry grin and muttered, "I was afraid he'd say somethin' like that!"

The swamper asked, "You kids waitin' on somebody special?"

Josh said, "Don't know."

"You kids don't know who you're waitin' for?"

"Know who we're waitin' for. Don't know as she's all that special. It's our Aunt Molly. She's on her way from Chicago."

"Chicago, you say? That's a far piece. What's she comin' out here for, son?"

"To visit, we hope. Maybe to stay. She never said in her telegram. Didn't even ask if she was welcome. Just said she was comin', dang it."

"From the long faces hereabouts I'd say none of you was all that anxious to meet up with your Aunt Molly, huh?"

"We ain't. If she's comin' to take care of us, we don't need her. We don't need anybody. We can take care of our own selves just fine!"

Old Amos chuckled and opined, "Kids always says that. Said it my own self when I was a boy. You'll larn better with time. How come your big brother, Luke, ain't with you today?"

"We sent him to fetch our Uncle Zeb. Ever'thing's gone wrong of late, Amos. First Ma gets kilt in that thunderstorm, then Luke goes off to fetch Uncle Zeb and neither one of 'em's here. Now Ma's durned old sister's comin' in on that durned old stage, and none of us even knows what she looks like!"

Amos shrugged and said, "If she's kin to your poor ma, she'll likely be a handsome gal. I'm glad I ain't her, though."

"What are you talkin' about, Amos?"

"She's comin' all the way from Chicago to comfort her orphaned kin an' here you three is on your high horses, too ornery to make the poor woman welcome. Decent kids'd be proud to have folks that worried about 'em. Decent kids'd likely know their kilt ma's own sister might be feelin' poorly her own self 'bout what happened to your ma!"

Josh frowned as the old man's wisdom sank in. Then he nodded and went over to where his sisters waited listlessly. Josh said, "I want you gals to listen up! I know how you both feel about some stranger comin' all the way out here to poke her nose in our lives, but she is our kin, and Ma was her sister, so she's likely as cut up about what happened as we are. I want you gals to make her welcome."

The two girls exchanged sullen, stubborn glances. Josh insisted, "We don't know her, but she may not be so bad. If she was Ma's kid sister, she might even be as nice as Ma was!"

Jessie pouted, "Nobody was ever as nice as our Ma, 'cept Pa and maybe Uncle Zeb!"

Laura nodded in agreement and said, "Uncle Zeb should have been here by now. Luke's been gone for weeks!"

Josh said, "Pa's been dead for years, and you know Uncle Zeb's wanderin' ways. Likely Luke's had trouble trackin' him, but they'll be along directly."

He broke off as the swamper yelled, "Stage comin' in!"

Josh went back to the porch rail as, sure enough, the swaying Wells Fargo rig thundered down the street in a cloud of dust and pulled up at the station.

The driver called down to the swamper, "Howdy, Amos!"

"How do, Rocky. Had some trouble, did you? You're a mite late."

"Bridge was out agin, and we come around by way of Curry. Don't know why nobody hereabouts can fix that damn bridge proper!"

During the exchange the shotgun rider had dismounted to unload the passengers' luggage from the boot. Josh and the girls watched warily as a young dude in a dusty suit climbed down, followed by a portly man in a wilted collar. Both men stood by the doorway to help the next passenger alight.

She was a living fashion plate in a huge black picture hat, and although she, too, was covered with a film of trail dust, her expensively tailored traveling suit was unwrinkled and she still looked as if she'd just stepped from the fashion pages of *Lesley's Illusstrated Weekly*.

The two men fell over each other trying to help her down, and she favored both with a gracious smile of thanks. The devastating creature looked over at the awe-struck Macahan kids and started to move toward them as the younger passenger ran after her to hand her a black lace sun parasol. She accepted it with a queenly smile that made him blush before she turned once more to the children and asked, in the accents of some fairy princess, "I do so hope you three are named Macahan?"

Josh stammered, "I'm Josh Macahan, ma'am. This here is Laura, and the little one's Jessie."

"I'm so pleased to meet you all. I'm your Aunt Molly. Molly Culhane. Did you think to arrange transportation to the ranch, Josh?"

"Our buckboard's yonder, by the livery stable, ma'am."

"That's fine, dear. Would you be good enough to see about my luggage? I hope it's not too much for you. You see, I came to stay awhile."

CHAPTER 23

On a distant mesa a young Dakota scout reined in his pony and frowned at the sound of a distant rifle shot. The brave was puzzled, for he knew the elders of the medicine lodge hadn't authorized a hunt at this time. Unlike the strangers from the east, his people did not hunt alone as the spirits moved them. Hunting was a serious matter, and it was foolish for people to scatter game before the chiefs smoked pipes to Wakan Tonka, Tunkanshe, and the other gods of the Black Hills.

The puzzled scout rode slowly toward the sound of the shot and heard several more in rapid succession. Topping a rise, he looked down at a terrible scene.

A small tight herd of buffalo were running in a circular milling stampede, hemmed in by galloping men on horseback. The Dakota knew how easy it was to fix a herd that way. What he didn't, couldn't understand was what white men were doing down the slope. There were many white men, many, and off in the distance they'd drawn up a caravan of brightly painted wagons. As the oddly fur-hatted riders kept the herd from scattering, some others stood at ease with smoking rifles, dropping buffalo after buffalo in a frenzy of killing. Some of the white men wore the blue sleeves of the army. The others wore funnier clothes. None of them had any right to be where they were, and the buffalo they were killing were the children of Wakan Tonka.

Down amid the noise and dust, the Russian adventuress, Valerie, stood by the wagons with a disgusted

Major Poynton, the U. S. Army's representative to His Highness, the Grand Duke Dimitri Romanov. Although the other court ladies tittered their approval as the grand duke and his nephew, Count Sergei, brought down another bull, Valerie's voice was filled with distaste as she asked, "Good heavens, how many of those poor brutes do they intend to kill?"

The young officer shrugged and asked, "How many bullets did His Highness bring, Miss Valerie?"

Like the Russian girl and their leader, the small detachment of U.S. Cavalry troopers detailed as escort watched with curled lips. Not because of pity for the helpless buffalo, but at the poor sportsmanship being displayed. The only American who seemed to approve was the new guide, Coulee John Brinkerhoff. He'd led the expedition to this draw between the mesas, and the grand duke had promised him a bonus for every head they took.

Between the wagons and the milling herd, the grand duke braced his expensive rifle on its tripod mount and turned with a smile to a nearby court follower, asking in French, "Natasha, my dear, what would be your next preference?"

The bosomy girl tittered and pointed her fan. "That one with the crooked horns, Uncle Dimitri! He's the biggest one left!"

The grand duke nodded, drew a bead on the big bull, and fired. The bull was hit and staggered, but it recovered to wheel away in the dust as the count turned to his uncomfortable gun bearer and snapped, "You fool! This rifle fires low!"

The gun bearer stammered, "No excuse, sire. It was my fault, of a certainty!"

Count Sergei laughed and called over, "You're supposed to aim at the shoulder, Your Highness!"

"I *did* aim properly, damn it! This peasant handed me a gun with a crooked barrel!"

Major Poynton, who knew his duty when he saw it, shouted, "Coulee John?" and the scout snapped off a hip shot that brought the bull down with smile.

Poynton strode over to the grand duke and said, "Congratulations, sir. That was a fine trophy you just shot."

"I did?" The duke frowned. Then he laughed boyishly and said, "Why, bless me, so I did. For a moment I thought I'd only wounded the brute."

"Your shot killed him, Your Highness. Brinkerhoff's simply put him out of his misery."

"Ah, we do understand about sportsmanship, Major. You are most accommodating, for a Yankee.

"Those are my orders, sir."

"I still fear that bull was not all mine, however. Why don't we move in a bit closer?"

Coulee John was close enough to hear the exchange. He called out, "We'd best not, Duke. We'll spile the stand!"

"Good Lord, spoil the *what?*"

"The stand, sir. Your Cossacks has 'em all mixed up an' millin' in one place. Buff don't recognize a man afoot unless he's close. We can shoot all day from here, but do we move in closer, they'll git so spooked they'll likely bust out through the riders!"

"Why don't they do so in any case? I've never seen such stupid animals. I swear, this is less fun than shooting penned swine! At least swine squeal when you shoot them. These creatures simply lie down like placid cattle going to sleep."

But, while he found buffalo poor sport, it didn't stop the duke from suddenly swinging his fresh rifle up and firing at a pale-pelted cow, saying, "By Jove, that one's good for a pretty throw rug!"

The herd had been cut by perhaps a third when a Cossack made a wrong move and a lead bull suddenly saw an opening. Head down, the herd bull bellowed and ran, with the others following in an unstoppable stream.

As the Russians watched with dismay, Coulee John shifted his cud and said, "That's it for now, gents. That there herd's long gone!"

The grand duke rubbed his aching gun shoulder and

sighed. "I was getting fatigued in any case. I trust you'll find us another herd as good, young man?"

Coulee John shrugged and said, "That's my job, ain't it?"

"Good. Let's go over to the wagons for refreshments. I see the servants have chilled more wine."

Coulee John Brinkerhoff knew he wasn't included, so he pulled out his skinning knife and went to work as the Russian nobles drifted off to their repast. Major Poynton lingered behind, staring soberly around at the blood- and buffalo-littered grass as he marveled, "Almost thirty head. I hope his nibs isn't serious about wanting to go back with a full two hundred trophies!"

Coulee John began to skin out a carcass as he replied, "If it was up to me, we'd wipe out ever' buffalo left this side of the U.P. tracks. I likes to see Sioux beggin' fur a handout at the Injun Agency!"

"That's not a very charitable view, Brinkerhoff."

"I don't like Sioux. Iffen I had my way, we'd take back some Sioux hair to hang on them Rooshun castle walls, Major."

"I'm afraid I can't agree with you, John. There's good and bad in all races. And we're at peace with the Sioux, just now."

"Haw, that'll be the day. The only good Injun is a daid Injun. This chile goes along with General Sheridan on that. Some day they oughtta strike a medal to us buffalo hiders. Picture of a daid buffalo skull on one side and a discouraged beggin' Injun on the other. Yep, ussen killen off the buffalo'll likely bring peace sooner'n all the soldiers west of the Big Muddy!"

But the major wasn't listening. His eyes were wide and his jaw was open as he stared off across the rolling prairie and whispered, "Oh, Lord! Brinkerhoff?"

"I see 'em," grunted the scout, continuing to skin out the carcass as the line of mounted Indians slowly approached from the north horizon line.

Poynton asked, "What do we do, John?

"We don't do nothin'. Theres a mess of ussen, an' they ain't wearin' paint. Likely we'll have to powwow a mite."

"What do you suppose they want? We're not on their land, are we?"

"Hell, Major, it don't matter where we are. You ain't skeered of a few pesky Injuns, is you? I'll jaw with 'em. I know enough Dakota to cuss 'em out."

"Be tactful, Brinkerhoff. I'm moving over to the wagons to reassure our guests. We've killed an awful lot of buffalo, and they don't look at all happy about it!"

But before he could move away, the scout warned, "Stand your ground, son! You move anywheres away from them jaspers an' they'll have you down as a man with squaw thoughts! You jest pay them no mind an' let me handle it. I've outbragged Sioux before"

Over by the wagons, Valerie was the first to see the mounted band of Dakota coming in at an ominous walk. She pointed and laughed. "Oh, look, Indians! Aren't they romantic-looking?"

The grand duke turned and muttered, "Oh, I say, they do seem rather savage, don't they? I wonder what they want. Do you suppose they'd like some caviar?"

Count Sergei snapped his fingers, and the nearby Cossack guards sprang to attention, wary hands on sword hilts, as the count soothed, "I'm certain they're just beggars, sire. Perhaps we can persuade them to entertain us with their funny dances."

Suiting action to his foolish words, the brave but not-too-bright young count swaggered over to join Coulee John and the major as the others, somewhat uncertainly, followed.

The leader of the cossacks barked an order in his own dialect, and his men fell in around the soft aristocrats as they awaited the next move of the mysterious mounted Indians.

The leader of the Indians raised his hand to halt his comrades, and the Dakota lined up, staring soberly down at the dead buffalo as if they'd hardly taken note of the large white party. The leader spoke to Coulee

John in his own tongue. The scout answered in the same, then spit a stream of tobacco juice on the carcass at his feet.

Poynton flinched and asked, "Why'd you do that? Spitting on their food strikes me as an insult, Brinkerhoff!"

The scout said, "I meant it as sech, Major. This big horrah with the red roach says his name is Drives-His-Horses. He says we've shot some buff belongs to Satangkai's people. So I showed him what I thought of him *and* Satangkai!"

Count Sergei blurted, "What does he mean about someone owning these animals? Just what is he claiming, Brinkerhoff?"

"I jest told you all, Count. Satangkai's kin to Red Cloud, war chief of the Sioux Nation. These buggers claim we're on Satangkai's huntin' grounds."

Major Poynton said, "You told me we were on open range, Coulee John. What's the meaning of all this?"

"Hell, Major, simmer down. Of course it's open range. I disremember jest where the treaty line was on the map, but what the hell, you never seed no signposts, did you!"

"Oh my God! Tell them it's an honest mistake, Brinkerhoff. Tell them we'll be glad to pay them for these buffalo we just shot!"

Count Sergei sniffed in contempt as he opined, "This whole thing's ridiculous. Anyone can see we have every right to be here. We're of noble birth!"

Coulee John began to palaver in Dakota, but Drives-His-Horses looked pained and said, in English, "Your words are badly fashioned, Buffalo killer. This person is waiting for a straight-tongued answer. What are you people doing on Dakota land?"

The grand duke stammered, "We'll offer you compensation, my good man."

His nephew sneered, "Compensation, sire? You'd submit under duress to a band of naked savages. The House of Romanov has never negotiated under such conditions. Brinkerhoff! Tell these men to be off before I lose my temper!"

Poynton tried to shush him, saying, "Your Highness, please, the U.S. Army will bear the cost, and it's really a minor matter, if you'll be good enough to let us handle it!"

"There is nothing here to handle, Major. These lice won't dictate to us! They trifle with the honor of the Czar!"

Drives-His-Horses obviously neither knew nor cared who the Czar was. He said, "You will come with me, all of you. Our leader, Satangkai, shall decide your fate!"

Poynton muttered, "All right, everybody ease back slow."

He spoke too late. As the Indians saw that the whites meant to resist them, Drives-His-Horses shouted, "Ah-ta-nag-hree-tah-wa-hen-dee!" and the stolid-looking line of hitherto motionless Dakota moved in a blur of feathers, dust, and shouted commands.

Count Sergei exclaimed, "How dare you?" as an Indian grabbed his reins. Another Dakota, with a grin, slammed a clubbed rifle across the back of Sergei's neck.

A Cossack drew his sword, to die in his tracks with a Dakota lance through his chest.

The grand duke scrambled under a carriage as another thrown lance buried itself in the wood above his frightened rump.

Major Poynton stared in horror, shouting commands as a bullet slammed into him, knocking him out of the fight.

Dancing his pony around in a circle, Drives-His-Horses chanted, "Hey-yo-ha-ya-ha-ha-ya-ha!" as both sides milled for a mad few moments of utter confusion amid a haze of dust and gun smoke.

And then the Indians were off at a dead run, leading Sergei's horse with the count an unconscious captive in his saddle. Another brave had scooped up

Valerie. He laughed as he rode off with the girl across
his knees, kicking and screaming, head down.

Coulee John rose from where he'd taken cover behind a dead buffalo and walked over to the fallen
officer, holstering his gun as he said laconically, "Told
you we was too big a boo for 'em, Major. You hurt
bad?"

"I'm dying, damn your eyes! They got the girl, and
Count Sergei!"

"Well, we winged more'n one o' them, and his nibs
is safe, save for wettin' his breeches. I see one of
them Cossacks is down, too. You'd best let me take a
look at that hole in your chest, old son."

"It's too late. Get Macahan, Zeb Macahan! He's
the only white man Satangkai might listen to."

But as the officer fell back, closing his eyes forever,
the scout spit and muttered, "That'll be the day, sojer
boy. Nobody but you ever guessed we sort of strayed
on treaty land."

Poynton's junior officer, Lieutenant Carstairs, limped
over to where the scout stared morosely down at the
fallen officer. Carstairs asked, "Is he?" and Coulee
John nodded.

He said, "Reckon this puts you in command, Lieutenant. What are your orders?"

"Orders? Jesus, Brinkerhoff, didn't he say anything before he died?"

"Nothin' I could make sense from."

Carstairs looked about him at the shambles the
sudden attack had made of the hunting expedition.
He licked his lips and asked the scout, "Where do
you think they'll take the count and the girl, John?"

"Don't have to think. I know. Satangkai's stronghold's up in the Black Hills, thirty, mebbe forty miles
from here."

"God, I don't know what to do! What do you suppose those Indians are liable to do to the captives?
That boy is related to the *Czar!*"

Coulee John spat again. "The gal ain't bad-looking',

they'll likely jest rape her, and if she rapes nice, they might let her live."

"And the count?"

"Oh, hell, he's as good as daid. We drawed blood on 'em in that fight jest now. Iffen he's mighty lucky, they'll jest kill him and to hell with it. Iffen they hand him over to the squaws . . ."

He didn't finish. He didn't have to. Carstairs had seen photographs of a hunter handed over to the squaws. Even in black-and-white, it had made him want to puke.

CHAPTER 24

Molly Culhane hadn't lied when she'd said she had a lot of luggage. As young Josh rode his pony beside the buckboard, Laura drove and little Jennie pouted, riding high on the trunks and carpet bags filling the wagon bed. Aunt Molly, of course, rode at Laura's side on the spring-seat, her delicate features shaded from the western sun by the dainty black lace parasol.

The ride from town had been in awkward silence up to now. Molly Culhane knew it was up to her to set the children at ease.

Turning to the tall blonde Laura, Molly smiled and said, "I can see my sister, Kate's, eyes in yours, Laura dear. It's more than just the same hair coloring. You really bear a striking resemblance to your mother. Has anyone ever told you that?"

Laura nodded sullenly but didn't answer. What was the matter with the fool woman? Didn't she ever shut up? 'Course she looked like Ma. Who was she supposed to look like, Queen Victoria?

Molly continued, "Of course, I can see there's a lot of Macahan in all of you. I met your grandparents at your mother's wedding, did you know that, Jessie?"

Young Jessie snapped, "No, I didn't know. Us kids wasn't invited to Ma's weddin'." Then she looked away with an impish wink at Josh, who tried to stare her down sternly before he grinned himself and turned his face away.

Molly ignored the sass for the moment and gazed around at the rolling prairie around as she observed, "My, the hills are so green for this time of year on the High Plains. Have you been having lots of rain?"

Laura stared ahead and clucked to the buckboard mule to hurry. Jessie snapped, "Lots of rain, with thunder an' lightnin', ma'am."

Molly blanched and said, "Oh dear, that was awkward of me, wasn't it?"

Jessie was about to agree. Then, taking pity on the strange, unwelcome woman, she added, "We had some nice spring rains, too, ma'am."

"Is that a happy omen for you farm folk, spring rains?"

Before Jessie could screw herself in deeper, Josh called over from his pony, "Be in a bad fix without no rains, Aunt Molly."

Pleased that he had used her name, Molly Culhane beamed at Josh and blurted, "Oh, I can see that, indeed I do, Josh."

To herself she wondered, "What's wrong with these children? What have I done? And why am I chattering on like a bashful schoolgirl all of a sudden?"

Aloud, to the nubile Laura, Molly tried to come up with something less inane than the weather. "You've grown to be quite a young lady, Laura. Is some special young man paying court to you yet?"

Laura shrugged and said, "Guess not. I mean, nobody special."

From her awkward perch behind them Jessie teased,

"She's got more'n one boy moonin' over her at the Sunday go-to-meetings on the green, Aunt Molly!"

"I can see why. Both you girls are growing up to be real belles."

Laura blushed, frowning, and Jessie said, "Aw, mush!"

As Molly laughed, Josh kneed his pony in beside her and asked, "Uh, was you plannin' on stayin' with us long, Aunt Molly?"

Molly Culhane looked uncomfortable. Then she brightened and said, "My plans are flexible, Josh."

"Flexible, huh? Does that mean you'll be stayin' long or leavin' soon?"

"It means I'm not sure, dear. I wasn't sure what kind of a welcome I'd receive and . . . What do you three want of me, staying or leaving?"

Josh stammered, "Well, you're right welcome to stay as long as you've a mind to, Aunt Molly. Ain't that right, gals?"

There was a long awkward silence before Jessie blurted, "Sure it's right, Aunt Molly's kinfolks, ain't she?"

Laura's jaw was set stubbornly, but she was not in truth a mean-minded miss, and fair was fair, so, licking her lips and crossing her fingers, Laura managed to turn with a wan smile to the woman at her side and murmur, "You're as welcome as the first spring robins, Aunt Molly. You just come or go as you've a mind to, hear?"

Molly Culhane's eyes welled with tears, but she managed to control herself as she put a hand on Laura's wrist. "Thank you, dear. Thank all of you for such kind words. You see, you three children are all the kin I have now."

Josh pointed with his chin as they topped a rise and could see the Macahan homestead snuggled in the foothills of the high country beyond, and said, "We're almost there, Aunt Molly, and— Blue blazes! I see horses tied up out front! One of 'em's Luke's! The other one must be Uncle Zeb's."

The boy rode forward at a gallop as Laura whipped the mule into a trot with a glad smile on her pretty face.

Over at the house, Luke was coming in from his room, buttoning a fresh shirt, as Zeb, lounging in the open doorway, said, "Yonder comes your brother and the others on the buckboard, Luke." He stepped out on the veranda, peered hard, and added, "Bless my britches if that don't look like Molly Culhane with the kids!"

"Aunt Molly, here? I wired her about Ma's death, but I never figured she'd come all the way out here! The funeral's over!"

Josh galloped in, slid his mount to a rearing stop, and yelled out, "Uncle Zeb! Luke! Where in tarnation you been?"

Zeb laughed and shook hands with Josh as he dismounted, turning to Luke to say, "The way your kid brother's fillin' out since last we met, I wouldn't lay odds agin him bestin' you in a Green River roughhouse, Luke!"

Luke grinned and snorted. "Be a cold day in the Bad Place when he bests me at eatin' pancakes, Uncle Zeb!"

And then the two girls had leaped down from the buckboard and were wrapped around their uncle from either side as he hugged them both to his broad rawhide-clad chest. They'd both burst into tears and were trying to tell him, at the same time, how they felt about their mother's grisly death.

Zeb noticed Molly sitting lonely and seemingly forgotten on the buckboard seat. He soothed the girls with "Now, now, I know how you both feel, but let's bite the bullet and take it like Macahans. Don't you aim to help your Aunt Molly down, Luke?"

Luke flushed and hurried out to the buckboard to hold a hand out to Molly Culhane as she smiled down at him and said, "Luke Macahan, you're going to be the spitting image of your father in a few years."

"I take that proud and kindly, Aunt Molly. Come in

and set yourself down whilst Josh and me see to your possibles!"

Zeb disengaged himself from the two girls and joined the youth at the buckboard, doffing his battered hat as he nodded and said, "Molly Culhane, I must declare you ain't changed a hair since I seed you last."

Molly allowed both of them to help her down as she told Zeb, "There's more flattery than truth in your words, as always, Zeb, but Lord, it's good to see you again. Well, Macahan blarney aside, it's good to see the two of you don't think I have the plague!"

As he escorted Molly to the house while Luke unloaded the buckboard, Zeb murmured, "What's wrong, Molly?"

She sighed. "I'm beginning to realize I'm here without a formal invitation, Zeb."

"Come on, the kids ain't been rude to you, have they?"

"No, they've tried very hard, but they're not very good little actors, Zeb."

"Give 'em time, Molly. They're likely still cut up about Kate's death and, well, you always have sort of made most folks shy."

"I don't try to do it, Zeb. Why don't people like me? I try so *hard* to make friends, but . . ."

"Mebbe you try too hard, Molly. You've always been too pretty to be real and, well, you sort of make folks wonder if you know about the holes in their socks. Just simmer down and let things happen."

On the veranda, Molly stopped for a sweeping view of the house and huge barn of raw lumber. She dimpled and said, "Oh, it's a lovely house. I'll bet you girls made the window curtains, and isn't that a brand-new barn?"

There was an awkward silence. Then Jessie said, "Ma made the curtains. The neighbors had a barn raising for us just after Ma's funeral."

"Oh, I didn't know."

Laura blurted, "You likely think it's a small house, after what you've been used to back east, huh?"

"Why, no, dear. I think it's a lovely little house. It has such charm, and it's exactly as I pictured it from your mother's letters."

Zeb tried to smooth things over by quickly adding, "This family's worked like beavers to make a home here, Molly. I'm kind of proud of them all."

"You mean you and Kate and the children *built* this house?"

"Ever' stick and most of the furnishings, Molly."

"Heavens, what a lot of work! Where did you children sleep while you built the house?"

Laura's voice was sullen as she said, "Out there on the ground."

"Oh dear, that must have been most uncomfortable!"

Josh smiled a trifle smugly and explained, "You get used to it, Aunt Molly. Uncle Zeb, here, never sleeps anywhere else, lessen it's in a holler log during a hard rain!"

"Dear me, where did you and my sister sleep when it rained, Josh?"

Jessie said, "There's a cave hole up the hill, Aunt Molly. We use it for a root cellar now, but we used to have to sleep in it when it got raw hereabouts. Old Laura never liked that much, though, she was afeared the bats'd tangle in that long blond hair she's so stuck up about!"

Laura snapped, "Don't sass your elders, snippy missy!" as Molly gagged and asked, "Oh, dear, are there really bats around here?"

Jessie grinned wickedly and said, "Yes, ma'am. Lots' of bats. Fly all over us, come midnight!"

Zeb saw their guest from the east was really upset and cut in. "Ain't that many bats about, Molly, and besides, there's no reason to fear such as there be."

Molly shuddered and said, "Glugh! The thought of having things like that tangled in one's hair . . ."

"That's jest an old wives' tale, Molly. Bats have no call to get their fool selves tangled in a lady's hair.

They can see in the dark, and besides, they can be real helpful!"

"Helpful?"

"Oh sure. I remember a friend I had once who lived down in a holler as was always full of fog. Some days it was too durned foggy down there to see to do his chores. So he trained him a team of bats to lead him about his spread. They'd lead him from the house to the barn, the barn to the chicken house, and sech. It worked out right well for a while, but it cost him a busted leg in the end."

Molly's eyes were amused as she said, "Zebulon Macahan, I have a feeling this is another of your tall stories, but go on."

"It's the honest truth, Molly. You see, he forgot them bats was only critters. Not much smarter than a pair of dogs. He jest started puttin' too much faith in them bats. You see, one foggy day he decided to repair the roof with a new coat of shingles, so there he was, up there in a pea-soup fog, jest a-hammerin' and a-shinglin' away whilst his pet bats flew around, makin' sure he set them shingles straight. The bats was smart enough to know the shingles should go on straight, but the poor little critters never knowed their friend couldn't *fly,* like them! Poor old boy got to the 'end of the roof and the bats never knowed to warn him. He shingled ten feet out on nothin' but pure fog afore he discovered there was no roof under him at all. Took a turrible fall and broke his fool leg!"

There was a happy roar of laughter from everyone listening. The tension broken for the moment, Laura said, "Well, I'll be getting supper on."

"I'll help," said Jessie.

Molly asked, "Can I help too, girls?"

Laura said, "No need to, ma'am. You're *company!*"

Zeb noted the stricken look on Molly's face and took her arm, saying, "Come on, I'll show you around the spread, Molly."

The unhappy woman waited until they had inspected the new barn and wandered down to the nearby brook before she sighed and said, "I told you my arrival wasn't an overwhelming success, Zeb."

Zeb chewed a grass stem and said soothingly, "Well, Kate's death was an awful blow to 'em, Molly, and they've never seen you before. I reckon you'll have to give 'em more time to get used to the idea of you bein' here."

"The blame is mine, I suppose. I really had no right to expect them to treat me like a member of the family, but . . ."

"Hell, you are a member of the family, Molly. You'll just have to give 'em time to figure that out for their own selves. Ease up and let the kids get to know you afore you go givin' up on 'em!"

Molly paused by a willow and shook her head. "When I heard of Kate's death, all I thought of was the children, out here alone and maybe needing help. But I see I was a fool. They're not the children I remember. They're almost grown young men and women!"

"I wouldn't say they was all that growed up. Mebbe they do need your help more'n they think just now."

She shook her head. "I'm not being honest with any of you or myself, Zeb. It's *me* who needs help, if the truth be faced squarely!"

"*You* need help, Molly? Seems to me you've always been one gal who never needed help from nobody."

"I wish that was true, Zeb. It's been six years since my husband died."

"I know about that, Molly. Kate told me. She said she was proud of you for bearin' up so well and takin' command of your own affairs without a whimper."

"It's all a hollow mask, Zeb. My whimpers have been hidden well behind a fan and laughter, but, dear God, I've been so *frightened!*"

"You, frightened? What scares you so, Molly?"

"Loneliness . . . Not just the loneliness of a widow, Zeb. I'm honest enough to look in the mirror and judge my chances of getting another man."

"You wouldn't have much trouble *there,* Molly."

"I know, but I'm not lonely for anyone who *wants*

me, Zeb. I need to feel that someone, anyone, *needs* me. I have no roots. Since Kate's death, I have no family left, save for those four young total strangers. I guess, to be honest, I never asked if I was needed here or not, because I was so afraid I wasn't! I was so afraid the answer would be no, I just came, uninvited and, I see, unwanted."

"Molly, you're givin' up too easy. There may be all the roots you need hereabouts."

"Don't try to comfort me with hollow words, Zeb. I'm an expert with hollow words. I had no right to intrude like this."

"You're no intruder. If you'd give yourself and the kids some time . . . But never mind, I think I can see how to hurry things up a mite."

"You're going to talk to the children about me?"

"Nope, Molly. You are. This is my plan . . ."

CHAPTER 25

Later that night, after supper, as the family relaxed around the table, Zeb filled his pipe and gave Molly Culhane a silent signal from where he lounged in a corner. The girls had done the dishes, refusing help from their guest. Molly put down her after-supper cup of coffee and smiled across at Josh, saying, "Oh, before I forget. You asked me on the way out how long I planned to stay, didn't you, Josh?"

Josh nodded quietly and murmured, "Don't matter, I reckon."

"Well, I wasn't sure myself at the time. You see, I remembered all of you as, well, babies. But now that

I'm here, I can see you're all young men and women."

All eyes were on Molly as she continued.

"Now that I see you're able to take care of yourselves so well, I've made up my mind. I'll be going back at the end of next week, if my staying that long won't be a bother."

"End of next week?" Josh frowned. "That's only eight or nine days, Aunt Molly."

Laura said, "All that way for only a week's visit? We thought you'd stay longer than *that*, Aunt Molly!"

Jessie blurted, "Can't you stay at least *two* weeks, Aunt Molly? Two weeks and we'll be havin' a calvin'! You ever see a baby cow git bornded, Aunt Molly?"

"No, dear, it sounds very interesting, but you see, I'm really not needed here, and I did so want to get back to Chicago for the fall fashion shows!"

The girls exchanged stricken glances, and Laura was suddenly very aware of her neat but homespun dress as she asked, "Oh, do you know what the new hemline's going to be next year, Aunt Molly?"

"The skirts will be the same length, but cut narrower, and the bustle is most definitely coming back, at least not quite so padded."

Josh blurted, "I hear tell folks is wild in Chicago. Heard some cowhands boastin' of a trip back there, and they said the bawdyhouses was— Oh-oh, sorry, ma'am."

Everyone laughed as Josh reddened. Then, the ice broken, Jessie asked, "Is it true Lillian Russell has a six-story house in Chicago, Aunt Molly? How in thunder does a body git up six flights of stairs in a corset and bustle like that woman wears?"

Molly explained, "The servants live on the top floors, dear. I've never met that actress, but I have seen the house she keeps by the lake. She has another just as grand in New York City. They say her lover, Diamond Jim Brady—"

Josh gulped and cut in: "Have you been to *New York City,* Aunt Molly?"

"I've visited it once or twice. You wouldn't like it, Josh, it's very wild and dirty."

"Oh boy, tell us about wild and dirty old New York, Aunt Molly!"

Luke, who'd been listening in dignified and lofty silence up to now, couldn't restrain himself. "Is it true they have a Chinatown, like San Francisco, ma'am?"

"Yes, dear, but I'm afraid I never went there. My late husband and I visited some business associates of his near Gramercy Park and took a carriage ride along the waterfront."

"You mean the *ocean* waterfront? What's the ocean like, Aunt Molly? We're stuck out here smack dab in the middle of the country, and it's hard to picture nothin' but water clean to the horizon!"

"Oh, we saw the ocean from Coney Island later. New York is up between two big rivers, and it was the ships I loved to look and dream about. There were so *many* ships in the harbor. Long black clippers in the China trade, oceangoing paddle wheelers, funny squat Dutch craft filled with cheese and chocolate, and so many flags. Flags from all over. England, France, Norway, even Constantinople—"

"Laura cut in with "Never mind the boys, Aunt Molly. Tell us about the ladies in New York. Were they pretty? Were they as fast as folks say they act?"

Jessie blurted, "I want to hear about the zoo! I've seen pictures of the animals in the zoos back east, but what's it like to really see an elephant?"

Zeb struck a match with his horny thumbnail and puffed his pipe alight before he harrumphed and said, "Now that's about enough, you kids. Can't you see your Aunt Molly's tuckered? You'll have a whole week to ask her all those things afore she has to leave."

Laura looked stricken as she pleaded, "Only a week? But there's so much she can tell us! Can't you stay at least two weeks, Aunt Molly?"

"Can't you stay a month?" asked Josh.

Molly said, "I don't know. I'm afraid I'm causing

you all a lot of bother even staying a week. I know how awkward having guests underfoot can be, and—"

"Aw, hell, Aunt Molly," blustered Josh. "You ain't no guest. You're *family!* You'll be no trouble hereabouts at all!"

"That's right," insisted Laura. "It's not fair of you to leave us just as we're getting to know you! Why, in a week we'd hardly have time to show you around Elk Creek! There's a dance at the settlement bein' held right after the harvest, and I'd planned on, well, you showing me how to fix the ribbon bows on the dress I'm making for it."

"You've got to stay and watch my cow give birth!" pleaded Jessie.

Molly smiled over at Zeb and said shyly, "Well, I might be able to stay a while longer."

Josh shouted, "Hot dang! You stay as long as you've a mind to, ma'am!"

CHAPTER 26

The main street of Elk Creek was twisted and studded with boulders too big to be moved. It made it rough to move a wagon through, but most folks this far west rode horseback. The town was an improvised ramshackle collection of jerry-built raw lumber. The frontiersmen who came down from the mountains to the foothill trail town didn't need a fancy saloon for their serious drinking. There were a bawdyhouse, a general store, the usual livery stable, a weekly newspaper printed as the occasion moved the town barber, who owned the printing press, and a sort of barn that called itself a hotel.

Molly Culhane had seen only a dusty corner of the town between getting off the stage and riding out to the Macahan farm, but she rose above her surroundings on her first serious shopping expedition with Zeb and the children.

Following her gentle-on-the-reins strategy, Molly deferred to the girls on what should be purchased for the household and to Luke and Josh about such manly mysteries as feed and fertilizer. There was a moment of awkwardness when Molly offered to pay, but Zeb cut in to suggest that their Aunt Molly be allowed to pay for a one-fifth share, her being family and all. Luke and Laura were old enough to realize, with a trace of guilt, that the few more dollars made the difference between enough and skimp.

As the storekeeper's young helper and the boys loaded the buckboard with supplies and staples, and the girls inspected a rack of new dresses wistfully, Molly, with Zeb lounging by, insisted on a few small luxuries bought with her own money on her own.

Goods transported this far west were dreadfully expensive, compared to the prices Molly was used to in Chicago, but she bravely bought ten pounds of orange tea at fifteen cents a pound, explaining in an aside to Zeb that a few small luxuries made the difference between economy and feeling poor.

Zeb didn't argue. Like most mountain men, he believed in spending when he had it and toughing life out when he didn't. Unlike many of his fellow westerners, Zeb's habits were tempered with a certain prudence. Hence, since he seldom gambled for high stakes or drank more than a man needed to feel a friendly glow, Zeb usually had a few coins clinking in his pockets long after the average trapper, scout, or cowhand was broke and borrowing against next payday.

As Molly bought the tea and started dickering with the storekeeper for some outrageous ribbon bows, Zeb spied a nickel-plated hunting knife on a counter, scooped it up, and wrapped it with a sidelong glance out front, where Josh was tying a feed bag on the buckboard mule.

Easing in beside Molly, he slipped the wrapped gift to her and said, "Josh has a birthday comin' up next week. His old hunting knife's wore down to a nub. Got him a new one, here. Better if you gave it to him."

"Oh, thank you, Zeb, but I insist on paying for it."

"Won't let you. How do you reckon things are coming with the kids?"

"It's still a bit early to tell, but I think we'll make it."

"So do I. Uh-oh, I see Sheriff Colter headed our way. You go on about your shopping, Molly. I'll see what he wants."

"Oh dear, you're not in trouble with the law again, are you? Kate wrote about the trouble you and Luke had a while back with that bounty hunter."

"That's not likely it. But if I ain't in one scrape it's another. I'll tend to it, Molly."

He strode out to greet the approaching sheriff, who offered his hand with a "Howdy, Zeb."

"Howdy, Abe. How's the law business these days?"

"Quiet enough, considering. Sure was sorry to hear about your sister-in-law, Kate. She was such a fine and healthy gal, but you jest never knows, do you?"

"Even in the midst of life, Abe. Likely the Lord had his reasons, but I aim to ask Him why, do we ever meet up, farther along."

"Is that Kate's sister, the one the kids and ever'body's been talkin' of?"

"That's her. Molly Culhane."

"I can see she's related. She's a fine-lookin' woman, like her poor daid sister."

"Yep, I'll allow she is, but you're a married man, Abe. You'd best be careful with that rovin' eye."

The sheriff chuckled and said, "Lookin' don't count, Zeb. I love my old woman, but she knows damn well that when I quit lookin' it'll be time to bury me."

Then, the civilities out of the way, Sheriff Colter took a folded reward poster from his vest and handed it to Zeb. "By the way, just got this new flier in the post about your nephew, Luke. It's got his picture on it this time."

Zeb unfolded the poster and studied the line drawing of what could have been nearly any youth Luke's age. "Ain't a very good likeness, Abe."

"I know, but somebody back east purely wants that boy bad, Zeb."

"Yeah, I noticed the reward's gone up. You tryin' to tell me somethin', Abe?"

"Hell, I know the boy's innocent of that fool charge. Even iffen he wasn't, what the hell, he never gunned that bounty hunter in *my* county! I jest showed you the damn poster so's you and him'll know he'd best keep his haid down!"

"I'll tell him, Abe, and I'll be thanking you, too. You've been a real friend, considering."

"Shoot, I may be a lawman but I ain't no skunk. You don't thank old friends for jest doin' what's right, Zeb."

"Mebbe, but I'm thankin' you anyways. Guess you know if the shoe's on the other foot . . ."

"Course I know, you old fool. Let's not go blubberin' up about it. We've been through the fire together more 'n once, and we both knows where we stand if things git hot agin hereabouts!"

A shout drew Zeb's attention over his old friend's shoulder, and he saw that a knot of townies had gathered in front of the newspaper office just down the street. Colter turned to follow his gaze and said, "Looks like somethin's goin' on down there. I'd best have a look."

The sheriff strolled down the boardwalk, with Zeb following after a quick backward glance assured him Molly and the kids were still tied up at the general store.

A news broadside had been tacked to the printshop wall:

GUESTS OF AMERICAN REPUBLIC ABDUCTED BY SAVAGES!

In smaller print, it read:

An incident of savagery has taken place in the Dakota Territory. Although details are still lacking, it is known that the sad mishap took place while his Imperial Highness, the Grand Duke Dimitri Romanov, brother to the Czar of All the Russias, and Duke Dimitri's nephew, Sergei, Count of Kiev, were on a royal hunting expedition near the Black Hills.

Zeb muttered, "What in hell were they doing near the Black Hills?" and read on.

A party of Sioux Indians came upon the Russian party as they were engaged in the sport of hunting buffalo and there ensued a bloody skirmish leaving one Russian guardsman and a U.S. Army officer dead, with several others of the party wounded. Before they were beaten off by our brave guests, the Sioux managed to abduct Count Sergei and a young woman of the Russian Court.

No word has been received from the Sioux Nation as to the meaning of this savagery or the fate of the captives.

In Washington immediate outcries have been sounded against this shocking and repulsive deed. The Russian Embassy has demanded an explanation.

At this moment the President and his cabinet are conferring with the War Department as to what action is to be taken against the Sioux.

The printer, Dave Wordly, was trying to clear space in front of his door by shouting, "All right, folks, you can read about it in my paper, if I ever git the durned thing all printed. Tarnation! I only put the first news up to sell the papers, you know!"

Wordly was an old friend of Zeb's. He caught the

harassed printer's eye and asked, "Anything else come over the wire on them Russian captives, Dave?"

"Last I heard, Zeb, the Secretary of War's ordered the Second U.S. Cavalry to Fort Sully on the quick march! Wasn't you up there, recent?"

"I was a few weeks back. The whole damn regiment's headed for Fort Sully, Dave?"

"That's what come over the telegraph, Zeb. General Stonecipher hisself is leadin' 'em."

"Stonecipher? The rough old cuss called Brandy Jack?"

"That's him. And if I know Brandy Jack, the Sioux Nation has about six minutes to hand over the captives and the Injuns who done the killin', only the six minutes was up three days ago!"

"Anybody pin the exact place down on the map, Dave? I mean, there's a heap of prairie around the Black Hills."

"Near as they can figure, it was north of Sully, near the treaty line."

Zeb looked disgusted and snorted. "North of Sully and *near* the line? Fort Sully's not more 'n a few steps south of the line! Them fools up and done exactly what I was afraid they'd do."

Zeb went back to the general store, where he'd tethered his pony, and explained what had happened to Molly and the kids in a few terse sentences. Then he mounted and announced, "Don't know how long I'll be. I'm hopin' to come back by harvest time."

But before he could ride out, Luke ran over from where he'd been talking to friends at the telegraph office. He called out, "Wait!" and as Zeb turned in the saddle, reining in, Luke said, "More trouble with the law, Uncle Zeb!"

"I heard. Don't let it worry you, son. As long as the county sheriff's a friend of our'n—"

"It ain't me, Uncle Zeb. It's *you!* You know that trouble you had in Three Rivers?"

"What about it?"

"The telegrapher says a message just come over the

wire ordering you brung in for that hearing you told me about!"

Zeb thought a moment. Then he nodded and said, "That circuit judge sure takes hisself important. Must be aimin' to run for governor! Luke, you go back to the telegraph office and telegraph the marshal's office. Tell the law I'm headed for Fort Sully and that from there I'll mosey down to Three Rivers for the hearing. Save ever'body a trip an' hard words over nothin'. By the way, I got somethin' for *you*."

He took out the reward poster, handed it down to Luke, and warned, "The reward's gone up. You'd best stay out at the spread an' keep a sharp lookout for strangers."

Luke studied the picture of himself for a moment, nodded, and asked, "Where are you off to in such an all-fired hurry, Uncle Zeb?"

"Fort Sully. Trouble's broke out and I have to see can I keep some friends of mine from gettin' kilt."

"I heard about the Indian trouble at the telegraph office. Don't see why you're so worried, though. With a whole regiment of U.S. Cav under a fightin' general, your friends at Fort Sully figure to be safe enough from the Injuns."

Zeb swore softly and said, "It ain't my white friends at Fort Sully I'm worried about, damn it! It's my Dakota friends in the Black Hills I got to try and save!"

CHAPTER 27

The harvest was almost ready, but meanwhile the expanded Macahan clan had to eat, so later that afternoon, after Molly and the kids returned from Elk Creek, Luke put on his buckskins, got a rifle, and allowed it was time he put a side of venison in the larder.

Molly intercepted him in the kitchen and insisted on making him a poke of vittles once she understood his hunting trip could last overnight. As she prepared some sandwiches, Luke decided he might as well set a few things straight in his head. Clearing his throat, he asked, "Aunt Molly, you're closer to Uncle Zeb than most folks. Uh, did he ever say anythin' about me bein' wanted?"

Molly looked up with a puzzled frown and stammered, "Wanted, Luke? You mean wanted by the law?"

Luke nodded, helped himself to a cup of coffee, and explained. "I don't stay around much. Sheriff Colter's all right, but there's this reward, and some old boys'll do most anythin' for money."

"Oh dear, you're so young to be wanted by the law! Whatever did you do, Luke? What laws have you broken?"

"Not a one that's in the Good Book, ma'am. I kilt some owlhoots near the Black Hills, but I done it tryin' to save a gal's life . . . and my own. Afore that, I had to shoot a sheriff in Missouri."

"My God, you shot a lawman?"

"That's what he called hisself. He was dead set on

135

hangin' me without no trial when I shot him. Didn't kill him, more's the pity. I only shot him in the arm some, but he's too mean-hearted to forgit it. Keeps sendin' out reward posters on me."

"Oh, Luke, that's terribly unjust!"

"I was hopin' you'd see it that way, Aunt Molly. You see, I like you too much to lie to you. I mean, it's sort of nice you're here. I hope you ain't aimin' to leave us too soon."

"That's up to the children, Luke."

"No it ain't. They think they're pretty big for their britches, but they need somebody to look after 'em when Uncle Zeb and me ain't about."

"I'll try to stay as long as I'm needed, Luke."

"It ain't just bein' needed, Aunt Molly. You're kin, and a real nice lady. I reckon we're right glad you come to stay with us."

"Thank you, dear. I . . . take that kindly. Here's your sandwiches."

"Thanks, Aunt Molly. Reckon I'll be movin out, then."

Molly smiled, her eyes blurred, and said, "You'd better, before I start to cry like a silly fool!"

But even as Luke rode off, a creaking Conestoga wagon was moving toward the Macahan homestead. The covered wagon was overloaded, and the woman on the plank seat was middle-aged and worn by life. The man walking out front, leading the ox team, was younger than she, tall and ruggedly handsome, with a hint of boyishness to his big-boned face. He wore a severe dark suit covered with trail dust. There was pride as well as strength in his slow strides beside the plodding oxen, but his face was troubled at the moment with uncertainty and weariness.

As he spotted the homestead he hesitated, then led the team in.

Molly Culhane was hanging out some washing, now that the girls had accepted her help without obvious protest. As the man in the dark suit led the wagon team into the yard, he doffed his cap and called out,

"Excuse me, ma'am, but we used up our last water yesterday and we was wonderin' . . ."

"Of course! The well's just behind the house. Why don't you both come in out of the sun and set a spell. We have some coffee on."

"I thank you kindly, ma'am, but we'll jest fill our canteens an' be on our way."

"If you wish, sir. It's none of my business, and I'm city bred, but if those poor oxen haven't had water since yesterday, aren't you liable to lose them if they don't have a good long drink and some shady rest?"

The haggard woman on the wagon seat leaned out to call, "Can you tell us how far we are from Spring-Flats, miss?"

Molly frowned and said, "Spring Flats? I'm a stranger in these parts, but I've heard my nephews mention it. I'd say it was a good two weeks by Conestoga."

The woman gasped and slumped, defeated, as she marveled, "Two weeks? Oh, Lord!"

"I'm sorry, folks, but it's beyond the pass, and since you're lucky to make fifteen, twenty miles a day with oxen . . . But why don't the two of you come in and rest a spell. We'll talk about it over supper."

The young man hesitated, the hope of a warm meal and a night's rest overwhelming him. Then his companion called, dully, "Tell her, Jeremiah. Tell her and get it over with!"

Jeremiah sighed and told Molly, "We'd like nothin' better, ma'am, but I'd best confess we've been refused water at four homesteads in the past fifty miles!"

"Heavens! I was wondering why you were out of water this close to the mountains. I can't believe anyone would refuse a simple drink of water to passing travelers!"

"I can, ma'am. You see, Maggie and me are . . . Mormons."

Molly smiled and said, "Oh, is that all? From the way you were acting I thought you must be lepers!"

"Beg pardon, ma'am?"

"The way you poor folk have been treated. I know very little about your faith, sir, but mine teaches something called the Golden Rule."

"So does ours, ma'am, but some folks don't see things that way."

"Then they have no faith, whatever they may call themselves. Come inside. Your religious persuasion is no concern of mine. Your thirst and weariness is!"

The woman on the wagon started to sob, and Jeremiah choked on a lump in his throat before he murmured, "We both thank you from the bottom of our hearts, ma'am. My name is Jeremiah Taylor, and yonder's my wife, Maggie."

Molly was too sophisticated to comment on the obvious disparity in their ages. She nodded and said, "I'm Molly Culhane. Those children out there working in the fields are my nieces and nephew, the Macahans. We'd be honored to have you for supper and the night. Do please come inside."

Jeremiah Taylor helped his tear-stained wife down from the wagon tenderly and said, "I'd best water the stock first, ma'am. You go on in with the lady, Maggie."

Out in the field, little Jessie saw Laura's interest in the visitors and said, "You just keep workin', girl. We'll never get this chore done if you don't put your prissy back into it!"

Laura sighed. "I'd just as soon the harvest was in and it snowed horned toads! Every durned year's the same out here. Don't you ever get tired of how nothing ever seems to change, Jessie?"

"Oh, it changes. It's dark at night and sunny or raining in the day. 'Sides, Aunt Molly says she'll take us to Chicago someday."

"Someday. It's always someday. You know what I found in my hairbrush this morning?"

"I hope it wasn't nits. I used the same brush."

"I found a *gray hair!*"

"Well, it wasn't mine!"

"I know. It was likely mine. See what I mean?"

"Sure, you had a gray hair an' it come off on the brush."

"It's more than findin' a gray hair. It means things are passing me by. I'm getting *old* waiting for someday Jessie!"

"Oh my, yes! At this rate you'll be a grandmother afore you're twenty, won't you?"

Josh was coming out of the barn with a bucket of manure when he found himself confronted by a tall stranger leading a team of oxen. As the boy stopped, gaping, Jeremiah Taylor smiled at him and said, "Excuse me, son. Miz Culhane said I could water these oxen."

Josh nodded and said, "Sure, mister. Well's right over here. I'll help you."

Inside the house, Maggie Taylor sat at the table, drinking a glass of water that tasted sweet as wine. She sighed and said, "Oh, I can't tell you how good that tastes, and you've such a lovely house. Is that an organ over there under that Spanish shawl?"

Molly nodded, and the thirsty woman took another sip before asking warily, "Are you sure your family won't mind us staying over, miss?"

"Please, it's Molly, Maggie. I've told you, you're welcome to stay as long as you like."

Laura came in from the fields, and was suddenly aware of the dirt on her work dress and hands as she gasped, "Oh, golly!"

"Laura, this is Mrs. Taylor. She and her husband will be staying for supper and bedding down for the night."

Laura gulped, and stammered, "How do. Excuse me, ma'am!" She ran to her room.

Maggie Taylor sighed and said, "She knows."

But Molly said, "Of course not. Not that it matters. It wasn't poor manners. Laura's at that age where a girl starts worrying about her appearance, and she was sort of filthy for a great lady. She wants so much to be admired as a woman, but it's so isolated out here, and I gather there haven't been many visitors."

"Oh, I understand. You're so lucky to have the sound of children around you, Molly. I love the company of young people, but the Lord never blessed me with children."

Molly nodded but didn't answer. Politeness forbade her asking, but what on earth had possessed that handsome young husband of hers to marry a woman old enough to be his mother?

Laura had donned her best dress with company nigh, content to pose as Molly's ladylike co-hostess. Jessie and Josh were less constrained. As Molly set the table once more, Jessie asked, "Why's that lady all the time layin' out in her fool wagon, Aunt Molly?"

"I'm sure I don't know, dear. They've come all the way from Missouri, and I suppose she's very tired from the long trip."

Josh said, "They're Mormons, ain't they, Aunt Molly?"

"Yes, dear, and our guests."

"Last time I was in town I heard some old boys talkin' about the Mormons."

"What's a Mormon?" Jessie asked with a frown.

Molly explained, "It's a faith, dear. A New York man named Joseph Smith had a revelation back in 'thirty-nine. Mormons are the folk who believe he received a message from the Angel Moroni. That's why his followers are called Mormons. They call themselves the Latter-day Saints."

Josh snorted. "Some saints! They aim to have their own state out in the Great Desert and have nothin' to do with the rest of us!"

"The rest of us haven't been to kind to them, Josh. Joseph Smith and his brother were murdered by a mob in Missouri, and the poor folk have been driven from one land to the other as if they were some sort of terrible outcasts."

"Well, from what I hear, they likely brung it on

their own selves, Aunt Molly. They act right spooky an' have all sorts of outlandish notions!"

Before they could go into it further, Jeremiah Taylor appeared at the door. He broke the awkward silence by saying uncertainly, "I hope I'm not too early . . ."

Molly said, "Not at all, Mr. Taylor. Come right in! Isn't your wife going to join us?"

"I'm sorry and so is she, ma'am. She's feeling poorly and asks to be excused."

"I'll have one of the children take her a plate, then. Is there anything else we can do for her?"

"Thank you, but I think a good night's rest is all she really wants, ma'am."

Jessie said, "I'll take something to her, Aunt Molly."

Molly said, "Thank you, dear. Suppose the rest of us sit down then?"

Molly hesitated, then said grace, noting that the Mormon made no objection as he bowed his head to her own faith's prayer. Then she smiled and said, "Well, let's dig in then!"

Taylor insisted that the others help themselves first; then he sighed and said, "This certainly is good. We'd had nothing but rabbit and salt pork for weeks."

Molly said, "The compliments must go to Laura, here. She cooked it."

The Mormon smiled at Laura and said, "And beautifully, too. Your cooking does you credit, Miss Laura!"

Then, before tasting a bite, he took a deep breath and said, "It may not be seemly, but may I offer my own grace to this table before I eat, Ma'am?"

Molly managed not to show her confusion as she nodded and said, "Certainly, sir." She wondered what had been wrong with her own words.

The children exchanged puzzled glances as Taylor clasped his hands and lowered his head, but they were polite enough to do the same as the Mormon said, "Blessed be the name of our God. Let us sing His

praise, yea, let us give thanks to His Holy Name, for
He doth work righteousness forever, amen."

There was a chorus of amens from the Macahan
clan. Then Molly said, "That was lovely, Mr. Taylor.
What part of the Bible was it from?"

"It's from the Book of Mormon, Alma 26:8."

"Oh, is that your Bible?" asked Laura.

Taylor said, "It's holy scripture delivered into the
hands of our prophet, Joseph Smith. It's our scripture,
along with your Bible."

He saw the blank looks his words occasioned and
explained. "Despite what you may have heard, we
are Christians. The Prophet Joseph's revelations
merely added to the original scriptures of the old and
the new testaments."

Josh frowned and asked, "What's in your Book of
Mormon that ain't in *our* Good Book, mister?"

Taylor smiled easily and said, "No deep dark
secrets, Josh. We're not the witches and warlocks folk
accuse us of being. Our ceremonies are different in
some matters. We're forbidden many things the earlier
prophets may have not thought to include. For instance, we don't take tobacco or coffee, in addition to
being forbidden strong drink."

Molly brightened and said, "Oh! That's why your
wife would only let me serve her water! I hope I
didn't offend her when I asked her if she wanted some
coffee, sir."

He laughed. "We don't impose our rules on others,
ma'am. Getting back to our mysterious Book of
Mormon, it was taken down by the Prophet Joseph
Smith as the Angel Moroni revealed it on the golden
tablets in a forgotten tongue of ancient wisdom."

"Have you seen the tablets, mister?"

"No. Have you seen the tablets of Moses, Josh?
The Prophet Joseph rendered them in English for us.
Aside from new commandments which I assure you
don't conflict with those of Moses, many mysteries of
history were revealed. For instance, did you know the
American Indians were one of the Ten Lost Tribes

of Israel? In ancient books the discovery of America and many other wonders were foretold—but forgive me, I'm so used to teaching that I tend to pontificate."

Laura smiled radiantly at the handsome stranger and said, "It sounds just fascinating, Mr. Taylor! I'd love to read your book someday!"

"Well, if it's all right with Miss Culhane, here, I'd be proud to see you get a copy."

Molly nodded her assent, then asked, "Do you have others of your faith in these parts, sir?"

Taylor shook his head sadly and said, "No, ma'am. Most of our people are out in the Great Salt Desert with Brother Brigham's flock. My mission is to start a new center for our faith at Spring Flats."

Josh looked startled and said, "Spring Flats? There's nothin' there but grass! Used to be a post office, but it's been deserted since the Pony Express was stopped after the wires went up. Nothin' over there but some cattlemen, last I heard."

"I know, but with God's help I intend to make it another city, like the one by Salt Lake."

"You and just your wife aim to build a Mormon *city,* mister?"

"A tabernacle first, Josh. The city will come later."

Laura asked, "What's a tabernacle, Mr. Taylor?"

"I may be quibbling with words to you young people, but if you read the Old Testament carefully you'll see the children of Israel worshipped in tabernacles, rather than in churches."

Josh said, "Oh, a tabernacle is a Mormon church, right?"

"I don't tike to seem pedantic, but a tabernacle isn't quite a church. Just as we're really not Mormons, but members of the Church of Jesus Christ of Latter-day Saints."

"But you just said you had no churches, didn't you?"

"I know it's hard for a gentile to understand, Josh. But to us, the church is our faith. The *buildings* are tabernacles and temples, as they were in the olden days of Israel."

Laura said, "I understand, and I think it's marvelous!"

"Thank you, Miss Laura. You see it's not just empty words and dreams with us. It's a necessity. We've been driven from so many places, we must create our own world in the wilderness or be destroyed once again, as we were at Nauvoo."

Molly said, "Nauvoo? It seems to me I heard something about Nauvoo when I was living in Chicago."

"No doubt you did, ma'am. Nauvoo was our town in Illinois, not far from your Chicago, albeit farther west on the prairie. The gentiles attacked one night and burned us out. Maggie's first husband died there. He was among those killed when the night riders came with burning brands and lynch ropes. They dragged him to death behind a horse. Later, as you may know, we were driven from Missouri after another mob hurled the Prophet Joseph Smith and his brother to their deaths from a window."

The Macahans exchanged stricken glances, and Molly gasped. "How terrible! How you must feel about us . . . gentiles."

"We know those of you who persecute us are a misguided minority, but perhaps you can understand now how much we appreciate your hospitality. Like Jesus, the Prophet Joseph instructed us to forgive our enemies, but one does become cautious in the face of constant enmity."

Laura asked, "But why do so many people hate you, Mr. Taylor? I mean, if you're just another Christian sect, it makes no sense."

"It makes little sense to us, I assure you, Miss Laura. Perhaps we frighten ignorant folk because our ways are not their ways and because we keep to ourselves. The leader of the mob who killed the Prophet said a man who didn't like corn likker was some unnatural kind of heathen. To be fair, we were saved in the end by U.S. Army troops of much the same persuasion. One of them seemed to think I'd done something terrible by marrying an older woman, but he allowed it was my right to be mad, and he was decent enough to enforce my right to live, and for that I'm grateful."

Laura lowered her eyes as she murmured, "I s'pose a man can marry who he has a mind to."

Taylor smiled understandingly and explained, "Our faith teaches us it's wrong for a woman to remain unwed. When Maggie's first husband was murdered, the elders chose me to take his place."

"You mean you had no choice?"

"Of course I had a choice, Miss Laura. Our elders don't dictate to us. They merely suggest what the wisdom of the Prophet indicates. I was the oldest bachelor in our community. It was fitting that I take Maggie to wife. Nobody made me do it."

"You mean you could have refused?"

"I suppose, but why would I have wanted to do such an uncharitable thing?"

Molly was afraid she knew where this line of discussion was in danger of leading them all, so she chose to change the subject. "You're both welcome to stay as long as you like, Mr. Taylor, but just what are your plans?"

He took a sip of water and said, "Naturally, we'll be leaving in the morning, ma'am."

Laura gushed, "Oh no, it will take several days at least to rest your tired oxen, and you really shouldn't leave before your wife feels better, too!"

He hesitated and suggested, "Several days would be an imposition on you all, Miss Laura."

"It wouldn't be any such thing, really it wouldn't!"

The Mormon looked at Molly, who nodded and said, "Naturally you'll stay with us until your wife feels better, sir."

But she wondered, even as she said it, why Laura was looking at the young stranger that way. Hadn't the fool girl just heard him say he was a married man? Of course Laura had. Perhaps she was just flirting with him so obviously for practice. Doubtless getting ready for the dance.

CHAPTER 28

Josh and his sister Jessie watched, puzzled, from the dimly lit house as Laura and Jeremiah Taylor returned from the Mormon's Conestoga wagon. Laura was fingering a thick leather-bound book, and Josh whispered, "Likely it's that crazy Book of Mormon he keeps jawin' about! I thought they was just goin' out to see how his old wife was and there he goes, a-tryin' to convert her."

Jessie smirked and said, "A lot you know about gals, smarty. Old Laura don't give two shucks for his old *Bible*."

Jeremiah and Laura mounted the veranda steps, and as they said good night he offered her his hand and said something the others could't hear. Laura laughed lightly, and Jessie whispered, "Well, they're sure gettin' along fast enough, ain't they?"

Josh frowned and agreed. "Yeah, considerin' he's already got hisself a wife bedded down in that durned wagon!"

Later, up in the girls' room, Jessie watched her older sister thoughtfully as Laura combed her long blond hair at the window, gazing down at the Mormon wagon parked in the yard.

Jessie trilled, "Well, well, it's a mite past spring, tra la, but I see old Laura's in love agin!"

"That's enough out of you, smart miss!"

"Well, it's true, ain't it? If you're not in love, why are you moonin' down on lover-boy Taylor right this instant?"

"What a thing to say, Jessie! We only met him today! Sometimes you really are a silly child!"

146

"Likely he's got gray hairs in his brush, too. He's sort of old, ain't he, even for old Granny Laura?"

"Old? What are you talking about? He's not old at all!"

"Is too. Bet he's at least thirty. 'Fore you know it he'll be forty!"

"That's enough, Jessie. Good night!"

"He'll likely be fat in a few years, or bald."

"Will you be still, brat?"

Jessie giggled and bored in with "See you've got his Good Book. Is it true Mormons is allowed more'n one wife?"

"What are you talking about, you silly child?"

"It's true. Josh told me. Mormons marry up like A-rabs. Keep regular harems, like the sheiks of Araby! They say Brigham Young has hisself two dozen wives or more, out Salt Lake City way!"

"Oh, for Pete's sake get in bed and be still!"

Jessie got onto her bunk, but bounced up and down on it instead of getting under the covers as she insisted. " 'Course, maybe you'd like that, Laura. You'd git to spend the rest of your days locked up in a tent or somethin', wearing baggy britches and pointy-toed slippers, with a veil over your face and all!"

Laura threw a pillow with an angry pout. Then she snuffed out the lamp and got into her own bed, filled with wonder and strange feelings she couldn't explain even to herself.

Down the hall, Josh was still dressed as he knocked softly on Molly's door. Molly called out to come in, and Josh found his aunt propped up in bed, reading by the coal-oil lamp.

Molly noted the anxious expression on his young face and asked, "Is something wrong, Josh? You look like you've seen a ghost!"

"Seen a saint, mebbe. Aunt Molly, I don't know what's got into Laura!"

Molly knew what he meant, but she asked anyway. "What's wrong with Laura, dear?"

"That's what I was hopin' you could tell *me*, Aunt

Molly. Since we haven't got our ma no more, I think you'd best have a little gal-to-gal talk with the fool mooncalf!"

"And what would this gal-to-gal talk be about, Josh?"

"About, you know, things gals should know about when they ain't kids no more."

"You don't think she knows the facts of life, Josh?"

"Well, she purely don't act like she does! I mean, you can't hardly blame a man for . . . well, wantin' to do more'n look when a likely gal keeps shovin' the real good in his face!"

"The real . . . what?"

"You know what I mean, Aunt Molly! Laura was makin' doe-eyes at that Mormon all through supper. It was plumb sickenin', and, Aunt Molly, that old jasper was *looking* too!"

"Your sister's a very pretty girl, Josh. You're going to have to get used to the idea of men looking her way. If you were a guest in some strange house and a girl as pretty as Laura was sitting across the table from you, wouldn't you, well, look?"

"That ain't the point, Aunt Molly. For one thing, I ain't married!"

"Oh, Josh, poor Josh, I *do* understand what you're worried about, but let me tell you a secret about us wicked grown-ups. You know I was married once, don't you?"

"Of course."

"Well, I was happily married and I loved my husband. I was faithful to him, as I'm sure he was to me."

"What's that got to do with that durned old Mormon, Aunt Molly?"

"Looking, Josh. You see, grown-ups do look. There'd be no point to the vows of marriage if it wasn't only natural for a healthy man or woman to look at and, well, admire each other."

"Gosh, you mean you looked at other men when your husband was alive, Aunt Molly?"

"Of course I did, just as he looked at pretty women. If you see a man on a fine horse ride by, don't you stare and admire his mount, Josh?"

"Sure, but Laura . . ."

"Do you want to *steal* his horse, Josh?"

"Steal a man's horse? Heck no!"

"Why not, Josh?"

"Why not? Shoot, that's dumb, Aunt Molly. It's wrong to steal another man's horse!"

"All right, maybe now you understand about looking. It wouldn't be natural for anyone not to admire a pretty face, but we all know better than to let ourselves do more than look. At least, most of us do. It's not the looking, or even the wanting, that's a sin, Josh. As long as there's no *doing!*"

"Well, mebbe *he* ain't more'n lookin', Aunt Molly, but Laura's actin' shameless!"

"I'll talk to Laura, but you have to understand she's almost a grown woman, and there's no boy her age for miles around. Jeremiah Taylor's handsome, educated, and charming. It's only natural for Laura to be impressed and, well, sort of want to look at him. Do you see what I'm getting at, dear?"

"Mebbe so, but if that fool gal carries on like that with ever'thing in pants she meets, she's likely to git herself in a heap of trouble!"

"I promise I'll talk to her, Josh. Why don't you go to bed now?"

"Can't, ma'am. Still have a few chores with the stock to tend to. I'll git to bed directly."

They said good night, and Josh went out to the barn to check the water troughs and secure the livestock for the night. As he crossed the barnyard Josh failed to notice the mounted stranger watching the moonlit homestead from a nearby rise.

At least, he did at first. Then the distant figure's mount nickered to the horses in the barn, and Josh froze in the shadows, peering in the direction of the sound.

Josh frowned as he stood there, waiting for the

mysterious mounted stranger to do or say something. The man was almost within hailing distance as he sat up there, outlined by the moonlight. But he wasn't moving. He wasn't coming and he wasn't going. He just sat his horse up there on the rise, like some sort of spook, and Josh felt the hairs on the back of his neck tingle as he gulped, took a deep breath, and called out, "Howdy, stranger!"

The night rider didn't answer, and after a time a cloud passed over the moon's face, darkening the sky. When the light returned, the stranger wasn't there any more.

Josh walked back to the house, closed the door behind him, and bolted it. Then he got a rifle and loaded it before going to his room. He didn't undress for bed. With Luke and Uncle Zeb away, he was the man of the house, and if he hadn't seen a haunt, he'd likely seen trouble on horseback!

CHAPTER 29

At sunup Josh rode out, doubling on his tracks a few times before making a beeline for the valley he knew his elder brother would be hunting in.

He found Luke gutting the carcass of a buck he'd hung from an aspen tree and got right to the point, bringing Luke up to date on the Mormon visitors and the mysterious stranger. Like Molly, Luke was inclined to view Laura's present flirtation as one of those girlish notions she was always having. The stranger was another matter to a boy with a price on his head.

As the two brothers hunkered down by Luke's

campfire, Luke asked, "Did you git a good look at the jasper, Josh?"

"Nope. 'Peared to be a man on a big horse, but that's all I can tell you. He just sat up there in the moonlight, watchin' the house from the ridge. I figured you should know."

"You figured right, kid. It was just a matter of time afore another bounty hunter turned up lookin' to collect my scalp for that damn reward."

"I know, Luke. I was a-feared you'd ride in blind. That's why I lit out at daybreak. I made sure I wasn't follered, too!"

"You're growin' up on me, little brother. You can take this here carcass back to the spread for me, Josh. Say it's my goin'-away present."

"Wait, maybe iffen I ask around town I can find out who he is. We don't know he's after *you*, Luke. Could be he's hauntin' them old Mormons or—"

"You said they was bedded down outside, in the wagon, didn't you?"

"Sure, but what does that— Oh, I see what you mean."

"Yep, it's a bounty hunter, most likely. Save ever'body a lot of trouble if I'm long gone by the time he gets around to poking his nose in deeper. I've been hereabouts too long as it is."

"Take me with you then, Luke."

"Are you crazy, boy? Why would I do such a fool thing?"

"You said I was almost growed, and if I rode at your side—"

"Cool down, Jesse James. We ain't ready for a brother act just yet. You don't ride with a man who's wanted by the law, Josh. You don't know what it's like on the owlhoot trail, and Lord willin', you never will!"

"I ain't scared. I can handle a firing piece, too, if I has to!"

"You *don't* have to, kid. You're still clean, and I aim to keep you that way! I ain't puttin' you down

as a man, Josh. I know you got the sand in your craw
to ride with me through hell, but I can't ask you to.
It ain't just the cold dark nights and loneliness, kid.
It's the lookin' back over your shoulder and the look
a man on the run gets in his eyes after a time."

"I could take it, for kin."

"You got kin back at the spread, kid. We can't
leave Aunt Molly and the gals alone back there without at least one man on the place, can we?"

"Reckon not, but dang it, I'll miss you, Luke!"

"I'll miss you too, brother. Make sure you get this
deer back afore the flies get at it. Make sure the gals
treat Aunt Molly right, too. I'll try to come back afore
winter, hear?"

As Luke threw a saddle over his bronc and cinched
up, Josh swallowed hard and asked, "Did you really
mean it when you said I was fit to be called a man,
Luke?"

"I said you was, didn't I, brother?"

"Not *kid* brother this time?"

Luke turned and held his hand out, his own voice
choked as he shook his head and said, "Nope. Not
this time. I'll be seein' you, brother."

"So long and good luck, then . . . brother."

CHAPTER 30

Zeb Macahan rode hell for leather into Fort Sully on
the lathered pony he'd half killed with hard riding
getting there. Ignoring the sentry who challenged him
at the gate, Zeb galloped inside, slid to a stop by the
livery stable, and dropped to the ground lightly as he
tossed the reins to a startled soldier and snapped,

"Soldier, cool this horse down with a walk around the parade, rub him down, and don't overwater him. Tell the hostler I'll expect my saddle and gear on a fresh mount at the postern in ten minutes flat!"

"Sir, I don't give orders to the stablehands and—"

"I said ten minutes flat, soldier! You got that loud and clear?"

"Yes, sir."

Zeb strode in giant limping strides to the orderly room, where a posted guard made the mistake of trying to bar his way with a rifle held at port arms, saying, "You can't go in there, sir. The officers are in con—" And then he was sitting down as Zeb threw his rifle aside and stepped over his legs, bulling his way through the orderly-room door.

As he entered he spied Major Drake, Captain MacAllister, Grand Duke Dimitri, and Coulee John Brinkerhoff, as well as a handful of cavalry officers, grouped around a map table.

Drake gasped. "Macahan, what are you doing here?"

"Trying to make sense out of lunacy! What in thunder's going on?"

"You know or you wouldn't be here with that fire in your eye, Zeb. Your Sioux friends have kidnapped Count Sergei and his . . . ah . . . fiancée."

"Yeah, I heard. They likely did it for no good reason at all!"

Drake said, "As I understand it, it was something to do with the Duke, here, hunting buffalo. But you know—"

"No, I don't know. *Where* were they hunting buffalo?"

"Look, Macahan, you can't just quit and join up again as the spirit moves you! I've got a handle on it. It's none of your business now."

"I'm making it my business, damn it! I was one of the fools who persuaded Red Cloud, Gall, Roman Nose, Crazy-Horse, and my old friend Stanangkai to sign that empty treaty promising them no white man would ever set foot in the Black Hills. It hasn't been a full six months since the treaty was ratified by Washington!"

"I know that, Zeb. But what's done is done. It's out of your hands now. It's out of my hands, too."

"Then these silly sons of bitches *were* hunting on the reservation!"

Duke Dimitri scowled and snapped, "See here, I am a brother to the Czar of All the Russias, peasant!"

"Shut up afore I spit in your eye and drown you, you moronic twit! If I had the time, I'd send my condolences to the Czar's mamma for havin' a halfwit for a son, but I ain't got time, so shut your face and let me talk to the *menfolk* hereabouts!"

MacAllister grinned, but Drake snapped, "You can't talk that way to His Highness, Macahan!"

"I just did! Let's get back to them prissy dudes killing meat on the Dakota's hunting grounds!"

"That hasn't been confirmed, Zeb."

Zeb scowled at Coulee John and said, "I'll confirm it for you if *this* bucket of piss guided the party!"

Brinkerhoff reddened and put a hand to the hilt of his bowie as Zeb whirled on him and sneered, "Pull it, Brinkerhoff! Pull your blade like a man and let me feed your heart to the hawks!"

Coulee John snatched his hand from the knife hilt as if he'd suddenly remembered it was red hot. Zeb turned his back on him and snapped, "This skunk's an Indian-hater as well as a yellow-belly, Major! What in thunder made you send them dudes out with him leading? Don't you know he's been saying for years that the only way to whip the Indians is to kill their buffalo and force a showdown?"

Brinkerhoff stared daggers at Zeb's back as he blustered, "See here, Major! I don't have to stand here an' take this rawhiding!"

Drake said, "He's right, Macahan. This is *my* office, in case you forgot! Did you just come here to insult us all or is there some reason for your paying us a call?"

Zeb pointed at the duke and said, "Depends on this idiot?" Then he asked Duke Dimitri in a less-insulting tone, "How 'bout it, Duke? You just want the Dakota punished, or do you want your nephew and the Rooshun gal back in two whole pieces? You can't have both."

The grand duke surprised Zeb by sounding quite reasonable as he said, "I want my nephew, Sergei, alive and unharmed, of course. I have been trying to tell everyone I am willing to negotiate, but they are waiting for some general and his regiment."

"The Dakota won't negotiate with no regiment. They'll mebbe run or mebbe fight, but they'll leave Count Sergei staked out on an ant pile either way, if he's lucky and they ain't got time to think of somethin' ornerier!"

The duke nodded and said, "I am not unaware of savage ways. We have had our own experiences with the Siberian Tartar tribesmen. Tell me, Mister Wild Man, will those Indians negotiate with *you?* You say their chief is your friend. I don't find this hard to understand."

Zeb shrugged and said, "Satangkai used to friend. Likely he has me down as a damn They might kill me. They might be willing to worth a try."

Drake said, "Get Satangkai to come in and I' to him under a safe conduct, Zeb."

"He won't come in. He won't be listening to white men's promises just now. You couldn't talk to him anyways. Satangkai don't talk our lingo."

"Oh, come on, most of the Sioux chiefs speak at least a little English. They tell me Sitting Bull can read and write.."

"He can. His name ain't Sitting Bull. It's Buffalo-Bull-Who-Waits, and he ain't their chief. He's their high priest. Satangkai's a War Chief. He don't savvy English on account he don't want to. He don't have use one for our lingo or our ways."

Duke Dimitri asked, "Do you speak Sioux, then?"

"Some."

Duke Dimitri snapped, "Suffice to say you can talk to this man who hold my nephew and the girl!"

"If he don't put an arrow in me on sight. Want me to give it a try?"

"Of course! Major Drake, I demand you call off your military expedition. I want this man to have an opportunity to try it his way!"

"Your Highness, it's not *my* expedition. It's Brandy Jack Stonecipher's, and he outranks me. He'll be here in about forty-eight hours, and if I know my General Stonecipher . . . Um, what about it, Zeb?"

"Can you hold Stonecipher here till I get back?"

"You know the answer to that one, Zeb. Besides, you said yourself you might not be *coming* back!"

Zeb nodded and said, "Well, Major, I don't hold with telling a man his job . . ."

"But you're going to, Zeb. What's your plan?"

"We both know Brandy Jack's an Indian-killing idiot, but you got yourself a telegraph line to Washington, ain't you?"

"Good God, are you suggesting I go over my general's head?"

"Ain't suggesting. Telling. You can take a chance on hurtin' old Brandy Jack's feelings some or you can see can you hold this fort in the face of an all-out Indian war!"

Harry Drake looked like a man trying to wake up from a bad dream. But he turned with a sigh to his adjutant and asked, "What about it, MacAllister?"

"We'll likely both be busted to buck-ass privates, Harry, but I'm for it."

"Jesus, I was afraid you'd say a dumb thing like that! All right, compose a telegram explaining our position to the War Department. Tell them Zeb Macahan's negotiating with the Sioux for return of the captives and ask, very delicately, if they can delay Stonecipher's attack until Zeb comes back. Oh, and on your way back, drop by the officers' canteen and fetch me a bottle of anything strong and wet!"

The grand duke said, "Forgive me, I know something of such intrigues. I think it would do no harm, Major, if my demands were added to your message." The portly Russian frowned in thought. "Inform Washington there will be serious international complications if the Russian subjects of His Majesty the Czar are harmed because of hasty and ill-timed efforts on the part of this thrice-accursed and no doubt unwashed General Stonecipher!"

MacAllister grinned and said, "I'll put it just that way, Your Highness, but Brandy Jack won't like it!"

"Bah, I am used to dealing with generals. If you gentlemen will permit an old courtier to interfere, it might help when your general gets here if I, how do you say? Catch the hell?"

"That's close enough, Your Highness, and mighty white of you."

"*Da,* I am a White Russian, *nyet?* But let us have no more jokings. Be on your way, young sir!"

MacAllister nodded and said, "I'll get it right on the wire, sir!" as he jogged out of the office on the double.

Zeb frowned thoughtfully at the old nobleman and said, "I ain't wrong often, but when I am, I ain't too proud to say it. I owe you an apology, Duke."

"Of course you do. And you are still quite uncouth. Just make certain my nephew and the dear girl are not harmed. I must repair to my quarters."

Drake asked, "Is there anything else we can do for you, Your Highness?"

"Nothing, thank you. I have sent one of my cossacks with a message to the Czar. I hope this entire nasty business can be over before my royal brother receives it."

"I'm certain it will be, sir."

"Really? If the efficiency of your War Department has any relationship to the efficiency of how this garrison guarded our safety, I hardly share your confidence, Major. Good day, gentlemen!"

As he left, Coulee John snickered and said, "Snooty old egg-sucker, ain't he?"

Drake snapped, "Brinkerhoff, get the hell out of my sight! I see now it's thanks to you we're in this mess. The last thing I intend to do before the War Department has my oak leaves will be to have you fired and make sure you never scout for this man's army again!"

Brinkerhoff sniffed and said, "Hey, don't you try and lay any of this on *my* haid, Major! It was made plenty clear to me I was to take them dudes out and find 'em buffalo. Don't you lie and say you thought I'd find enough buffalo to be worthwhile anywhere's *but* the Sioux reservation, damn it!"

"Get out, you bastard!"

Coulee John left, muttering under his breath, and Drake turned to Zeb. "All right, Macahan. Show me on this map where Satangkai's encampment is."

Zeb looked down at the map and said, "Can't do it. For one thing, like I said, Satangkai's a friend of mine, or used to be. For another, your dumb map's all wrong."

"What are you talking about? This is a U.S. Government Survey map."

"Yep, likely surveyed on the run by some greenhorns more worried about keepin' their hair than runnin' a contour line. The Black Hills ain't lined up like that map shows 'em, Major. You see, the Black Hills ain't a spur of the Rockies like this map shows. It's a sort of mountain island, set out all by itself on the prairie. The hills ain't black at all. That's another white man's mistranslation. The Indians use the same word for 'black' as they do for 'blue,' figuring black is just a darker shade of blue. So they call them hills up to our north the Black Hills 'cause they's *blue*. Mostly blue-gray granite in the center, with ring after ring of rimrock foothills all around 'em, sort of like the rings of a target or maybe a heap big fingerprint left east of the Rockies by Wakan Tonka. It's ridge an' flat valley after ridge an' flat valley, all the way in to the big granite peaks in the bull's-eye. The Indians never go up to the high middle mountains. That's where Old Woman, Rock Spirit, Thunderbird, Lord Grizzly, and such other spirits guard the high lodge of Wakan Tonka."

"I see. You figure Satangkai's band is hiding out in one of the grass-filled long valleys between the rim-rocks, right?"

"Wrong. Satangkai ain't hiding. He's waiting. You can't just move anywheres through them castle walls of hogback ridges. You got to ride in through the passes, and Satangkai'll have them passes guarded."

"How do you know he's expecting Stonecipher's attack if he doesn't speak English, Zeb?"

"I said he don't speak English—never said Satangkai was stupid. First place, there's Dakota as does talk our lingo, and more'n one can read a newspaper if they've a mind to. Second place, Satangkai don't have to have it spelled out in fine print for him. He's fought us afore and he knows our ways. Likely that's why he don't like 'em, much. When the Dakota wiped out Fetterman's command a few years back they wasn't even holding captives. They hadn't done nothing 'cept make some demands for simple justice, and Washington's answer was Fetterman's cavalry troop!"

"I think I see your meaning, Zeb. Satangkai took those captives because he wants Stonecipher to attack! He's deliberately provoking a war!"

"Yes and no. He expects us to explain about the invasion of his hunting ground, or fight. My hope on getting back with the hostages and my hair is that he'll listen to reason."

"And if he doesn't, General Stonecipher will lead a regiment of cavalry into a natural fortress, with no real notion of the lay of the land and the Indians set to ambush him in any of a thousand places!"

Zeb nodded grimly and said, "I reckoned if I gave you a mite more time out here you'd start to think like an Indian, Major."

CHAPTER 31

Zeb rode in bold as brass. There was no other way to ride in. The smoke talk went up before he'd passed through the first range of the whirlpool ridges of the great Black Hills massif.

By the time he'd ridden through the second pass he knew they aimed to see what he had to say before killing him. He'd spotted the scouts watching from above as he passed under them within easy arrow range.

Zeb rode all morning and into the afternoon, ignoring the puffs of smoke that rose about him, reading, "American coming . . . Alone . . . One rifle . . . Gun belt . . . He takes no cover . . . He shows no fear . . ."

Then Zeb rode over a rise between two nearly vertical walls of shale, ignoring the impassive Indians who watched from above on either side with casually flexed bows, and headed for the tipi ring in the grassy mountain meadow by a sluggish brook.

As the white man rode into the encampment, a yellow Indian dog barked twice before being shushed by a child. Those Indians in view went on about their business as if Zeb were invisible. Zeb rode by the rope corral of the band's many ponies, noting the cavalry bay Count Sergei had been riding, in with the others. He guided his own mount toward the white buckskin lodge with Satangkai's mark and feathered medicine shield over the door flap and reined in a few paces away, sitting his pony quietly.

A tall muscular Indian with traces of iron-gray in his long black braids came out of the lodge, stripped to the waist. His chest bore the scars of sun dance, for Satangkai was a man, and all real men who wished to be called Dakota faced many tests of their courage. Zeb knew his old friend was entitled to the grizzly-claw necklace and the coup feather bonnet of a great warrior, but Satangkai dismissed such badges of his rank among the Real People. Every man who spoke Dakota knew his rank and station among the great chiefs. Satangkai didn't care what his enemies thought when they saw him. Satangkai's enemies were not in the habit of living long. A man fought best in the simple garb of a warrior.

Zeb dismounted as the Indian came over to him with a thin smile. He held out his hand, and Satangkai grasped his forearm, their palms to crook of elbows, as men greeted one another, but he said in his own tongue, oddly high-pitched to a white man's ears, "White Eagle, you come among us at a bad time between our peoples."

Zeb answered in Dakota. "I know this to be true. Am I welcome in your lodge this day?"

"White Eagle is always welcome, but I greet him with a heavy heart. Come, we shall smoke together."

Zeb followed the Indian into the spacious lodge, where a pretty young woman kneeled by the central fire pit, nursing a child. Satangkai said, "The woman is called Shewelah. She is young, but she is a good wife. The child will be a man someday, if he is brave."

Zeb nodded a greeting to the shy young squaw and hunkered down beside his host as Satangkai took up an already lit pipe with a red stone bowl and drew a lungful of smoke before passing it silently to his guest.

Zeb took a deep drag on the strong tobacco and said, "My heart soars that you share calumet with me, Satangkai, old friend."

"My spirit flies with the hawks to see you once again, White Eagle. Have you hunger?"

"This person has had good hunting and has no hunger, save for the company of his old friend. How has it been with the Dakota since the making of the marks on paper?"

"A little better than war. Much worse than peace. Your people do not keep their word. I know you to have a good heart, White Eagle. Why are your people so wicked?"

"Not all my people are wicked, Satangkai. You know how it is with the changing of our chiefs in the Great White City."

"I know. It seems a foolish thing, this changing of chiefs all the time. How can we have peace with your people if they dismiss the chiefs we just dealt with? Is it true there is a new Great White Father?"

"It is true. I don't think he is a bad man. They say he has a good heart, but he is perhaps ignorant of what the last Great White Father promised my friends."

"I hear your words but I do not understand them, White Eagle. Our high chief, Red Cloud, still leads our nation. Our high priest, Buffalo-Bull-Who-Waits, still speaks to the spirits for us. Your people must be fickle to keep changing their chiefs and laws all the time. How do they keep from becoming confused?"

"They don't, always. To explain it in Dakota is to try to catch a flea on a running dog."

"Your people are as many as the leaves of the forest, and in some ways wise. If they can make an Iron Horse and speak over copper wires, why can't they find one man wise enough to lead them until his vision dims? Why can't they choose a chief whose words will last longer than the summer storm on the mountaintop? Why do you change your laws and treaties with the wind? Hear me, many summers before we drew breath my people lived far to the east, on the shores of the Minni-Tonka where the wild rice grows, and we hunted deer and Chippewa in the forests instead of buffalo on the greasy grass. In those long-ago times we had laws and customs and prayed to our Great Spirit and his children."

"This is known to me, Satangkai."

"We moved west, giving way to the Americans and their Chippewa and Crow and Pawnee allies. We moved far. We changed our ways of hunting, and when we got horses from the Comanche we changed our way of life, but we did not change our laws. What a Dakota said a hundred summers ago in truth is true to this day. What is the matter with your people? Are they children? Are they mad?"

Zeb thought hard, sorting out his thoughts as he tried to form them in Dakota words his friend might understand. He took a drag from the calumet, blew it out, and said, "You have more than one lodge to your nation, Satangkai. There are the Dog Soldiers and the Contraries and the Crooked Lances, true?"

"This is so."

"My people have two great lodges. They are called Republicans and Democrats. They oppose each other like fire and water. Every four harvests my people gather to choose which lodge shall lead our nation. If fire replaces water, the laws are changed. The Democrat lodge does not feel bound by the promises of the Republican lodge, as fire does not keep the word of water."

"Heya! It is *harder* than catching the flea of a running dog! How can the chief of fire make words to live by if the chief of water may wash away his every word?"

"He can't. It is hard, but it is so with my people."

Satangkai shook his head wearily and said, "My warriors are angry. It is only five moons since the Great White Father said these mountains shall forever be for the Dakota alone. Yet he has come into our land to kill our winter meat for the love of killing alone. When my young men spoke to him, he spat upon our meat and called us names. Because of this, men died. You must know my young men took two prisoners, a man and a woman. Many of my people counsel me to kill the captives. Your chiefs spoke to us with forked tongues, and some of my young men were wounded in the fight at the funny painted wagons."

"I understand this, Satangkai. Do you think this is wise?"

"No, but when the heart is filled with anger, the

mouth speaks with the tongue of a child. You know I lead my people because they look to me to do the just thing and be brave. Some of the young men say I am squaw-hearted for not letting them kill the man, at least."

"But you agree then, he should not be killed?"

"No, the man is bad and should be killed. The woman is only a woman. Her fate is not important. If I gave you the woman, do you think the Great White Father would forgive my young men's hastiness? They acted foolishly, but justice was in their hearts and they fought well."

"Satangkai, many soldiers are coming, many."

"I know. My scouts have seen them. I know it is not wise for me to kill the white man, but he has been evil, even as a captive. If I don't kill him, my young men will be filled with scorn. If I do, the blue sleeves will come and many men will die on both sides, but my young men are angry and not afraid to die like men!"

"Hear me, the white man is not an American. He is a great chief from another nation, far across the great bitter water. If he dies, there may be more than a war between your people and mine. It may mean a long bloody war between his tribe and mine as well as yours. In the end, there's no telling how many people, innocent people, may die."

"Heay, the ways of the white men are mad. But what can I do? The blue sleeves are coming in either case."

"I have spoken to my chiefs. Some of them want war, and others are willing to forgive the Dakota if the two captives are returned unharmed."

"Many of my people speak for war, too. They say it is better to die as Dakota than to live on in shame forever. We have bent before the white man's winds like the reeds, but no matter how far we bend he always pushes our faces deeper into the mud."

"But this time you may make the white man bend. By giving back the captives you may count coup on your enemeies among my people."

"By surrendering to their demands? How does a warrior count coup on an enemy who gets what he wants from one?"

"By making others laugh at him. Do you remember the time when you were a young untested warrior and you humiliated that Crow chief?"

Satangkai smiled and chuckled. "Heya, that was a shining afternoon! He was big and had many coup feathers, but I rushed up to him, unarmed, and took his shield from him after slapping his face with my open hand, as if he'd been a child. Ha! How everyone laughed at him! Even his own friends laughed at him. It was a good fight!"

"Then hear me, Satangkai. Among my people there are men who hate you and want nothing more than another war. The man who spat on your buffalo was one. Another is a great chief of the blue sleeves who boasts of many victories. He is a man who lives for war. He is leading many soldiers against you, licking his lips like a hungry coyote and famished for another fight."

"He will have one then. We are not afraid."

"I know that, Satangkai, but what if you made a fool out of him?"

"As I did that Crow? How is this thing possible, White Eagle?"

"Hear me, as I said, the man you hold is the nephew of a great chief from a faraway land. If he gets his kinsman back alive and unharmed, he will tell the Great White Father not to let the blue sleeves fight you. Their great war chief will have marched for days for nothing, and he will feel like a fool. Even some of the blue sleeves hate him, and they will laugh at him behind his back and call him funny names. Tell me, who would be the victor then, you or him?"

Satangkai nodded and said, "I would enjoy counting this coup on a man I do not know who hates me. I think if I put it that way to my young men they will see the humor in your plan, but hear me, I must have my own terms, so that my laughter shall not be the empty laughter of a cowardly dog who barks but is afraid to bite."

"I listen, old friend."

"Then hear. We shall return this stupid bad man from across the bitter water, and the woman too, but we will not return them under threats from those we do not fear. Have your people meet us at the Painted Meadows with no guns or more people than can sit about the fire in one lodge."

"You words are good. Is that all?"

"No. In the past, weak chiefs have handed over young men who did bad things to be hanged like dogs. Drives-His-Horses and the others shall be pardoned by the Great White Father. We must have a paper with words saying it was the white men who broke the peace. It must all be written down. All of it. The paper must say our young men were right in what they did and that the white men who caused the fight were in the wrong."

"I hear, Satangkai."

"Then hear yet more. The paper is not enough. Winter is coming, and many of my people will go hungry unless we get food. For what those evil men have done, we must have tribute. I want them to bring some of the green paper the traders value so much, to buy food and blankets against the coming of the frost spirits."

"That sounds reasonable. How much green paper do you want?"

"I don't know. You must tell me, White Eagle."

Zeb grinned and said, "You ask *me* to fix the price of those buffalo they wasted, Satangkai?"

"Yes, White Eagle. Since first we met as enemies and became friends you have always spoken fairly to me. My people do not sell buffalo for green paper. How much should we ask for?"

Without hesitation, Zeb said, "Ten thousand green papers."

"So many? We can buy much food with so much green paper. Your words make my heart laugh."

"Then both our hearts laugh, Satangkai! As decent men among my people shall laugh at your enemies for a thousand sunrises! You shall have more green papers than there are people in your nation, and the evil men of war will be made to look like fools. You count a great coup, Satangkai!"

"Then we have spoken here. Now let us go to where I hold the captives so that you can tell the Great White Father you have seen them alive and well."

Zeb followed Satangkai out and to another lodge, where he found Count Sergei and the girl, Valerie, looking a little the worse for wear.

The bosomy Valerie was unharmed and unbound, but she could have used a bath and a fresh gown. It was obvious that no serving maid had been helping her with her tangled hair, either.

Count Sergei, being male, was bound, but loosely enough for him to attend to his own needs. His clothes were torn, he needed a shave, and he'd lost some of his dignity with that halter around his neck. A Dakota guard had the other end of the halter rope. He'd obviously been led about like an animal since his capture, and the bandage around his head bespoke the hard knocks he had taken in the capture.

As Zeb and the chief ducked in, the captives looked up in mingled fear and hope. Count Sergei said, "A white man at last! I hope you've come to affect our release, my good man?"

Zeb said, "I don't know as I'm anybody's good man, but I've come to get you outen this fix, in a manner of speaking. You and the gal here, all right?"

Valerie said, "They haven't tortured us, but my God, get us *out* of here!"

"Just simmer down, missy. The chief here's lettin' me see you so I can tell the army you're both still breathing. You'll both be freed if I can get the army to agree to their terms."

"Terms?"

"Yes, ma'am. Ten thousand dollars and a signed statement admitting your guilt."

Count Sergei exploded. "Incredible! It was a common kidnapping for ransom after all!"

"Mister, you don't hear so good, if that was all you heard."

"Macahan, I've had about enough of your arrogance! You're no better than your savage friends! Don't you know who I *am?*"

"Sure, you're likely a big frog in your own little puddle, but out here, a *who* don't pick a tick off a buffalo rump. It's *what* you are that matters, and from what I've seed so far, you ain't all that big a shucks."

"Damn you! You'll find out how powerful I am when the Czar of all the Russias hears what's happened here! A nephew of the Grand Duke Dimitri Romanov and the Count of Kiev, bound and treated like a captive beast!"

"Boy, like I said, there's somethin' likely wrong with your ears! These so-called savages had an empire from the Great Lakes to the Rockies when your Czar was collecting tribute for the Mongol hordes. They're noble as you are, and likely got more honor, but if you'll give 'em your word not to try to escape they'll likely untie you and treat you more neighborly till I can arrange your exchange."

"A Romanov give his gentleman's word to naked savages? Never!"

"Then you'll likely have to stay trussed till I see if you're worth cold cash to anybody interested enough to put it up. If it's any help, I reckon they will and you two will be out of here in mebbe forty-eight hours."

Valerie brightened. "Forty-eight hours! Do you think it's possible?"

"Fair chance, ma'am, provided your proud friend here can keep his mouth shut just long enough to hang on to his fool scalp till I get back!"

Zeb ducked out, followed by Satangkai. Count Sergei scowled after them and muttered, "By God!

We'll see a day of reckoning yet! That arrogant Yankee shall pay for his arrogance if it's the last thing I do, and that's a promise I make on my father's grave!"

Valerie sighed and said, "If anyone's to blame here, it's certainly not that brave man who rode in here alone to help us!"

Then, realizing what a tender toe indeed she might have stepped on, she quickly added fawningly, "I didn't mean that as it may have sounded, Your Highness."

Count Sergei stared at her with narrowed eyes, and there was a sinister cast to his smile that even their Indian guard recognized as pure evil as Count Sergei purred, "I know just what you meant, and *do* mean, my dear. Arrogance is not confined to the Yankee peasantry, it seems."

"Count Sergei, I'm so frightened and weary, I don't know what I'm saying lately."

"I know, there's truth in wine and in a woman's hysteria. Don't worry about it, little peasant. I promise to remind you of it later, at a more . . . convenient time."

CHAPTER 32

Back at the Macahan farm, young Josh and their Mormon guest, Jeremiah Taylor, were splitting a cord of wood against the coming winter. Josh had protested that the severely dressed older man was "company," but the Mormon insisted it was his duty before the Lord as well as his pleasure to take part in the manly chores of the homestead.

What his wife, Maggie, was doing was anybody's

guest. She'd hardly stirred from her pallet in the Conestoga wagon since they'd arrived.

In the kitchen, Molly Culhane came upon Laura, dressed in her finest Sunday-go-to-meeting dress, long blond hair freshly washed and combed. She was busily stirring something sweet and spicy-smelling in a mixing bowl. As the older woman came in, the girl smiled brightly and said, "Good morning, Aunt Molly, isn't it a lovely day?"

"You're up early, dear."

"Well, seeing we have guests, I just thought I'd need a mite more time to fix breakfast. I'm makin' batter cakes from a recipe I cut out of *Godey's Lady's Book*. Do you think Jeremiah will like 'em?"

"I'm sure he will, unless he counts cinnamon as wicked as coffee, tea, and tobacco."

"You're just funning, aren't you? I've been thinking I really ought to do more cooking hereabouts. I mean, I can cook, but not near as good as you or Ma, and every woman my age should be a regular cook and homemaker, don't you think?"

"Laura, sit down. I'll mix the batter for you."

"Really, Aunt Molly, I'd rather do it my own self."

"And I'd rather you sat down and listened to me," Molly said firmly as she took the mixing bowl from Laura and indicated the kitchen chair with a brisk nod.

Not looking at the girl as she took over the mixing chore, Molly said, "It's time we had a little talk, dear. I know that Jeremiah Taylor is a handsome, rather fascinating man—"

"Fascinating? Aunt Molly, I've never met anyone like him in my whole life! He's so interesting, and he wants to do such wonderful things!"

"I suppose he does, dear, but aren't you being a little, well, obvious?"

"Obvious? What are you talkin' about, Aunt Molly?"

"I think you know, dear. I was younger than you when I fell madly in love with my schoolteacher back home in Illinois. I thought he was the most perfect man I'd ever seen. I thought I'd never get over the fact that he'd married someone else while I was in the third grade."

"Aunt Molly, it's not the same!"

"It's never exactly the same, dear. The details are always as different as the people involved, but the feelings, and the mistakes, run pretty true to form."

"But, Aunt Molly, I haven't done anything wrong! Is it wrong to admire someone because they're strong and intelligent and brave and good and—"

"We're not talking about right or wrong, dear. I'm talking about your getting hurt! I know I'm not your mother, and perhaps it's not my place to interfere, but face it, Laura, Mr. Taylor is a married man."

"I know that, Aunt Molly, but I can't help the way I feel. I know Jeremiah would never want to do anything sinful, and neither would I, but we can't help it if, well . . ."

"*We* can't help it, child? Just how deep have *we* been getting into this, uh, fascination?"

"Oh, he hasn't said anything, but I can tell. I've seen the way he looks at me, and when our eyes meet . . ."

"Oh dear, forgive me, Kate, but this daughter of yours is about to be taken in hand! Laura, I'm going to put it to you woman to woman with no beating about the bush. You're making a damned little fool of yourself!"

"I don't know what you mean, Aunt Molly. Jeremiah—"

"Jeremiah Taylor is a healthy man, married to a sick old woman, and you are healthy, young, beautiful, and offering. Of course he's attracted to you. What man in his position wouldn't be?"

"Aunt Molly! What are you suggesting? How dare you say I'm offering anything? I mean, anything sinful?"

"Young lady, you've been throwing yourself at the good-looking young Mormon like a barroom tart!

Maybe a bit more obviously, in fact, since at least a tart knows what she's doing. You've probably got that poor young man so confused he doesn't know *what* to think of you!"

Laura's eyes widened in dismay as she blurted, "That's not so! He's never said or done anything disrespectful!"

"I never thought he had, or he'd be off this spread with a load of buckshot bidding him godspeed Don't you understand a thing I've said? Of *course* Jeremiah Taylor's going to treat you with respect. He's some sort of minister, for heaven's sake!"

"Oh, I thought you thought we—"

"No, I didn't, but you're going to get hurt either way, honey! You have to snap out of this foolishness. The man and his wife will be on their way any time now, and you'll want them to remember you as a decent, sensible young woman, not a silly lovesick child!"

Laura started to protest. Then her aunt's words sank in, and she gasped. "They? What they, Aunt Molly? I've hardly spoken word one to his old wife!"

Molly made her voice deliberately mocking, for the girl's own good, as she nodded and said, "Married people call it 'pillow talk.' When a man and woman sleep together, it's only natural they exchange little jokes together. I remember, once, having a good chuckle with my late husband over a silly girl who'd been throwing herself at him. She was the young daughter of a business associate. My poor husband was a little worried about her advances, until we talked it over and—"

"Oh, Aunt Molly! You don't think Jeremiah would repeat any of our conversations to old Maggie, do you?"

"Why not? She's his wife, and they sleep together, don't they!"

"Oh! Oh, Aunt Molly!"

"Well, as you say, since you've neither done or said anything wrong . . . Let's see about the rest of the breakfast, shall we? The menfolk will be coming in with a good cold-morning appetite any minute."

Laura took the bowl from her and started beating the batter furiously, blushing scarlet from her hairline down.

Molly Culhane turned away with an understanding smile. If the poor little thing felt anything like what she'd felt about that teacher from the ninth grade, she'd doubtless bat her eyes a few more times by suppertime, but, hopefully, she'd be a little less effusive.

As for Jeremiah . . . well, they were leaving soon. She'd cross that bridge after she'd watched them both a lot more closely for a time.

CHAPTER 33

Hale Burton was something of a power on the Elk Creek neighborhood. He owned a significant part of the range land within a day's ride of town, and had a finger in many of the town's businesses. Such business as he didn't own outright might still be his business, to Hale Burton's way of thinking. Rich men can afford to be nosy. Big *tough* rich men can be as nosy as they've a mind to be.

Hence, he rode into Elk Creek with a certain confidence. He was flanked by his ramrod, Woodley, and a couple of hands named Banes and Plante. Some town loafers near the general store saw the four riders coming and decided it was time to end their spitting and whittling. Hale Burton was a cross-grained cuss at best, and right now he looked like he purely aimed to cloud up and rain all over somebody.

Burton reined in at the saloon and slid out of his

saddle, leaving it to his hands to tether the pony. The big man stamped up the wooden stairs, spurs ringing and a tie-down holster riding low on each hip. He came through the swinging doors and stopped. So did the rinky-tink piano as the the big and obviously annoyed rancher loomed in the doorway, getting his bearings in the gloom and smoke of the crowded saloon. His foreman and hands waited outside. Hale Burton had told them to.

He clanked over to the bar, scowled at the bartender, and snapped, "Well?"

The bartender pointed with his chin at a stranger seated alone at a corner table, playing solitaire. An empty plate had been shoved to one side, and a bottle sat before him as he toyed with the cards and smoked a black cheroot. He had the waiting look of a professional gambler or a hired gun.

The big rancher strode over to him and got right down to it.

"The name's Hale Burton!"

"Good for you."

"Don't mess with me, boy. I'm the big frog in this puddle, and when I yell froggie, most folks jump!"

"Must be a comfort to you, huh?"

"What's your name, stranger?"

"You can call me Smith. What's your pleasure?"

"You've been askin' around town about Mormons who're supposed to be coming through this territory."

"I was?"

"I told you not to mess with me, stranger. Like most decent folks, I hates Mormons more'n I hate liars, thieves, or cowards. If I had my way I'd hang every last one of the heathens!"

Smith shrugged and said, "Well now, if I was a Mormon that might make this conversation right interesting. I ain't."

"I never said you was, but if you be huntin' Mormons I want to know about it. I got me plenty of good gun hands and—"

"Sorry, friend, I work alone."

"You do, huh? Let me tell you something, sonny. I own this town and most of what's around it for a long day's ride. That means if there be Mormons hereabouts, they're likely on *my land!*"

"That's your problem. Not mine."

"It'll *be* your problem iffen you know of Mormons squattin' on my range and I find out you've kept it from me! I don't take kindly to be being crossed, god damn it to hell!"

The stranger reached casually for the bottle and poured himself a drink. He met the rancher's gaze calmly and said, "I'll keep your words in mind, Burton. Now, if it's all the same to you, I not only work alone, I drink alone."

Hale Burton reddened. His hand hovered like a hawk over the ivory butt of his six-gun as they sized each other up. If he pushed it any further, Burton knew, he'd have to either draw or crawfish in front of everyone in the saloon. Like most bullies, Hale Burton had a well-developed sense of survival, and there was something lethal in the cold gray eyes of the stranger. Something that told him now was as good a time as he'd ever see to let things be.

With a curt nod at the stranger, Burton clanged outside.

His foreman almost snapped to attention as he came out, clomped down the steps, and snapped, "Round up ever' rider we has. I want ever' man who owes me, too. I want ever' square foot of this neck of the woods gone over with a fine-tooth comb. Search ever' canyon, ever' draw, ever' water hole. Make sure they ride by ever' ranch an' homestead, too. I want ever' thing within fifty miles of where I'm standin' searched and searched good!"

The ramrod nodded and said, "It's as good as done, Boss, but what are we searchin' for?"

"God damn it, what do you *reckon* we're searchin' for?"

"Mormons?"

"Mormons!"

"I'll git right to it, Boss. If we find us any Mormons, are we to bring 'em in to you fust or do we jest string 'em up where they's at?"

"God damn it, Woodley! Why do you keep askin' fool questions any decent Christian knows the answer to?"

CHAPTER 34

Zeb Macahan topped the rise north of Fort Sully and reined in a moment, a morose figure against the sky-line as he took in the imposing sight below.

A long blue column of mounted cavalry was approaching the fort from the east. Zeb didn't need the red-and-white guidons fluttering at the head of each troop to know he was looking down on the U.S. Second Cav. All of it. Six hundred sabered troopers followed by a large support train and a heavy-weapons detachment bringing up the rear behind the covered wagons. Brandy Jack was loaded for bear all right. In addition to a battery of mountain howitzers Zeb could see the sunlight glinting on the polished brass of a pair of Gatling guns.

Watching from the parapet were Major Drake, MacAllister, and the sullen Coulee John, whose status remained in doubt as Drake shifted with every wind from Washington. Beside the officers stood Grand Duke Dimitri and some of his entourage.

MacAllister's voice was neutral as he muttered, "Well, he got here. Very impressive, eh?"

Drake said, "Very. I wonder if the general missed his telegram or just ignored it."

Coulee John spat a stream of tobacco juice. "That's the way to do her! Turn them yaller laigs loose on the damn Sioux and teach Satangkai and all a lesson! Yessir! Cut 'em down with Gatling fire and saber anythin' that's still movin', after!"

Drake shot him a disgusted look and asked. "Will you tell me something, Brinkerhoff? How the hell does a man get to be your age without a brain in his head or a heart in his chest?"

Coulee John laughed and said, "Lucky, most likely. Man don't have to think all that much out here, as long as he jest larns to shoot anythin' with feathers fust and study whether it's a bird or an Injun later!"

A few minutes later General Brandy Jack Stonecipher in the flesh rode in at the head of his long column, accepting the salute of the garrison with a curt nod. He was a bowlegged bantam rooster with a drinker's nose. The rest of him was made of whalebone and rawhide. He'd shown how good he was at killing people during the Civil War, and had no intention of letting Washington forget, or of getting out of practice.

Drake and his adjutant had hurried down to the parade ground to greet him. As Stonecipher dismounted, a junior officer took the reins of his big bay and led it off to be pampered and petted with a good rubdown and a bucket of oats. Despite the latrine rumors in the lower ranks, it was not true the general's horse drank more strong spirits than its rider.

As Drake attempted a formal welcome, Stonecipher cut in. He spoke almost with the speed and authority of a Gatling gun. He snapped out, "Got your wire saying there was no hurry. Don't believe in coddling these troops. The colonel I relieved to take personal command of this expedition let the Second Cav go to wrack and ruin, but I've legged 'em up with a good forced march. When men march with me they march sudden! Proved that way to handle troops in the Shenandoah campaign. You'd be Drake. Introduce me to your adjutant, here!"

"Uh, this is Captain MacAllister, sir."

"Glad to know you, Captain. I hope both you men are brandy drinkers?"

"I have some in my office, General."

"Then what are we standing out here for? Who're them dudes staring down on us from the parapet?"

"That's the Grand Duke Dimitri and his party, Sir."

"Oh, the jackass who decided he needed two hundred buffalo heads to take back to Russia?"

MacAllister said in warning, "Yes, sir, and he speaks English."

"Don't care if he heard me or not. Might save us a lot of wasted motions if *everyone* around here got to know up front there are only two authorities out here right now. The only other one's God. What's this bull from Washington about him making trouble for us?"

"He's supposed to be very important, sir."

"All right, I won't turn him over my knee and give him a spanking. I'll even smile at the silly son of a bitch, if that's what the State Department wants. If either of you ever reach my rank you'll find half your duty is smiling at idiots. Let's go put our guts around some of that brandy you mentioned while we plan this operation, Major!"

By this time Zeb Macahan had reached the fort and ridden through the gate. As he dismounted and headed for the office, the grand duke intercepted him to plead, "My nephew, Count Sergie? . . ."

Zeb paused long enough to say "He's faring as well as can be expected for an idiot, Duke. The lady with him's bein' treated better, but then, she ain't got such a mean mouth. And talkin' on mean mouths, you'd best sit in on my talk with the general. They say he can be a cross-grained piss-ant, too."

The Russian agreed and followed Zeb into the orderly room and back to Drake's office, where they found the three officers drinking brandy and poring over the inaccurate map of the Black Hills. Drake and the adjutant were on their first snifters. The general had stolen a march on them and was working on his second. It was a canard that he drank brandy like beer, but he consumed it faster than most men drank sherry.

After the greeting and introductions were out of the way, Zeb got down to cases and explained the deal he'd made with Satangkai. General Stonecipher slammed his glass down on the table and snapped. "You offered terms like those to the Sioux? Jesus H. Christ! Why didn't you throw in a night in bed with the President's wife?"

Zeb sniffed at the glass MacAllister had handed him. "Good stuff, Major. I didn't offer Satangkai the President's old woman 'cause he's got hisself a pretty little squaw of his own. I reckoned ten thousand dollars was a fair price for enough meat to feed the whole band through the winter."

Major Drake, seeing the way the general's wind was blowing, shook his head wearily and asked, "Why not twenty thousand, or thirty?"

" 'Cause I knowed you'd likely have trouble raising ten. But I figure Wahington will go along with them numbers, Major."

"You do, eh? And just how did you arrive at such a magic number?"

Zeb grinned at the general and explained. "Added the figures in my own head. I figured the base pay of thirteen dollars and all the beans they can eat a month for a regiment on campaign, throwed in a campaign bonus, pensions for the likely wounded, enlistment bonuses for replacements . . . Then quit when I seen I was well over ten thousand for a short and lucky campaign. Won't take Washington too much bookkeepin' to see they're gettin' off cheap at ten thousand by callin' off an Injun war!"

Stonecipher glowered and snapped, "Damn it! Who gave you the right to offer terms at all? You had no authority to treat with the enemy in our names, Macahan!"

"I know that, General. I rode in there to see if the captives was still breathin', and I said my piece to keep 'em doin' so until I could make it back. I know you folks has to approve the terms. I'm only Satangkai's messenger boy."

He took another sip of brandy and added, with a sidelong glance at the grand duke, "When you git down to cases, I don't reckon the duke, here, will be all that happy about a mess of powwows draggin' on for days and weeks with his nephew sitting in a tipi without champagne and caviar worth mention."

The grand duke stepped forward, regal in his stance, and nodded as he said to Stonecipher, "General, do you consider such a piddling sum too much to pay for the lives of my nephew and that poor young girl?"

"Of course I don't Your Highness, but I'm, ah, a little put off by not being consulted and not having a say in the proceedings. It's important for the army to keep its face with the Indians, you see!"

"These Sioux of yours are Japanese?"

"No, but they're arrogant as any damned samurai about their own fool notions of honor." He frowned at Zeb. "You knew I'd look like a horse's neck when you agreed to those terms, didn't you, Macahan?"

Zeb shrugged and lied. "Wasn't thinking about your façade, General. Wasn't thinking much about you at all. My job, as I saw it, was to git them captives back with no more bloodshed on either side."

"Damn it, son, it's not my own image I'm concerned that much about! I've got my medals, should I bother with wearing them like a Mexican second lieutenant! The image I'm worried about is that of our army and our race. We can't have these children of the plains looking down on us for a minute!"

Zeb scowled and snapped, "Children of the plains, General? You call Satangkai a child? You think Red Cloud, Yellow Hand, Gall and Crazy Horse are children? You're talking about *warriors,* General! And if you do force an all-out war with this fool campaign you're spoiling for, you'll find they lead the finest mounted troops in the world!"

"Man for man, my horse soldiers can lick any cavalry, red or white, in this world or any other I can lead them to! But that's not the point!"

"What is your point then, General? What are you tryin' to prove?"

"That we're not afraid of the Sioux or any other Indian who ever drew breath. It's more than a point of honor, Macahan. I'll concede some Sioux are decent men. I'll concede mistakes have been made on both sides, but face it, son, their whole culture is based on the fine honed art of bully and brag!"

"Takes one to know one, likely."

"I don't take that as intended, son. When you get down to it, every soldier lives for either cowing or killing other people, and the Sioux Nation is a nation of soldiers. Right now they've had enough and we have 'em sulking up in their reservation, but let someone like that troublemaker, Sitting Bull, get the idea Uncle Sam's had *squaw thoughts,* lately, and I won't have to carry warfare to the Sioux. They'll come boiling out of those Black Hills like red ants from a crowded nest! You remember how Little Crow and Red Wing took advantage of our thin-spread western troops during the Civil War to massacre the settlers in Minnesota that time?"

"Yep, 'Minnesota' is a Dakota word. Means 'white water.' Likely Little Crow reckoned the land they'd named was theirs, but we're jawing ancient history, General. The Dakotas was pushed clean out of Minnestota in the end, and Little Crow and Red Wing was executed. It's another day and other chiefs we're dealin' with."

"I'm not so sure. A Sioux is a Sioux, and you know what General Sheridan said."

"I do, but makin' good Indians out of the whole Dakota Confederacy seems a hard row to hoe, next o settling this peaceable."

"We both know it's got to be done sooner or later, Macahan. The Lord never meant ranchers and wheat farmers to live side by side with Stone Age nomads who live for war and roaming pillage!"

Macahan nodded soberly and said, "I know. Likely the day of the mountain man and even the cowboy will have to pass in time. Along with the beaver and the buffalo. I reckon the Dakota knows it as well as we do, General. But while we've got these last few years left . . ."

The grand duke cut in to insist, "Gentlemen, all this is very interesting, no doubt, to a historian! But can we get back to here and now and what is to be done about my nephew, the Count of Kiev?"

Stonecipher poured himself another drink as the duke said flatly, "If I have to inform my brother, the Czar of All the Russias, that you allowed our mutual noble kinsman to perish, horribly, over a point of ethnic nit-picking—"

"All right, damn it, don't declare war on us for a few more days and I'll see what we can do about the count and that girl. I don't like it. I don't like it one little bit, but I'm not an unreasonable man. I'll recommend the terms to Washington. Captain MacAllister can put it on the wire as soon as this meeting's over."

Both Drake and his adjutant looked relieved. The general caught the look that passed between them and added, "I keep a shitlist in a little black book, gents. Doubtless you'll know whose names just went in. Now that Macahan, here, has wrung such astonishing concessions from the Sioux, let's get down to the details. What exactly are the terms aside from the money, Macahan?"

"Painted Meadows."

"What's that supposed to mean?"

"It's on the treaty line. Just north of Bear-Creek, General. Satangkai says he'll meet us there with the captives, providing—"

"Providing what, damn it? Am I to pull my britches down and bend over, or will the greenbacks be enough?"

"You're to bring no more men than can fit comfortable in a tipi."

"What the hell kind of a number is that supposed to mean?"

"Not more'n a dozen, General. Satangkai'll ride in with the captives and braves. There's to be no firearms on either side."

Stonecipher nodded curtly and snapped, "Agreed. I'll be there."

The grand duke protested, "If there is agreement to the terms, why does not this savage simply bring his prisoners here to Fort Sully?"

Zeb answered dryly, "Mangus Colorados tried that one time, down Arizona way. Officer named Bascom had him kilt. Likely our children of the plains heard about it, somewheres. Not many Indians trust a safe-conduct pass these days. Likely they been *humored* a mite too often."

Major Drake snapped, "You're treading on dangerous ground, Macahan!"

"The ground I'm interested in is Painted Meadows, tomorrow. I'll guide you and do the talkin' if you want, General. You got that about no more'n ten of us all told, right?"

"I said I agreed, damn it! Do you want it in writing?"

"Nope, but Satangkai wants somethin' in writing. A signed statement that the treaty was broken by our side. White men invaded their lands and killed their buffalo without permission. They want the warriors who shot up the duke's party pardoned unconditional, too. In other words, they want a full confession that what happened was a mistake on the part of the U.S. Government!"

, There was a long stunned silence. Major Drake was first to break it when he thundered, "You mean you agreed to that proposal, too?"

Zeb shook his head and said, "I keep telling you gents, I never agreed to nothin'. It ain't up to me to agree or not. It's up to the general, here. Not that he's got much choice, and not that I see anythin' so all-fired wrong with bein' man enough to admit an honest mistake!"

Stonecipher glared, red-faced. His eyes were volcanic craters fixing to erupt as he said ominously, "Now you just listen and you hear me good, Macahan! You've got me by the short hairs, but as far as I'm concerned this whole thing started when you refused to act as guide for the hunting party! I don't like you much, but from what I hear of you, I don't think you'd have gotten them into this fix if you'd have been there. So put away that superior smile!"

"I'll bite the bullet and take that, General, but what's done is done. Do you agree to all them terms, General?"

"I have no choice. But from this point on, Macahan, I'm holding you personally responsible. If anything else goes wrong, anything at all, I'm taking a hundred percent of your hide! Is that understood, Macahan?"

"I reckon it is."

"Good, and understand, I'm a man who always, repeat, always, keeps his spoken word! So help me God, if you mess up again—"

MacAllister cut in to ask, "Uh, isn't the general's agreement contingent on word from Washington, sir?"

"That's a formality. But, yes, we'll have to observe it, Captain. We don't have Macahan's luxury of a free rein hereabouts!"

Turning back to Zeb, the general said, "You'll be our guest while great minds ponder your amazing notions back east, Macahan. Consider yourself confined to the post until I tell you different!"

"I had a few errand to tend to between now and the meeting with Satangkai, General."

"I said you're confined to the post. I don't want you riding back to your Sioux friends and making them any more nervous than they already are!"

Zeb shook his head wearily and said, "I get a mite tired of explainin' that Indians don't *git* nervous, much. They've been taught what it means to wait. 'Sides, I don't have no more to say to Satangkai. The words has all been said. The rest is up to both sides showin' good faith at Painted Meadows."

CHAPTER 35

As Zeb argued with the officers at Fort Sully, his nephew, young Luke, rode uneasy through a sea of flowers toward a purling brook in the middle of the parklike mountain meadow.

He'd been on the run long enough to have the haggard look of those who ride the owlhoot trail. In addition to being on the run, he was lost.

But a lone fisherman was working the stream near a clump of lodgepole pine, his back to Luke as the youth spotted him, and after an undecided moment, Luke spurred his pony forward and hailed the angler standing knee-deep in the burbling water.

The man turned as Luke approached. He was a tall, lean, weathered man just past his prime. His smile was relaxed and friendly, and his eyes held malice for naught but trout as they stared at Luke from under a set of impressively bushy brows. He nodded to Luke and said, "Mornin', son."

"Mornin', mister. How are they biting?"

"Not good, not bad. Can I help you?"

"I seem to be turned around. Is there a town near here called Jimson's Break?"

The fisherman nodded and pointed to a pass in the rimrocks to the west, saying, "Jimson's Break is that cut over yonder, the town lies jest the other side. You're new in these parts, ain't you, son?"

"Just passing through, sir. I'm riding to visit kin up in Idaho Territory, but I'm runnin' short of supplies."

"Well, you'll likely find what you're lookin' for in Jimson's Break then, son. Take care of yourself."

"I aim to. By the way, I spied some real old lunkers in a riffle hole upstream just now. You might have better luck if you worked your way up past those boulders on the rise."

"Well, I thank you kind, son, but I ain't just after trout. I'm after Old Elmer."

"Old Elmer?"

"Yep. That's what I calls him. Don't know what he calls his own self."

"Oh, you're talking about a *fish?*"

"Hell, son, this stream is filled with fish! Old Elmer is somethin' more like a whale. Biggest mossbacked trout ever spawned this far from the deep blue sea."

He pointed downstream with the tip of his rod and added, "You see that big rock, half awash in that there boil? Old Elmer's layin' down there ahint it, grinnin' at me, most likely. He reckons I don't know he's there. But I'm damn near as smart as he is."

"Near as smart as a fish?"

"Now don't go puttin' Elmer down until you gits to know him, son. He's there all right, layin' in the shade an' laughin' at the two of us. Trouble is, he gits smarter ever' year, and he's likely older than both of ussen put together."

Luke laughed and asked, "Do you mean to tell me you've been fishing for the same damn trout more than a year?"

"I purely do, only it's more like nine years, son. I been comin' up here after Old Elmer since the North started up with the South, or whichever."

"And you've never caught him in all that time?"

"Nope. Been tryin', though. You can scoop a dozen skillet-worthy trout outten this stream 'most any stretch to cast your fly, but I ain't after pan fish. I'm after Old Elmer, and he knows it. He's likely enjoyin' our feud as much as I am. Old Elmer's what makes the fishin' hereabouts worthwhile!"

"Well, good luck with Elmer, then. I'd best be on my way."

The fisherman nodded and cast again, with the wistful expression of a poor child at Christmas with a nose pressed against the window of a toy shop and his old man out of work.

Luke rode perhaps a hundred yards before he heard a wild scream of mingled surprise and triumph behind him. Reining in, the youth turned to see his fishing friend braced against a rod bent like a Cheyenne's buffalo bow, leaning back against some great weight on the singing end of the taught line as he gasped and chortled. "I hooked him! Great jubilation day in the mornin', Old Elmer took my fly this time and I've purely *hooked* the son of a bitch!"

Luke laughed and sat his pony easy, enjoying the innocent, amusing scene immensely as the fisherman fought the big invisible mossback. The man was soaked to the chest as he stumbled downstream over the slippery rocks, playing the twanging line like an obvious expert.

Then, suddenly, Old Elmer leaped, and Luke gasped in admiration and astonishment as the huge trout rose a full six feet from the surface, shaking his head like a terrier with a rat between its jaws. Luke knew trout simply didn't grow to that size, and the gray-green algae masking Elmer's scales bespoke years of feeding, and growing, in his small wet empire.

As the big trout crashed down with a mighty splash the fisherman who'd hooked him took a wrong step, twisted an ankle on a moss-covered rock, and went down, full face in the white water.

Still hanging on to the submerged line, the desperate man rose partyway from the water boiling over him, like a surfacing sea lion among ocean breakers, and yelled, "God damn it, help me, boy! Git back here an' help me! I've hung my fool ankle in the rocks!"

Luke laughed and spurred his pony back across

the flower-spangled meadow as the fisherman called'
out, "Hurry up, boy, hurry up! Iffen he gits any slack
he's gone! I lose that mean old son of a bitch agin and
I'll likely kill my own self!"

Luke reined in and slid from the saddle, wading
out into the knee-deep water as his boots filled with
cold and wet. He reached down and caught the fisherman's ankle, wedged between two boulders. The foot
was caught fast, and Luke had to pull with all his
might before he suddenly felt it slip free. Then Luke,
too, was down, sitting on the bottom with the water
boiling over his chest and shoulders in a freezing
frenzy of foam.

The other man somehow got his feet back under
his center of gravity and struggled upright against the
current and the pull on his twanging line as he
screamed prayers and curses, reeling in an inch at a
time. Luke floundered over to the bank and stumbled
out of the brook, dripping and shaking himself like a
cold, wet bird dog. He watched in wonder as the
older man slowly gained the upper hand on the leap-
ing, fighting mossback.

More than once Luke moaned, sure that this time
Elmer would throw the hook or break the line, but
each time he leaped, the fisherman reeled in savagely,
gaining on the monstrous trout.

And then, to Luke's amazement, it was over. The
fisherman suddenly whipped his dip net from his belt,
smashed it down in the water boiling around his waist,
and lifted it with a triumphant yell of "Gotcha! Gotcha
again, you muley mossbacked cuss! Thought you was
too smart for me this time, didn't you?"

Luke stared at the big trout fighting to free itself
from the net like a drowning cat in a gunnysack, and
called out, "What do you mean, 'got you again'?
You haven't caught that thing afore, have you?"

The fisherman nodded, holding Old Elmer up for his
admiration in the sunlight. He called back, "Hell, I've
caught him *twice* afore this shining day! Caught you
the first time nigh nine years ago, didn't I, Elmer?

Then, lessee, I caught him again three years later. No, four, by jimmies! Been tryin' for him since five years an' three months! Ain't that about right, Elmer?"

Then he wet his free hand to protect the protective mucus of the great fish as, with infinite tenderness, he removed the lure from the huge trout's jaw.

Holding it before the trout's round golden eye, he chortled. "You see that fly, Elmer? Thought it was the real thing, didn't you? Took me months to tie this here fly right, but I knowed when I had it done it would purely be your downfall! You ain't as smart as you figured, are you, you sassy old bastard!"

Then, with the reluctance of a lover parting at dawn from the girl of his dreams, he lowered the net into the current, tipped the trout free, and sighed. "Off you go, Elmer. But I'll be back after we've both had time to git our wind back a mite!"

Luke shook his head and said, "That's the most purely loco thing I've ever seen! What in thunder did you want to catch him for if you aimed to let him go?" The beaming fisherman reeled in the last few inches of the line and began to wade out to Luke, saying, "Hell, I wanted to catch him, and by jimmies, I done it, too. You seed your own self I caught him fair and square. That'll larn him not to be so sassy!"

"But what's the point? Most folks I know catch trout to cook and eat 'em."

The fisherman looked horrified. "Cook and eat a friend! Why, son, I'd sooner eat my old hound dogs! What do you take me for, a cannibal?"

Luke smiled wryly. "No, I can see you're a natural-born fisherman. Likely cannibals have more sense! You aim to try for him again, huh?"

"'Course I do, boy, and I'll catch him again, too!"

"If you live that long."

"I'll catch him, and Old Elmer knows it. Sometimes I think he jest takes my fly fur the pure hell of it. He knows I don't aim to hurt him all that much. He never bites on nobody else's line hereabouts. Some

old boys think I made Elmer up, but you've seed him
with your own two eyeballs."

"Yeah, that's for sure, but I've got to be getting on.
It was interesting fishing with you, mister . . . ?"

"Gant, Orville Gant."

"They call me Luke. I'll see you, Orville."

"You got soaked pure through helping me, Luke.
Why don't you come on home with me and dry your
own self off around some corn squeezin's?"

Luke was sorely tempted, but a man on the run
has no business gettin' in too thick with strangers,
so he shook his head and insisted, "I got to be movin'
on, Orville, but I thank you kindly for the offer."

The fisherman's eyes narrowed a thoughtful hair as
he said, "You was riding into town to git them supplies
anyways, wasn't you? My place is on the way."

Luke shook his head firmly and said, "I thank you
again for the kind offer, but I'm in a hurry and I'm
mounted up. Don't worry, I'll likely dry out in the sun
afore I get to the settlement!"

Then, before the argument could continue, Luke
stepped over to his pony, hauled himself into the
saddle, and rode off, not looking back. He squished
some where his saddle met the part he sat on.

Luke was still damp, but not quite dripping snow-
melt water, as he rode into the sleepy little one-street
town of Jimson's Break.

It wasn't quite as sleepy as usual this noon, however, as the board sidewalks were filled with people.
They weren't shopping or drinking. They were just
strolling or standing, as if they were waiting for someone. Luke didn't think it could be him.

He reined in and dismounted near a boy of perhaps
ten who sat perched on a barrel near the general store.
As the boy's curious eyes met his own, Luke nodded
and asked. "What's all the excitement about?"

The boy shrugged and said, "Nothin' much. Just a
horse race."

"You don't say? What's the race being held for,
money or fun or both?"

"Shoot, it's for an old *girl!*"

"A horse race over a girl?"

"Yeah. Dumb, ain't it? By the way, mister, your pony's fixin' to throw his left hint shoe on you!"

Luke turned to examine his mount and said, "By thunder, you're right and I thank you, son. Is there a smithy hereabouts?"

"Yep, cross the street near the livery. 'Cept the smith ain't here."

"Oh, do you know when he'll be open?"

"After the horse race, most likely. Nothin's gonna git done in this durned town till after that durned old race!"

"You said the race was over a girl."

"Yep, my dumb old *sister!* If Tobe Harker wins, he gits to take her to the dance next Saturday night."

"Your sister sounds like she's some girl. Can't she make up her own mind who she wants to go to the dance with?"

"Reckon not. She allowed she'd go with the one who wins the fool race. I don't reckon she likes old Tobe Harker. I knows I purely don't. But she gave her word. Ain't it all dumb, though?"

"What, giving her word?"

"No, havin' a fool horse race over a stupid old dance. I swear, I don't understand growed-ups!"

Luke chuckled, reached into his pocket, and took out a five-cent piece. He tossed it to the boy and said, "Why don't you walk my pony over to the forge and see if someone over there can't tap that shoe nail a couple of good licks. Tell 'em I'll be by to pick him up and pay in an hour or so."

The boy nodded agreement and dropped off the barrel, taking the reins of Luke's pony. But as he started to lead it across the dusty street there was a roar from the crowd, and the boy froze in place.

Two riders dressed in cattlemen's garb tore around the bend riding hell for leather, neck and neck, fanning their mounts with their hats and whooping like Comanches.

As the young boy fought to control Luke's plunging, frightened pony, the riders bore down on him at a dead run. Luke's pony danced back and grazed the forequarters of one of the speeding racehorses, shying it into a stumble-buck that threw its rider headlong in the dust near the bewildered boy as the other rider, laughing, tore on toward the finish line up the street.

Luke and some of the townies ran out into the cloud of dust as the thrown rider staggered to his feet, dazed. Luke grabbed the cowboy's shying mount by the reins and steadied it, calling, "I got him. Are you all right, cowboy?"

But the thrown rider wasn't a cowboy. It was a girl—a perky brunette of about twenty dressed in hickory shirt and jeans. As she dusted herself off she glared at Luke and demanded. "Are you the idiot that belongs to that horse, stranger?"

"Yes, ma'am, only he belongs to me."

"Are you trying to get somebody killed? Everyone in town knew the race was about to start!"

"I'm sorry, I just got here!"

"Then you'd better be leaving, pronto! I ought to have my pa lock you up as a public menace and a fool who has no call to be running free without a leash!"

"Your pa sounds plumb dangerous, ma'am."

"He is. He's the sheriff!"

Before Luke could think of a suitable reply, the other rider cantered back from the victory line with a crooked grin. He reined in near the furious girl he'd left behind in the dust and said, "Too bad, Hillary! Looks like I'm the winner!"

She shot a withering look up at the sturdy youth on the other mount and snapped, "You did not neither win, Tobe Harker! I had at least half a length on you!"

"Mebbe, but I crossed the finish line first. It ain't my fault you cain't stay aboard a hoss! You made yourself a bet, Hillary. Are you aimin' to stand by it?"

The girl pleaded, "Let's run the race again, with this fool out of the path!"

But Tobe Harker laughed easily and shook his head, saying, "I'm satisfied with the way the last one turned out. Hope you ain't too bruised up to dance and what all."

"You can damn well forget the what all, Tobe Harker. I'm warning you of that right here and now!"

Harker laughed again. He caught Luke's eyes with a friendly nod and said, "If that was your pony, mister, I reckon I owe you for a favor."

Luke shrugged and said, "Don't mention it. My pleasure, amigo."

The girl called Hillary turned, eyes spitting anger, and snapped, "Well, I likely owe you too, jackass!"

With that, she gave Luke a sharp kick in the shins.

Then, as Luke gritted his teeth with pain and the townsfolk laughed, she stalked off, leading her pony.

Tobe Harker chuckled down at Luke and asked, "Ain't she the sweetest little thing you ever laid eyes on, stranger?"

Luke gave him a withering look of his own, limped over to the boy, who still held the reins of his own mount, and took them from him. The boy asked, "Do you want your nickel back, mister?"

Luke smiled and shook his head. He said, "No, but I'll take care of it, son."

"I saw Hillary kick you a lick. Lucky she was so vexed with you she never noticed me. Lucky for both of us she didn't have a fence post handy. I purely can't figure why all the fellers is chasing that old sister of mine!"

"She's your sister? Well, if you was a few years older you'd likely understand. I'll get this pony over to the smithy."

Luke found a helper waiting for the missing blacksmith across the street and left his pony in the hand's charge, saying he'd be at the saloon if they needed him.

He went over to the saloon, bellied up to the bar, and ordered a beer, nursing it along with his still-throbbing shin as he killed some time.

While he was waiting, a freight wagon stopped out front and three hard-cased types piled off to have their own drink and what seemed to be a running argument. They were dressed like mining men and ranged in size from their big obvious leader down to a narrow-eyed terrier with a Green River knife tucked in his belt and the look of a man who knew how to use it. The bigger man wore a patch over one eye and a Navy Colt. The one between them in size looked as if he had the consumption. He was sallow and lean, with crazed and nervous eyes. As they joined Luke at the bar, the big man with the patch stood next to him. He yelled at the bartender, "Redeye! And keep it comin'!"

He caught Luke's eye in the pier glass behind the bar and turned to him to ask, "Hey, what time is it?"

Luke said, "It's Tuesday," and went back to his beer.

The big man frowned, but as Luke tensed for a hoorah, the miner grinned and said, "Tuesday, huh? Whatever happened to Sunday or Monday? Well, hell, it don't make no never mind, boy. My name's Booster McDonough. This here scrawny cuss is Hub, an' the runt down thar's calt the Nugget. We-uns been workin' up to the mine for slave wages an' we've had enough. Got fed up and quit 'em cold last Friday. Disremember where we been drinkin' since. Name your pizen an' join in!"

Luke shook his head and said, "I thank you kindly, but I'm leavin' town."

"There something 'bout me you don't like, boy?"

"No, you look fine to me."

Booster laughed and said, "You hear that, Hub. Boy here says I look fine to him."

He turned back to Luke and roared, "Why, boy, you must be blind as a bat! I'm so ugly I sour milk! I'm so ugly women scream an' dogs howl! I takes *pride* in my ugly, boy!"

He waited a moment before he asked, ominously, "Now how do I look to you, boy?"

"Pretty damn ugly."

Booster howled with delight and slammed a fist on

the bar, calling out, "Hey there, Charlie! Put another beer aside the one my buddy boy's a drinkin'!"

But another voice cut in: "Never mind that beer, Charlie. He won't have time to drink it!"

Luke and the others turned to see Orville Gant, his fisherman from earlier that morning, down at the far end of the bar. Gant wasn't holding a fishing rod just now. He held a double-barrelled sawed-off shotgun, pointed at Luke's belt buckle. He'd changed his clothes since Luke had seen him last. A tin star was pinned to his vest. Nodding at Luke, he said, "Lay your pistol on the bar, Macahan, and do it careful. I owe you for helpin' me catch Elmer, and I'd hate like hell to have to blow you in two!"

As Luke slid his revolver down the bar toward Gant, the big miner, Booster, frowned and asked, "Now what's this all about, Sheriff? The boy here's old enough to drink!"

Orville Gant said, "I don't know you, friend, but if you're lookin' for a piece of this action, jest say so."

"Shoot, I don't even know the kid, and I jest decided I don't like him all that much!"

Gant nodded and said, "Let's go, Macahan."

"Sheriff, I'm sorry about your daughter losing that race, but this is silly!"

"Talk later, Macahan. Let's go."

As the sheriff frog-marched Luke past the smithy, the boy who'd held Luke's pony turned to the blacksmith, who'd just returned, and sighed. "I don't reckon there's any hurry with that loose shoe now, Mr. Dodge. When my sis gits vexed with someone, she can purely be mean as all hell!"

Gant marched Luke to the jail and ushered him to a seat near the desk. He racked the shotgun, came back over to his desk, and held up a reward poster, saying, with a touch of pity, "Ain't much of a likeness, but it's enough to keep you runnin', likely. You shoulda come by the house and dried out like I asked you, son. I might never have suspicioned you was on the run."

Luke stared numbly at the older man as the sheriff

added, "I been a lawman thirty years, now. Learned a mite about men in that time. 'Bout the good ones as well as the bad ones. This paper says that shootin' happened when you was about sixteen. Ain't that a mite young to start shootin' folks, son?"

"I didn't have much choice. They were Southerners, I was a Yankee. It was shoot or die, so I shot. It's a long story, Sheriff."

"I got time. Neither one of us is goin' anywhere afore you tell me all about it."

Luke started from the beginning, telling how the war had caught the family moving west and how his father had died and all the trouble he'd been in since. By the time he'd finished Orville Gant had brewed a pot of coffee on his potbellied stove. He poured out two cups as Luke explained, "I woke up in that barn to find the Missouri sheriff and three unreconstructed rebel good old boys standing over me. They said the horse I was riding had been stolen. I don't know if it had been or not. I'd come by it honest. When I offered to tell my story to a judge they laughed and said no trial was needful, as they aimed to hang me on the spot as a horse thief, or maybe just a Yankee."

"I see they didn't manage it, son."

"No, I didn't think much of their notion. I grabbed the sheriff's gun and fought my way out. I winged the sheriff in the arm and just kept going. I've been going ever since. If you send me back to Missouri they'll likely hang me."

"Yep, I'd say that was a right good guess, son. You're in a pure fix, ain't you?"

"I don't reckon you could do by me the way you done by Old Elmer this morning, huh?"

"Like to. Cain't. Old Elmer wasn't wanted by the law, and I take my job serious. I'll tell you what I will do. I got friends back Missouri way. Suppose I wire them afore I notify that ornery sheriff I'm holdin' you on his warrant?"

"I'd say that was tolerable Christian of you, Sheriff."

"Shucks, call me Orville. You understand I've got to

lock you up till I find out you ain't stretchin' the truth on me, don't you, son?"

Before Luke could answer, the sheriff's daughter, Hillary, came in, to say insistently, "Pa, I need to know when you're expected for supper . . ." Then she saw Luke sitting there and stared, surprised. He grinned up at her and said, "You didn't have to get your pa to arrest me, ma'am. He took it on his own self!"

Orville looked equally surprised as he asked, "How come you two know each other?"

Hillary snapped, "We don't!"

Luke explained. "Your daughter blames me for losing a horse race. She like to broke my fool shin!"

The girl snapped, "Wish I had!"

The sheriff grimaced and said, "I heard about that race, young lady. I've told you, I won't stand for fool commotions in this here town. It ain't ladylike! You're gonna purely git your own self hurt one of these days!"

"Oh, Pa, it was only me an' Tobe Harker!"

"And you *lost,* girl?"

"Thanks to this fool and his damned old pony!"

"All right, let's drop it, girl. And that's enough of that kind of language, hear?"

"I'm sorry, Pa, but he made me mad. Why's he in jail?"

"It ain't your concern, honey. Why don't you git on home and warm up some of that beef pie? I'll be along directly. Oh, and fix a plate for this young feller here, with a dish of that apple cobbler you got in the pantry."

"What's wrong with feedin' him from the saloon? When did we start feeding apple pie to every saddle tramp you lock up in the tank, Pa?"

"Honey, I don't know what this boy is, but he helped me catch Old Elmer this mornin', and that's worth apple pie whatever he is or done!"

"You mean I have to cook for criminals just because of that durned old fish?"

Luke said, "Forget it, Orville. Considering Miss Hillary's temper, I might be safer eating beans from the saloon. At least I don't have to worry about 'em poisoning me!"

The girl stamped out in a huff as Luke chuckled, adding, "I hope you ain't lookin' forward to grand-children, Orville."

"Son, let me tell you somethin' about that little girl of mine. She's a hellcat. Takes after her mother. None of the boys hereabouts seems to catch Hillary's fancy, which may be lucky for 'em, as she's stubborn as hell, too. If she ever does set her sights on a man, he's a goner! Now, I'm fixin' to lock you in that cell over there. Your supper will be comin' directly."

Luke walked into the cell and sat down on the cot as Orville closed the barred door on him with an apologetic look. He said, "You just rest easy whilst I send that wire to my friends in Missouri, son."

He left, and Luke explored the possibilities of busting out. There were none. Old Orville's methods only seemed casual. The jail was stout. Luke was there till someone got him out.

Less than an hour later, Hillary came in with a tray of food. She still wore an angry pout, but Luke noticed she'd changed to a fetching dress. She'd tied her hair with a nice new ribbon, too.

Luke said, "Howdy, ma'am."

"Don't you say a word to me, jailbird!"

"Suit yourself. Just tryin' to be neighborly."

"I want you to know serving supper to a gunfighter's not the way I usually enjoy my evenings!"

"Who said I was a gunfighter?"

"I did. I read what Pa sent to a Federal marshal he knows back east. He's askin' about you gunnin' down some sheriff!"

Luke took the tray through the bars, sat down, and proceeded to eat.

The girl asked, "Well?"

"Well what? Did I shoot that sheriff? Hell yes, I shot him. I'm a regular Jesse James."

"You don't look like no gunfighter."

"What's that supposed to mean? What does a gunfighter look like?"

"Oh, you know, all squinty-eyed and dangerous. You look sort of dumb and harmless to me."

"You think what you like. This sure is good eating."

"Is it poisonous?"

"Hope it ain't. I purely aim to eat every bit."

"Then you apologize for saying I'd likely poison you?"

"Sure, if you'll say you're sorry for bustin' my leg."

"That'll be the day!"

"Well, you've started lookin' like a lady, leastways. Did you put that dress on for me?"

"I did not! I hope my pa sends you back east to Missouri and that they string you up by the neck, you sassy thing!"

She started to storm out, but Luke called out gently, "Hey, Hillary?"

"What is it? I suppose you want to say you're sorry?"

"Ain't got nothin' to say I'm sorry about. You wouldn't have any more of this apple cobbler for me, would you?"

The door slammed hard enough to shake the jail house. Luke laughed as he finished the dessert. Then he frowned and asked himself, "What's so funny, you idiot? Can't you see you're in one hell of a mess?"

CHAPTER 36

"How dare you threaten me, peasant?"

"Mister, I'm *telling* you! Which way do you aim to ride? It's up to you!"

Valerie called out, "Please, Your Highness, do as he says!"

The count arrogantly allowed the Indians to boost him up to the saddle pad as he snapped. "None of this shall be forgotten or forgiven, Macahan!"

"You can be sure nobody's forgettin' in these parts, either, but lucky for you, these Indians are more civilized than you, so you're forgiven. Let's try to keep it easy for 'em not to lift your hair, though. Huh? Just behave yourself and you'll be sippin' champagne an' eatin' fish eggs soon!"

Now that his captives were prepared to move out, Satangkai went back inside his own lodge to bid his young wife farewell. Shewelah wore a worried look as her husband smiled down at her.

Satangkai said gently, "You are still troubled."

"You go to sit in council with the whites. How many of our chiefs have trusted the word of those forktongued ones husband? How many wives among our people are still weeping for them?"

"I have given my word, Shewelah."

"But their word is no good! They hate you for being strong. They hate you for being the leader of our people!"

Satangkai nodded and replied, "That is true. They would rather our Nation had no voice. No head. But they know they must deal with me."

"And that is why I fear for you so, my husband! They have broken their word so many times before!"

"The terms have been decided. If the long knives have evil in their hearts, my friend, White Eagle, will tell me."

"Then if you trust White Eagle, let him take the prisoners in and come back with the tribute!"

"Hear me, Shewelah. I ask more than green paper from the long knives. The white chief I go to meet is very powerful. I must face him like a man. He must meet my eyes as he says it is proper for us to defend our land. When the child you bore me has become a man he must be able to live as a Dakota. The long knives must promise me this thing. We must know and respect one another as men. Men do not send others to do their bidding. I must go myself and face them all."

The girl was silent as she picked up their child to nurse it.

Satangkai's face was soft as he sighed. "Take care of my son, my woman! I will return to you soon. I will always return to you."

Shewelah didn't follow as her husband went back out to join Zeb and the captives. Unlike Satangkai, she knew Zeb Macahan only by repute. It was said among the Real People that the heart of White Eagle was good. But he was a white man. Could a coyote be trusted not to eat meat? Could the hawk be trusted not to fly?

At Painted Meadows, General Stonecipher waited with MacAllister, the grand duke and his Cossack bodyguards, and a handful of junior officers. Since the general was a political animal as well as an officer and gentleman, he'd included an army photographer in the small party to record the historic event. What the general said to the Indians and what would be put in the captions of the news photographs might not have to agree too closely. It was said the camera did not lie. In the recent War Between the States, Stonecipher had learned different.

Despite the agreement regarding firearms, the officers wore dress sabers. Zeb had not been there to consult on the matter, and by jimmies, if the duke and his Russian guards were going to be photographed with sabers, the general had no intention of looking like a sissy!

As Duke Dimitri anxiously scanned the horizon for sight of his long-lost nephew, Stonecipher murmured to MacAllister, "When this nonsense is concluded we say hail and farewell to this royal pain in the butt, right?"

"Lord, I hope so, sir. Those so-called ladies of the court are drivin' our men to drink. Look-but-don't-touch vexes any man when a gal's in a low-cut gown with bedroom eyes a-batting!"

"Hmm, just how high in rank does that look-but-don't-touch go, Captain?"

"I'm sure a general's not included, General."

"Couple of those doxies ain't bad-looking. You been to that well yourself, Mac?"

"I doubt my wife would like that, General."

"Son, every man in this man's army ought to have an understanding woman. Next to celibacy, or being queer as Caesar, an understanding wife can help a lot."

"I'll keep your advice in mind, sir. Oh, I see them coming in! It's Zeb and the Indian with half a dozen Dog Soldiers. Looks like that's the count and the girl captive, too!"

As the Dakota party approached, the photographer set up his tripod and measured out flash powder. The army officer entrusted with the payment counted and noted the greenbacks once again as the grand duke waved to the incoming party.

Satangkai turned to Zeb as they rode side by side and said, "I was taught to hunt near here by my father. There are no buffalo here now."

Zeb nodded and said, "I remember those times. It was fat-cow time in the shining days, but everything changes, for better or worse."

"Our bellies were filled then. Now when the buffalo do not visit us we must eat our ponies in the winter. The food the Indian Agency promised us does not come."

"This winter you will buy food enough with the green paper, Satangkai. This winter your people will grow fat."

"Heya, and next winter?"

"Two winters is a long time. Take them one at a time."

"You speak with a straight tongue, White Eagle. Tell me, what do you see in the future for my people? How long can we go on like this? How long will the army let us live as men?"

"I don't know, Satangkai. With luck, perhaps your lifetime."

"And in my son's lifetime?"

"You want the truth?"

"Always."

"All right, I see your son growing up as something new. Not a white man, not a Dakota as you and I know Dakotas."

"I would rather see him dead in his cradle board!"

"Don't be too hasty. We can't see that far, and it may not be as bad as you think. The world is changing fast. In our lifetime we've seen the talking wire and the Iron Horse come. Who knows what your son and his sons will see? It may be a better world than this one."

"Heya, it may be worse, too!"

"Your words are true, but while we live we can hope. I want you to live, old friend. Don't give up on the future just yet. Someday our two peoples may understand one another better."

"Heya, that is a dream worth waiting to see come true!"

As the duke started forward, Stonecipher called out, "Stand your ground, sir! Let them come to us!"

The grand duke shrugged, perplexed as always by the nit-picking of these Americans. He'd cheerfully agreed to sign a full confession of his transgression on the Dakota hunting ground, for to a man of his rank the opinions of lesser beings were unimportant. A Romanov was always right.

As the Indian party rode into hailing view, the photographer fired his flash, spooking several ponies and causing a moment of milling confusion as the general roared, "Easy, damn it! Can't you take a picture in broad daylight without scaring everybody out of a year's growth?"

As the photographer sheepishly got out of the way, Satangkai calmed his own followers and reined, staring impassively at the white men awaiting him on foot. Zeb Macahan called out, "General, I want you to meet up with Satangkai, war chief of the East Wind Clan of the Dakota Confederacy!"

Stonecipher came forward and said, "I have heard of my little red brother and I welcome him, wishing the reasons for our meeting were different."

Zeb said, "He welcomes you," in Satangkai's language, leaving some of it out to be diplomatic.

From where he squirmed angrily between two braves on either side of his pony, Count Sergei called out, "For God's sake, what are we waiting for? Now that we're here, why doesn't somebody untie me?"

"Get the count down off that pony, Zeb," said the general, adding, "The girl, too. It's over now."

"Not quite, General. First there's the little matter of the money and the written apology."

Stonecipher nodded and removed a sheet of paper from his tunic, holding it up to Satangkai, who merely stared at it coldly.

Zeb explained, "He expects you to read the words, General, like he would if the shoe was on the other foot."

"God damn it, Macahan, there's a full explanation here."

"What do you mean 'explanation'? Does it admit the fault was on our side or don't it?"

"We admit a mistake may have been made."

" 'May have been'? Hell, Coulee John knowed he was killin' buffalo on Dakota land! What about it, Captain MacAllister?"

MacAllister flushed and said, "Don't mix me into this, Zeb. I didn't write it and I wasn't there. I'll read the statement aloud for the Indians, General."

But Zeb shook his head and said, "Satangkai don't want it from you, Mac. He don't savvy English, but he knows what your bars mean. He wants the apology from a heap big chief!"

Stonecipher muttered a curse and said, "All right, here goes." Then he read aloud: "Greetings to the chiefs of the Sioux Nation . . ." This is to acknowledge an inadvertent error on the part of this authority in the incident occuring on the southwest sector of the lands held in trust for the Sioux and Cheyenne tribal groups. It is with personal regret that we acknowledge the misunderstanding resulting in the deaths of several persons. Signed, Brigadier General Marcus Stonecipher, on behalf of the U.S. Army personnel at Fort Sully, Dakota Territory."

Zeb shook his head and said, "Sure is a heap of words to say so damn little."

"Macahan, I'll put you under military arrest if I hear one more derogatory remark out of you!"

"Hell, hold your hosses, old son. I'm gonna advise Satangkai to accept the fool thing, knowing he'll likely never get nothin' better. But it wouldn't have cost you much to have drawed up a paper as meant a bucket of warm spit!"

Satangkai asked Zeb something in Dakota, and the scout added, "He just asked me if you agree the white men were at fault. He may be your little red brother, but he ain't so dumb. I've promised him I'll translate your words the way they fall, General. I can shave a hair for you, but I can't just plain lie. What's it gonna be?"

Stonecipher nodded at the Indian and said, "Tell him I said what happened was wrong. Tell him it will never happen again. Tell him I have the money right here and that the payment will acknowlege a serious wrong as well as partly pay for it."

Zeb translated to Dakota, and Satangkai nodded, calling to his followers, "The blue sleeves has spoken well. Release the captives."

Stonecipher turned to an officer and snapped, "Paymaster, turn the money over to the chief. Unless you want to count it first for him, Macahan?"

"Nope. I'll allow you're too big a man for that, General. It ain't your money, and it would look right petty in the newspapers iffen you played a shell game on your red children. I reckon we can trust you."

The grand duke moved forward with a glad smile and a wave to his nephew as the braves began to cut Count Sergei free.

The count remained on the pony, heeling it forward to join the group around the general, the duke, Zeb, and Satangkai, as Valerie followed, teary-eyed with relief.

The young nobleman smiled cunningly as he asked the general, "Is it over, then? Am I truly free and under the protection of the United States Army?"

"Of course you are, Count Sergei."

The Russian nodded slyly as he shot a sidelong glance at Satangkai, leaning forward to accept the notes from the paymaster. Then he swung a length of rawhide he'd been saving for the chance and caught the chief right across the eyes with a vicious slash.

Satangkai reeled from the blow and almost fell as his pony shied and danced back from another attempted blow. A red streak across his eyes half blinded Satangkai with blood as one of his braves screamed out, "Ah-ta-nag-hree!" and threw his lance, almost without thought.

The lance tip took Count Sergei over the heart and passed on through, leaving him transfixed and dead even before he could slide from his saddle pad with a bewildered expression on his haughty face.

MacAllister sprang forward to catch the falling body as Satangkai, raging with pain and anger, flung the money in a great green cloud at the white men and roared out, "So be it! Hear me, White Eagle! Tell your people this is war and that I think this is a good day to die!"

There was a howling moment of total confusion as Satangkai danced his pony around, shouting insults and orders in Dakota. Then the Indians were dashing off as the general and some of the other offers produced hidden guns and began to fire at the fleeing Indians.

Zeb Macahan swore and interposed his own mount between Stonecipher and the galloping Satangkai, yelling out, "You wasn't to bring weapons, you sons of bitches!"

For a moment it looked as if the general intended to fire right through Zeb. Then he lowered his smoking muzzle with a glare and spat, "Don't hand me that bullshit, Macahan! Look at what they did to Count Sergei!"

Zeb stared down at Valerie and the disconsolate grand duke kneeling over the count's transfixed corpse and said, "The fool had it coming years ago!"

"Agreed. But that's neither here nor there. What was all that Sioux yelling about?"

"He was telling you he'd declared war." Zeb sighed, pointing with his chin at a still, tawny form in the grass a few yards out. "This time he likely means it, since you fools just kilt one of his young men. I don't know why it should surprise me that you gents brung guns along. I ain't one of your little red brothers."

Zeb rode over to the fallen brave and dismounted, hoping he was wrong about the stillness of the body in the grass. He wasn't. He knew even before he rolled the Indian over that the body was dead.

MacAllister joined him, saying, "The general told me to take your horse, Zeb. I'm sorry."

"The general told you *what?*"

"The horse. It belongs to the army, and he just fired you again. He says if you aim to join your Indian friends you may as well walk."

Zeb straightened up and judged his chances. They didn't look good, since he'd come unarmed to the meeting and the general and his officers were packing shooting irons.

He said, "Leaving a man afoot on the prairie with both sides likely sore at him ain't neighborly, Mac."

"I know. It's not my idea, Zeb, but I have to follow orders."

"Well, you just follow them, sonny. Only, you'd best pray I don't walk out of this fix with my hair!"

"No hard feelings, Zeb?"

"Sonny, when I pay you back for this I don't reckon you'll feel a thing!"

CHAPTER 37

That same morning, in Jimson's Break, Sheriff Orville Gant came into the jail house with Luke's breakfast and a big grin, saying "I reckon this just ain't my week, son. First I had to turn Old Elmer loose, and now it's your turn."

Luke sprang from the cot as the sheriff unlocked the door. "Are you really letting me go?"

"Yep. Federal marshal in Saint Joe backs your story enough for me. He says the sheriff back there you had trouble with is an ornery cuss with a bad rep. He's an unreconstructed rebel, like you said, but what can anybody do? The folks in his county who keep electin' the cuss are Yankee-haters too! Federal man tells me the sheriff you shot has lynched more'n one passin' stranger with a northern accent, whilst he turns his back on the Younger-James gang as they rob the Glendale train."

"Does this mean I'm not wanted anywhere, Orville?"

"Hell, you're wanted, son. But you're wanted in Missouri, and I'm satisfied you're innocent. Eat them eggs and git. You're wastin' the taxpayers' money clutterin' up *this* county jail!"

As he watched Luke demolish the light repast and coffee, Orville Gant added, "I hope you don't hold the night ahint bars agin me, son. You know it wasn't personal, don't you?"

"Of course, sir. If half the lawmen in this neck of the woods were as fair-minded as you, I'd sleep a lot easier in or out of jail!"

Orville got Luke's gun belt and other personal belongings from his office safe and put them on the desk. "I've been studyin' on the fix you're in with bounty hunters, Luke. Just what are your plans, once you light out from here?"

"I don't have too many plans worked out, Orville. I reckon my best bet is to move far and move sudden and keep on moving."

"I'll tell you something, boy. I've sort of took a shine to you."

"Well, I like you too, Orville."

"Yep, I been thinking'. I been thinkin you ought to stay on here in Jimson's Break."

"Stay on? I don't savvy you."

"Where else can you go that you won't run the chance of gettin' picked up by the law agin? I don't need that fool reward, but there's some piss-ants would deliver you dead for it, and some of 'em wears badges!"

"Don't I ever know it! But what can I do?"

"Like I said, stay here. You know I don't aim to arrest you again. I got enough trouble tryin' to catch Old Elmer! You come on home with me, now, and we'll see what we-uns can work out!"

"You're offering to have me under your own roof?"

"Sure. Wouldn't look right boardin' you here in the jail." He saw the look of uncertainty in the youth's eyes and quickly added, "You got a better place to bed down tonight, boy?"

Luke grinned, and they both knew the answer. There wasn't a safer hideout west of the Big Muddy than the private home of the county sheriff!

Hillary didn't like it all that much. She waited until her father had gone out to make his rounds before she let Luke know what she thought of them both. She was serving the noon meal to Luke and her kid brother, Tommy, when she suddenly couldn't hold it in any longer and snapped, "I'd say you really must have told my poor pa a whopper! You start out being thrown in jail and wind up eating in the sheriff's own kitchen! Does this happen every time you get arrested?"

"Well, not every time. Most places, the lady of the house ain't such a good cook!"

Tommy snickered. "Ha! I'd like to see the day old Hillary acts like a lady!"

Hillary picked up a saltcellar to throw at her little brother, but Luke caught her wrist and said, "Hey, easy there! Boys will be boys!"

For a long moment in time they froze in place, eyes locked in something between mock anger and . . . something else?

Then Hillary twisted away and flounced out of the kitchen.

Luke turned to wink at Tommy. Then he noticed something was bothering the boy. Something other than his big sister's tantrums. Luke asked, "What is it, Tom? You've been edgy as a hound with worms since your pa lit out."

Tommy Gant said, "It's Pa I'm worried about, Luke. You likely figured he ain't no gunslinger."

"He got the drop on me with no trouble, Tom. Said he'd been a lawman for thirty years."

"I know. That's the trouble. Pa married late. You might have noticed he ain't such a young feller, even if he is my Pa."

"Get to the point, son. Your father's not a youngster, but he looks to be in pretty good shape to me."

"Mebbe, but pretty good ain't good enough, the way things is gittin' hereabouts. The town's been growin'. Lots of strangers comin' in these days."

"You mean hard-cased strangers, like those miners I met up with in the saloon?"

"Yeah, and others jest as ornery. Others who don't look like they'd back down from an old man who talks about fishin' more'n gunplay."

"I see. Don't you reckon your father's man enough to stand up to the new rough elements in town?"

"Oh, he'll stand up to anybody, only . . ."

"How many fights has your father won, Tommy?"

"Not all that many. Jimson's Gap was a peaceable place up to the gold strike over on the foothill reef. I mean, sure, Pa's pistol-whupped his share of crazy-drunk cowboys in his time, but, well, you're a gunslinger, ain't you, Luke?"

"Not if I can avoid it. What are you tryin' to ask me, Tom?"

"Well, if you was to sort of watch out for my pa, I'd take it neighborly, Luke."

"I see. You're askin' me to stick my nose in where it ain't been asked, son."

"I'm askin' you, ain't I?"

"It ain't the same. If your father wanted a nurse-maid, he'd have likely told me."

"Shucks, he's too proud to ask anything of anybody. He's too proud to talk about his hands, too. But me and Hillary knows."

"Know what, Tom? What about your father's hands?"

"They're stiff with age and somethin' the doctors call arithmetic."

"You mean arthritis, Tom?"

"Yeah, that's what the doc called it. Said it comes with gittin' old and freezin' your fingers in thirty-odd hard winters. Pa says it don't bother him none, but I knows better."

"He seemed in pretty good shape when I watched him catch Old Elmer."

"Mebbe, but Old Elmer wasn't tryin' to beat Pa to the draw. I'm skeered skinny, Luke. I jest know that one of these nights one of them muley cusses from the gold mines will call Pa, and that Pa won't back down. He's too durned stubborn to back down. And too old and stiff to stand up to a real gunslinger! You see what I mean?"

"Yeah, kid. I see what you mean, and I owe him."

CHAPTER 38

After sundown, Luke made it his business to stroll through town with his friend, the sheriff. Orville Gant aked Luke how he liked the town from the outside of the jail house, and as they passed a door filling the night with fiddle playing and raucous laughter Luke said, "It's lively enough, for such a little town, Orville."

"I know. Used to be a quiet county seat. Still is, most days of the month. But comes payday at the gold mines and things git a mite noisy."

"Some of the miners troublemakers?"

"Yeah, sort of. You was holdin' a conversation with a mean bunch when I had to take you in, remember?"

"I remember."

"Couple of years back they hit gold-bearing quartz on the headwaters of Stone Creek. Not far from where I was fishing. It's brung in a wild bunch. Not jest the miners. Folks from all over, uprooted by the war. We got men as fought for the North and men as fought for the south here in Jimson's Break, these days. Likely you know what that can lead to, Luke!"

"Yeah."

"Trouble. More trouble than a town this size can shake a stick at, but it won't always be like this. This town'll be something grand one of these days!" Orville's voice held the hope of a man with a dream. "Aside from the rough bunch, most of the folks in Jimson's Break is decent, law-abiding folk. There's plenty of fertile soil and good water. Whole kingdom waitin' to be claimed and cleared. There's talk of the Union Pacific running a spur down this way from the south pass. When that happens, watch out!"

"Town'll likely grow some, eh, Orville?"

"Won't be a town. It'll be the county seat and a *city*. Good place for a young feller to start buildin' a new life. If he was to git hisself started right and play his cards right, might amount to an important man in this territory someday."

"You talking about me?"

"Why not? You got friends here, which is more'n can be said for some other places you might run for."

"I'll tell you the truth, Orville, I've been running so long there's nothing I'd like better than to find a place I could call my home. A place where I wouldn't have to keep looking over my shoulder."

"You keep thinkin' on it, boy. Meanwhile, I'd best see what all the ruckus is over in the saloon!"

Luke followed as the older man went up the walk and through the swinging doors. Inside, the fiddler was drunk and sawing away at his instrument as if his life depended on it. It might well have. Booster, Hub, and Nugget had taken over the saloon, and obviously aimed to keep it open and noisy all night.

The lean consumptive, Hub, had his eyes on one of the dance-hall girls as she came down the stairs with a customer. The girl was pretty in a painted, weary way, and the man she'd been entertaining in the cribs upstairs was, like most of the others in the place, a miner.

As the satisfied miner said good night to the girl and swaggered out, Hub sidled over to her and asked, "How's about it, Ruth?"

The girl shook her head. She didn't turn down many such offers, but Hub looked sick, crazy, and mean. A girl had to think about her health.

As she tried to walk around him, Hub's hand snaked out and grabbed for her, tearing the shoulder strap of her sleazy gown as she pulled away from him in mingled annoyance and disgust.

The bartender, Charlie, frowned at the exchange and reached for something under the bar, but the girl caught his eye and shook her head in a silent message. She could handle it. At least, she thought she could.

The old drunk playing the fiddle suddenly stopped, exhausted, and collapsed in a chair, saying, "Whooey! I'm drunk as a skunk and twice as wore out! I got to take a break, gents."

Booster glared at the weary fiddler with his one good eye and shouted, "Well, the trouble is, I ain't tired! I ain't even got started! My name is Booster and I'm a regular rooster, and you'd best git back to playin', friend, 'fore I gits annoyed!"

He picked up the fiddle, shoved it in the bewildered and frightened drunk's face, and roared, "I said *play*, god damn your eyes!"

Orville Gant thumbed the hammers of the shotgun hanging loosely at his side and cut in with "I can see as you're a music lover, Booster, but I 'spect the man's earned a rest. It's gittin' a mite late, anyways. Let's save some fun for tomorrow night, eh?"

Booster turned with an ominous frown as, in a corner, Nugget started cleaning his nails with his big Green River knife. Booster nodded at Orville and said, "Well, how do, Sheriff. Ain't that boy with you the one you throwed in jail?"

"That's my own business, friend."

"Shucks, it don't make no never mind to ussen do you aim to sashay about with criminals as fierce as him. Why don't you both mosey on, Sheriff? This here's a private party."

"Well, the party's about over, friend. I've got better

things to do than quiet down a passel of drunks. It's late and, like I said, I reckon it's time to call it a night."

"Do tell? How come you're all the time totin' that sawed-off shotgun ever'where you go, Sheriff? You scared of somethin'?"

"Not with a shotgun in my hands."

"Whoooo-wheee! Ain't you fierce? How come you don't pack a handgun like ever'body else, Sheriff? Don't you reckon you're fast enough on the draw to keep a bitty town like this tamed down?"

"The job gits done, mister. You boys mess with me and you'll find out!"

"Do tell? I cain't help noticin' them old hands of yourn, Sheriff. Knuckles big as hickory nuts. Fingers startin' to twist up some. They don't work the way they used to, do they?"

"They work well enough, mister. And you're treading on the tail of my coat with that loco line of talk!"

People in the line of fire began to move to either side as Booster laughed and faced the older man on widespread boots, one hand out to the side, perhaps six inches from the grips of his Navy Colt. Booster sneered. "I'm scared, Sheriff. Purely scared outten my mind. I'm likely drunk, but I have this crazy notion. I have this notion I could somehow put three rounds in you afore you could swing that there gun up and fire once!"

Before Orville could answer, Luke stepped out by his side and said casually, "The sheriff's a friend of mine, Booster."

"Now what's that supposed to mean, sonny?"

"You take it any way you like."

It got very quiet, and time seemed to hold still for a very long time as nobody bothered with breathing. Then Booster laughed easily and said, "Boy, I thought you and *me* was friends. You are a pure fundamental disappointment to me."

Orville said, "Like I was saying, the party's over.

You boys finish your drinks and then Charlie's gonna close down for the night. Ain't that right, Charlie?"

The bartender said, "We'll keep the noise down, Sheriff. The boys never meant no harm."

Orville nodded and said, "All right. I'm gonna make my rounds of the town now. Next time I pass this way I want to hear a heap of silence!"

He waited until he and Luke were outside before he turned to him and asked, "What's the matter with you, son? What are you aimin' to do, git kilt?"

"I was trying to help you!"

"Yeah, well from now on you jest let me run the show. I thought we was about to have a showdown. Know it's comin' with them three sooner or later anyways, but I had to back off on account so durned many folks was buttin' in!"

"What are you talking about? You could have been killed just now?"

"Why, because that idiot said so?"

"No. I was lookin' at your hands too."

"Well, you're both right about these hands not bein' all they used to, but they ain't quite gone yet. I'll tell you somethin' else, Luke. It ain't the hands, or a ready gun, as makes a lawman. It's the pride that makes him hold his ground, no matter what. That loudmouth wasn't gonna draw on me!"

"How could you be sure?"

"'Cause I'm a man and he ain't! Oh, he's got a gun and a sassy brag, but he knows once push comes to shove I aim to be standin' there, facin' him down. Not many bullies like the odds of kill-or-be-killed. Booster knows the night he draws on me, one of us gits buried."

Luke shook his head and said, "I've faced a few gunslingers. He was going to try for you. I felt it in my gut!"

"Mebbe, mebbe not. I thank you for siding me, anyways, Luke."

They finished their rounds and went back to the house, leaving the town to sleep it off. Orville Gant seemed drained, once the exitement of the close call had worn off. He seemed if anything older as he said good night to Luke and headed directly to his room, feet dragging just a mite.

Luke went to the kitchen to make himself a sandwich.

He noticed that the oil lamp in the kitchen was still lit. He assumed Tommy or Hillary had left it on for them. A voice from an alcove just off the kitchen called out, "Pa?"

Luke called back, "No, it's me, ma'am," as he walked over to the alcove. Then he froze in place. Hillary Gant sat naked in a big oak tub, taking a late-night bath.

"I'm sorry!" Luke stammered as he leaped back into the kitchen.

Hillary screamed, "You animal! What do you mean by spying on me?"

"I said I'm sorry! How was I to know you was taking a bath?"

The girl got out of the tub, wrapping a towel around her as she snapped, "Don't you ever knock?"

"I was just going to fix a bite to eat! Your father said you was likely in bed. I told you I was sorry, damn it!"

"Well, keep your voice down! You're going to have him down here in a minute, and I purely don't aim to have to explain a scene like this to him.!"

"What's to explain? Nobody's done nothing wrong hereabouts!"

"Oh no? There's a name for men who sneak about for a peek at a gal in the altogether!"

"Sneaking? Damn it, gal, there's a name for women who play such tricks on fellers, too!"

"Tricks? What tricks? There I was, mindin' my own business, washin' my own self, and you—"

"Oh, hell, you knowed good and well I was comin' back tonight!"

"What are you saying?"

"Figure it out for your own self. If you needed a

bath you could have shut the door, or taken it another night. I notice you had that there nice big towel handy, too."

Hillary exploded, "Why, damn you!" and rushed over to slap Luke's face. Instinctively, the angry youth raised his own hand; then he stopped himself with a scowl.

She gasped. "Why, you were aiming to hit me!"

"No, but it's time somebody did," Luke snapped. Then, turning on his heel, he stomped out to go to bed, hungry and most annoyed.

Hillary stared after him with a puzzled frown. Then, slowly, the frown faded, to be replaced by a mysterious little smile.

CHAPTER 39

Nobody at the Gant house got much sleep that night. In the wee hours everyone awoke to frantic pounding on the front door. A female voice sobbed out, "Sheriff! Sheriff! Please hurry, Sheriff!'

Orville Gant reached the door first, in his nightshirt. He found one of the bar girls from the saloon in a state of hysteria on the veranda.

He said, "Calm down, Mina! What in thunder's all this about!"

"It's Ruth, Sheriff! I think they killed her! She's bleedin' awful bad!"

"Ruth? That new gal at the saloon? What happened to her, Mina?"

"It was them miners. The ones you had the words with! It was that skinny one with the scary eyes. They called him Hub!"

"I know the cuss. What happened, damn it?"

"He wanted Ruth to go upstairs with him, but she wouldn't. She said he was dirty and mean and likely crazy. I reckon he was, and likely drunk, too! Hub cut her with his knife. Charlie sent her to the doc, but she was bleedin' so bad . . ."

By this time Luke had joined the sheriff. He heard Orville ask in a quiet tone, "All right, where are those miners now, Mina?"

"They're waitin' for you, sheriff!"

"Waitin' for me? Where?"

"At the saloon. They got Angie with 'em, and they said if you don't come right now they aim to cut Angie, too!"

By now Hillary and Tommy had joined everyone else in the doorway. Orville shot his daughter a glance and told Mina, "You go along with my daughter and she'll fix you some coffee, Mina."

Hillary gasped. "Pa, what are you aimin' to do?"

"Git dressed, fust. Then I'll be goin' down to see what them three lunatics want!"

"Pa, don't do it!"

"Take your brother an' this gal to the kitchen an' stay there, girl. I'll be back for breakfast, one way or t'other."

A few minutes later, as Orville Gant strode from the house with the shotgun crooked under an elbow, Luke fell in at his side. Orville asked, "Where you headed, boy?"

"With you."

"In a pig's eye, son! I'm the law in this town, and it's my job."

"It's three to one, Orville."

"Don't make no never mind iffen it's three or thirty. It's my job, and I'll ask you to stay outten it."

As Luke hesitated, the older man strode away in the cold gray light.

Hillary came out to where Luke stood, bemused, and asked, "Who are they, Luke? Who could do something like that to any woman?"

"Ain't got time to explain. You'd best lock and bar the door as soon as we're out of sight."

"But Pa told you to stay here, Luke!"

"I know what he told me. Now I'm tellin' you. Get inside and bar the door!"

"Are you aiming to follow him, Luke?"

"Is there anything else I could do?"

Luke walked away from Hillary without another word, keeping to the shadows as he followed Orville's tall, proud figure at a discreet interval. Had it been up to Luke, they'd have circled in and scouted some. Orville Gant strode straight to the saloon, stood in the middle of the street outside, and bellowed, "All right in there, McDonough! This is the sheriff! You send that girl out first, then all three of you follow with your hands above your heads!"

A voice from the blacked-out saloon called, "Why sure, sheriff. Happy to oblige!"

There was a blur of motion, and the bar girl called Angie rushed out and ran over to Orville, sobbing, "Sheriff! I thought they'd kill me!"

"Get out of here pronto, gal. All right, McDonough. Come on out!"

Two of them did, but none of them had raised a hand. Booster McDonough said, "Understand you want us, Sheriff."

"Where's your little sidekick, Nugget?"

"Inside. He's scared. Let's talk this over, Sheriff. I'm halfway sober now, and right sorry for what Hub, here, done to that gal."

"You two throw down your guns!"

"Aw hell, Sheriff, can't we talk this over like gents?"

Before the sheriff could answer, Luke stepped out from the shadows, shouting, "Orville! Behind you!"

Nugget had been waiting in ambush, outside the saloon and directly across the street, behind the false front of the livery. As Orville whirled, the little miner fired the rifle in his hands. The bullet slammed into the sheriff's hip and spun him like a ballerina as Luke drew and fired, his shot pitching Nugget off the building and into the dust.

Hub stood frozen by the gunfire as the giant Booster went for his own gun. But even on his side in the street, Orville Gant was still a man to be reckoned with. He fired both barrels from where he lay, jackknifing Booster McDonough at the waist with a double charge of number nine buck.

As Hub threw up his hands and started whimpering for mercy, Luke ran over to the wounded sheriff and dropped to one knee at his side.

"Lay still, Orville! I'll get the doctor!"

"Calm down, boy. I'm all right. You ain't one for takin' orders, are you."

"But, Orville . . ."

"I said I was all right, damn it. Help me to my feet and let's put this surviving bucket of scum in jail!"

CHAPTER 40

Orville Gant had been right. The doctor came out of the sheriff's bedroom with a smile and told Luke and Hillary, "He wants to see you both."

"How is he, Doctor?" asked Hillary.

"Your father's going to be fine, Miss Hillary. Bullet went clean through, just above his hip. He may be gimpy for a spell, but he'll be up and around and chasing Old Elmer up the creek before you know it."

"Oh, I feel so much better. Thank you, doctor."

"Thank this young man here, Miss Hillary. The way your pa tells it, he'd have caught that bullet betwixt the shoulder blades had not this feller warned him about that rascal tryin' to ambush him from behind!"

And then the doctor bade them both good day and the young couple went into Orville's room.

The sheriff was propped up in bed, looking fit but disgusted with himself. After assuring his daughter that he felt tolerable, Orville turned to Luke and said, "They like to took me like a greenhorn! How'd you know that Nugget was ahint me with that rifle gun, boy?"

Luke shrugged. "You get to where you feel things after you've been on the run."

"Well, you had them three sized up better than I did. What's the county done about 'em since I been layin' here? They ain't still layin' in the street, are they?"

"No, sir. The county coroner's taken Booster and Nugget off our hands. I got Hub locked up in the jail house. He's pretty scared, and the doc says he's got a bad case of consumption. Doesn't much matter how his trial turns out. Doc says he's got a year to live at the outside."

"You feedin' him, takin' care he don't bust loose?"

"Sure, but like I said, he's not much of a problem without his tougher sidekicks, Orville."

The sheriff reached in the drawer of the end table near the head of his bed and took out a nickel-plated star. "Well, as the circuit judge will be coming by any day now to try that poor idiot for what he done to Ruth at the saloon, you'd best pin this on."

Luke looked incredulous. "Are you serious? Me a lawman?"

"Hell yes, you. Who else in thunder's liable to be able to keep a lid on this here town until I'm on my feet agin? Besides, I owe you, Luke. Likely you savvy it ain't jest for helpin' me catch Old Elmer!"

"Come on, you don't owe me anything, and the truth is, I've been studyin' on movin' on."

"Don't you hear good, boy? I ain't askin' for a lifetime pledge. I need temporary help, and I pay good wages for a deputy I can trust!"

"But don't it matter that my face and name are on wanted posters over half the country?"

"Now, if you had the brains of a gnat you'd see the advantage of bein' my deputy, damn it! Who in thunder's likely to look for a wanted owlhoot wearin' a badge?"

"I dunno. Seems sort of weird, if you ask me!"

"Who's *askin'*, boy. I'm *tellin'* you! Hell, I know dozens of lawmen who've had some paper out on 'em at one time or another. Seems a man can't hardly larn to handle a gun hereabouts without some pesky nit-picker runnin' to the law about it. We'd have no law west of the Big Muddy if we insisted too much on every town tamer bein' a Sunday-school sissy! You gonna pin this here badge on or do I have to git up off my deathbed and do it for you?"

Luke took the badge with a grin and said, "I suspicion you're crazy, but you got yourself a deputy."

Hillary's eyes were moist as she held her hand out and said, "Let me pin it on you, Luke. You menfolk never get things straight."

Luke gave her the badge and stared down at her soberly as she pinned the star to his shirt, smoothed it with her fingertips, and added, "There. That looks about right. Likely you know what I'm trying to say, don't you, Luke?"

"I reckon. We can talk it over at the dance this Saturday."

"I'd like that, but Tobe's taking me, remember?"

"You mean he was. You didn't want to go with him anyway, right?"

"No, but he's likely to be awful mad, and Tobe's bigger than you."

"Don't worry on it, honey. He ain't that much bigger."

CHAPTER 41

Meanwhile, Luke's Uncle Zeb was covering ground at a tolerable pace, considering he was still on foot. He'd wasted a lot of time, he knew, in the big circle he'd made around Fort Sully during the first night of his consuming rage and poorly thought out plans. He'd told Beth and Marshal Logan he'd be back within ten days for the hearing over that shooting scrape and his time was almost up. So his first idea was to simply walk to Three Rivers and to hell with it.

But, damn it, they'd stole his pony! No matter what Stonecipher had told MacAllister, that mount hadn't belonged to no U.S. Army, it was his, and a tolerable old hoss!

He didn't have a gun. He was outnumbered a mite by the Second U.S. Cav, but, by jimmies, he purely aimed to get his pony back. He'd figure how once he got there. And so, footsore and still mad as hell, Zeb headed for the fort, ready to take on the army empty-handed if he had to.

At the fort, General Stonecipher was annoyed as hell, too. He balled up the telegram from Washington and threw it across the room, explaining to the other officers at the meeting, "Those silly sons of bitches are sending reinforcements! Washington's in a flap over the death of Count Sergei and Satangkai's open declaration of war, and we're not to move until they get here!"

Major Drake nodded and said, "That may be wise, sir. If Red Cloud, Crazy Horse, or any of the other Sioux leaders decide to throw in with Satangkai we could be in for more than one regiment can handle."

Stonecipher snorted. "God damn it, Major! You give me a corporal's squad and a Gattling gun and I'll take on every Indian west of the Big Muddy! This time I'm going to punish the heathen, gentlemen! The Sioux have been put down in the past, but this time I mean to shove them so far down they'll have to look up to see bottom! I mean to attack. I mean to harry and pursue. I mean to pin him down and utterly destroy him, once and for always. Is that understood?"

There was a chorus of agreement, and Stonecipher said, "All right now if only Washington will turn us loose, Satangkai's as good as dead or in jail, where he belongs!" He scowled around the table at his junior officers. "Until they let us move, I want all of you and your men to shape up or ship out! I want every soldier on or about this post ready to move at a moment's notice. I will personally eat the liver of any officer who's not one hundred and ten percent prepared to lead said men! You troop commanders are dismissed. I want a word with the Major and Captain MacAllister, here."

As soon as the lesser lights left, the general asked, "How's His Imperial Whatsis taking the death of his nephew, Drake?"

The major shook his head and said, "Not good, sir. He's demanding a personal role in the revenge. I gather in his salad days he was a cossack leader in his own right."

"Well, that gives him damned few rights out here! But you can tell him for me his nephew's death will be avenged as soon as they turn me loose!"

"I'll do that, sir. Have you any idea how long we'll have to wait?"

"It better not be long. By now every newspaper in the country is screaming about what happened out here. Any politician who isn't screaming right along with him don't figure to run for dog catcher in the next election! We'll get our orders and the reinforcements. After that it's a simple albeit long overdue mopping-up operation."

"Do you expect Red Cloud and the other Sioux leaders to stand by Satangkai, sir? What about the Cheyenne? They say Black Kettle and Dull Knife are on the prod, too."

"I hope every red rascal who owns a feather rides with Satangkai! This so-called Indian problem could be solved once and for all in six weeks, if Washington could ever make up its mind!"

Drake nodded wryly and said, "I know, sir. We feed 'em in the winter and fight 'em in the summer. Doesn't seem to make much sense."

"A sensible politician is a contradiction in terms, Major. Hell, I'm not an unreasonable man. I'd be willing to go along with civilizing the Indians with education, housing, and such. But those rascals in the Indian Agency keep most of the money and send the Indians just enough to keep them alive without enough to make it worth their while to do so. Silly bastards give 'em a sack of flour and a handful of ammunition and tell 'em to live offen the land. Meanwhile, another band of thieves in Washington take away another chunk of said land and call on us when the Indians jump the reservation lookin' for food or trouble."

"Then it's fight-em-in-the-summer time, right, sir?"

"Damned A. On a shoestring budget and all sorts of fool red tape to tie our hands so's we can't do it right. We're either going to have to turn them into civilized farmers or kill every damned one of 'em, and there's no two ways about it, Major."

Drake nodded, sure he knew which method the general found most logical to his way of solving things.

But Stonecipher surprised Drake by adding, in a sadder, more subdued tone, "It's a pity, though. You only have to look at Satangkai to know he isn't going to let us tame him. Wouldn't it be grand if there was another way? Think what it would mean to have warriors like that fighting on our side!"

"Someday we may have Sioux in the army, sir. We have Crow, Pawnee, and Chippewa scouts now. Someday we may serve side by side with Sioux."

"I hope you're right, Major. But someday isn't now. Right now we have a nasty little campaign ahead of us. By the way, where is the duke if he's so all-fired anxious to help us slaughter Sioux?"

"He's in his quarters, sir, being consoled by the ladies."

"Well, I suppose that's one way of putting it. If you have to grieve, there's less-pleasant ways of doing it."

Outside a lookout called, "White man comin' in on foot!"

MacAllister went out to investigate and returned in a few moments to report, "It's Zeb Macahan! I can't believe it!"

Stonecipher chuckled and said, "I can." Then he turned to Drake and said, "You owe me a month's pay, Major. You should never bet against an old soldier like me. I've met Macahan's breed before!"

MacAllister said, "I don't understand it, sir. What's he coming in for?"

"I suppose he wants his horse. It's his property, after all."

"His property, General? But you told me—"

"I know what I told you, son. Let that be another lesson to you. Old soldiers never die, but old soldiers often lie. Go out and tell him I want to see him, Captain."

MacAllister went outside, bemused, and found Zeb swaying in the open gate, glowering. Zeb caught a passing soldier by the sleeve and spun him around, snapping, "You know where my pony is, sonny?"

"I think it's at the blacksmith's, sir, but—"

"But me no buts, god damn your eyes! I just walked mebbe fifty miles lookin' for that pony! You'd best go *git* it!"

Zeb strode to the orderly room, pausing along the way to fill his battered hat from a drinking trough, gulp a deep drink, and pour another hatful over his sweating frame as he clamped it angrily back on his grizzled head. He spotted MacAllister and snapped,

"I've come for my belongings. You got objections or have you tired of livin', sudden?"

"Zeb, we'll talk about the mix-up later. Right now the general wants to see you!"

Zeb nodded curtly and stamped inside, where he found a morose Major Drake counting out some money into Brandy Jack Stonecipher's hand.

Zeb snapped, "I've come for my property, General!"

"I know, I figured you would."

"You aim to try and stop me from takin' what's my own?"

"I think I could, but I won't. I commandeered your horse to make sure you came back to Fort Sully, Zeb."

"You what?"

"You heard me. I couldn't take the chance of you riding out after your Indian friends. Quanna Parker of the Comanche had an ex-army bugler riding at his side, and it purely complicated things for us at the time. I wanted you on our side."

"Well, you got me here. Don't know as I'm on anybody's side. I got my own troubles, and a lady and me has to see a judge about some other damn fools I met."

He waited for the general to object. Stonecipher was still looking smug and satisfied with himself. Zeb asked, "How soon you figure to ride out to meet Satangkai?"

"Don't know. Waiting on new orders and reinforcements."

"It could take some time."

"Not this time. The whole country's up in arms about this massacre."

"Massacre? You call stompin' on one piss-ant a massacre?"

"Washington does. Once they turn me loose I'll have the Sioux by their scalp locks within a week!"

"You talk a good fight, General."

"I fight a good fight, too, as your Indian playmates will discover."

Zeb shook his head in disgust as, behind him, the door reopened to admit Grand Duke Dimitri. Zeb ignored the Russian as he asked the general, "You're fixin' to wipe out half the Dakota in the Black Hills because of a man so stupid they should have shot him in his crib?"

The duke was outraged. "How dare you speak like that about a Romanov?"

Zeb shrugged. "Look, Duke, I'm sorry for your sake the boy's dead. But if ever a man committed suicide, it was Count Sergei!"

The Russian turned to the other officers for help as he all but shouted, "I will not stand for this! Count Sergei lost his young life as a direct result of this uncouth peasant's blundering!"

Drake said soothingly, "Your Highness, Macahan did everything he could to get the captives back safely. He very nearly succeeded, too."

"He succeeded only in getting my nephew killed! I demand this scoundrel be punished!"

Zeb snorted. "Oh hell, we all knew the idiot had been set *free* by Satangkai when he up and slapped him across the eyes like that. What in thunder's wrong with you jaspers? I can't be the only man in these parts with a head on his shoulders!"

The duke repeated his demand, asking, "General, what are you going to do about this arrogant lout?"

Stonecipher looked at Zeb and said, "Don't know yet. How about it, arrogant lout? Are you still scouting for me or not?"

"Scouting for you? I'd sooner eat skunk shit! I only come for my pony and possibles!"

"All right. Get them and get out then."

The duke protested. "You shall not release him! I will not have it!"

But Zeb had turned and was on his way. The duke took a deep breath and started to follow as Major Drake warned, "Uh-oh, we'd better stop what I think's about to happen, General!"

Stonecipher grinned, lit a cigar, and said, "I don't think so." They went to the window as the duke shouted orders to his nearby bodyguard, saying, "Vasili! That man in the buckskins! Take him!"

A huge bear of a Russian in a Cossack hat and steel breast plate moved to intercept Zeb Macahan as Drake said, "Zeb's unarmed, and he's been on his feet around the clock! He's in no position to defend himself against that giant!"

"I wouldn't worry about it, Major."

"But the Russian's wearing a steel breast plate!"

"So he is. Ain't he lucky?"

As they watched, the giant Vasili overtook Zeb and shouted in halting English, "You. Stop, *da?*"

Zeb ignored the command and kept on going for his horse.

The big Russian frowned, shrugged, and grabbed Zeb by the shoulder, spinning him around to face a huge right-handed swing.

Zeb ducked under the fist with a speed worthy of a smaller man and threw a counterpunch. It was a good punch, and the Russian's head flew back, dislodging the fur shako in the process.

But Vasili was neither too bright nor too badly hurt. He shook his bullet head like a bulldog and rushed Zeb again, wrapping both big arms around him in a bear hug.

Zeb swore, grabbed the lower edge of the breast plate, and heaved upward, cutting the Russian's jaw to the bone and knocking him out completely with the impact of the steel collar.

As the Russian's knees buckled, Zeb was left standing with the torn-off breast plate in his hands and an annoyed look on his face. He saw Duke Dimitri hesitating in the middle distance with his plump hand on the hilt of his saber. Zeb snorted in disgust and threw the breast plate at the duke's feet, turning to resume his pace as if nothing had even slowed him down.

The duke ran back toward the officers in the window, sobbing. "You are fools! He is riding off to join the Indians! He will help them against us all!"

Stonecipher shook his head and said, "He'll cool

off and be back. He's got a lot on his plate right now, but down deep I'm banking on him being a white man."

Drake asked, "But what if His Highness is right, sir? What if Zeb should join the Sioux against us?"

The general puffed on his cigar. "He may. It should make for a most interesting campaign."

CHAPTER 42

At the Macahan homestead young Josh and Jeremiah Taylor were working together on some worn-out harness. Despite his reservations about the way his sister mooned over the Mormon, Josh had taken a shine to the man. It was hard not to like Jeremiah. He spoke a heap in riddles, but he seemed one of those rare souls who've simply been created without malice in their hearts. Josh suspected the Mormon of being mixed up about the world, with all his going on about gold tablets and magic spectacles to read them by, but you had to admire a tree grown straight, and there seemed nothing crooked or devious in the tall man's soul.

Laura joined them as they worked together, sitting on the corral rail. She'd baked another tray of gingerbread and tied still another ribbon in her long blond hair. Josh took a piece, bit into it, and allowed, "Not bad, Sis!" as he reached for another.

But Laura had moved the tray out of the boy's reach and held it out to Jeremiah, smiling coquettishly as she said, "Won't you have some, Jeremiah? I made it my own self."

The Mormon took a piece and tasted, smiling as he

said, "Delicious, Miss Laura." Then he turned to Josh and added, "I can finish up this mending, Josh. I thank you for your help."

Josh caught the look that passed between his sister and the man. He didn't like it much, but he knew when he wasn't wanted, so he left, after helping himself to more gingerbread.

The Mormon smiled after the boy, then turned back to his sister and allowed, "You're a fine cook, Laura. In the few short days we've been here I've been eating like Solomon in all his glory. Everything you serve is just delicious!"

"Well, I didn't do it all. Aunt Molly's the real cook hereabouts."

"Maybe, but you've a certain touch there's just no mistaking. I, uh, planned to go out to the meadows to look for herbs this morning. There's thyme and mint growing wild all over these hills. Would you care to come along?"

Laura shot a backward glance at the house before she nodded and said, "I'd love to, Jeremiah!"

As they strolled uphill from the homestead, neither noticed the two riders watching them from a distant rise.

Laura seemed oblivious to the late-blooming flowers all around her skirt hem. She said, "Sometimes I wish I could get away from this place, pretty as it is, sometimes."

"It's beautiful country, Laura."

"I know, but it's awful lonesome. Not like it was back in Virginia before the war, when I was little."

"Do you ever feel you want to go back there, Laura?"

"Not really. It's likely all changed after all the fighting and the killing where we used to live. My father died not far from where I was born. He was killed in the war. I 'spect I'd rather go on instead of back. Go on to something new, I mean."

"That's the best way to think, Laura. You're young

and have your life ahead of you." He paused and added, "You're a fine strong girl, and very pretty."

"Strong?"

"Don't you think so?"

"I dunno. Everyone else . . . Josh, Jessie, even Aunt Molly seem to feel I'm foolish. They seem so satisfied with so little. I've always felt a mite guilty about wanting . . . well, *more!*"

"You mustn't feel guilty, Laura! The strong are never satisfied to just make do. They're meant to build. To create. To widen their horizons. That's what makes life worth living, Laura."

"Gee, ever' time I hear you talk I just get goose bumps all over! I've never met a man like you before, Jeremiah!"

"I've never met a girl like you, either."

As she blushed and turned her head away, Jeremiah Taylor suddenly and impulsively blurted, "Laura, have you ever thought about marriage?"

"Marriage?"

"Yes. You would make any man a splendid wife and helpmate, and you'd make a wonderful mother. A mother for my children."

Laura gaped at him, stunned, as he insisted, "I know we've only known each other for a few short days, but I've admired you from the first moment I saw you. Yes, and I know you've felt something for me, too. Do you deny it?"

"Aunt Molly will be wondering what's keeping me. I'd best get back."

"Laura, I have such a terrible need for a wife!"

"But . . . but you're already married!"

"I know, but surely you're aware of how it is with poor old Maggie and me?"

"She's too old for you, but . . . You married her, didn't you?"

"That's not the obstacle to us it might be to others. You know we Latter-day Saints are allowed more than one wife."

Laura shook her head and said, "That's easy for *you* to say, but I'm no Mormon!"

"Come now, you know we've spoken of my faith, and you've said how much of it you admire, darling."

"I like the hymns and all, but all them wives . . . It ain't natural!"

"Why not? David and Solomon had many wives. There's nothing in the Ten Commandments of Moses forbidding it. Monogamy is simply a rule someone made up in the Middle Ages, Laura. There's nothing in your Bible or mine forbidding us from getting married."

"I've got to git!"

"Please don't run away from me, dear. Try to understand. Maggie was an elder's wife. After he was killed by the gentiles she was old, alone, and frightened. She needed someone to care for her, and so I married her.

"But do you . . . love her?"

"We're the best of friends, but . . . Children are out of the question."

Laura blushed deep red as his meaning sank in. Then she shrugged and asked, "What about your other wives? How many wives have you got, Mister Latter-day Saint?"

Jeremiah hesitated before he sighed and said, "I have two, dear."

"*Two?* You've already married up with two other gals and you dare to court me like this?"

"I told you, it's not the same with us. My other wife, Ellen, is waiting in Burtonville until Maggie and I can get settled out here and send for her."

"I see, and what does Maggie think about having this other gal sharing your, uh, favors with her?"

"Darling, the two of them are like sisters. As a matter of fact, they're related by blood, and they love each other dearly. There's no place in a well-run Saint's home for the mindless jealousy of you gentiles!"

"It sounds crazy! I could never share a husband with another gal!"

"Perhaps it would seem awkward with a stranger, at first. Try to imagine what it would be like, though, if you and little Jessie were living together with one husband. Would that be so terrible?"

Laura laughed, a trifle hysterically, as she tried to picture it. She said, "Good Lord, we'd be having pillow fights on our honeymoon!"

He joined her in her laughter and quickly pressed, "Yes, but would you hate her?"

"Hate Jessie? Of course not. She's my little sister!"

"That's the way Maggie and Ellen feel about each other, dear. They're sisters under Christ. I assure you, they've never had a jealous word over me."

"Maybe not, but it still spooks *me!* If you want those children so bad, what's the matter with your second wife? Why can't she . . . Uh . . ."

"Ellen is barren," said Jeremiah bleakly. "I need a younger, stronger wife, Laura. I need children. I know the taking of more than one wife seems strange to you, darling, but with us it's not a matter of lust. It's a matter of need, and we must be practical."

"Practical? Beddin' down with a whole harem?"

"I'd hardly call two older women and a strong young beauty like you a harem, Laura. The same Bible you believe in ordered the sons of Noah to go forth and multiply, didn't it?"

"I don't know what the Lord told Noah, but neither him or his sons ever asked me to marry up with a traveling parlorhouse!"

"Ah, there you go putting sinful connotations to what's meant by God to be a holy sacrament! My people are so outnumbered, Laura. Our only hope is to be fruitful in the wilderness."

"I have to git back. You've got me all mixed up with all this talk."

"Laura, I'll be leaving here tomorrow."

"Tomorrow? So soon?"

He nodded. "Our oxen are rested, and Maggie's

feeling better. We can't go on imposing on your family forever, and I've so much to do where we're headed."

Laura stared down at the grass and murmured, "I hadn't thought about you leaving, Jeremiah."

"I know, that's why I had the courage to press you on the matter of coming with us. If you need more time, perhaps we could stay another day or so, but will you think about all I've said?"

Laura didn't answer. She was running for the house, her eyes blurred with tears and her pounding heart filled with mixed emotions.

But if Laura was confused, Molly Culhane had no such difficulty making up her mind when the bewildered girl repeated Jeremiah's proposal to her in the kitchen. She picked up a rolling pin with a determined set to her Irish jaw.

Laura pleaded, "Aunt Molly, don't go gettin' ugly! I don't want him to know I told you!"

"I don't care what he knows! Less than three days on the property and he tries to turn a virgin's head!"

"Aunt Molly, he asked me proper to marry him!"

"For land's sake, child! The fool's already married, more than once!"

"I know, but it ain't sinful to him and his kind, Aunt Molly. Neither of his old wives can give him children, and he says he needs another for reasons of the Lord!"

"I'll give him a reason of the Lord to get his polygamous carcass off Macahan property!"

"Please, Aunt Molly, you have to try to look at it Jeremiah's way. To his way of thinking there was nothing sinful in what he asked. You might say it was sort of an honor, considering."

"An honor? Have you gone crazy too, girl?"

"I don't know. I know he really cares for me, and he needs a wife who can bear his children and help him carve a home from the wilderness. You should be, well, proud a man like Jeremiah asked me to marry up with him!"

"Laura, the idiot's already got two wives to carve up all the wilderness he needs to! Why should I feel proud about his wanting to marry a third?"

"Aunt Molly, you haven't been listening! He married old Maggie out of pity. She was alone and frightened. You can see she's not going to ever have a child. His other wife, Ellen is barren too."

"I swear if that doesn't beat all! What's the *matter* with the young fool? Why does he have to keep marrying older women?"

"I don't know . . . or, yes, I do. It's 'cause he's kind, Aunt Molly."

"Hmmph! Kind of crazy, you mean! How's it supposed to work? They can be his unpaid housekeepers and you can be his little bed partner?"

"Aunt Molly! What an awful thing to say!"

"Child, I can't help being indignant. You're barely grown and you're talking about sharing the rest of your life, *and* a husband, with two strange women! And what about them? What makes you so certain they'd be so keen on sharing Jeremiah with a younger, prettier girl?"

"Oh, Mormons don't believe in jealousy."

"They don't, eh? Well, they'd best get cracking, then. I don't care what Joseph Smith got off that fool angel, Moroni. Jealous thoughts may be sinful, but they're human. Those folks may call themselves Saints all they like, but—"

"Oh, Aunt Molly, you don't understand. You're trying to make things look nasty, but if you'd been brought up a Mormon—"

"Honey, I wasn't brought up a Mormon, and neither were you. I'll say no more about how Jeremiah and his wives might or might not feel about plural marriage, but if I know a thing about the way my sister Kate raised you, and the way you keep your sister Jessie out of your dresser drawers, you're simply not cut out for such a life."

"Are you saying I'm too selfish to share, Aunt Molly?"

"I don't suppose you're any more selfish than most girls your age, dear. But sharing a man's not the same as sharing a dresser drawer."

"I wish you wouldn't make it sound so . . . so personal."

"Having children with a man *is* sort of personal, girl! Tell me something—is Jeremiah planning on building a small town for you three girls or are you planning on a very big bed?"

"That's disgusting, Aunt Molly. I happen to know Jeremiah and poor Maggie don't . . . you know."

"How do I 'you know'? Did Jeremiah say he'd never 'you-knowed' with his own wife, or wives?"

"He didn't have to. It's obvious the others are only his wives in name. It's *me* he asked to be the mother of his children!"

Molly shook her head and sighed. "Oh, Laura, Laura, you're such a child! I've never been a Mormon, but I've been married, and I've exchanged a few notes with other women who've lived with a man, too, in my time."

"Jeremiah's not like other men."

"Honey, I honestly don't know *what* kind of man he is, but if he's any kind of man, and he's been living and sleeping with any woman for any length of time, he's a liar if he says he hasn't touched her—or, in this case, them!"

"That's not fair! You're just prejudiced against him because of his religion!"

"Honey, I'm not talking religion. I'm talking about biology. That man and his two wives can do anything they like, but it's not going to include you if *I* have anything to say about it!"

Laura's face was flushed with mingled defiance and confusion as she blurted, "You don't have anything to say about it, Aunt Molly! I'm of the age of consent, and even if I wasn't, you're not my ma!"

"Then you're really thinking about going through with it?"

"I don't know what I'm thinking! But I have the right to make up my own mind!"

Molly shook her head wearily and muttered, "I'm not sure you have a mind, and I can see I'm not getting anywhere talking to *you!*"

Leaving Laura in the kitchen to sort her own thoughts out as best she could, Molly Culhane marched out to the yard, where she spied the young Mormon walking toward his Conestoga. She called out, "Mr. Taylor! I'd like a *word* with you!"

Jeremiah turned with a pleasant smile, which faded fast as Molly lit into him. He waited until she'd called him everything from a cradle snatcher to an idiot before he got a word in edgewise and protested, "I assure you my intentions are honorable, ma'am!"

"Mr. Taylor, I don't give two hoots and a holler for your intentions! Laura is a child! She has absolutely no knowledge about the world, or men!"

"You have every right to be angry, Miss Culhane. I should have spoken to you first. But when I walked out with Laura just now I just suddenly found myself proposing. It just happened. Of course, as Laura then went straight to you, I had no chance to prepare you!"

CHAPTER 43

"All right, what's done is done. It would have spared the child considerable confusion if you *had* come to me first, but in the end it probably wouldn't have made any difference. The whole idea is simply impossible!"

"But why, if we love each other?"

"I hardly think it needs explaining! We know abso-

lutely nothing about you, Mr. Taylor. The girl's only
known you a little over seventy-two hours. Even if you
weren't a Mormon, your proposal would be too sudden to consider."

"Aha! You *are* prejudiced because of my religion!"

"Sir, I don't know a thing about your religion. I'm
prejudiced, if you want to call it that, because you already have two wives!"

"Both of whom will receive Laura with love and
affection as a sister under God's love, ma'am!"

"I don't know about your wives, but I do know
my niece. It just won't work. Laura's not a Mormon.
She knows nothing of your—your—"

"Belief in the one true God? Our faith is Christian,
the same as your own, save for a few small details."

"Mr. Taylor, I'm not a theologian. I'm Laura's aunt,
and guardian with her uncle and elder brother gone.
I won't argue religion with you. I only know the idea of
this marriage is wrong for Laura and, believe me, sir,
for *you!* I want you to go this instant to Laura and
withdraw your proposal!"

Jeremiah sighed and shook his head. "I can't do
that, Miss Culhane. It wouldn't be honorable."

"In that case, sir, I must ask you and your wife to
leave this property at once! Do you understand?"

"Of course, ma'am. We shan't stay a moment where
we're not welcome, and despite our differences, I
thank you for all you've done for us in the past few
days."

Before Molly could answer, there was the sound of
pounding hooves, and they both turned in time to see a
quartet of horsemen riding into the yard.

It was the rancher, Burton, with his ramrod, Woodley, and two of his hired hands. Maggie Taylor peeked
out from the Conestoga as they came in, grim-faced.
She whimpered, "Oh Lordy, Jeremiah!"

The young Mormon strode over by the wagon as if
to protect his wife, although Molly knew there were
no weapons in the wagon, save for an old rusty fowl-
ing piece, and no powder at all.

As Josh, Jessie, and Laura appeared on the veranda, Molly stood her ground, smiling up at the four riders with a quizzical expression.

Burton held up his hand like a cavalry officer as he reined in, the other three riders following suit. Burton nodded curtly at Molly and said, "You and the children had best git inside, ma'am."

"Inside? Whatever for?"

"Kate Macahan was a good Christian woman, and we'-uns respect this family, ma'am. We don't want trouble with you all."

"We certainly don't want trouble either, sir. What's all this about?"

"Them folks there by the wagon. We'd like to have us a little talk with 'em. Best for you and the kids if you jest went about your own business!"

Now, while Molly had just had words with Jeremiah Taylor over articles of their two Christian faiths, Molly Culhane was a Celt, and the Celtic laws of hospitality went further back than Christ, or even Rome. Her voice held firm as she shook her head and said, "What happens to guests on Macahan land *is* our business, sir. Just what is it you'd be after?"

"Mormons, ma'am. Me an' the boys is huntin' Mormons!"

"Well, go and hunt them somewhere else! You're tresspassing on Macahan land!"

Burton shook his head and said, "It's no use, ma'am. You're givin' sanctuary to hypocrites and murderers!"

"Murderers! What are you talking about?"

"Mountain Meadows, ma'am. I had *kin* at Mountain Meadows!"

"I don't know what you're talking about!"

"I know that, ma'am. That's why I'm tryin' to be nice about this. Ask that mealy-mouthed Mormon hidin' ahint his woman's skirts over thar to tell you 'bout Mountain Meadows, if he dares!"

Jeremiah flushed and stepped away from the wagon, where he'd been comforting his frightened wife. He said, "I'm not hiding from any man, behind a woman's skirt or anywhere else!"

Burton sneered. "Likely you'll tell us, next, you never heard of Mountain Meadows, huh?"

"I heard of what happened there," said Jeremiah grimly. Then, noting Molly's and the Macahan children's confusion, he explained, "Mountain Meadows is a terrible blot on the honor of our church, Miss Culhane. Back during the gold rush, in the state of Deseret, or, as you folks call it, Utah, a small group of fanatics committed a terrible crime."

"You mean *Mormon* fanatics?"

"Yes, ma'am. I'm afriad there are fanatics in every faith. A Saint called Brother Lee disguised himself and a small handful of followers as Ute Indians and attacked a wagon train bound for California. It was said Brother Lee had been driven mad by years of persecution, and of course the elders of our church condemmed his actions!"

"Oh dear, what happened?"

"To face it squarely, it was a massacre. A massacre of innocent pioneers just passing through. These misguided Saints, dressed as savages and perhaps with a few real Utes as willing helpers, attacked the wagon train and killed a hundred and twenty people. To poor Brother Lee's dubious credit, he spared eighteen children, and that was his undoing. The children weren't fooled by the Indian costumes. When they were picked up by friendly people of our faith, they were able to describe their attackers all too well."

Burton snapped, "Not well enough by half! My own sister and her family, seven people in all, was murdered by them Mormon outlaws! Mormons just like these you've given bed and board to, ma'am!"

Jeremiah shook his head and said, "I'm sorry, sir but you have it wrong. As I told you, Brother Lee was disavowed by our elders. What's more, he paid for his crime, along with some of his followers. The army made him ride his own coffin to Mountain Meadow and made him dig his own grave at the site of th tragedy. Then they shot him. As far as the rest of *us* are concerned, the Mountain Meadows case is closed!"

Burton shook his head and said ominously, "Not by me it ain't! Your Brother Lee wasn't the only one to hit that wagon train! I know for a fact most of his so-called Avenging Angels was never caught!"

"Sir, if you're looking for any of the poor fanatic's followers, I assure you you won't find them here! I was only a boy at the time and, like most of my people, I only heard about it weeks after it happened."

Burton turned to his followers and said mockingly, "Will you listen to him, boys? Seems there ain't a Mormon alive who remembers bein' up in Mountain Meadows when my sister and her kids was killed!"

He swung around to Molly again, reaching for the rope on his saddle swells as he did so. "Like I said, you'd best git inside, ma'am. We don't aim to hang him on your land."

Molly shook her head and said, "You'll not do it anywhere! These people are our guests!"

"You reckon you can stop us, ma'am?"

There was a metallic snick from up on the veranda, and young Josh called out, "If she can't, I purely aim to try, Mr. Burton!"

The four riders stared open-mouthed at the very young but very determined-looking boy with the Winchester in his hands, and even as Burton started to laugh, little Jessie appeared at a window with a huge horse pistol gripped between her two shaking hands.

The ramrod, Woodley, warned, "These are Zeb Macahan's kin, Boss!"

Burton nodded, but said, "That's not the point. I'm only out to kill one kind of critter, and kids ain't them!"

Touching the brim of his sombrero to Molly, Burton said, "All right, young lady. Seeing as it's your land, and not wantin' to harm decent folks, we'll crawfish off polite like."

Then he turned a hard stare on Jeremiah. "We can wait until he leaves your property. Once he's off Macahan land he's on mine, and that wagon can't move fast enough to clear it in a night and a day! We'll be waitin' for you, Mormon. You can ride high or you can ride low, but whichever way you go from hereabouts, that's where we aim to bury you!"

Then, in a cold fury, Burton whirled his horse and, followed by his foreman and hands, galloped off without looking back.

Jeremiah Taylor sighed and turned to his wife. "Get in the wagon, Maggie. It's time we were moving on."

Maggie gasped. "But Jeremiah! They'll be waiting for us out there!"

"I know, dear, but we're not welcome here, and it's not God's will that these innocent people suffer on our behalf!"

As the frightened woman moved to obey her husband, Jeremiah turned to Molly with a gentle smile and asked, "Before I hitch the oxen up, may I say my good-bye to Laura, ma'am?"

Molly shook her head and said, "There's no need to worry about that right now!"

"But we have to leave at once, ma'am. You ordered us off your property!"

"I know what I ordered, but those men are waiting just out of sight to kill you. We may not agree about religion on a lot of points, Mr. Taylor, but if anything happened to you and Maggie it would be my fault. You'll just have to stay for now."

"Are you certain you're being wise, Miss Culhane? You have to think of the children, and it's not your fight."

"I'm making it our fight, then. Besides I don't think they'd dare attack you on Macahan land. That Mr Burton can't hold a candle to the children's uncle o: big brother when it comes to remembering dead kin folk, and I'm sure he knows it, too."

Jeremiah Taylor swallowed and murmured, " don't know what to say."

"Just say you'll stay until Zeb or Luke get back. None of us have any other choice!"

"Yes, ma'am, but, if you'll allow me, I'd like to thank a great lady, and some very brave young men and women!"

Molly shrugged, turned to the house, and shouted, "Josh Macahan, I ought to whip you, and your little sister too. Put those guns away this instant!"

As the children vanished into the house, abashed, Laura came out to join Molly and the Mormons, sobbing, "Oh, I was so frightened. I'm sorry we had such ugly words before, Aunt Molly!"

"Laura, will you for God's sake get inside? We have to move the wagon around to the back of the barn and prepare ourselves for a silent siege!"

Back up on the rise, Burton reined in once more and snapped out to his ramrod, "Woodley, I want this homestead surrounded by at least a corporal's squad of our best guns! I want 'em here at all times, day and night, savvy?"

"Sure, Boss. What do you want the boys to do iffen that Mormon makes his play?"

Burton's voice was cold and hard as polished steel as he said, "I want 'em to wait until the Conestoga wagon's at least a mile off Macahan property. Then I want that wagon burned."

"Sure, Boss. And the Mormons?"

"I want 'em held while someone comes to fetch me. I'll be riding in with a couple of ropes."

Woodley looked surprised and said, "A *couple* of ropes, Boss? Do you mean to say you'd string the woman up too?"

"Why not, she's a Mormon, ain't she?"

"Yeah, but, Boss, a woman?"

"My sister was a woman. So were her daughters, my dead nieces. At Mountain Meadows they was murdered and scalped!"

He spit and added, "Stringin' up the old cow alongside her mealy-mouthed husband is lettin' her off lightly, to my way of thinkin'!"

CHAPTER 44

The mysterious stranger Hale Burton had questioned
in the Elk Creek Saloon sat his black mare quietly as
he watched Burton ride by from the deep shade of the
lodgepole grove. The other riders were drifting back
from the Macahan homestead, too. The stranger
chewed his unlit cheroot and thought about that. From
where he'd watched the scene in the Macahan yard
he hadn't, of course, been able to hear a word. But
he could guess from the later actions what the conversation had been about. The stranger unlimbered
his sidearm and checked his brass. It was simply a
nervous habit. He knew how many rounds he had in
his guns.

He ran a thumbnail through the stubble on his angu-
lar jaw and mused, half aloud, "All right, they reckon
Zeb Macahan and the oldest boy are just too big a
boo for a frontal attack. That means a siege, and
since the wagons round in back and the oxen are
grazing in the meadow, I don't figure all that much
is fixing to happen hereabouts for at least the rest of
this night."

He patted the neck of his mare and added, "What
do you say to havin' supper with me, old gal? We got
us some work ahead of us, but it can keep till we've
et, back in town."

Down at the homestead, things were getting back
to normal with amazing suddenness. Young Josh left
off his weeding in the garden to run inside to Molly,
blurting out, "That fool Laura's sparking with that
Jeremiah agin, Aunt Molly!"

"Have you finished your chores, dear?"

"No, ma'am. That fool sister of mine is over by the barn, jawin' and talkin' with that Mormon and his old wife agin'!"

"I know, I saw it from the window. You'd better get back to work if you mean to finish by suppertime, Josh."

"Aunt Molly, don't you aim to put a stop to that there foolishness?"

"I'm not big enough to tie her up, Josh. I'm hoping letting her get friendlier with the young man's wife might help to clear her head."

"But Laura and old Maggie like each other, Aunt Molly! I seen them just now, laughin' and a-cuttin' up with Jeremiah! You got to put a stop to it, Aunt Molly! You can't let Laura marry up with Jeremiah, it just ain't naural!"

Just then young Jessie came in, buttoning her apron. She'd heard part of the conversation, and her own two cents' worth was, "You're not going to let her do it, are you, Aunt Molly?"

"Jessie, Laura's a young woman now. What do you think she'd do if I simply stamped my foot and told her I said no?"

"She'd likely run away with him, I reckon. Laura can be muley once she makes her fool mind up."

"I know. I think she'd run away, too."

"But, Aunt Molly, you know Laura's not cut out to share a husband with no two other gals!"

"You're right, Jessie, your sister is too immature and possessive to have an easy time in the most normal of marriages. But she's proud, too. Too proud to ever admit a mistake. Even if she were miserable with Jeremiah she'd try to stick it out. And if she had a baby . . . Well, our only hope is that she'll come to her senses by herself. I'm afraid I really messed things up by losing my temper with her earlier. There's nothing like having to defend a man to convince a girl she's in love with him!"

Josh shook his head and said, "We can't go along with it, Aunt Molly. It just ain't right!"

"We're all agreed on that, Josh. But we've got to stop driving her right into that young man's arms by opposing her so openly and so hard. Part of what she thinks is love is simply stubborn pride. We'll only drive her away from us unless we use our heads!"

Josh sighed. "But what can any of us *do*, Aunt Molly?"

Molly Culhane thought and suddenly said, "Jessie, would you go out to the wagon and tell Laura I want to see her? Tell her I'll be in my room."

"Yes'm. What do you aim to do, give her a good whippin'?"

"No, dear. Sometimes you can catch more flies with honey than you can with vinegar!"

When Laura came into the house she found her aunt waiting for her with an old but lovely wedding dress spread out on her Saratoga trunk. As Laura gasped at the beautiful sight, Molly smiled up at her and said, "Seems only yesterday I walked down the aisle in this."

Then she picked up the wedding gown and held it against a surprised Laura, musing aloud. "It'll need some new lace, and of course some ribbons."

Laura was close to tears. "Aunt Molly! Do you really mean it?"

"Well, I've had my say, but as long as your mind's made up, you may as well do it right, dear. I don't suppose it would do any good to ask you to wait a few weeks, until your Uncle Zeb and Luke can get back?"

"I wish we could, Aunt Molly, but Jeremiah, Maggie, and I was just talking about that. He says we must be on to found his new settlement, and I do so want to be a part of his dreams for that!"

"But, child, you know Hale Burton and his men are all around the spread. You can't leave now! Wait until your Uncle Zeb returns!"

"Aunt Molly, Jeremiah's not afraid of those cowboys. He says there's danger everywhere, and that we must all trust in God's mercy. What kind of a wife would I be if I couldn't be as brave as my husband and sister in Christ?"

"Oh, is that what you call Maggie now?"

"Yes, ma'am, it's the Lord's will that we all love one another."

"Hmmm. Why don't you try on this dress, dear. I have a few chores to do before suppertime."

Leaving Laura to moon over the dress, Molly went out to the Conestoga, where she found Maggie attempting to tidy up the cluttered interior. Molly said, "Good morning, how are you feeling?" and Maggie said, "Oh, I'm much better after a few days' rest, and so happy about the coming wedding!"

"You and your husband discussed it, then?"

"Of course. That's the rule. None of our men would dream of taking another wife unless his first wife gave her permission."

"I take it you've no objection, then?"

"To Jeremiah marrying up with your Laura? Of course not, she's a dear sweet girl and it will be so nice to have some young ones about."

"Well, Laura seems to have made up her own mind on the matter, but I'm concerned about the ceremony. I don't know of any Mormon settlements near here—do you?"

"We don't need to hold it in a tabernacle. Jeremiah is a bishop of our church, Miss Culhane. He can conduct his own ceremony anywhere."

"Oh, when one of your men decides he'd like another wife he just up and weds her on his own?"

"Not exactly. It's a very simple rite, but naturally I have to formalize it by being there to give my consent."

"It sounds simply charming. And you have no reservations whatsoever about sharing your husband with my niece?"

"How can I make you understand? Why on earth

should I object? Laura's such a loving, wonderful girl. It will be a joy to live with her and Jeremiah."

"What about Jeremiah's other wife? Won't she be concerned, either?"

"Ellen? Why should she? I wish you knew her, Miss Culhane. She's a lovely girl, too, and she'll probably be even happier than I am about the wedding. She'll have someone closer to her own age to talk with."

"Closer to her own age? Just how old *is* this other wife of Jeremiah's?"

"She's only twenty-one. They could almost be sisters. Ellen is an angel. One of the prettiest little things you ever saw, and Ellen's sweet soul is as lovely as her face. I love her as much as Jeremiah does."

Molly's heart skipped a beat as she digested this unexpected development, but her voice was cool as she asked, in a desperately casual tone, "Won't your little sister in Christ be upset by missing the ceremony? I mean, if a Mormon's other wives are supposed to give their consent, it seems as if—"

"Oh, Jeremiah and I were talking about that very thing last night in bed. We'd both dearly love to have Ellen here with us. But she's nigh forty miles away and there's just no help for it. As the eldest wife, I can speak in her name, but it would be nice if she could take part in the weddin', don't you think?"

"Oh, I so agree with you, Maggie! But maybe I can help you, if you think Jeremiah wouldn't mind putting off the wedding for just a little while."

"Put off the wedding? I don't understand, Miss Culhane. Why would we want to do that, now that our plans are all set?"

"I know the three of you would feel better if Laura joined your family without the slightest cloud in anyone's mind, Maggie. Why don't I send young Josh to fetch your Ellen in a fast light shay? I know where we can rent one cheap, and Josh is a fine fast driver."

"Oh, ma'am, that would be lovely. But Burtonville's so far!"

"Nonsense! If Josh left this afternoon he could have Ellen here in less than forty-eight hours!"

"Oh my, wouldn't that be grand? Wait till I tell our husband!"

"Uh, do you suppose he'd object? You might point out it's not safe for the, um, four of you to leave for at least a few days in any case."

"I purely will, Miss Culhane, but if I know Jeremiah there'll be no objections. He loves little Ellen as much as I do, and I know he misses her. I think it's a grand notion, but I don't know how we'll ever be able to thank you!"

Molly smiled like Mona Lisa as she murmured, "Oh, don't mention it."

CHAPTER 45

At the Elk Creek livery stable Josh occasioned some more than a little interest as he rented the light carriage from Mr. Greevy, the liveryman. He had to arrange the care and feeding of his own pony during the trip, and as Greevy got the story a monosyllable at a time from the boy he shook his head as he added his own two cents' worth, opining, "Don't know, Josh. I'm a live-and-let live hombre, but I'll be hogtied with barbed wire iffen I can figure your Aunt Molly goin' along with a Mormon wedding! If it was my own daughter, I'd likely run them Mormons off with a double charge of birdshot in their britches!"

"It ain't our idea, Mr. Greevy. That mule-headed sister of mine says her mind's made up. Aunt Molly and the rest of us are just bein' as friendly as we can in a bad situation."

"Mebbe, but I'd never go along with them Mormon folk degradin' one of my kinswomen, boy."

"I don't like it neither, but I reckon they don't figure it's all that degradin'. I'm off to fetch that jasper's other wife so's she can give her own consent to the fool weddin', and ever'body's over the age of consent, so what the hey? I's pure appreciate you puttin' my pony out to pasture while I'm gone, Mr. Greevy. Old Baldy's likely to miss me some."

"I'll do that, son. Take care with *my* horse and buggy, too."

Josh nodded as he threw his gear and the basket lunch Aunt Molly had made him in the rented shay. Then, with a last farewell, he climbed aboard, cracked the buggy whip, and lit out at a smart pacing trot. Had it been up to him, Josh would have walked the whole way to Burtonville and likely taken the long way round, but Aunt Molly had told him to drive like hell, and though she'd never said why, Josh suspicioned she had her own good reasons. Aunt Molly had turned out smarter than he'd expected, and Josh liked her. So, even though he didn't see why in thunder they needed even more fool Mormons on the spread, the boy was determined to make good time.

Over in the saloon a blowsy bar girl who'd never see forty again was racking half-cleaned glasses behind the bar. Hale Burton ignored the somewhat interesting rear view as he leaned against the bar, drinking himself mean.

The liveryman, Greevy, joined Burton and his ramrod and ordered a bottle with a morose shake of his head, saying, "It jest ain't right. I never thought the Macahans would take up with Mormons!"

Burton's ears pricked up as the liveryman added, "I jest don't savvy how them Mormon gals can abide by sech notions. I reckon most men would git away with sech foolishness if they could. But how in thunder do them Mormons *put* it to their old women? Why, my wife'd skin me alive with a can opener iffen I was to come home with a younger gal and jest say, 'Move over, honey. This here's yore new little sister in Christ!"

Woodley nodded and said, "Damn harem keepers is what them Mormons be! Lyin' wordsmiths, too. They keep mouthin' the Bible like an old hound gnawin' a boot until they twist the words around ever' which ways so's it gives 'em a different gal ever' night! They say Brigham Young keeps a wife for ever' day of the month! Ain't that a bitch?"

Burton shushed him with a look and asked the liveryman, "What's this about the Macahans, Greevy? Them Mormons still out there at the homestead?"

"Sure. I jest rented a shay to young Josh Macahan so's he can go and fetch that Taylor feller's extra wife. Seems the one he brung an' that pretty little Laura Macahan ain't enough for him to keep warm at night. Feller must be randy as a horny old billy goat!"

Woodley sighed. "Whooo-eee! A warm meal and a night in bed with that blonde little Laura Macahan would likely kill me! God knows what I'd do with two other gals at the same time!"

Burton snapped, "Shut up! I wants to hear! Let's git this straight, Greevy! Are you sayin' Laura Macahan's been trifled with by that damn Mormon?"

"Not exactly. She's marryin' up with him!"

"Marryin' up? You mean the Macahans has all become Mormon?"

"Never said that, Hale. Jest said Laura Macahan's marryin' up with him as soon as Josh gits back with the other wife. From what the boy tells me, the family's dead agin' it, but what can anybody do to stop a stubborn gal with a notion she's in love?"

Hale Burton thundered, "By God, *I'll* do somethin' Christian 'bout it! We'll jest invite our own selves to that there wedding!"

Woodley snorted. "Hot damn, won't that be a shivaree!"

"You're damned A! I'll jest drop by with mebbe a dozen riders, and we'll bring some rope and torches along! I aim to give that Mormon three widows exactly thirty seconds after that blasphemous wedding takes place!"

Woodley nodded and said, "And I'll help haul the rope, Boss! But what are we bringin' the torches for, to burn the Mormon wagon?"

"The wagon, the barn, the house, the whole damned spread!"

"Whoooo-eee! You're fixin' to do the Macahan family, too?"

"Cross that bridge when we comes to it. I know I aim to burn 'em out and run 'em outten the county."

"Zeb Macahan ain't gonna take that kindly, Boss."

"Can't be helped. Besides, Old Zeb's off fightin' Injuns. Read in the paper where the Sioux wiped out some folks in the Black Hills. Zeb's a scout, and he won't git back for some time, iffen he ever gits back at all."

As the cattle baron made his vocal plans at the bar, the doxy, Anna, waddled across to where the mysterious stranger calling himself "Smith" sat quietly in a corner at his usual table.

Anna asked the stranger, "You want another, mister?"

Smith shook his head politely and said, "No. I'm set for now."

Anna ran her fingers through her not-too-tidy hair and batted her eyelashes at the lean and hungry-looking man, saying, "I've been sort of watchin' you, mister. You looks like you're waitin' for somethin'."

"Maybe I am. Sounds like the boys are planning some fun for the weekend, don't it?"

"Who, that drunken cowpoke, Burton? He's just a lot of talk. Lissen, mister, I noticed you don't have no gal. I mean, iffen you're lonely . . ."

"I'm used to being alone, miss. Goes with my line of work."

"Do tell? Nobody here in town seems to know just what line of work you follow, Mr. Smith."

"Is that so? Well, it's likely because I haven't said."

He yawned and looked at his pocket watch before

he downed the last of his drink and added, "I'll be in my room, upstairs, should anybody calling me Smith come looking, miss."

Anna nodded with a secretive little smile as the tall stranger got to his feet, dropped some loose change on the table, and sauntered out of the room.

An hour later found the stranger fully dressed in his sinister black togs, seated at the window of his tiny room with a cheroot between his teeth as he cleaned and oiled a six-gun.

There was a soft rap on the door.

Smith snapped the loaded and freshly primed cylinder of his long-barreled Walker Colt in place and glided on the balls of his feet to the door. He moved to one side, out of the possible line of fire, and flipped the barrel bolt of the door with his free hand, saying, "Come in. It's open."

The door opened inward and Anna entered, freshly made up, with one shoulder exposed above the neckline of her loose but amply filled blouse. She licked her painted lips and said, "Howdy. I told the bartender I'd be gone an hour or so. He, uh, understand how it is."

"Is that so? Just how is . . . it, Anna?"

"Well, you know. You're lonesome for a little company, right?"

"Mebbe, when the company looks interesting."

Smith holstered his gun as Anna moved to the side of the bed in the little cramped room. Smith smiled crookedly and reached into his pocket. Then he placed a crumpled greenback on the dresser and smoothed it flat with his long fingers as Anna watched.

She smiled in delight at the size of the denomination and began to unbutton her clothes, saying, "I reckon I can stay longer than an hour after all. You want it all off, or do you like it with the lace stockin's and garters left on?"

Smith reached for a bottle on the same dresser and asked, "Join me in some decent brandy, Anna?"

"Sure, I understand. Some men likes to have a few

belts first. I'm used to this sort of thing, but some of you boys seem a mite nerous at first, so . . ."

"Anna, I'm not nervous. Leave your clothes on."

"Huh? You want to do it with my clothes on? Well, I aim to please, if that's your idea of pleasure, mister."

"Brandy?"

She took the bottle. "Sure. Mebbe if we both git drunk I'll understand."

"There's nothing to understand, Anna. I don't want you that way."

"You don't? What's the matter with me? Don't you think I'm pretty?"

"You're a handsome woman, Anna," he lied. "You may find this queer, too, but I happen to be a very moral man."

"A moral what? You're talkin' crazy, mister! What are you paying for if it ain't the usual?"

"Your company, Anna. Your company's for sale, isn't it?"

"Well . . . sure!"

"All right, have a seat in that chair by the foot of the bed."

The whore sat bemused in the straight-back bentwood chair as the tall stranger went back over to the window with a glass of brandy he'd poured himself and stared out into the street through the shabby lace curtains.

After a time he asked, not looking at her, "How well do you know the Macahan family, Anna?"

"Don't know 'em all that well. We ain't in the same business. I see 'em around the town sometimes."

"Are they Mormons?"

"Mormons? Hell, they're Christians, like most ever-'body hereabouts."

"I take it you don't think much of Mormons, then?"

She took a swig and wiped her lips with the back of her hand, asking, "What is there to think? Don't care much for their ways. You're huntin' Mormons, ain't you, Mr. Smith?"

"Who told you that, Anna?"

"Oh, there's always talk 'bout strangers in town. It don't make no never mind to me. You're sort of nice-lookin', and I knowed you was generous afore I come up here."

"I see. Well, let's just say I'm interested in Mormons, Anna."

"They do somethin' to your kin, like they done Hale Burton's? I can tell you're on the prod, but you purely act so strange."

The stranger's low voice reminded Anna of the dangerous purring of a great lazy cat as he mused, half to himself, "We live in strange times, Anna. When I was a boy, life seemed simple. You thought about getting by with hard work and the help of your neighbors."

"I know. You never said where you was from, mister."

"It doesn't matter. It was the same all over in those days. Things aren't like that today. Today folks are too busy worrying about each other's ways to think much of helping one another. Maybe it's because things have gotten easier, with most of the Indian troubles settled. Maybe it was the war. People all went a little crazy during the war."

"I remember. Was you Yank or Reb, Mr. Smith?"

"Let's say I was a survivor. The war didn't prove much, after nearly a million boys from North and South laid down their lives because our leaders were too stupid and too stubborn to talk things out."

"Well, the war's over now, and like you said, times is easier in some ways." She looked down at the shabby finery of her once-expensive red satin shoes and added wisfully, "In other ways, it's gotten tougher. I don't fret myself thinkin' on the might-have-beens, of late."

"Nobody bothers to think much any more. Maybe that's what wrong with the country today. The world's changing so fast around us that there's hardly time to think things through. We have to just move, and move pronto, just to keep our heads above water."

"You sure talk funny, and you looks so sad. Are

you sure it ain't my looks? I knows a little water has passed under the bridge, but what I lack in looks is made up in motion. I can move it like a saloon door on payday for a man I cottons to."

Ignoring the invitation, Smith continued. "We've been taught to hate people before we've even seen them. Before we know who they are and what they're really like. Then the hate comes back at us like an echo off a wall. We're born into this world with the battle lines all drawn for us. By the time we learn to talk, we know what side we're on, and so few of us ever bother to ask if it's the right side!"

"Listen, I ain't as old and wore out as I may look to you. I caught this, uh, illness off a dirty old man who said it was jest an itch, but the doc says I'm cured."

"Maybe humans are just wild animals at heart. Could be we're just born with an instinct to kill and all the rest of our high-sounding excuses are just the growlings of the wolf pack."

"My body's still right young-lookin' under these fool duds. I never had no kids and I'm right firm for my age, which ain't all that much, you understand."

This time the stranger heard her words, or perhaps realized she wasn't interested in his. He moved over to her and lifted her chin with his strong fingers, noticing the tears in her eyes.

His rawboned, wind-tanned face softened with bemused compassion as he said, "I think you're sort of nice, Anna. And you were right. I am lonely. More lonely than you could ever understand."

She pouted. "But you don't think I'm pretty, do you?"

"Don't see you as the pretty kind, Anna. 'Handsome' would be a better word. I'd say you were one handsome woman."

"Is that the truth, or are you just funning me?"

"I don't make fun of people, Anna. Our world is cruel enough without our adding to it with cruel jokes. The joke God played on all of us is cruel enough."

"I know. About the lonesome part, I mean. I don't rightly savvy much of what you've been sayin', but, Lord, I do know lonely."

He bent to kiss her gently on the forehead. Anna took his wrist in both her hands and murmured, "Come on, let's talk some more in bed."

"I just paid you for your company, Anna. I don't much like the joke you girls play with staring at the ceiling, hating every minute of it."

"Sometimes, when a man's nice-lookin' and sort of gentle, it ain't all that bad. Come on, take off your duds and let me treat you right."

"Anna, you don't have to."

"I know, mebbe that's why I wants to. I don't rightly know what half them big words you've been sayin' mean, but I know need, and I want you to forgit all that other hurtin' for jest a little while!"

CHAPTER 46

Over in Three Rivers, Deputy U.S. Marshal Logan greeted the severely dressed older man getting down from the stagecoach with a handshake, saying, "Hope you had a good trip down, Judge Rensen. We've sort of been waiting on you hereabouts."

The judge shot a murderous look up at the shotgun rider lowering his carpetbags to the station porch as he grumbled, "The trip was good as could be expected, with a rough road and a busted thoroughbrace. Rode the last twenty miles leaning like a drunk and getting kicked in the tail by every bump!"

Logan nodded to Bumper, his elderly office janitor, and said, "I'll have your bags delivered, Judge. Why don't we go down to my office and wet our whistles."

"Sounds like the first smart thing I've heard all day, son. What's on the docket for this circuit session, Logan?"

"Light docket, this time, Judge. Big Nose Annie says closing her parlor house down ain't a Federal case, but I done it on account the local constable's a regular customer and our jurisdiction's a mite flexible in a Federally administered territory."

"Hell, I've got more important things to worry about than whorehouses, Logan. Goddamn Sioux are cutting up again, and half the damned army's headed west. Figures to be an interesting season. What else we got?"

"Well, we pulled a dead body outten the river last Tuesday."

"Body, huh? Whose was it?"

"Can't rightly say. Nobody hereabouts could identify it. It was hung up on a sand bar and sort of gamy. Been in the water some time, I'd allow."

"More damn bodies turn up in these parts! We're getting one damn mess of scrofulous characters in these damn mountains of late!"

"Yes, sir, rough bunch movin' west these days. Oh, Zeb Macahan wired he's due in any minute, Judge. Took time off from the Injun war to appear at the hearing today."

"He is, huh? That's the point I'm just making. Bodies floating downstream with nobody to say who killed 'em, Zeb and that woman sayin' he killed two men and not body one to show for it. It's sloppy, Deputy! Sloppy as all hell!"

"I know, and the gal's story is a mite fishy, too."

"I read your telegram. Where's this Beth Smith now?"

"Under house arrest at the hotel. Every time I talk to her she gives me a new story. I can't seem to get any place with her, Judge!"

Rensen frowned and snapped, "I'll get somewhere with her! I think I'd like to question her before Zeb

Macahan shows up. Get a sworn-to statement before they can put their heads together for an agreed-on version."

"Good idea, Judge. I'll have Bumper fetch her from the hotel after he tends to your belongings."

The idea might have been a good one, but it didn't turn out simple.

When Beth arrived at the marshal's office she seemed composed but cagey. As Logan brewed coffee for all, the judge presided behind the deputy's desk and read off her first statement from a ledger. Beth listened from her seat across from him, hands folded in her lap and a carefully blank look on her otherwise pretty face.

When Rensen had finished, Beth nodded and said, "I would say you have it all correct, sir."

The judge studied a page and mused aloud. "Traveling between various jobs, teaching school in different settlements, eh?"

"Teaching is my profession, Your Honor. I don't see why you insist on questioning it."

"Miss, uh, Smith, I can question anything I've a mind to. You say you were teaching school near White River when those men kidnapped you."

"I may have . . . No, I did not say White River."

Logan looked up from his coffee-brewing. "You did so too, ma'am! I got it down in black-and-white!"

Beth shook her head and said, "You may have oversimplified my statement, Deputy Logan. What I meant to say was that I was *passing through* White River when it happened. I never meant I was teaching school there."

Rensen's tone was sardonic as he nodded and said, "Moving on, was you? You seem to move a heap, Miss Smith. Likely that's why nobody saw fit to report you missing. According to these reports, nobody said word one when you just vanished, sudden like."

Beth shrugged and said, "That's easy to explain, Your Honor. I'd said good-bye at the last place I was employed and was on my way to yet another when those men grabbed me. Naturally, nobody at either end missed me. Travel's so slow out here, and a few weeks either way—"

Logan cut in. "You see what I mean, Judge?"

Rensen nodded and with a smile asked Beth, "Miss Smith, perhaps you can enlighten me. Why is it I have this funny feeling that talking to you is like trying to hang on to a greased hog?"

"That's not a very flattering simile, Your Honor. And now may I ask you something? Why must I go over this so many times? I've given my statement to Deputy Marshal Logan, many times."

Logan snapped, "Yeah, and every time it's a brand-new story!"

"I'm sorry if your badgering confused me, sir. I thought my words were simple and to the point!"

The judge shushed them both and said wryly, "It's simple to the point of saying very little, Miss Smith. But let's get on to Zeb Macahan's statement. Briefly, he's stated that while traveling through Kettle Meadows he came across two hide skinners who were holding you a prisoner. The third man you say abducted you was not present. In attempting to free you, Macahan was forced to kill the two hide skinners."

Beth nodded firmly and said, "Yes, that's exactly the way it all happened, Your Honor."

"Then Macahan brought you here to town, where your minor injuries were treated by Dr. Cox."

"Of course."

"I see. Tell me, Miss Smith, did you know Zeb Macahan before? I mean at any time prior to his freeing you from those kidnappers?"

"Uh, do you mean had I heard of him before?"

"I do not. I ask you point-blank if you ever knew Zeb Macahan in the past. That's a very simple question, if you'd just be good enough to answer it, my dear."

"I am not your dear, and I'd like you to please tell me what possible difference it could make if I'd ever met Mr. Macahan before he rescued me."

"There's a great deal of difference, Miss Smith. By the way, is 'Smith' your real name?"

"Of course it's my real name!"

Before the judge could pursue the matter further, Logan, nearer the window, cut in with "Uh-oh, Zeb Macahan! He just rode in, Judge!"

Beth got to her feet with a relieved smile as an annoyed-looking Zeb Macahan stomped in. The judge said, "Resume your seat, Miss Smith, you're still under oath."

As Beth sat down, Zeb nodded to her, strode over to the desk, and scowled down at Rensen, thundering, "I've rode high and I've rode low! I've just taken time out from a full-fledged Indian War and I aim to get back sudden! What in the hell's wrong with you damned fools?"

The judge blinked and said, "I beg your pardon? You're talking to a Federal district judge, sir!"

"Yeah, and it seems like he's been making me out a liar!"

"Simmer down, sir. Nobody said anything about you being a liar. From the way I hear it, calling you a liar isn't healthy. Our only problem here is Miss Smith's part of the statement."

"Well, who the hell cares about what she's done said? She was out like a lamp when I took them two kidnappers apart up on the mountain! *I* killed 'em both, Your Honor. I cannot tell a lie, and I done it with my little bowie! Or, to set the record straight, I shot one of the bastards and put the other one's bowie in his fool chest with an overhand throw!"

The judge shook his head and said, "You don't understand. This is an official hearing on a double homicide, to determine whether there was justification or not."

"Hell yes it was justified. They'd kidnapped her and worse!"

"I understand that part. But there are so many loose ends."

"Well, god damn it! Tie up your fool loose ends and

let's hear no more about it! I've got me some real troubles to tend to up in the Black Hills!"

"All right, suppose we take up the vagueness of your relationship to Miss Smith, here."

"Suppose we don't! What's the charge, Judge?"

"The charge? Damn it, a witness before the court is required to tell anything and everything he or she knows about the case before the court!"

"And the case before this court is a double killing. It don't make no never mind if we jest met up that night or iffen I'd stolen her virginity ten years or more before!"

"Nobody's suggesting fornication, sir!"

"Shoot, you just go and suggest it all you god damned please! There ain't no Federal law agin my takin' this poor gal from this hearing to a Roman orgy and back, and you knows it. If it's all that important 'bout what's goin' on betwixt any man and woman in the territory, I'll take you down to Big Nose Annie's, just down the street, and show you more relationships than you can shake a stick at!"

"Now listen, Zeb. I'm not trying to ruin this lady's reputation. I just want to have a handle on what really happened."

"You know what happened. Had not we told this idiot, Logan, nobody on earth would know them rascals is dead! I killed the two of 'em. This gal here never lifted a finger agin either one, and the way we've acted together before or since can't have no bearing on the case."

"I'm afraid you're wrong, Macahan. There's a matter of motive."

"You know my motive! I killed 'em 'cause they needed killing. If you aim to arrest me for murder you're welcome to try."

"Let me put it another way, then. When you killed those men, it was not because of any prior understanding with Miss Smith, here."

"Now you're right on the mark, Judge. For one thing, she was out like a lamp. For another, I didn know who or what they had hid moaning under them hides. It could have been a man, a woman, or a sack of snakes. They tried to kill me when I started to look. That's when I killed 'em. I never asked nobody's permission first!"

"I'll accept that for now. What happened then?"

"I buried 'em, like I told you. Had not I buried them, they'd have likely left me to rot, but I seen my Christian duty to keep the neighborhood from stinkin'."

Rensen nodded and said, "Getting back to Miss Smith, here, she seems to be reluctant to tell us anything about her past."

Zeb shrugged and asked, "What if she is? Agin I ask you, what's the charge?"

"The charge? Withholding evidence, of course!"

"Evidence of what, that her name might not be Smith? Hell, if ever'body in this territory had to use their right name or go to jail, you wouldn't have the room to put 'em all!"

Beth murmured, "Please, Zeb, I can handle this . . ."

But Zeb said, "Honey, you don't have to answer nothin'! It says so right in the U.S. Constitution these jaspers are sworn to uphold! The only possible charge anyone could make agin a stranger with no job and sech is vagrancy, which ain't no Federal charge, an' besides, if you have over two dollars on you, the local county couldn't make it stick!"

Judge Rensen frowned and said, "You seem to be quite up to date on the law, Macahan."

"I have to be. Life was simple when I fust come out here. Since then the country's gotten cluttered up with nit-pickers who keep tryin' to make trouble over rifles for me and mine!"

"I see. This hearing is suspended until tomorrow, then."

"Suspended? I got to git back to the Black Hills, Judge! You got all you're gonna on them two dead skinners, and the cause of death was me and self-defense!"

"Mr. Macahan, I just heard a case where a trapper who claimed a man had tried to ambush him for his furs had been killed in self-defense. Upon exhumation the body was found to have been killed by strangulation and the rope was still around the neck. This hearing won't resume until I've had Deputy Marshal Logan up to Kettle Meadows with the coroner to report just how those men died."

Judge Rensen got to his feet and stomped out, saying he'd be at the hotel.

Zeb helped Beth to her feet as he shook his head and said, "I knew he was fixing to run for governor! But what about you, Logan? I thought you and me was friends."

Logan shrugged and said, "I'll tell you, Zeb. I believed it the way you and Miss Smith here told it, at first."

"What do you mean, 'at first'? You making me out a liar too?"

"No, Miss Smith here was the one as got me to wondering. The minute you left town she lit out for the livery stable and was set to cover ground sudden."

Zeb turned to Beth and frowned. "Ride out? I told you to wait for me, Beth."

Beth's eyes were pleading as she insisted, "I was coming right back, Zeb. I was only going for a ride out to the lake and back."

Logan snorted. "Listen to her, will you? This gal lies when the truth is in her favor, Zeb! She was wearing trail clothes and had her possibles with her."

Macahan shook his head and said, "We'll talk about it later."

Beth asked, "Don't you believe me, Zeb?"

"I said we'll talk about it later, Beth."

CHAPTER 47

As the grand duke had discovered at Fort Sully, champagne was hard to come by west of the Missouri, but the bottle Zeb had sent up to their room that evening was close enough. He grinned at Beth as he popped the cork and, pouring, said, "At least it's fizzin', sort of."

Beth laughed in the candlelight and said, "Beer was good enough for us back at Bent's Fort, Zeb."

"I know, but we was both fool kids back in them days."

"Was it just puppy love to you then, darling?"

"I disremember the details. I reckon love always hurts the same if it's puppies or old wore-out boots like I'm gittin' to be."

"I know how I felt, Zeb. I set my cap for you the first day I saw you, and it seems like yesterday!"

He sipped at his glass and nodded. "I remember too. First time we met I suspicioned you was the best-lookin' gal I'd likely ever set eyes on."

"That's understandable. You'd just come down off the mountain after living with beavers for five months. You never told me I was pretty, Zeb."

"Did too. Right after I fust kissed you."

"Oh, but that was days later."

"Not all that many, and you've got to admit I made up for lost time, once I come unstuck."

"I admit it in spades, but for the longest time I was afraid you didn't know I was there, or that you'd ever so much as want to hold my hand."

"Well, hell, I was scared!"

"Scared? Of me, Zeb? A man who'd been to the Shining Mountains and back with his hair? The first day I saw you, someone told me you'd already shot it out with Blackfoot."

"Shoshone, too, over in South Pass. Fightin' Indians was easier'n kissin' you the first time. A reckon that's 'cause I didn't want to go all the way with them braves."

"You certainly did with me! I've thought back to those nights a million times since then, Zeb. My Lord, the chances we took! I'll never understand how Pappa missed what was going on!"

"I got a feeling he wasn't all that dumb, honey. Seems he used to ask me an awful lot when I was fixing to go back up the mountain. I had me a hell of a time makin' up reasons for staying at the fort!"

Beth laughed and said, "I know, you were such a dear sweet fool about it, too! Remember the time you put a splint on your leg and hobbled about all month saying you were too banged up for riding out?"

"Hell, it worked, didn't it?"

"It did till Sergeant Cotter caught us climbing up to the haymow."

"Yeah, and you was up there laughing your fool head off whilst I tried to explain to Cotter how I aimed to exercise the stiffness out with some climbing practice!"

They both roared with laughter. Then Zeb shook his head and sighed. "Those were shining times, Beth. The world seemed greener then. Likely 'cause we was a mite green our own selves. Ain't it a shame that bein' young has to be wasted on kids?"

"We didn't waste it all, Zeb. Did you really love me as much as you said you did, back there in yesteryear?"

"You know the answer to that one, honey."

She put down her empty glass and snuggled against him on the bed, staring soberly into the flickering candle flames as she murmured, "It's so strange to remember us as we were then. So many years have slipped by u since then. So many things have happened, and here we are. You a famous scout, almost as well known as Buffalo Bill or Kit Carson, and me . . . Well, things happen."

Zeb trid to brush the uneasy thought back into the shadow of his mind, but it wouldn't stay there. Gently, he asked, "This teaching you've been doing . . . You said along the White River Valley, Beth?"

"What . . . ? Oh, that."

She suddenly got to her feet and walked over to the window, pausing to pour herself another drink. Not facing Zeb, she sighed and said, "I'm what you might call a horse-and-buggy teacher. I sort of travel between farms and settlements—"

"Teaching?"

"Of course teaching. Why do you question it? I may never get rich at it, but it's a living, and I enjoy it well enough."

Then she turned and added, "Why do you keep harping on it, like the others, Zeb? Don't you believe me?"

Zeb shook his head and said, "Honey, it's no never mind of mine whatever you've been doing. Just seems odd the way you can't seem to settle down no place. Good-lookin' schoolmarms are scarce as hen's teeth in these parts, and I'd've thought they'd want to hang on to you some place."

Beth turned again to stare idly out the window into the dimly lit street as she murmured bitterly, "I told you, things happen, Zeb."

"Well, I never heard of nobody gittin' run outten town for teachin' kids the alphabet. You have trouble with menfolks gittin' fresh with you on the job?"

"I can handle most men, Zeb. You were one of the few I never could."

"Well, the important thing is that we've met up agin, after wastin' a few good years. So here's to us, old gal!"

Beth started to turn from the window to return his toast. Then she suddenly froze and gasped, "Oh my God!" as she spotted something or someone from the window.

Zeb was on his feet and at her side with the bewildering speed he was noted for. He caught just a glimpse of a slinking form in greasy buckskins before the man scuttled away in the shadows up the street.

Zeb frowned and asked, "Who was it, Beth?"

"Who was it? How should I know, Zeb? Just some ugly little man, I suppose. Why?"

"He had the look of a buffalo hunter, and he was moving off like he'd just seed a ghost. Who was he, Beth? The third man of them as held you captive up in the hills?"

"I wouldn't have been able to recognize him if he had been, dear. It's very dark out there, and—"

"Beth, don't lie to me! If there's something I should know, something I can help you with—"

"There's nothing you can do anything about, Zeb."

"I'd know that better if you was to level with me, honey. Maybe it's your own business, but it's a mistake trying to live under another name. What happen to you back when the Indians killed your husband and used you as a love toy is long forgot, Beth. Besides, it ain't anythin' to be so all-fired ashamed of. I met a gal in California once, was not only held by Mojave but tattooed by 'em to boot. She was married up with a rancher, and nobody ever asked about her tattooed chin all that much."

"But, Zeb, I'm not married to an understanding rancher. I've made a whole new life, with new friends. It would be too much to explain after all these years."

"Don't see why. You explained to me, and I didn't fall down in a dead faint, did I?"

"You're different, darling. You've been to the Shining Mountains and seen the white buffalo. Most folk live their lives in tidy little worlds with no room for understanding . . ."

"I know. Things happen. We'll just have to figure some way to git that damn judge to buy your story, but you might have picked a better name than 'Smith'!"

Zeb took his gun belt from the bedpost and slipped it around his waist before putting on his jacket. As he picked up his hat, Beth frowned and asked, "Where on earth are you going, dear?"

"Got somethin' I forgot to check on, Beth. But I'll come back with another bottle, in case you're still awake."

"You know damned well I'll be awake!" she answered, with an impish little smile.

He grinned back and said, "I'll try to make it fast then."

He went out and down the stairs, heading over to the livery stable as Beth watched, puzzled, from the window.

Zeb found the liveryman oiling a harness and said, "Evening. I'm lookin' for a hide skinner who just rode into town. Figured he might have stabled his pony with you just now."

"Short feller smellin' of dead buffalo about as far as you can see him?"

"That's him. I'd take it kindly if you could put me on to him."

Zeb took a gold piece from his pocket and plunked it on the table between them. The liveryman nodded and said, "His horse is in back. I got to reshoe him. Been ridden hard. The skinner's name is Growler. Ned Growler. Funny name, ain't it?"

"Old Ned's a funny feller. You know where I can find him?"

"Sure. Parlorhouse. Said he was pining for a woman, and I sent him over to Big Nose Annie's. From the way he was talkin', he's likely to stay there till his money runs out."

Zeb thanked the liveryman and ducked out the door. But he'd moved only a few paces up the walk before he spied the buckskin-clad figure he was looking for, coming his way at a fast walk, head down and keeping to the shadows as he warily eyed the façade of the hotel across the street.

Zeb slipped into a narrow space between two buildings and let the skinner pass. Ned Growler entered the open door of the lamplit livery stable and called out,

"I've changed my mind about stayin' the night in town. Are them my horse's shoes a-heatin' over thar in the forge?"

The liveryman put down the harness he'd been working on to point with his jaw at the horseshoes soaking in the glowing charcoal of his corner forge. He explained, "Those are for a freighter's draft horse. I've been heating them so's to spread them for the bigger hooves. I figured shoein' your cayuse later on."

"Well, you can shoe him now. I got to light out!"

Zeb Macahan came in from the darkness, slid the stable door shut behind him, and asked ominously, "Light out to where, friend?"

Growler turned with a frown and asked, "Who the devil are you?"

" 'Devil' might be a good name for me, mister. Why are you in such a hurry to leave town?"

"What business is that of yourn?"

"It's been my business since the lady at the hotel and you recognized each other just now."

Growler went for the gun in his belt. He never made it. Zeb's big hand shot out like a striking sidewinder and ripped it from his side. Then, with the man's own gun, he pistol-whipped him into a corner, sobbing in pain.

Reaching down, Zeb grabbed the skinner by the front of his buckskin shirt, hauled him back to his feet, and grated, "You were one of 'em weren't you! The one who got away!"

"Please, mister! I don't know what you're talkin' about!"

"You know. You recognized the girl in the window. The one you and your friends raped!"

As the skinner protested his innocence, Zeb backhanded him again and sent him flying across the livery stable and almost under the hooves of a frightened horse. The liveryman, who, like everyone else in town, had heard the story, gasped. "By jimmies! Is he one of them skunks who trifled with that lady, mister?"

Zeb nodded and said, "Yep. Seems like he's havin trouble rememberin' it though, don't he?"

The terrified Growler gasped, "What—what—what are you sayin' about me? Have you both gone loco?"

Zeb dragged him over to the forge and bent him over the bricks of the fire pit, snarling, "You might say as I'm loco, friend. Then again, you might say I'm using my polite methods to git the truth outten you!"

Zeb held a free hand out to the liveryman, snapped his fingers, and said, "Hand me a hot iron!"

Growler whimpered. "Wait, for God's sake, wait! What's this all about?"

"You know what it's about. You know what you done to that woman, too, so, once the iron's white-hot—"

"Oh God, please, God!"

"You ain't talkin' to God. I'm likely closer to the devil! I reckon I'll start with the iron where you'll never do it to another woman!"

"Stop! What in hell did she say I done to her?"

"You know what you done, boy!"

"I didn't! I never! I never tetched her! Never got the chance!"

The liveryman handed Zeb a red-hot branding iron. Zeb held it close enough to Growler's face to singe his beard and said, "Tell it, boy. Tell it all just like it happened!"

Growler winced at the heat and stammered, "I never was in on it! Honest to God I wasn't! I never knowed they even had the gal with 'em when I jined 'em at the forks!"

"Forks? What forks?"

"The North Forks, of course. Didn't she tell you, mister?"

"Just keep talking, 'fore this iron cools an' we have to start all over! You say you met them other hide hunters at the North Forks. Then what?"

"There ain't all that much to tell, damn it! She was too sick for me to tetch her by the time I came along."

"But those others, Krater and Horn?"

"Hell, like the old song says, they'd been doin' it layin' an' doin' it liein', an' if she'da had wings they'd'a done it flyin', but I purely wasn't in on it. I swear to God! As soon as I seed what was goin' on I lit out!"

"All right, let's go back to them North Forks. Your story sounds good, but it won't hang together. The way I hear it, Krater and Horn kidnapped that woman from near White River."

"White River? How could they have? There's no buffalo that far south, damn it. Ain't been a skinner down in the White River Valley for years!"

"Then where did they say they'd kidnapped her?"

"Like I said, near North Forks. They catched her washin' herself in a stream, nekked, and likely lost their haids. I've never been a man fur rape, my own self!"

Zeb stared long and hard into the frightened little man's eyes. Then he lowered the still-hot iron and straightened up, releasing Growler. The skinner sniffed and asked cautiously, "You ain't goin' to kill me, mister?"

Zeb shook his head and said, "Not just now I ain't. Not till I know who's been stretching things a mite, and why. You said somethin' about wanting to go to the parlorhouse before. Why don't you just do that?"

"I don't want a woman now. I jest want to put a lot of miles betwixt the two of us, iffen it's all the same to you, mister."

"I wouldn't like that, Growler. I reckon you'd best stay here in town for a time."

"What, and have you bendin' me all outten shape agin?"

"If you've told me the truth, you've got nothing to worry all that much about, old son."

"Honest, I ain't lied word one!"

"Let's hope not, Growler. There ain't enough miles from here to hell for you to run if I find out different. Now *git*. I've got some other fish to fry this night."

"Can I have my gun back, mister?"

"No. You don't look growed or smart enough to tote a gun, and if you've lied to me, it don't figure to do you all that much good in any case!"

CHAPTER 48

In the alleyway beside the hotel, old Bumper from the marshal's office met the woman calling herself "Beth Smith." Bumper was on his way home from sweeping out Logan's office and locking up for the night. Beth was loading her bedroll on a familiar horse.

Bumper tipped the brim of his hat and said, "Howdy, ma'am. Ain't that Pop McShield's hoss there?"

"Uh, yes, I believe it is, Bumper. He said he'd lend it to me."

"You know Pop McShields, from the parlorhouse, ma'am? I mean no disrespect, but McShields is . . . uh . . ."

"I think 'pimp' is the word you're looking for, Bumper. Don't worry, I'm not stealing the horse. McShields and I have . . . a relationship."

"Do tell? Well, I never . . . You ain't one of Big Nose Annie's workin' gals, is you?"

"I haven't time to talk. Look, I have a note here. Would you make sure Zeb Macahan gets it, Bumper. It's important."

As the old man nodded, she handed him the folded note and mounted the horse. Then, not looking back, she spurred off at a gallop and was soon out of Bumper's view.

He shook his head and marveled, "Do Jesus! Who'd

have thunk it? One of 'em like *that* would be worth a month's pay!"

On the other side of the hotel wall, Judge Rensen and Deputy Marshal Logan were drinking quietly at a corner table. They'd gotten around to the subject of Zeb and the girl again, and the judge was saying, "I'll concede your point about Zeb telling it as he saw it, but we all know the woman's story is as twisted as a sidewinder's trail in sand. I doubt if there's an honest bone in that shapely form of hers, and I'm a man who's studied the female form in as much detail as the Lord and my old woman have allowed!"

Logan said, "I'm sure you have, sir. But I'd stake my hide on old Zeb's word!"

"So what? If Macahan's telling it like he sees it, she's likely pulled the proverbial wool over his eyes, too."

"Judge, I just don't have an answer to that one. I don't suspicion Zeb's an easy man to fool, though."

"Son, anything that smells as pretty and looks as pretty as that lady can likely turn any man's head till he unscrews it for her. Come to think on it, most women can do that to most men. The Good Lord saw fit to provide 'em with weapons fearsome to behold. How does that line in the Song of Solomon go . . . 'Thy beauty is more terrible than an army with all its banners'?"

"They got us whupped afore we start, I reckon, sir. Likely the reason I try to stay clear of 'em."

"Deputy Logan, a woman is the closest thing to heaven as well as the nearest thing to hell most men will ever know. They got just the right equipment to treat us either way!"

"Well, I'll allow the, uh, equipment comes in handy, used in moderation. I like a little peek at the heaven part occasionally."

"Occasionally, son? Damn it, boy, nothing on this earth can compare to it. Except maybe the joy of watching a hoss thief's legs thrashin' when you've strung him up legal!"

Before Logan had to answer that, Zeb Macahan came in, wearing a scowl and holding Ned Growler by the nape of his buckskins. The skinner was protesting, "But you said you'd done with me, damn it!"

Zeb shoved him in front of the judge's table and snapped, "Let's say I changed my mind. I won't be quite done with you till you've told the judge the whole story!"

The buffalo skinner sniffed, wiped a hand across his bruised face, and said, "All right, I'll tell him, damn it! Jest don't go hittin' on me ever' other word!"

He told his story to the judge and deputy. When he'd finished, Zeb handed the judge the note from Beth. He said, "Bumper gave this to me outside. That's why I ran after this runt and brought him back. It sort of all fits together now, fool that I am!"

The judge smoothed the paper out and read: "Dear Zeb: There's so much I can't explain to you. I thought you were dead and, well, like you said, things happen. I'm sorry about the lies I had to tell you. Sorry for a lot of things it's too late to mend now. I can only say I have always loved you and always will, no matter how you must feel about me now. Please forgive me, if you can find it in your heart to remember the innocent girl I once was. Beth."

As the judge handed the note to Logan, Zeb said bleakly, "Bumper says she just rode out, on Pop McShield's pony."

"McShield? The man who plays piano in the house of ill repute?"

"Yeah. Answers us a lot of questions, don't it?"

Judge Rensen nodded and said compassionately, "Well, as she said, things happen. The fact she ain't a schoolteacher after all has nothing to do with your killing those two weasels, as you aptly named them."

Logan had finished with the note and handed it back with a frown, asking, "But how could they have been guilty of rape iffen she was . . ."

"What the lady might have been is not the question." The judge sighed. "The statutes on rape are

quite specific. You're not supposed to do it to *anybody.*
Besides, Macahan here acted in good faith, and hell,
she *could* have been a schoolteacher!"

Zeb said, "I'd like to git it over with and forget it,
Judge. I'll ride up with you at daybreak and show you
where I buried the bodies."

But Judge Rensen shook his head and said, "No,
son, as far as I'm concerned, this case is closed."

Logan asked, "What about McShield's horse? Don't
you want me to ask if she borrowed it or stole it,
Judge?"

"No. I don't much care. If McShields led a cleaner
life he'd likely keep better tabs on his property. Unless he files a charge, I'm willing to leave that sleeping
dog alone. Besides, I have the odd notion Zeb, here,
might be thinking of riding after that horse to, ah,
discuss its ownership with the lady."

Zeb thought a wistful moment before he shook his
head and said, "I might, I might not. Some questions
are best left unasked, most likely."

"Ah, then you do intend to just forget her?"

"I'd purely like to, Judge. Only, somehow, I doubt
I ever can."

CHAPTER 49

Nobody ever rightly remembered just who had built
the little shack on one of the foothill rises overlooking
the Macahan homestead. It had been there when the
late Kate Macahan and her children had come west,
and since it wasn't on their claim, they'd never paid
much mind to it. Once Josh and Jessie had walked up
the hill to explore it, when they'd first arrived. They'd

found it empty save for wasps' nests and the stale, dusty, vinegar smell of spider webs. It was too far to visit often, and seemed just a smudge on the ridge line from down in the Macahan dooryard.

The old shack wasn't empty any more, however. The gun hands called Banes and Plante had been using it for a lookout since Hale Burton had posted them there to watch the Mormons.

They'd brought some crates, folding cots, and other crude furnishings in under cover of darkness and were making themselves at home. Very much at home, as the row of empty bottles on the shelf above their seated heads now testified.

They were seated on boxes at a small folding camp table, playing poker for matchsticks and from time to time casting a glance down at the Macahan spread through the partly-boarded-over window on that side.

Plante displayed a winning hand. "Ladies and sixes."

Banes sighed. "You sure you ain't got them cards marked, boy?"

"Hell yes, I always cheat when I'm playin' for matches. Did you hear somethin'?"

Then both of them stiffened. There was no mistaking the sound of a rifle being cocked!

Both the gun hands slowly turned to see the mysterious stranger calling himself by the all-too-common name of Smith. He was standing in the open doorway with a cocked rifle in his hands and a six-gun hanging at his side.

Before either of Burton's men could ask what he wanted, Smith said, "You two had best pack up and *git!*"

Banes gasped. "Git? We're workin' for Hale Burton mister!"

"You just quit. Get your gear together and get outten the county! Come on, move your tails afore I shoot 'em off!"

The two gun hands stared at him in disbelief, so Smith started shooting. He shot the deck of cards off the table between them in an explosion of tattered pasteboard. He shot a can of beans to a big wet brown blob in the air. He shot high and he shot low as the two frightened hands scrambled for cover behind the little table. Then he commenced shooting the bottles over them as if they'd been lined up in a shooting gallery, showering the wildly protesting Banes and Plante with shards of broken glass.

As he finished emptying the rifle for effect, he dropped it to his side and whipped out the six-shooter in a metallic blur of motion, saying, "Ain't got time to waste on you pilgrims. You fixin' to get aboard your broncs and ride, or do you aim to die right here and now?"

Banes made the mistake of reaching for the gun belt he'd been careless enough to hang on the end of his cot. The six-gun roared, and the belt exploded into tattered leather as the holstered gun it had held dropped to the floor with a dull thud.

Banes snatched his hand away as if it had been burned. As Plante staggered to his feet with hands raised and a pleading look in his frightened eyes, Banes asked, "Hey, are you *crazy,* mister?"

"Lots of folks has told me so. They may be right. If you're hoping the friend you have covering the Macahan spread from down the slope is likely to slip up ahint me, forget it. Him and me has already discussed his future movements on this here planet. He's likely halfway outten the territory by now. I, uh, had to scare him some afore he'd listen to sweet reason."

"Thunderation! What do you want from us, mister?"

"I want you to do as I say. Have you both got wax in your ears? You aim to go on living, you'll be moving on with the fear of God in your black hearts!"

"Hell, you can't run us out. We're on Boss Burton's land! Just who do you think you are?"

"You can call me 'Death,' if 'Smith' don't take your fancy. I'm tired of talking, but I'll say it one more time. You can move or you can die, so what's it gonna be?"

Plante edged toward the other door, on the far side of the shack, saying, "Hell, you got the drop on us, so there's no other sensible answer we can give. But Hale Burton ain't gonna like this much."

"You let me worry about Burton and just keep riding if you value your own hides. I'm telling you with sweet reason that I'll kill you on sight the next time I see either of you this side of the county line."

As Banes began to follow his frightened partner, the stranger added flatly, "Don't either of you stop to say faretheewell to your old boss, either. I'll know if you did, and don't make book on me not being able to track you down!"

Banes, the braggart of the two, attempted to save face, saying, "We're leaving, on account you got us cold, but next time we'll be ready for you, mister."

"No you won't, old son. You see, I'm a killer, not a talker. If you boys do anything dumb enough to make me come for you again, you won't get off this cheap. I'm going through all this foolishness because I'm a man who don't like to kill unless he has to. If you make me think I have to, you won't ever know what hits you."

"I figured you for a hired gun. What do you do when you kill most men, shoot 'em in the back?"

Smith's voice was cheerful, considering, as he said, "Back, front, sideways, it don't make no never mind. Just take my word for it, old son. If I ever see you in these parts again, you'll be dead, and you won't see me at all. I speak sweet reason only once."

Banes nodded, a cold fuzzy ball in his guts as he dropped his eyes from the stranger's catlike stare. There was no sense jawing further. There was nothing to do but light out. Smith, or Death, meant every last word he'd said

CHAPTER 50

Over at the Burton spread, a new foal had been born and was just learning to suckle the mare who'd borne it. A handsome woman watched them fondly as she stood just outside their stall in the darkness of the stable.

Hale Burton came in from the corral and joined his young wife in enjoying the scene. He put his arms around her from behind and nuzzled her neck, saying, "Well, your favorite mare's done proud by you, but do you aim to stay out here all day?"

The woman sighed and said, "Oh, Hale, isn't she beautiful? She's going to be even prettier than her ma!"

"Yep, but neither of 'em can hold a candle to my own sweet kind of mare. How do you feel about serving your old stud, honeybuns?"

She tried to twist free, still smiling. "Now, now, there's a time and place, as the saying goes, but this ain't it, Hale."

"Hell, woman, I don't see nothing wrong with time *or* place!"

"Hale, you fool, be serious!"

The big rancher scooped her up in his strong arms, laughing. "Honey, you ain't never laid eyes on a more serious man than me in your life!"

He carried her over to a stall filled with sweet-smelling new-mown hay and dropped her in it, falling half on top of her.

She gasped. "Hale, please, for heaven's sake!"

"You don't have to say 'please' to me, old woman! I'm ready to oblige most any time!"

"Hale, for God's sake, not here in the stable!"

"What's wrong with here in the stable? Methinks the lady doth protest too much, like that furriner says."

She resisted, but only feebly, as he began nuzzling away at her. Then suddenly she stiffened. "Someone's coming! Good Lord, did you sell tickets to this show?"

Not stopping what he was doing, and thinking it was one of the hands, Hale Burton called out, "Whoever that is, git!" in the no-nonsense tones of a man whose whim is law.

A rifle hammer snicked in the semi-darkness, and Smith said gently, "I sure hate to interrupt important moments like this, folks. But I aimed to get us an early start. You was going to a wedding today, remember? It's my understanding you're bringing a rope as a wedding gift. Shall we look for it?"

Burton's frightened wife said, "Hale, dear, who is this man?"

Burton rose to his feet, growling, "Beats the hell outten me! This Mormon business is my own pleasure, Smith, or whatever in tarnation your name might be!"

"Some people call me 'Death.' "

"Yeah? Well we'll just see who winds up dead hereabouts! How'd you git on this ranch, Smith? I don't pay my hands to let folks creep up on me in my own stable like this!"

"You don't have any hands working for you at the moment, Burton. I took the liberty of running them out of the county."

"You what? Oh, I get it, you're a lawman after all! What are you, a Federal marshal? Take at least a marshal to spook my boys out of a shootout!"

"Mr. Burton, I am a man of sweet reason and infinite patience, as witness I didn't kill a single one of your men. It's true that three got slightly wounded. A fourth was kicked by his horse when he was in too much haste to mount and ride out. A fifth lost a few front teeth before I persuaded him of the error of his ways, by sort of pushing his handgun down his throat a mite, to emphasize a point of order. The others all

agreed with no real violence on my part that workin'
for you just now might be a losing proposition."

"All right, so you're a right spooky feller. What
your game?"

"We'll talk about it as we ride over to the Macaha
homestead. I reckon you'd best start to saddle up
as my angelic patience is gettin' a mite wore out."

Burton's wife shook her head in wonder as, smooth-
ing her dress with a bashful blush, she asked, "Youn'
man, do you mean to tell me you ran every one of
those gunslingers my husband hired off this ranch?

"No, ma'am. I ran them outten the country. Wasn'
too hard, being they was cheap help to begin with
and I thank you for the 'young man.' Most folks ca'
me awful things."

Burton said, "Stay out of this, honeybun." But hi
wife persisted.

"I told you we were getting more mouth than gu'
when you started hiring those drifters, Hale. If yo'
really mean to start these wars of yours, dear, you'
do better to hire an obvious professional!" She dim
pled at the man in black. "When this business yo'
have with us is settled, whatever it is, would you con
sider working for us?"

"Work for you, ma'am?"

"Why not? My husband and I are the biggest an'
the richest. We pay the best wages, and like to thin'
we have the best help."

Burton looked at his wife as if she'd gone insan'
and blurted, "Hey, honeybun, the man is holdin'
gun on me!"

"Oh, don't worry about it, dear. You can see he'
not given to rash moves, and you know what the'
say—if you can't whip 'em join 'em. How about i'
young man? We need a real man to ramrod this out
fit."

Smith pondered before he said, "Don't reckon I'
like to work for your husband, here, ma'am. But as h'
may not live through the day, I may be comin' bac'
this way to talk it over with you."

Then he nudged Burton with the muzzle of his cocked rifle and added, "Let's go, old son."

He sounded as if he meant it. So Burton did as he was told.

CHAPTER 51

When the mysterious stranger and Hale Burton reached the Macahan spread, Molly and the children were busy inside, getting ready for the wedding planned for as soon as Josh got back with Jeremiah's other wife, Ellen.

The bridegroom-to-be was out in the yard, helping his first wife, Maggie, put the freshly patched canvas top back on the Conestoga in preparation for what promised to be a crowded but interesting honeymoon trip.

As Jeremiah Taylor spotted Burton riding in ahead of the man in black, he stepped away from the wagon warily, warning Maggie, "Keep clear of me, dearest. It looks like trouble, but we must trust in the Lord's will!"

Smith called out pleasantly, "Jeremiah Taylor? Mr. Burton, here, would like some words with you!"

Burton reined in and scowled down at the Mormon couple as he snapped, "If the truth be known, I'd rather see you in hell! I don't like you, Mormon, but it seems I have no choice." He licked his lips and continued. "I reckon our feud is off. I've given my word you can pass over my land without no harm from me or mine. I still hope someday somebody puts you where you belong, meaning six feet underground, but I give my word it won't be by my hand or the hand of anyone I hire."

As this odd conversation was going on, Molly Culhane had spotted the visitors from a window and come out warily to join the group.

Smith nodded as Burton finished, and said, "Very graciously stated, Hale Burton. But I reckon Miss Culhane and Macahans are due an apology and some assurances they, too, won't have to keep an eye peeled nights for, say, a barn burning under mysterious circumstances, or other unexplained misfortunes."

Burton nodded down at Molly and said, "I never had nothing agin the Macahans. I just gave my words on these damn Mormons, didn't I? As far as I'm concerned, if I can't kill Mormons, I don't want to kill nobody. Nobody but a yaller dog burns barns."

Molly smiled up at the uncomfortable rancher and said, "Then the whole thing's settled. I for one am willing to forget anything any of us may have said in anger and start all over. Can I take it we're still friends, Mr. Burton?"

Burton shrugged and said, "I ain't one for makin' war on women and children, like some Mormons I could mention, ma'am. You got my word I'll not lift finger one agin you or yourn."

Then he turned in the saddle to glare at the stranger and add, "As fur you, Mr. Smith, Mr. Death, or whomsoever. You don't rate promise one from me!"

The stranger nodded pleasantly and said, "All I wanted was your word about these innocent folk. I know you pride yourself on the keeping of your given word, but I just may be riding this way again, some dark moonless night, but if you've kept your word, there's little chance we'll ever meet face to face again."

Burton snapped, "Mister, I purely hope you *do* pass by this way a second time. Sometime when I'm packing a gun! I aim to keep my word to these folks here, but I'm giving you my word too! The next time I see you, stranger, one of us figures to wind up fairly dead!"

"I'm pleased to hear you aim to fight me fairly, sir. I offer you no such assurances. Think about that some dark stormy night when you next take a notion to bully innocent folk."

"We know just where we both stand. Can I go now?"

"Of course, with my regards to your wife and my apology for interrupting your, uh, discussion."

Burton rode out fast, not looking back, his neck beet red.

Molly looked up at the stranger with a smile and asked, "Who are you, sir, a lawman?"

"No, although I live by certain Old Testament laws, ma'am."

Jeremiah had been staring at the stranger thoughtfully since he'd first appeared, and now he nodded and said, "I think I know you, friend. You must be the Avenging Angel called Stover!"

The politely sinister stranger nodded and said, "Some folks call me that, too. I knew you'd have trouble in these parts, Bishop Taylor. I knew what you thought of my methods, too, so I tried to leave you on your own as much as I could."

"Stover, you had no right to interfere in the Lord's Will!"

"Who are we to say what His Will may be, Bishop Taylor? To rest your mind, no one was killed, this time. And, by the way, associates of mine inform me young Josh Macahan and your other wife, Ellen Taylor, were escorted safely and without incident out of Burtonville. They, of course, were unaware they were being guarded. They should be here almost any minute now."

Maggie Taylor blurted, "Oh, how wonderful, the wedding can take place this very afternoon!"

Molly said nothing. She appeared to study her fingernails.

Stover touched the brim of his black hat to both women and said quietly, "I hope everyone enjoys the festivities. And now, as I see my presence disturbs Bishop Taylor, I'll be saying farewell to you all."

As he turned and loped his horse off, sitting ramrod straight in the saddle, Molly turned to the Mormon couple and asked, "Who is he if he's not a lawman, Jeremiah?"

Jeremiah Taylor's face was pale as he said soberly, "He's a vicious amoral killer, ma'am. They say Stover's killed over thirty men, and I believe it! He'll do anything in what he conceives to be his duty."

"What was that about an avenging angel? Was he a member of your faith, then?"

"There's a great difference of opinion on that point, Miss Culhane. You see, like the misguided elder Brother Lee, a small clique of, well, fanatics have taken it upon themselves to protect the rest of us. The so-called Avenging Angels have been excommunicated by the elders assembled in the Salt Lake Temple, but what can I do? One of my own uncles was with Brother Lee at Mountain Meadows, and despite my protests, the Avenging Angels seem bent on protecting me and mine, even against our will!"

"You really do belong to a most odd church, Mr. Taylor. I mean, heavens, I just get used to plural marriage, and now Avenging Angels?"

"Damn it! *Excuse* me, ma'am, but the Avenging Angels are most certainly *not* members of my church! Let me ask you something. Would you consider it fair-minded to call the men who murdered those accused witches in old Salem true to their Puritan faith?"

"Oh, heavens, they were misguided fanatics who . . . Oh, I see what you mean."

"Exactly. Just as the European fanatics who saber Jewish villagers in the name of Christ, forgetting in their hate and madness that Our Savior and His followers were Jewish, can hardly be said to represent the teachings of any Christian church! There are madmen everywhere. No doubt that unfortunate Hale Burton considers himself a decent Protestant. As far as I'm concerned, Stover is at best a fanatic and at worst a hired killer. It's said he drinks coffee, and smokes, too. In my opinion he's simply a born killer with some lamebrained attempt at justification on semi-moral grounds."

"Brrr! Even now that he's gone I have this odd feeling he's still watching over us all. My niece has been asked to share a most uneasy life with you."

"That is true. I cannot guarantee it will ever be any different. Yet, even in the midst of life, we walk with death. It's God's Will, and farther along we'll understand why."

Inside the house, Laura, with little Jessie's help, had finished donning her wedding dress. As Molly came in, Jessie seemed close to tears. Taking Molly to one side, the girl held out her fist and whispered, "I got somethin' for Laura, Aunt Molly."

She opened her palm, revealing a small cameo brooch. As Laura primped, oblivious, in the pier glass across the room, Jessie explained, "It belonged to Ma. She gave it to me just before . . . Well, I been saving it."

She turned to call out, "Laura? Here, Ma would have wanted you to have this, I reckon."

Laura came over, looked down, and felt her eyes brimming suddenly with tears. Jessie worked as hard not to cry as the two sisters embraced for a bitter-sweet moment. Then, still hugging her little sister, Laura said, "I'm going to miss you, brat!"

"I'll likely miss you too, prissy!"

Then, overcome, Jessie suddenly wrenched free and ran out of the room, bawling like the baby she'd been only too short a time ago.

Molly seemed to be having trouble with her own eyes as Laura sobbed and said, "It's all happened so fast, Aunt Molly! I can hardly believe I'll be a married woman before night must fall! I sure wish Luke and Uncle Zeb could have gotten home in time for the wedding!"

Privately Molly wondered if any such wedding could possibly take place with either of the Macahan menfolk present. Aloud she said, "That would have been nice. You're going to make a lovely bride, dear!"

"Oh, Aunt Molly, I'm going to miss you all so much!"

"It's not too late to change your mind, dear."

For a moment Laura hesitated and Molly could hope. Then the girl's jaw set with the determination the Macahan clan was famous for, and she said, "It's too late to even think of it, Aunt Molly."

Before Molly could think of a suitable reply, little Jessie burst in with "Aunt Molly! Laura! They're here! Josh just rode in with that other Mrs. Taylor!"

Molly heaved a sigh and said, "Good. The groom's getting dressed out back in the wagon, with the other wife. Will you run and fetch him, Jessie?"

Laura missed the look in her aunt's eye as Molly added, "Come, Laura. It's time you met your other sister in Christ, you know!"

As Josh drove the rented shay into the yard, Molly and the young bride-to-be stepped out to greet the bride-who-already-was.

Josh reined in and with unaccustomed gallantry jumped down to hold a hand up to his passenger. The other Mrs. Taylor was a petite girl whose face, at the moment, was hidden by her sunbonnet, but Josh was obviously on best of terms with her after their long ride together.

Laura hesitated. Then Molly elbowed her and asked, "What's the matter, jealous?"

"Of course I'm not," Laura sniffed, moving forward in her bridal gown to meet her disturbingly shapely little co-wife-to-be.

She called a greeting. Then, as Ellen Taylor looked her way with a radiant smile, Laura blanched, visibly staggered.

Ellen Taylor was not only young, she was gorgeous. Like Laura, she was a blonde, but her luxurious head of hair was the color of warm honey and set in natural waves. Her complexion was peaches-and-cream, and her elfin heart-shaped face came complete with

huge innocently sultry eyes that seemed capable of
melting most men to mush in their boots. Young Josh
was obviously smitten with adoration as he finished
helping her down.

Molly noticed that Laura had frozen in her tracks,
so she went forward to extend the Macahan welcome
to the beautiful stranger.

Ellen Taylor smiled at Molly and held out her delicate hand, saying, "You must be Molly Culhane. I'd
know you anywhere from the description young Josh,
here, gave me. You're one of the things he constantly
talked about. How nice it must feel to have your
nephew so taken with you!"

"Good God!" Molly thought. "It needed *charm* with
a face and figure like that? Some girls just seem to
get it all, god damn it!"

Aloud Molly said, "We're delighted to have you,
Mrs. Taylor. And this is my niece, the Mrs.-Taylor-
to-be."

But before Laura could say anything, Jeremiah
Taylor came into view around the corner of the house,
hastily buttoning his sleeve. He called out, "Ellen!" in
a happy tone, and the lovely little thing held out both
arms and called back, "Oh, Jeremiah darling, I've
missed you so!"

They ran toward each other, like the long-separated
lovers they were, and met in a tender embrace as
Laura gaped at them, thunderstruck.

Molly glanced at her niece, who stood there dying
in her borrowed wedding gown; though she'd planned
so much of it, Molly died a little for Laura, too. She
really hadn't hoped in her wildest dreams that Jeremiah
would be so blatant about everything!

Pretty little Ellen moved her lips from those of her
ardent young husband and murmured, "Jeremiah,
we're in public and you may be upsetting, uh, my
bonnet," as she shot an arch look in Laura's direction.

Jeremiah kissed her again and said robustly, "Nonsense, my darling. With or without your bonnet, you

could never be anything but ravishing. Now, I want to introduce you to another lovely girl who's going to be your sister!"

Jeremiah turned to where Laura had been standing. He frowned and muttered, "That's odd. She was standing right there."

Molly's eyes met those of the young Mormon wife, and for a tiny moment their female minds met in mutual understanding. Ellen Taylor's eyes were triumphant as Molly murmured, "She, uh, had to go inside. I'll be right back."

She went back to the house and tiptoed up to Laura's room, where she found her niece sobbing full-length on the bed in her rumpled bridal gown, the veil discarded on the floor.

Molly sighed and picked up the veil she had worn herself so long ago. She began to fold it as she sat on the edge of Laura's bed, murmuring, "Honey?"

"Oh, Aunt Molly . . . How could I have been such a fool? How could I have thought . . . Oh God, I don't think I was thinking at all!"

"You were thinking with your heart instead of your head, dear. You weren't the first of us who's done it, and I doubt you'll be the last."

"But, Aunt Molly, he said he loved me!"

"Doubtless he does, in his fashion. He told you he had two other wives already, didn't he?"

"Yes, but I thought—"

"That they were both old and ugly and wives in name only? Face it, dear, you were capable of considering plural marriage only if you could think of yourself as the only bride that really mattered. No doubt that's why 'most every other faith on earth decided long ago on monogamy. You see, your feelings aren't so unusual or unnatural after all."

"You knew what Ellen would be like, didn't you?"

"I suspected. Jeremiah didn't look to me like a compulsive martyr. Being stuck with one old Maggie would be enough for any healthy young man."

Laura wiped her face and sobbed, "Oh, Aunt Molly, how could I have been such a blamed *fool?*"

"You may have been a bit foolish, child, but nobody has the right to blame you. Jeremiah is an attractive, magnetic young man, with the added glamor of always being *right*. It must feel ever so comfortable to know that you and your best friend, God, have everything all worked out in detail."

Laura asked, "Why didn't you tell me, Aunt Molly?"

"If you'll remember, I tried to, dear. You seemed to have your mind made up, and, unlike Jeremiah and so many other people I've met, I just don't know the Lord's Will down to the fine print!"

"I'll bet you sent for Ellen on purpose, hoping it might make me change my mind!"

"Yes and no, or not exactly. I really didn't know what she'd be like or what might happen, but I did think you deserved the chance to meet her before you committed yourself to such a serious step. If a girl intends to share her husband with another woman, she really should make such a choice with her eyes wide open, don't you think?"

"I don't know what to think, Aunt Molly. I don't know what to *do!*"

"Yes you do, Laura. You're going to tell Jeremiah you made a mistake and that you've changed your mind about the wedding."

"Aunt Molly, how can I? What can I ever say to him, to everybody? I'm in a wedding dress! The house is decorated for a wedding, and the wedding cake's been baked! Poor Ellen's come all this way, and I gave my *promise!*"

Molly's voice was firm but gentle as she said, "Now listen to me, Laura. When you agreed to marry Jeremiah you were sincere. You thought you were in love with him."

"But I am in love with him, I think. It's just that . . . Ellen . . ."

"Laura, if you loved him with the sincere, well,

faith he has in communal marriage, Ellen wouldn't
make any difference, would she?"

"I don't know. Maybe I'm just selfish, but she's so
pretty and I saw the way he held her and this ugly
picture formed in my mind and—"

"Laura, there's nothing ugly in the way Jeremiah
feels about his wife, or wives. The young man is per-
fectly sincere in his belief that his way of life is right
and proper. He was brought up to think that way.
You were brought up another. You're simply going to
have to explain that to Jeremiah, and if he has any
true feeling for you at all, he'll want you to be
happy."

"Aunt Molly, I just can't face him now! Won't you
go out and break it to him gentle for me?"

"No, child, I can't. It's your mistake, not mine or
even Jeremiah's. If you ever mean to grow up, you're
going to have to learn what it means to be an adult.
You have to show the courage it takes to face the
embarrassment you've caused others as well as yourself. So dry your eyes and off you go!"

"Aunt Molly, please . . . ?"

"I said go!"

And so, caught between the hard place and the
rock, Laura went.

CHAPTER 52

It was getting on toward maybe ten at night, and the
children were in bed at last. Molly Culhane walked
out to the veranda and sat herself down for a quiet
albeit improper smoke. She knew her society frowned
on a woman smoking, but her late husband had taught

her the soothing habit, and it wasn't as if she were in public.

All in all, it hadn't ended badly, although Molly's nerves were badly frayed. The Mormons had left before supper, Jeremiah a bit annoyed but smugly satisfied he'd only meant to do right by Laura. Old Maggie had seemed saddened by the thought of losing her new little sister, although Molly had detected a certain sardonic contentment in the glorious eyes of pretty little Ellen as they'd said good-bye.

Laura had shown herself to be a brave and proper young lady when the chips were really down, and Molly was proud of her. She was proud of Josh and Jessie, too, for they'd helped her take down the paper wedding decorations without comment and forsworn the golden opportunities presented by their older sister's embarrassment. Josh had asked who was going to get to eat the wedding cake, but, mercifully, it had been when Laura was changing her clothes. Both Josh and Jessie had been surprised at their aunt's somewhat hysterical laughter as she said she'd put it out in the barn for them to eat in secret, and hopefully over a period of several days!

Well, she supposed she could relax again. The strange young Mormon and his wives were free to work out their destinies, safe, for now, from persecution. Laura would get over it all with a little more time and tears. Molly would worry about Luke and Zeb Macahan when she heard just where they were and what they'd been up to. She'd worried and done enough for one day.

Molly bit the tip off Zeb's cigar, taken from the kitchen humidor, and reached into her apron pocket for a match.

Damn! She'd forgotten to bring a light out here. She was comfortably settled in this old rocker, and it seemed a shame to move an inch just now. It was a balmy evening, and the crickets were serenading as the moon rose over the pines of the rise to the east.

But she really would have enjoyed that smoke.

Molly flinched in surprise as a lighted matchstick suddenly appeared, as if by magic, before her startled eyes. A voice said, "Allow me, ma'am!" and Molly saw the match was held in the black-gloved hand of the dark figure who'd stepped from the brushy shadows beyond the porch rail to offer her a light.

Molly put the forbidden cigar to her lips and accepted the light, puffing twice before she murmured, "Thank you, Mr. . . . Stover?"

The mysterious stranger in black extinguished the light, becoming once again a mere dark outline, as he answered, "Some folks have called me that, ma'am. I disremember who I was before the war."

"We thought you'd ridden off. You said good-bye, remember?"

"I remember. I say good-bye a lot. Sometimes I ride here. Sometimes I ride there. I reckon you could say I ride where I'm needed most."

"Why aren't you following Jeremiah Taylor then? Isn't it your job to protect him, Mr. Stover?"

"I protect who needs protecting, ma'am."

"And you're watching over us? But I thought the matter with Hale Burton has been settled peacefully!"

"Likely it has been, ma'am. They say he's a man of his word. We'll know better come a morning or two, won't we?"

"Brrr! You Avenging Angels certainly take your duties seriously. But you know my family and I aren't Mormons, don't you?"

"I know you're gentlefolk, who got mixed up in things you can't understand through the goodness of your hearts. Where'd you get the notion I was one of the Avenging Angels?"

"Aren't you one of those Mormon, uh . . ."

"Fanatics? No, ma'am. I don't hold much with Bishop Taylor's faith. As for the Avenging Angels, the ones I've met have run to beards and Bibles. I used to work for Allan Pinkerton, afore I went into business on my own."

"Good heavens, are you a private detective, then?"

"Never said that. Used to be. The Pinkertons fired me. Said my methods were . . . unconstitutional."

"Then could you tell me who you are working for?"

"I could, ma'am, but I won't. Wouldn't be ethical. Let's just say someone who don't want Jeremiah Taylor killed has asked me to make sure he don't get that way. You likely noticed he's inclined to get into weird situations, with his funny notions about having the Lord in his hip pocket."

"He did strike me as a bit smug about some things. I'll bet the elders in Salt Lake hired you to protect him, right?"

"Nope. Bishop Jeremiah Taylor's been excommunicated from the Mormon church."

"He's been *what!*"

"Excommunicated. Throwed out. That's likely why he's wandering about so much, lookin' for a place to start his own New Zion."

"I can't believe it! He seemed so devoted to the Prophet Joseph and the Book of Mormon!"

"Oh, I reckon he's as devoted as they come. Maybe a little more than the elders in Salt Lake consider healthy or even proper. Like we both agreed, the man's a mite convinced he's on the inside track with God. It sure makes keeping him alive a bitch."

"Mr. Stover, you've got me completely turned around! There are so many wheels within the wheels, I'm ready to give up! I guess I've a lot more to learn about the Latter-day Saints than I thought possible!"

Stover shrugged in the shadows and said, "The Saints is just folks, like most others. They just take religion sort of serious, and religions of any notion seem to attract all sorts of queer birds. John Brown attacked that arsenal in Harper's Ferry and helped to start a Civil War in the name of his God. It's funny, when you think about it, but I can't remember an inquisition or a witch burning run by atheists. Likely God moves in mysterious ways His wonders to perform."

"But what did Jeremiah do to be condemned by

his own church? He was odd, but he didn't seem an evil man."

"Bishop Jeremiah's not evil, ma'am. He's just sure of himself. The elders in Salt Lake condemned him for his views on marriage."

"You mean polygamy? I thought that was a pillar of the Prophet Joseph's revelations!"

"Lots of folks think that. It's caused a heap of trouble for the Saints. You see, Joseph Smith never wrote a word on paper one way or the other. After he and his brother were lynched and martyred, other elders read where Solomon and such had lots of wives and . . . well, it's too complicated to go into. The elders at the Salt Lake Temple have given up on the fool idea."

"Just a minute! Are you saying the Mormons no longer practice polygamy?"

"Not outside the Provisional Territory of Utah. Brother Brigham aims to make Utah a state of the Union, and one of the things it says in the Book of Mormon is that every Latter-day Saint must obey the law of the land."

"But polygamy's against the law almost everywhere."

"There you go, ma'am. That's why Jeremiah Taylor's always gettin' into trouble. The Mormons moved out to the Great Salt Desert so's they could practice their own odd notions without breaking the law of any land. Polygamy bein' legal in Utah. Brother Brigham and the others set up their own land, with its own laws, in unclaimed territory. Now that they aim to become a state, the practice we're talkin' about is bein' discouraged, and it'll likely be forbidden outright, sooner or later."

"But Jeremiah wanted to marry Laura here. Are you saying the wedding wouldn't have been a legal one, even in the eyes of Jeremiah's own faith?"

"Well, I'll tell you, ma'am. Jeremiah Taylor's faith is sort of hard to follow, even for a Mormon, which neither of us is. His reasons for aiming to start his own New Zion are on account he don't see eye to eye with *anybody* on the word of the Lord. They run him out of the Salt Lake Temple for telling Brigham Young he had things wrong."

"My God, poor Laura! She had a narrower escape than I'd even imagined! What on earth is wrong with Jeremiah Taylor? Do you think he's insane?"

"Don't know. Might be crazy. Might be the Messiah he reckons he is. I ain't paid to convert or be converted, ma'am. My job's to see no harm comes to him or his. That keeps my mind busy enough."

"I shudder to think how busy. But they left hours ago."

"I know. I know where they're headed, too. They'll likely be safe enough for now in empty open range. You likely noticed Bishop Taylor doesn't like me all that much, so I like to keep him on a slack leash."

Molly blew a thoughtful smoke ring and said, "It's all becoming clearer to me now. I guess I wasn't the bigot I thought I might be when I tried to put a stop to what I felt was nonsense."

"You just acted like the lady you was, ma'am. Your intuitions about his hasty notions was good ones. Bishop Jeremiah's a caution when it comes to making up his mind on the fly."

"There's one thing left that puzzles me. If you're a hired bodyguard, what keeps you here? The people who pay you to keep poor Jeremiah breathing surely didn't pay you to watch over us, did they?"

The dark sinister shadow sighed gently and said, "No, ma'am. You might say I do some things sort of . . . on the house."

CHAPTER 53

Later that night, many miles away in the Black Hills, a circle of worried men sat in desperate council around the central fire in the camp of Satangkai. Save for a few representatives of the allied Cheyenne Nation, all were high-ranking chieftains of the Dakota Confederacy. Satangkai had summoned, or, rather, invited them to the meeting to decide on what was to be done about the situation.

After laying out the facts leading up to the killing of Count Sergei and his own unthinking declaration of war, Satangkai addressed his fellow chieftains humbly, saying, "My words were spoken in the anger of the moment, but I can never swallow them back. There are many blue sleeves, many, and they have the wheeled guns that spit death from clustered barrels. I could forget the insult of a whip across my face while treating under safe conduct, but one of my young men was killed. He was shot by a blue sleeve who'd sworn no firearms were to be at the meeting. My heart is heavy. My young man's spirit cries out for revenge. I have sworn to the blue sleeves' faces I shall fight them to the death. But, hear me, this is not the fight of any other Dakota or Cheyenne. I think it will be a bad fight. I think my band will lose it, but there are less-honorable ways to die. I have spoken."

As he fell silent, another chieftain stood in the firelight and said soberly, "Hear me, I am Yellow Calf and I will speak what is in my heart. My people have tried to avoid trouble with the strangers. They come to this land and they change it. Where there is timber,

300

they cut it. Where there was once green grass, they overgraze it with their short-haired buffalo with long horns. Or rip it open to the wind with the iron claws they drag behind their animals. Where once the buffalo and other meat roamed in uncounted numbers, they have left a desert of bleaching bones. For they kill like weasels for the pleasure of it and leave the meat to rot. When we go to the posts to trade with them for the food we need they cheat us, and they often abuse our daughters. Hear me, we have tried to love with them in peace. But can a man live in peace with such people? We are like foolish men who have invited thieves to live in our tipis with us! I say throw them out or be left with nothing!"

A dapper Cheyenne with a red quill roach in his oiled hair was awaiting his turn. Now he asked politely, "Has Yellow Calf spoken?"

The older Dakota shook his head and said, "No, hear me further. Satangkai suggests he fight alone and that the rest of us leave this land of our fathers forever. He says we could go far north, to Canada. To live under the red coats of the Great White Mother, Victoria. Satangkai is wise. I respect his counsel. I know he means us well, but I, for one, do not intend to leave these hills where I grew to manhood and dance the sun dance to Wakan Tonka! We have moved before, seeking peace with the strangers who know not what the word means. Our grandfathers dwelled by the Minni-Tonka, where the wild rice grew lush above the heads of the women gathering it in plenty from their canoe. Our grandfathers' bellies were fat with wild rice and venison from the happy forests all around. There were Chippewa, but we laughed at them and beat them as if they were children, until the fur traders sold them guns."

There was a growl of long-remembered grudge from the others, old and young, around the fire. Yellow Calf held up a hand for silence and continued. "Then the settlers came to cut down the happy forest and turn the land upside down with their iron claws. Little

Crow and Red Wing fought them and died. The rest
of us decided it was not a good fight and decided to
join our western cousins on the prairies across the
Great River where the Minni-Ha-Has fall down from
the north. We got horses from the Cayuse in trade
and took them for ourselves from lesser men. We
learned new ways and began to fatten once more on
the buffalo sent to us by Wakan Tonka and the other
spirits, Old Woman, Thunderbird, and He-Who-
Dwells-in-the-Rocks. Then, in our father's time, we
had to move farther west again, here to these Black
Hills, where the dream-singers say Wakan Tonka
rested after creating the rest of the world. Today it is
not our grandfathers' time. It is not our fathers' time.
It is *our* time. I do not wish to move again. I will
die here, where my father's bones were laid to rest
after many fruitless wanderings. I will die where I
was born, here on Wakan Tonka's last gift to his True
People, with my weapons in my hands and my death
song on my lips! That I have spoken!"

There was a low murmur from among the others,
and another man stood up, resplendent in coup feathers and scalp locks. He waited until the others had
fallen politely silent before he said, "Hear me, I am
Medicine Mark and I have killed many enemies. I
have horses. I have many wives. My heart is with
Satangkai and Yellow Calf! When I was very young I
roved the prairie at will, seeking honor. I rode to the
south, below the Cimarron, and stole many horses
from the Comanche! I fought Pawnee by the Great
Muddy River! I stole my first wife from the Crow,
leaving them dishonored by my mischief! There was
nowhere I could not ride, for the world was larger
then."

There was a sigh of nostalgia from the older men
at the fire.

"Now our world has shrunk to this small but beautiful land we still hold, with the promise of the Great
White Father. But the promises of most white men
mean nothing!"

"What about White Eagle?" protested Satangkai, lowering his eyes as he realized he'd been impolite by cutting in while another spoke.

But Medicine Mark was Satangkai's friend and knew his heart. So he nodded and said, "Your friend, White Eagle, is a good man. It is of the others among his people I am speaking. They speak to us of peace with forked tongues. Even as they promise one thing, they send soldiers with guns against us! Hear me, it is a fine clear autumn for battle. I think it is a good day to die. I, too, have spoken!"

One of the Cheyenne delegates rose, his Algonquin accent making it more difficult for him to be as eloquent as he spoke in Dakota, saying, "Hear me, I am Crow Tears. I shall not count coup on the numbers of my slain enemies or how many horses I have. I am speaking for my people now. Long ago, as all of you know, we Cheyenne dwelled far to the east in the game-filled hunting grounds of the once-great forest that is no more. Like yourselves, we were driven out on the prairie to starve, but learned new ways and became new men. We who are known to our enemies as the Cut-Fingers were few in number, and our Dakota brothers took us in as allies. In many a fight, when things looked bad for the Cheyenne, our Dakota brothers have fought bravely at our side! Hear me, when the hunting has been poor and our lodges held no food or blankets, Dakota friends have shared with us. I, too, have hung by the flesh skewers from the sun-dance pole and the one you call Wakan Tonka, known by us as Manitou, gave me a vision in the hour of my pain!"

All eyes were on the Cheyenne as he spoke, now, for visions were important things to consider among the Real People.

Crow Tears said, "It seemed I saw a bundle of sticks, tied together with a blood-red thong. Great Manitou made me understand its meaning. The sticks bound together were the bands of our people, Dakota and Cheyenne. The red thong was blood and battle, binding all together in a bundle too strong to be broken. I think we should keep our bánd of blood and battle and, yes, brotherhood, around us all. I think one small stick is easy to break between the white man's hands. I think we should stay and fight or die together. The Cut-Fingers fight at the side of Satangkai. We have no other honorable choice. Now, *I* have spoken!"

One by one, the other chieftains rose to make their formal declarations. When the youngest warrior of the Dog Soldier Clan had finished, and the formalities were out of the way, Satangkai nodded soberly and declared, "It is settled, then. No one speaks for peace. We shall therefore paint our faces and compose our death songs like True Men. Hear me, we shall fight. Though we win or lose, they shall pay many lives, many, to our medicine and weapons. Let their women keen many songs for their dead. For every young man we lose, make them pay tenfold in blood!"

Yellow Calf said, "You have been chosen to lead us. Tell us where you think we'd have the best fight. Speak. We listen."

"The Pa Sapa would be best, for there the mountains cradle us in arms of steep cliffs. At the Pa Sapa, the blue sleeves will have to come at us in the open, man to man. The riders with the long knives won't be able to use that trick of riding against our flanks as the big guns fire to confuse us."

There was a chorus of agreement, but Satangkai held up a hand and said, "Wait. To reach the place of our best fight holds danger. We have our women and children to consider. We must think of the old ones, whose bones are brittle and who must rest along the way! We cannot reach the mother of the mountains in less than three days, and the army is on the march against us already. If the long knives catch us in the open plains between the ridges, we may die like fish in a drying pond, and the Pa Sapa lies three days from here!"

A new voice from the shadows called out, "The three days you need can be bought, Satangkai!"

Satangkai gasped, "White Eagle! Is it really you?" as Zeb Macahan stepped into the firelight, grim-faced and firm of jaw.

As others made room for him, Zeb hunkered down in council with his friends, saying, "Yes. I have come because my Dakota brothers and their Cheyenne friends are in trouble."

"Then tell us what we should do, White Eagle. Your medicine is mighty and your heart is good!"

Zeb stared into the fire and said, "Hear me, then. I know better than you how the white man thinks and how he fights. Give me some of your young men. Brave men who are not afraid to die. With their help I can harry the long knives for you. I can hold them off your trail until you reach the stronghold of the Pa Sapa!"

"You would do this for us? You would fight against your own people?"

"Who is to say who my people are? I am a man who stands by his word and his friends. If anyone, anyone at all, comes to kill my friend, red or white, to cover up his own mistakes or evil heart, I, White Eagle, shall fight him. I shall fight him if he is my brother. I am bound by friendship more than blood."

Satangkai stared for a long time at the white man, his sober face carved in pipestone even as he fought not to sob aloud. At last he recovered enough to say to the others, "You have heard the words of my brother, White Eagle. He would risk his life and more for us, but it is not just to ask it of him! It is I, Satangkai, who should harry the long knives to buy us time."

Zeb shook his head and said, "No. My brother, Sa-angkai, is brave, but I dispute his wisdom. He does not know the white man's army as I do. Hear me, I have served as a blue sleeve. I have scouted for the men who seek you in these hills. More importantly, Satangkai is needed here, among his people. I am better able to confuse the long knives. Satangkai is your great leader who knows these hills as well as he knows

the palm of his own hand. Every man should do what
he does best. Would you ask a dream-singer to lead
you into battle? Would you want to go on a pony raid
under a Dog Soldier instead of a Crooked Lance, or
ask a Crooked Lance to guard your camps instead of
Dog Soldiers? I, White Eagle, shall play hide-and-seek
with the soldiers. Satangkai should lead you all in
safety to the Pa Sapa. I have spoken!"

There was a murmur of agreement, but, of course,
each chieftain in turn had to rise to make another formal statement of agreement. Zeb had learned to be
patient with his Indian friends. At least, thank God,
neither Red Cloud nor Crazy Horse with their larger
bands had joined just yet with these chieftains from
the eastern slopes of the Black Hills. Despite his sworn
friendship to his Dakota friends, Zeb was in no great
hurry to see an all-out Indian war. He knew, better
than either the proud Satangkai or the stubborn General Stonecipher, where this horns-locked position was
taking both races.

Lord willing and the creeks don't rise, there was
still time to save the situation.

CHAPTER 54

Zeb Macahan sat his pony on a rise at dawn, watching
the long line of Indians file northwest to the higher
country on horseback or travois. A less experienced
scout might have been dismayed at the numbers of the
great procession, but Zeb knew that fewer than a
quarter of the mounted figures were actual warriors
Like any nation, the Dakotas included women, chil
dren, and old folk. Doubtless Satangkai's little army

could fight better if they left their dependents behind, but if the war leader of the Dakota had even considered it, he'd not be leader long, and there'd be no point to having a war in any case.

As he thought of Satangkai, the chief appeared downslope at the head of a small war party. He led the dozen painted and befeathered young braves up to Zeb and reined in, saying, "Many of my young men fought to ride with you. These you see have been selected by me as best for the task White Eagle has taken upon himself. All have counted coup in battle. All have proven themselves disciplined on the buffalo hunt. You will find no young man here who loses his head in battle through fright or too much bravery."

Zeb nodded to the young warriors as they circled him, and was met by friendly smiles. His reputation as a fighting man was known to the young men, and they were honored that someday they would be able to tell their grandchildren of this shining time.

Satangkai held out a beaded buckskin medicine bag to Zeb, saying, "The feather of an eagle. The tooth of a wolf. The musk glands of a fox. A piece of pipestone. A white shell from the Great Bitter Water. They are all good medicine. Take it. No bullet can find you if you carry it with you into battle!"

Zeb took the medicine bag reverently and tucked it away before he asked, "Do any of your young men speak the white man's words?"

Satangkai indicated a bright-looking youth and said, "This is he. His name is Dancing Wolf. He speaks English."

Zeb handed the young Indian a small packet and said, "Hear me, Dancing Wolf. I am giving you the white man's words on paper. I am giving you green paper to pay the people at the end of the singing wire. Do you know where the telegraph station is on the other side of Fort Sully?"

Dancing Wolf took the packet with a nod and said, "I know the way. What am I to do there?"

"First, make sure you ride far around the fort. I

know the soldiers couldn't catch such a man on such a pony, but I don't want them to know or even guess a telegram's been sent. When you get there, give the money to the telegrapher and have him send what's written on the paper. Do you understand?"

"Heya, consider it done!"

Satangkai said, "If Dancing Wolf says a thing is done, it is done, but why? What medicine is on your paper?"

"It is for the eyes of a powerful white man. Many moons ago this man made me a promise. Perhaps he still remembers."

Dancing Wolf asked, "Have you spoken, White Eagle?"

"I have spoken. May the spirits ride with you!"

Dancing Wolf whipped his pony into a full gallop and quickly vanished in a cloud of dust, riding hell for leather with Zeb's message.

Satangkai waited until the boy was gone before he turned soberly to Zeb and said, "May the spirits ride with all of us. I must leave you now, White Eagle. Would it insult you if I begged you to be careful?"

"No. You be careful, too. Your young men and me will be all right."

Satangkai nodded good-bye to each of the small party in turn and wheeled his pony to rejoin the column winding up into the Black Hills.

Zeb turned to the expectant young warriors with a grin and said, "We'd better be on our way. Do any of you know a good campsite well away from the main Dakota party's trail?"

One of the braves nodded and said, "I know a sheltered glade with good grass and clear, clean water. Are we not going to fight with the blue sleeves then, White Eagle?"

"First we have to make our headquarters camp in a safe hidden place. We'll talk about our plans after we get there."

"*Our* plans? Does White Eagle ask for our counsel?"

"Why not? Satangkai said you were among his best, didn't he?"

"You honor us, White Eagle."

"That was my intention. I always honor my friends. It's my enemies who have to watch out for my nasty side!"

CHAPTER 55

Coulee John Brinkerhoff would have said he was just doing his job. It was likely a weasel sneaking into a henhouse might have had his reasons too, albeit more noble ones.

It was late in the day, and Coulee John had a right too be keeping his head below the skyline. He was scouting deep into the Black Hills on General Stonecipher's orders. Coulee John was not a nice man, but he knew his business well enough to have held on to his hair long after he should have been scalped.

Tethering his mount in a grove of cottonwood, Coulee John moved up the steep slope of a hogback ridge, slithering on his belly in a water-worn rill between the tawny clumps of summer-killed buffalo grass.

Belly down, Brinkerhoff eased his head over the edge of the rimrock, hat removed and face shaded by a clump of soap weed.

Down in the glade on the far side, Zeb Macahan hunkered on his boot heels, drawing in the dust with a stick as the assembled braves of his little guerrilla force watched intently.

Alert against surprise attack, but unaware of the white man peeping down at them, another young Indian guarded the ponies, tied head to head a short distance away. Even as they listened to Zeb, some of the Dakota were working on their weapons, rebinding arrowheads or fixing fire bundles to the shafts.

Coulee John had seen enough. Crawfishing back through the grass to his own mount, the treacherous Indian-hating scout rode off on muffled hooves.

A short hard lope away, the U.S. Second Cav was winding its way through the rolling grasslands of the Black Hill's piedmont. The column was moving slowly, for aside from the mounted troopers, there were the caissons, wagons, and carriage guns to consider.

Near the head of the column, under the fluttering red-and-white guidon, Captain MacAllister spotted a distant figure on a rise and said, "Brinkerhoff's coming in, General!"

Brandy Jack Stonecipher nodded and said, "Rest the column, then."

MacAllister held up his gloved palm, and the order to halt was repeated down the long blue line.

Coulee John came down the slope, reined in, and shouted, "Whole Sioux Nation's pulled up stakes, General! Satangkai's likely running fur the Pa Sapa!"

Stonecipher growled, "I'll bite, what in thunder is a Pa Sapa?"

"Busted-up big granite range, back deep in the Black Hills. They packed and moved all through the night and int' morning. Likely figuring the landlord's come to collect the rent!"

"You mean Satangkai's giving up without a fight?"

"Oh, he's in a hell of a good spot for a fight, General! The Pa Sapa's a natural-borned ambush of big growly gray rocks and hidden hidey-holes! He's out to get a good lead on you with his women and kids and old folks tucked away for safety. If you don't catch him afore he's well dug in, he figures to claw you a mite. You aim to follow him to the Pa Sapa, General?"

"I aim to follow him as far as the north pole, or any other goddamn place he thinks he's going! I don't intend to fight the goddamn Sioux every summer until hell freezes over or Washington decides on a consistent

Indian policy! As long as we're out here after Satang-kai, we may as well wrap it all up once and for always!"

Coulee John grinned slyly as he nodded and said, "You an' me is agreed on Sioux, sir. By the by, I spotted Zeb Macahan over on them hills up yonder, too."

Stonecipher frowned and said, "I wish he'd make up his mind if he's working for us or not! Where's he scouting, Brinkerhoff?"

"Uh, he ain't rightly scouting for ussen, General. When I last seed Macahan, he was powwowin' with a passel of Sioux. Crooked Lance Clan, I'd say. Found 'em with their heads together in a valley."

Stonecipher scowled as Zeb's friend, MacAllister, said, "Zeb siding with the Indians? I find that hard to believe!"

Coulee John shrugged and said, "I don't. Always figured that squaw man for a renegade."

Stonecipher's face was grim as he snapped. "Where was Macahan, with the main party?"

"Nope. Like I said, riding with a war party of Crooked Lances. Come on him an' about a score of Sioux in this glade about four miles from here. Jest this side of Three-Scalps Creek. You know the place, don't you, Captain?"

MacAllister nodded, with a puzzled frown, and said, "I know the glade. We'll be passing within a mile of it, General!"

The general nodded, turned to the scout, and asked, "No more than ten or twenty braves with him, Brinkerhoff? You're sure about that?"

"General, I was too intent on keepin' my hair to count 'em off on my fingers. I'd guestimate no more than twenty. No less'n a dozen. I lit out as soon as I seed old Zeb down thar with his redskin friends."

"Do you suppose they know we're coming?"

"Don't suppose it, General. I knows they're expectin' you. Some of Zeb's Injuns was fixin' fire arrows!"

MacAllister's eyes narrowed as he gasped. "Fire arrows! You're sure?"

Coulee John nodded and said, "Yep. Arrow shafts wrapped in cottonwood wool, dipped in pine pitch. Didn't look like they was fixin' 'em to cook buffalo on the run."

Stonecipher said, "I can't believe he means to attack this column!"

But MacAllister said, "Not in the open in broad daylight, General. Those fire arrows figure to be meant for later on tonight, when our wagaons are circled up as sitting targets!"

"I have it on good authority that the Sioux never attack at night!"

"I read Colonel Custer's book too, General. I doubt if Satangkai and his braves have, and, in any case, Macahan's not a Sioux."

"A no-count renegade is what he is!" agreed Coulee John.

Ignoring him, Stonecipher turned to MacAllister and said, "You know the man, Captain. What in thunder do you think this means? Has Macahan gone mad?"

"I'm not sure what I make of it, General. As a guess, I'd say old Zeb intended to slow us down by harassment. I doubt if he'd want to kill a fellow white man, but if he burned our supply wagons in the night he'd have us in one hell of a fix, with or without bloodshed!"

Stonecipher prepared to dismount as he called to a junior officer, "Fetch me my ordinance map, Lieutenant."

The general and his staff soon had the maps spread out on a folding camp table while the men fell out to graze their mounts and rest a bit.

As MacAllister's finger traced the contour lines he was familiar with, he told the general, "You can see how these ridges act as a sort of funnel into that glade, can't you, sir?"

"What you're saying is that it's not a bad hide-out

but a lousy stronghold! I don't see any place in the area for them to make a decent stand."

"There isn't, sir. You can see they likely gathered there because of the shelter, grass, and water. They'll be on the lookout, of course. A frontal attack up the valley between the ridges would just have them fanning out and away, over the hogbacks on either side. I'd say it was even-steven. The glade's not a likely place for an ambush *or* a stand."

Stonecipher pursed his lips in thought as he studied the situation. Then he said, "We don't win battles by picking and choosing our battlefields, Captain. We win by hitting hard and by surprise!"

"But any approach we can make will be spotted in ample time, sir."

"I'm not so sure of that. There's only a handful of them in that glade. Zeb Macahan knows our style, so he'd expect me to send no more than a troop at the most to disperse what I might think of as a scouting party ghosting our flanks."

MacAllister nodded and asked, "What's the real plan, sir? One obvious force sent up the valley to scatter them while we circle the whole area with dismounted pickets on foot, with rifles?"

"You're learning, son. All but the scattering part. I want to keep the rascals bunched. Trouble with any mad scramble is that you're likely to let a few slip by, and one of those Crooked Lances getting away would be too many. They're the eyes of Satangkai. I aim to put 'em out and leave the whole Sioux Nation blind to my every move."

"I see the need, sir. I'm a mite fuzzy as to method, though."

"Hell, didn't they teach you anything at the point, boy? We circle 'em tight with only one apparent avenue of retreat left open. Then we hit 'em with a strong force, and drive 'em up the glade like steam drives a piston in an engine."

"And as they ride out the other end, we have still another troop laying for them!"

"You're learning, Captain. Only, the troop we send the long way round to ambush 'em will be dismounted and dug in. The noisy sabers and bugles comin' up the glade from the other way should run those rascals into my ever-loving embrace!"

MacAllister nodded and said, "It ought to work, sir. But what about Macahan? Remember, he's in there with those young Sioux. Isn't it likely he'll be caught in our cross fire?"

"Likely? Captain, I'm counting on catching the son of a bitch in our cross fire!"

Coulee John chortled, "Hot damn! That'll larn the turncoat to ride with Sioux! It's his own blamed fault if he gits kilt!"

MacAllister sighed and said, "Well, *we* certainly never sent him into that glade. What are your orders if we take him, General?"

"Alive? You know the answer to that, don't you, Captain?"

"I suppose I do, sir. Do we offer him a chance to explain before we hang him?"

"What do you take me for, a barbarian? Of course he'll get to have his say. I intend to give the son of a bitch a proper drumhead court-martial."

Stonecipher lit a fresh cigar before he added, "And then we'll hang the rascal high!"

CHAPTER 56

A little over an hour later Zeb Macahan and two of his Crooked Lances sat their mounts in the shadows of a cottonwood grove as, down at the open end of the funnel-shaped glade, the Second Cav passed as if in review. One of the braves muttered, "They march as blindly as owls in the brightness of Shu-nah!"

Zeb said, "Steady. They may not be as blind as they act."

Over in the army column, mere blue-gray blurs among the rolling dust and confusion from where Zeb could have been watching, Coulee John reported in from another one-man patrol on pony, foot, and belly to say to Stonecipher, "They's still thar, General. Zeb's got 'em up to the far end of the glade, under some trees."

Stonecipher nodded and said, "Good. Rather a stupid tactical error on Macahan's part. I expected better of the man."

The general gave a hand signal and the column halted in place, lined up across the open end of the funnel-shaped valley like the crossbar of a gigantic letter A. As a troop of saber-wielding shock riders wheeled into a wall-to-wall position between the wall of wagons and gun limbers, the general gave another signal, the young captain in command of the troop selected for the frontal attack raised his sword, and a bugle began to sound the stirring notes of "Charge!"

Stirrup to stirrup, guidon pennants fluttering bravely in the breeze of their own making, B Troop tore up the valley in a hell-for-leather cavalry charge fit for poetry or a Napoleonic battle print.

Zeb Macahan and his handful of braves had neither guidons or bugles, of course, but the plains tribes were used to signaling at a distance with their intertribal sign language. Zeb began to signal now as his widely scattered Indians responded from various points of cover in what seemed to be a very confused disposition of his limited forces.

General Stonecipher and his staff followed close on the heels of the charging line of cavalry, for the general's plans seemed to be going well and he wanted to be in at the kill, in the point of the valley.

As the walls of the valley closed in, Indians began to break cover, milling in and out in utter confusion.

To the displined troopers charging up the valley, the dogfight dancing back and forth and all around seemed mindless panic on the part of the Dakota.

Stonecipher suddenly spotted Zeb Macahan and what looked like the main party of his Soux. They were moving, as expected, up toward the point of the valley, and the general chortled, "Got you now, you rascal!"

A mounted Indian appeared as if by magic from the dust and confusion between the general and the flying hooves of the line of troopers just ahead. Even as he wondered where in thunder the young brave had been concealed as the troop apparently charged right over him, the general, who was a man of action if nothing else, drew his saddle gun and fired. He grunted in satisfaction as the yipping Soux seemed to fall off the far side of his pony. But then the Indian was coming in from another angle, hanging by one leg on the far side of his well-trained painted pony. The general gasped in shock as still another Indian overtook him from the rear and snatched the pistol from his hand to join his partner as both rode, laughing, into the galloping men of B Troop, from behind!

"I count coup!" whooped a boy called Beaver Tail as he snatched the hat from a startled trooper and threw it to his friend, Plenty Fish.

As a trio of troopers fell out of line to chase the two young braves, the general yelled, "Reform your line, god damn it! They _want_ you to chase 'em! Hold your formation and keep moving up, you dumb bastards!"

Ignoring the two young braves who whooped and hollered at him from the slopes on either side, Stonecipher bulled through with a grim little smile. Knowing his trap was about to be sprung, he could afford to ignore the coup counters. It was Macahan and the other leaders he wanted, and they were riding right into the ambush he'd sent around to the point of the funnel. He'd have them any second now.

The general laughed aloud as a line of blue-clad figures suddenly appeared against the skyline to his right. The eastern slope was secured. A moment later a bugle sounded and more troopers popped over the ridge to the west. There was no way out now. Macahan and his Indian friends were in a triangular box, or perhaps "coffin" would be a better word. There was nothing left for the Second Cav to do but mop the rascals up.

And then a great wall of dust rose like a mushroom cloud at the head of the valley and the slopes echoed to what sounded like a sudden thunderstorm, even as the sun stood shining from a bowl of cobalt blue.

Amid the dust and milling confusion the general saw some of his forward troopers riding back. Back in haste, as if the devil in the flesh were in pursuit.

Stonecipher reared his mount and screamed, "God damn it, men, you're going the wrong way!" even as he wondered what had turned his charge back on itself. What had gone wrong? What could have gone wrong? He knew Macahan couldn't have more than a squad or two of Sioux against nearly two thirds of his whole regiment.

And then the general saw them: buffalo. A whole herd of buffalo coming his way from the far end of the valley, heads down and wicked black horns tossing over thousands of razor-sharp and thundering hooves! Behind the stampeding buffalo rode a mere handful of Indian boys, yipping and waving blankets in the dust cloud of their passing.

Let it be recorded that Brandy Jack Stonecipher was a good officer and a very brave man. Let it also be recorded that he was not given to suicide under most unpleasant conditions. As his charging troopers had just discovered, there was nothing left for any man on the wrong side of a charging buffalo herd to do but run like hell.

Cursing, sobbing, the general wheeled his mount and rode for his life down the valley, with the hooves and horns of a thousand head of frightened buffalo in hot pursuit.

As he tore out into the open he waved his hat and

screamed, "The guns and wagons! Get those con-
founded vehicles out of the way!"

But his orders came too late. As the men and horses
of the Second Cav fanned out of the path of the thundering herd to either side on open ground, the herd
hit the supply wagons, caissons, and gun limbers in a
heads-down wall of brown wool and black horns.

Wheeled vehicles turned over. Canvas tops were torn
off and scattered to the winds, as were supplies, ammunition canisters, and all sorts of military gear. Some
buffalo broke their necks or legs on impact. Others
were shot running by those few troopers with enough
presence of mind to turn and fire as they ran for their
lives, and then the buffalo, too, began to fan out
across open prairie, their Indian tormentors no longer
herding them.

When it was all over, the proud Second Cav had
been scattered from hell to breakfast over more than
a square mile of rolling grassland!

As the scattered military drifted in warily from
every point of the compass, Captain MacAllister found
General Stonecipher sitting his charger, sobbing, amid
a littered scene of total chaos. MacAllister guided his
own mount around an overturned Gatling gun as he
called out, "Are you all right, General?"

"God damn it to hell! Does it look like I'm all right?
Look what that devil, Macahan, did to my column!
What's the casualty figure?"

"We're still trying to get all the parts back together,
sir. So far, there's been no report of any casualty. We
don't seem to have any killed or even wounded."

"That son of a bitch! Oh, that dirty son of a bitch!
You know why that fool, Coulee John, is still wearing
his hair, Captain?"

"I think it's obvious, sir. Zeb knew our scout was
there. The whole thing was an act, put on for Brinkerhoff's edification."

"He slickered us, Captain."

"I know, sir. They didn't let Coulee John see the
buffalo they had penned up ahead. Do you want me to

get a work detail together and start righting the wagons, sir?"

"Why, hell no! I was sort of planning to let them right and repair themselves! God damn it, at the best it's going to take us the rest of the night and into tomorrow to put this Humpty Dumpty mess back together!"

As other junior officers drifted in, eyeing their general and the shattered debris around him warily, Stonecipher roared, "Any of you gentlemen care to write a report on this action that won't leave us looking like a posse of halfwitted schoolmarms?"

There were no takers. Stonecipher nodded and said, "I know, I'll have to figure that out myself."

MacAllister suppressed a smile as he said, "I don't envy you *that* chore, General!"

"You just see to the repairs while I get drunk enough to write a report that won't get us all cashiered for general stupidity!"

He spotted and signaled to an abashed and wary Coulee John, who rode in hesitantly as the general whip-cracked, "And here's our expert on Indian warfare in general and the Sioux in particular! In the future, Brinkerhoff, I'll take your advice with a grain or maybe a barrel of salt! Have you any explanation for what just happened?"

"I reckon Zeb Macahan kind of tricked us, General. Don't you figure what he done here rates as pure and simple high treason to these here United States?"

"He'd probably argue you committed treason against your country when you started this whole mess by leading those fool Russians over the treaty line and busted things wide open. But we'll worry about that later. I'd like to hang you, Coulee John, but that'd leave me with no scout at all, and riding against the best in the business!"

He suddenly whirled on MacAllister, caught the captain smiling, and said, "Wipe it off, mister! I'll give your old friend his due and allow it was a slick military maneuver. Letting this idiot see those fire arrows he had no intention of using on us was a master touch, too, but, damn it, you don't have to look so all-fired pleased about it! I know Macahan is a friend of yours!"

MacAllister sobered and said, "A very good friend, General, but I'm a soldier first, and my duty is to this army!"

"Hell, son, nobody's accused you of being an Indian spy. I'll be double damned if I know what your friend Macahan is, either. We'll worry about it later. Right now you're detailed to put things to rights around here, on the double. Feed and water the men and mounts, but no man's to sleep a wink until the damage is repaired."

"Yes, sir. Double watch on all outposts tonight?"

"Better. Though I doubt he'll hit us again till we're ready to move out. Couple of his Indian kids had the chance to lift my hair and passed on the matter. The way I see it, he's out to delay us, not kill us. He'll doubtless get a good night's sleep, feeling smug as all hell. But a single skirmish don't make a war, as my old war buddy, Sam Grant, was fond of saying. You ever study up on Sam Grant's strategy, Captain?"

"General Ulysses S. Grant? Of course, sir."

"Well, you might remember what his secret was. Up to when they put Sam Grant in command, them Johnny Rebs had our boys runnin' about in circles, like Macahan means to do. You know what Grant's answer to guerrilla tactics was, don't you?"

"Yes, sir. He ignored 'em. Just kept bulling through till he had Bobby Lee pinned down at Appomattox with all the fight knocked out of him!"

"By jimmies, Captain, that's how I mean to fight this war! I was with Grant at Shilo. Rebs had us all mixed up till nobody knew what was going on. One of our officers said it looked like the rebs had us surrounded. You know what Grant said? He chawed his cigar and said it was impossible. He had no more notion than the rest of us what in thunder the rebs was up to, but he knew we outnumbered 'em two to one. He said no matter what the enemy done, it was impossible for a smaller army to surround or whup a bigger one. So we just kept fighting. And after it was over, guess who'd won."

"I know we did, sir. It was a costly victory."

"Yep, costly to both sides, but the point is still that we won. You keep that in mind and you'll know how I make war, mister. I'll be in my tent if you need me!"

Stonecipher rode away, softly singing, "Oh, I put my head to a cask of brandy . . . It was my fancy, I do declare . . . For when I'm drinking, I get to thinking . . . and wishing Peggy Gordon was there!"

MacAllister suppressed a shudder, but one of his fellow junior officers caught it. He asked, "What's wrong Mac? Doesn't the old man's way of fighting suit you? It seemed to work pretty well for General Grant."

MacAllister nodded and said, "I know. But every one of his battles was a bloodbath, for both sides."

CHAPTER 57

Coulee John Brinkerhoff found General Stonecipher in the command tent, scowling down at his unfinished report. The general had half finished a bottle of brandy, too. He stared up at the scout and asked, "All right, what is it, Brinkerhoff?"

"Well, General, I heard somethin' about a reward being posted for deserters and renegades. You heard anything about it?"

"Of course. The standing offer runs about two hundred dollars, dead or alive."

"Dead or alive, huh? That sort of makes things easier, don't it?"

"Get to the point. You're smelling up my quarters. Don't you ever take a bath, damn it?"

"Been a long day, General. Do you mind?"

Stonecipher slid the bottle over to him and waited until the scout had gulped a few swallows before he said, "How do you suppose you're going to collect that two hundred dollars, Coulee John?"

The scout wiped his mouth with the back of his sleeve and said, "Two hundred ain't all that much for Zeb Macahan, General."

"I see. What amount did you have in mind?"

"More like a thousand. Is me bringin' him in, sorta, worth a thousand to you, General?"

"Brinkerhoff, you're a fool! We both know you're just not up to it, for any reward at all. You'll just get yourself killed, and I still need your dubious services riding out on point."

"Now hold on, General. I never said I aimed to take him alone!"

"How else do you plan to do it? I don't have any men to spare, and if I had, sending them behind Sioux lines doesn't sound very smart."

"I don't need no white help, General. I got me some Sioux might be willin' to work for me, for a split of the reward."

"You know some Sioux renegades who'd betray their own side?"

"Let's say I got me some Injun friends who've had enough and aim to be on the winning side. Injuns is a lot like womenfolk in some ways. You know how it is with a popular gal? How they's always other gals in the pack who'd like to see her with acid in her face?"

"I see, there's a faction among the Sioux who are jealous of old Satangkai."

"There you go, General. Just like gals. Anyways, iffen I could pull it off, would it be wuth a thousand to you?"

"You bring in Zeb Macahan and you'll get a thousand dollars. You have my word on that."

"Might not be able to deliver him with all his skin left on. The reward's dead or alive, right?"

"Damn it, Brinkerhoff. The U.S. Army does not condone coldblooded murder!"

"Do tell? Must be a new policy I ain't heard about."

"Get out of here, you bastard. And leave the tent flap open. I need some air in here now!"

The scout left, sneering, "You just sleep on it, General. We both knows you'll come around to my way of thinking. Zeb Macahan's all that stands betwixt you and a mess of shiny new medals for another easy victory!"

He scuttled to safety, laughing, as Stonecipher hurled the bottle after him.

Brandy Jack was truly indignant, at the time. Later, as MacAllister gave him a full damage report, he sighed and said, "Brinkerhoff knows some renegade Sioux he says can be bought to kill Macahan."

MacAllister grimaced and said, "Every time I hear that man's name, of late, I sort of start to itch and want to take a long hot bath."

"I know what you mean, Captain. But I'm almost tempted to turn Coulee John loose like the mad dog he seems to be."

"It sounds like an ugly way to make war, General."

"All ways of making war are ugly, Captain. I doubt if it matters all that much whether women and children are trampled to death by a knight in shining armor, hit by a canister round, or murdered by scum like Coulee John and his renegade friends. You know what tempts me the most? It's that Noble Savage notion of Zeb Macahan's. He's taking a chance with hanging as a traitor to us because he's so all-fired sure his redskin friends are more honorable and just than his own kind."

"You mean, if Brinkerhoff's Sioux traitors . . ."

"Yeah, wouldn't that be a bitch! God, how I'd love to show him how little difference there is between his Noble Savage and the white scum of our city slums when it comes to the almighty dollar!"

CHAPTER 58

Before high noon the next day the damage had been repaired and the Second Cav was once more on the move. At least, they were on the move until they found their progress blocked by a mountain-spawned river at flood stage.

As the picket riders fanned out across the rolling grassland swells to secure the flanks of the halted column, General Stonecipher glowered at the muddy flood barring his advance and told MacAllister, "I don't like this, Captain!"

"I know, sir. But I doubt if Zeb Macahan had anything to do about thunder on the mountains last night!"

"Don't be funny, son. Where's that goddamn scout?"

Coulee John rode forward from where he'd been skulking amid the column and asked, "What can I do for you, sir? You changed your mind about my notion about that reward?"

"Never mind that just now. What have you to say about this river?"

"Too deep to ford right here, General. We could swing down through bear-grass flats, where it's shallow."

MacAllister said, "We could, but that's three days out of our way."

Stonecipher shook his head and said, "I'm not wasting three minutes if I can help it. Brinkerhoff, just how deep is this flooded ford right now?"

"Up to the head and shoulders of a mounted man, if his pony could walk underwater."

"What about swimming the mounts across and floating the wagons?"

324

"Be a mite less work a mile or so upstream, towards them hills. There's another ford up that way. It'll be flooded high, but not too high to cross without swimmin' if you like wet britches."

"God damn it, why didn't you say so! Why were you about to lead us way out of our way?"

"I ain't leading nobody, General. You ask me a question and I'll likely answer it. I didn't reckon you wanted to get your powder in them caissons wet, or your own selves, for that matter. I can take you through this country comfortable or I can take you sudden. I cain't do both!"

Stonecipher stared for a time at the hillier country indicated. Then he snapped, "MacAllister, I want those flank riders farther out. I don't like my flanks exposed in rolling country like this."

"Yes, sir, I'll have men posted on each rise as we go by."

Satisfied, the general gave the signal to swing the column north over the rolling swells of summer-killed grass.

In a shallow draw upwind, a young Indian set fire to a clump of grass and crawled away through the knee-high straw.

A soldier shouted, "Smoke off our point, sir! Looks like a smoke signal!"

"Ignore it!" snapped Stonecipher. "That damned Macahan's trying to spook us with his smoke talk. We know the main body of the Sioux are too far off to read any signal from here."

MacAllister said, "There's another column of smoke, General."

Coulee John added, "There's two more off on our east flank!"

Stonecipher snapped, "You know what's he's trying to do, damn it. Press on! We know he hasn't more than a score of braves with him, and six hundred would be fools to attack us in the open like this!"

One of the outriders was coming in at a full gallop,

and MacAllister called out to him, "What is it, Trooper? What did you spot out there, Indians?"

The rider reined in to blurt, "No, sir. Never seen Indian one! It's a grass fire! Whole damned prairie's been set alight, upwind and blowin' this way!"

Stonecipher cursed and stared in horrified anger at what now had blended into a solid wall of smoke just over the horizon. Coulee John said, "I'll bet Macahan's Injuns done it! They's worked around upwind of ussen and set the prairie blazin'! Picked him a day with the east wind blowin', too, the ornery cuss! It blows from the west six days outten seven in these parts!"

MacAllister gasped. "General! We're going to be trapped between that fire and the flood to our west if we don't move fast!"

"I can see that, god damn it to hell! What do you think our chances are on racing the fire to the water by running north toward Satangkai's stronghold?"

"Pulling guns and wagons? No good, General. The corridor he's got us boxed into is shrinking while we're talking about it! What are your orders, sir?"

"Jesus H. Christ! What other orders can there be! He's done it to us *again!* The bastard!"

As the smoke drifted closer and the first line of red flames topped the rolling rises on the horizon, Stonecipher turned to his bugler and snapped, "All right, god damn it, son. Sound retreat!"

The long blue column once more recoiled on its own length, like a big blue snake that had stuck its head into a hornets' nest by some ghastly error in judgment.

By the time they had themselves headed the right way, if there was such a place with Zeb Macahan's trick in mind, the smoke lay in thick acrid clouds over and between the men, mounts, and wagons. The animals, panicked by the smell of fire, were hard to manage. The men who had to try were nearly as confused as they stumbled, rode, or simply cursed with tear-filled eyes and gasping lungs.

Nobody noticed the Dakota brave who leaped up

from a clump of beargrass, sliced through the reins of a smoke-blinded teamster, and ran off, grinning, through the pungent grass smoke, leaving the teamster sitting on his caisson, swearing in fright and wonder with the severed reins in his hands, unable to control his stampeding team.

The runaway caisson crashed into a fieldpiece, overturning it with a broken wheel.

A trooper fired at something moving in the choking smoke. He'd never know what he'd fired at or if he'd hit it, but Beaver Tail rolled safely away, laughing, counting coup on the white man's sword he'd just snatched.

It was every man for himself now as, blinded and choking, singed by falling embers and terribly aware of what would happen should the fire reach one of the ammunition caissons, the Second Cavalry simply tucked its tail between its legs and once more ran like hell.

An hour later an abashed and smoke-stained Captain MacAllister found his general nursing a torn sleeve and a badly bruised ego in the shelter of a ravine beyond the reach of the grass fire burning itself out against the river just to their north.

Stonecipher glared at his junior officer through red-rimmed eyes and snapped, "All right, report!"

"No killed or wounded, sir. A few men singed. A few others bruised and shaken. It's a miracle we got off so easy, though. I was sure one of those damned caissons was about to blow!"

"What about our equipment?"

"Lost some sidearms in the route. Couple of wagons and a fieldpiece left to the flames. I imagine we'll be able to salvage the gun barrel, but I'd hate to think of firing it before the ordnance men examined it for loss of temper!"

"Well, that field gun's not the only thing that's lost its temper, now, god damn it! Get me Coulee John! I have a piece of work for him to do for me!"

"Sir, I hope you're not thinking what you're likely thinking!"

"I'll do all the thinking around here, Captain. And if I have to repeat another order to you, you just made corporal, the hard way!"

When Coulee John came in, the general was still fuming. The scout grinned slyly and said, "If this keeps up we won't have all that much of a war with Satangkai and his Sioux, will we? I mean, we seem to be gettin' whupped like hell by a passel of Injun kids!"

"God damn it, Brinkerhoff, we both know who's been whipping our tails off and making a fool out of this man's army!"

"Yup, they say the Injuns calls him White Eagle, but we knows he's jest old Zeb Macahan."

"Listen to me. I want him, Brinkerhoff! I want him alive to face trial if it's possible."

"But iffen it ain't, General?"

"You just get him, mister! Whether it's alive or dead will be up to him. You'll order your Indian friends to try to take him alive, won't you?"

"I'll tell 'em what you said, General. But you know Injuns."

"In other words, they'll think it's a lot easier to murder him than to try to capture him in a fair fight?"

"Well, I'll tell you, General, iffen you had the job to do your own self, would you be all that fired up to face Zeb Macahan in a fair stand-up fight?"

"I wouldn't like it at all, but I'd still like him alive, if it's possible."

"There you go. We got a deal, General. I'll git him. But you jest let me study on what's possible."

CHAPTER 59

Bone-weary and black with smoke, Zeb Macahan sat his singed pony on a distant rise north of the fire. A blue haze of cooling but still smoldering sod hung in the sky as a great gauze screen between his small guerrilla band and the Second Cav.

He'd taken his prominent position to make himself a visible rallying point for his widely scattered young followers. As they rode up to him from every direction Zeb greeted each by name and listened solemnly as each recited his claims of coup against the blue sleeves. One boy proudly displayed the saber he'd snatched from a bewildered trooper in the smoke. Another wore a cavalry sombrero at a jaunty angle, laughing as he spoke of how pretty his new hat would be once he'd stuck his coup feathers in the band of yellow braid. All agreed, modestly, that Beaver Tail's capture of a squadron guidon was the most astounding and praiseworthy event of their bloodless attack. He waved the red-and-white pennant in a circle over his young head and sang, "I count coup! I have stolen the flag of the blue sleeves! I could have taken the hair of the man who carried it, for I knocked him from his pony and had him at my mercy in his smoke-blindness! I claim a scalp coup, for hear me, I only spared him because White Eagle told us not to kill!"

Zeb nodded formally and said, "Your words are heard, Beaver Tail. I shall speak for you in council with your elders and I shall plead for a red-tipped eagle feather for you. Discipline in battle calls for more bravery than merely taking a scalp at opportunity."

Then, seeing that all his braves had straggled in and were circled around for further orders, Zeb said, "Hear me, I shall speak for all of you at the council of the chiefs! You have all done well, and your praises shall be sung by the squaws around many a campfire in the years to come! I see blood as well as smoke on many of my brothers. Are any of you wounded badly?"

There was a chorus of indignant denials. One youth who'd caught a lucky trooper's round in the thigh shouted, "We are Dakota!" and no further explanation was necessary, although Zeb made a mental note that Little Bear would be tended to and left in camp until his wound healed. He did not insult the proud young warrior by bringing it up in front of his comrades. Zeb knew it would take hysterical demands by admiring young squaws to keep the boy bandaged and resting for a time. No doubt all involved would enjoy the dramatics immensely.

One of the braves asked, "What is our next move, White Eagle? When do we hit them again?"

Zeb said, "You have all been brave, but we have done enough for now. The long knives have been delayed, and by now your people are safe with Satangkai in the high Pa Sapa. That is where I mean to lead you now."

"Can't we hit them one more time? It's so much fun to make fools of the long knives!"

"I know, but the wise horse thief heads for home when he's taken as many ponies as he can herd. We have done well. It's time to break off the action before someone gets hurt."

"We are not afraid! All men must die one day. At worst, we go to meet Old Woman just a little sooner! It feels so good to play tricks on the white men after all they've played on us. Can't we kill just a few of them before we go to join our people?"

"Hear me, I have sent words on paper to a white chief who can put an end to this war before things get really ugly. It is most important that we keep the bloodshed from growing, for the larger the wound, the longer the healing. I know all of you are faithful and would die for Satangkai. Would you ask your chief to die for you, if I can find a way to prevent it?"

There was a murmur of denials. Zeb nodded and said, "Then hear my words. Satangkai is brave and very angry. The white chief who leads the soldiers against him is made of the same clay. Both are brave and stubborn. Both are good men who must be saved from their own unthinking hate. If we can keep the two great chiefs, red and white, apart until my greater chief from the east can speak and be listened to, all may yet be well with both our peoples. Once let this fight get out of hand and it will not be a good fight. Satangkai and many of you will die, because past a certain point, a war is very hard to stop. War is a hungry wolf. We must try to keep it leashed. Now, come, we ride to the Pa Sapa!"

Traveling light, Zeb and his young warriors made good time to the high country in the center of the Black Hills massif. The last of Satangkai's tired, heavy-laden tribespeople had just filed wearily into the dubious safety of the great granite stronghold by the time Zeb's band caught up with the chief.

Zeb and Satangkai met on a level glade of wind-blown loess soil between great potato-shaped boulders higher than the tallest tree. One end of the great horseshoe-shaped area looked down on the lower ridges to the south. Zeb and the chief rode to the edge of the overlook and reined in. Satangkai sighed and said, "I wish I could have been there with you! You have given us the time we needed, White Eagle. From where we stand, the coming fight should be a good one. Look down there at the broken ground the blue sleeves must ride over to get at us! Heya! They will not find this a good place for them to fight! Pa Sapa is a maze of great strongholds like this one. If they drive us from this place, we can simply fall back to the next one to the north and make them do it all over. Each time we have to give them another meadow, we shall make them pay with dead and wounded!"

Zeb nodded and said, "My brother has chosen his battleground well. Even our great war chief, Washington, told his soldiers to always take the high ground."

"You are wiser than I in the ways of the blue sleeves, White Eagle. Is it possible I have overlooked anything? I have prayed and smoked to Wakan Tonka! I have asked Tunkanshe, the rock spirit who dwells in this place, for a vision. I have asked the Old Woman who takes dead warriers to her ledge among the northern lights for a vision. No vision has been bestowed upon me, and my heart is worried. I fear in my ignorance I may yet destroy my people!"

Zeb considered and said, "My brother could not have picked a better place to stand and fight. It is good, but not enough. The white chief who marches against you is no fool, despite the trick we played on him. He will know how costly a frontal attack against this rocky stronghold will be. His men will ride no farther than that hogback just beyond rifle range. Do you see the one I mean?"

"Of course. What will they do when they top that rise, White Eagle?"

"I don't think they'll show themselves against the skyline. Certainly not mounted. The white chief will make his headquarters on the far side, as safe as you among the rocks. Then he will do two things. He will send in a skirmish line of dismounted troopers, crawling on their bellies as they take cover behind every boulder or break in the earth."

"You said two things. My braves can deal with enemies fighting on their bellies."

"I know. The soldiers have great guns on wheels. They will fire them from the far side of that ridge down there so that my red brothers cannot see them. The big guns throw three kinds of missiles. One is simply a ball of iron. Another is a ball of iron filled with powder. It blows great holes in the earth and shatters rocks. The most deadly is a thing called canister shot. It is like a little barrel filled with bullets. When it hits, it bursts open throwing a great cloud of bullets all around."

Santangkai nodded and said, "These things I have seen. When I rode against the army under Red Cloud before we made them give us the last promise, I saw men cut in two by the big guns of the blue sleeves. But what are we to do? We have no great guns of our own!"

"Hear me. The white men have learned a way to make it harder for the great guns to kill. You must have your people dig holes in the ground."

"Heya! You expect Dakota to fight from holes, like prairie dogs or badgers?"

"I know it is not your way. The white chief knows this, too. He will not be expecting trench warfare."

"What does 'trench warfare' mean? I have never heard of it before!"

"Have your women, children, and old ones well back and hidden in caves in the rocks, or deep pits if there are not enough natural caves among all those boulders. Here where we stand and in other places like it all around, have your warriors dig themselves into the earth as deep as a man's shoulders. When the great guns fire, they will duck their heads below the level of the ground, and the shot and shell will pass over them, leaving them unharmed."

"I see! And then, when the soldiers charge, thinking many of us are dead and wounded, we shall pop up and fire into them!"

Zeb contented himself with a nod. He'd sort of hoped Satangkai wouldn't make such a quick study of the arts of modern warfare! His original idea had been to buy time and keep as many as possible on both sides alive until another truce could be arranged. Between them, Satangkai and Stonecipher were shaping up as another Bobby Lee and U. S. Grant!

Aloud, Zeb said, "After you have your forces dug in, there is one more thing you should do."

"Then speak. My brother's words seem wise, and I am eager to learn how the white man wins so many of his wars."

"Then listen. You must buy even more time. You

should meet the approaching war chief under a white flag."

"A white flag? That means surrender!"

"No, listen, a white flag only means two opposing warriors wish to talk. You have two good reasons for talking once again with the chief called Stonecipher."

"I have spoken to him. Last time, it cost me a young man when he broke the truce through treachery! Why does my brother give such strange counsel at a time like this? Are we not in a grand position to fight? Is this not a lovely time and place to die?"

"You said you wanted to learn the white man's way of winning wars, Satangkai."

"I am sorry. I shall listen to all your words before I break in like a rude youth filled with foolishness and firewater. What is it I do not understand about the white man's way of making war?"

"Far across the Bitter Water lived a white chief who'd fought in many wars on many sides. He had won many battles. He had lost many battles, but always he got his young men safely back, with fewer killed or wounded than his enemies."

"He sounds like a good fighter!"

"He was. His name was General von Clausewitz. In time he grew old, as all warriors must. All the great chiefs across the Bitter Water had respect for his counsel, for he had learned much in his years on the warpath. They asked him to put his wisdom on paper so it would not be lost when the Old Woman took him to her lodge among the northern lights."

"I see, and has my brother read the words of this great white chief?"

"Yes, they were printed in many tongues and he died when I was but a child. Are you ready for the wisest thing he ever learned in all his battles?"

"Of course! Only a fool refuses counsel from his elder warriors!"

"Then hear me, von Clausewitz spoke a great truth all too many men who consider themselves mighty warriors tend to forget. He said never to forget one's reason for a war. All wars, he said, are fought simply to make the enemy give in to your demands. The number killed, the lodges burned, even the land taken, means nothing in the end. The point of all wars is to have your enemy say, I hear your words and I will listen!"

Satangkai thought a moment before he nodded and said, "I can see the wisdom in his words. If the Crow would only stop raiding us and give us all their ponies, we would not have to kill them."

"That's close enough. If my brother heeds my counsel, he will meet with the white chief who's coming to fight. If the Dakota win their point without a battle, they will have won as the white man has so many times, at no cost to them in blood or keening widows."

"This victory I would like to have, but how is it possible? We have spoken many times, many, to the blue sleeves. Always they press us further. Is is possible the chief who leads them intends to ride all this way just to talk?"

"He will if he is wise. We will make him see in his head how many soldiers he must lose to take these last rocks and ridges. Like me, he will have read von Clausewitz. He, too, will see the advantage of trying to win his victory with words when guns may not be enough."

"But won't all our words be empty bags of wind? I have been backed as far as I can move. He is a stubborn man who means to humble the proud Dakota. I can see our talk taking many days! And in the end, all must be decided in our last great battle!"

Zeb shook his head and said, "No, for even as you keep him talking, you'll be beating him! Battles are won with blood, supplies, and time. Stonecipher will not give in to your words. You, of course, will not give in to his. Meanwhile, his soldiers and their ponies will be eating green paper as well as food and grass. No man will be killed on either side. Tempers on both sides will have a time to cool."

"But in the end, won't he want to fight us anyway?"

"Yes. He won't be allowed to. I have sent for

help from an even greater chief on the singing wire. When our friends in the east learn of what they call a stalemate, they will wonder if this war is wise. They will ask for all the facts in the matter. Once they learn the truth about the army's mistakes and Satangkai's good heart, they will tell the blue sleeves to leave you alone."

"Because they wish to be friends with the Dakota?"

"To save the green paper from being wasted. You see, my brother, the way your people have been fighting does not impress them. You can kill many soldiers. You can wipe out many settlers. It only makes them angry, and they send more white people to replace them."

"I know. There seems to be no end to the white people."

"I don't think there is. But there is a limit to the green paper, and some men value it much more than human lives. Will my brother meet with the blue sleeves under the white flag?"

"Heya, I shall try once more to fight as the white man does, with empty words and promises!"

CHAPTER 60

No North American Indian Nation had ever invented the concept of a jail or prison, but every tribe had laws. A Dakota brave who hunted on his own against the orders of his elders had his bow broken by the Dog Soldiers for a first offense. A warrior who disobeyed a command in battle might be disgraced by being made to dress as a woman for a time. Usually such mild punishment sufficed, but there were men among the Real

People, as among all people, born with something twisted in their souls. Criminal or antisocial Indians might be killed if their crimes were truly outrageous. Others were simply banished—told, "Go from us, you are not a person!" and left to fend for themselves as best they could, as Cain was sent into the Land of Nod by an earlier tribal society.

It was to the squalid camp of such outcasts that Coulee John Brinkerhoff made his cautious way that afternoon. The exiled band of thieving or degenerate Dakota had formed a loose-knit band of perhaps a half dozen renegades and their unhappy dependents. They were camped in a cottonwood draw, living, or, rather, surviving, in a makeshift shantytown of lean-tos and dugouts. Unable in such small numbers to form a proper hunting band, they survived on handouts from the Indian Agency and what they could beg, steal, or sell their women's services for to passing whites. As Coulee John rode in, even his not-too-particular nose wrinkled at the smell of filth and vomited firewater. The men and women in the little camp were clad in scraps of white man's castoff clothing or, as in the case of one drunk and lewdly grinning squaw, were simply naked.

Coulee John dismounted and strode over to where some braves sat dully around a small buffalo-chip fire, passing a jug of trade whiskey back and forth. Coulee John hunkered down by the leader of the desperate band and said, "I have words for Little Dog."

Little Dog wiped the back of his hand across his mouth, handed the white man the jug, and said, "Did you bring us matches? Did you bring us firewater?"

"No. Your brother is a poor man, like yourselves. But he knows where we can find a lot of green paper."

"Heya, you talk. We listen."

"Satangkai is making a stand up in the Pa Sapa. He is badly outnumbered by the blue sleeves. Any Dakota riding in to join him would most likely be forgiven a few little things like sodomy or cowardice against the Crow."

"What is this to us? Do we look like fools who rush to join the chief who banished us in the Old Woman's lodge of death?"

"I have not spoken. Zeb Macahan, the one called White Eagle, is with Satangkai in his mountain stronghold. The blue sleeves know he is a great warrior. They don't want him at Satangkai's side when they do battle with him. The army wants White Eagle to go to the Old Woman."

"The blue sleeves want a white man killed?"

"Yes. They gave me some green paper for saying I would do it. They will give us all more green paper when the deed is done."

He took out a modest roll of bills and peeled some off for Little Dog. "There's more where this came from. Enough to buy new dresses for your squaws, new rifles, ponies, more firewater than you could drink in a long cold winter."

"The green paper sounds good. Killing White Eagle in the camp of Santangkai does not."

"Come on, you'll be getting good money for what comes natural to your breed! How is he to suspect Dakotas are out to do him in? You and your boys will never be noticed up there in the Pa Sapa. Bands from all over are drifting in. They even have some Cheyenne nobody can hardly talk to. Most of the warriors are wearing paint. You can paint yourselves and use new names. If you use any care at all . . ."

"It begins to sound possible. How much do we get for his scalp?"

"Now that's another point, Little Dog. You have to kill him with no trimmings. I intend to say I did it, after giving him a chance to surrender alive to the army. It's got to look like a fair fight."

"The killing is unimportant. Little Dog knows how to kill. I don't like the idea of trying to fool Satangkai with such simple pranks. If we are caught, after being banished on pain of death if we return . . ."

"All right, let's try it another way. Like I said, Satangkai needs all the warriors he can get. I know you don't intend to stand by him in any fight against the blue sleeves, but how is he to know that? You take a couple of your braves with reputations for being fighters. Never mind what naughty tricks they may be guilty of, just so Satangkai thinks they're tough and mean. You ride in openly, demand hospitality as men who wish to speak. Then you tell Satangkai you're sorry for having been such bad boys. You tell him you may be outcasts, but that you're still Dakota and that it's a good day to die. He'll likely swallow your story."

"Swallow story?"

"Believe you. He's got more on his mind right now than a little rape and incest or the filching of another man's pony. You tell him you want a chance to prove yourselves worthy of his friendship and— Hell, Little Dog, you know how to lie!"

"Hmmm. Do you really think he would restore us to our manhood as his warriors?"

"You bet your life he would! He needs every man he can get on the Dakota end of a rifle, and you boys have firearms! He'll welcome you back with open arms, now that he needs you. Macahan won't be expecting trouble in Satangkai's camp. Once things cool down a mite, couple of you just grab him while another slips a knife in his gullet. Will you do it?"

Little Dog shook himself, as if trying to clear the fumes from his brain. Coulee John was too insensitive to notice the dreamy look in some of the other renegades' eyes as they listened to the talk.

Little Dog sighed and said, "We have spoken about such things among ourselves. Not of killing White Eagle, but of what Satangkai would say if we approached him."

"I told you, he'd likely take you back with open arms."

"By Wakan Tonka! If only this was possible! To be as we were! To be once more respected Dakota warriors in our paint and coup feathers! Satangkai stripped us of our honors when he banished us. Yet now you say he needs us!'

"To lay rotting with the other corpses after the army wipes the whole tribe out? You just said you had no hankering to be going to the Old Woman's lodge, didn't you, Little Dog?"

"Yes, but those were the words of men without hope! A man who lives as the white man's cur has no need for an honorable death, since a dog is but a dog, no matter how he dies. Your words have lifted a stone from my heart! How often we have talked about it, without hope!"

Another outcast managed to sit straighter as, with the gravity of the semi-sober man's attempt at dignity, he cut in. "I too have often dreamed of being a man among men once more. If our brothers need us, we should go back to them and fight at their side. Are we not Dakota? Are we not men?"

Damn it," insisted Coulee John, "you boys are all mixed up. I only came to you because you're outcast renegades! I've been banking on you being just as willin' as any other exile to pay back those who wronged you!"

Little Dog was almost sober now. His eyes gleamed with a long-abandoned hope as he said, "Hear me, Coulee John. You just don't know what it means to be a Dakota, or a man!"

Coulee John snorted in disgust and snapped, "Don't you get all high toned with me, boy! Who was it had your squaw for a night for a bottle of firewater less than a moon ago?"

"I am ashamed. I was not a man then," said Little Dog with simple new-found dignity, adding, "The actions of a beggar are without meaning. An outcast lives as best he can. Let us forget the matter. Let us consider how we can help Satangkai, our chief!"

"Damn it, the plan I just gave you was meant to be a trick against Satangkai!"

"I know. I am rapidly becoming sober. Tell me, Coulee John, will the death of White Eagle help or hurt our people?"

"What are you talking about? You're renegades! I

told the general I was counting on you to help me take Zeb Macahan!"

Another Indian said owlishly, "We waste time in idle chatter. The white man has spoken. We know Satangkai, and our people need the help of White Eagle." His voice took on an ominous edge as he stared at Coulee John and added, "We know this one is not Satangkai's friend, too."

Coulee John licked his lips and started to rise. "Well, hell, I'll just ride on and give you time to think about my proposition."

But they had already thought about it.

Coulee John didn't make it to his pony.

CHAPTER 61

The picket on the Second Cav's perimeter studied the distant mounted figure for some time before he called out, "Outpost number nine! A white man comin' in on a painted pony. Looks like the scout, Coulee John!"

The corporal of the guard moved over to join him, frowning as they both watched the meandering progress of the distant rider. The guard said, "Don't that beat all? He's walkin' that hoss all over Robin Hood's barn! Why's he driftin' around like that instead of making a beeline for ussen? Can't he see our guidons?"

"He's riding like he's drunk, or mebbe hurt," said the corporal. "I'd best get the O.D."

A few minutes later Captain MacAllister reported to the general's tent, saying, "Sir, it's Brinkerhoff. His pony just brought him in."

"Well, damn it, send him to me! I was about to have my orderly fetch me my supper, but it can wait."

"Sir . . . I'd like you to step outside a moment."

The general followed his junior officer out with a puzzled frown. Then he froze in shocked horror as he saw what the corporal of the guard had led to the front of his tent.

Coulee John Brinkerhoff was braced in his saddle with a cottonwood A-frame holding his body upright. He was dead. There was no mistaking that. His ghastly drained face still wore the terror of his last living moments, and they'd likely killed him slowly. The scout had been scalped. His chest had been ripped open from belt line to breastbone, and the lower part of his body and his leggings to the knees were caked with dried blood. In the ghastly open cavity of his ripped-open guts someone had stuffed bloody crumpled banknotes that Stonecipher recognized as the first advance on the reward for Zeb Macahan.

Stonecipher swallowed the terrible taste in his mouth and said, "Somebody tell my orderly I won't be eating my supper just now. Let the record show this man was killed in the line of duty. Then bury the poor son of a bitch!"

MacAllister nodded and said, "Yes, sir. It seems as if he misjudged those Sioux he thought were renegades, didn't he?"

"Captain, we'll never know just what happened. Could have been his tame Sioux turned on him. Could have been he got jumped by some of Zeb Macahan's bunch. It makes better reading in the report that way."

"But, sir, I hardly think old Zeb would have killed him with all the trimmings, do you?"

"Damn it, Captain, you really are bucking for corporal, aren't you? Didn't you hear what I just said? We can report this as treachery gone agley, or we can report it as a brave scout killed in the line of duty by a Sioux war party. Now, what's it going to be?"

MacAllister nodded but didn't speak. He was an old army man and knew the answer to that one well enough.

CHAPTER 62

Zeb Macahan and Satangkai rode slowly down the long slope of a mountain meadow with the rocks of the Pa Sapa at their backs. Zeb carried an improvised white flag on a lodgepole-pine staff, though both men were armed with rifles. Satangkai had had enough of meeting white soldiers without a gun handy.

Against the skyline behind them, the occasional flutter of a feather in the breeze or the flash of sunlight on a silver concho bespoke Indians in position among the great battlements of granite to the north.

Far down the slope and moving up the grassy incline to meet them rode a small party of officers a short way out in advance of the main column. But the Second Cav in all its glory was coming on right behind Stonecipher and his staff.

As Zeb and Satangkai halted a third of the way down, a lone rider detached himself from the military and loped up to meet them, his own white signal flapping over his head. Zeb said, "Looks like they mean to listen to us before they start shooting. Is my brother ready?"

Satangkai nodded and said, "Yes. You will have to speak for me."

"I will, my brother. I mean to keep the speaking going at least into sundown!"

Down at the head of the army, General Stonecipher studied the enemy positions with the practical eye of an old soldier before he turned to Captain MacAllister at his side and said, "They've got the high ground, but they'll be in a hell of a fix when it's time for them to retreat, Captain!"

"I can see that, sir. But I don't think they mean to retreat any more. Since our kind met the Sioux they've been pushed a thousand miles or more. There may be a limit to how far any man can be pushed, and they'll never find a better place to make a final stand."

"There's never a final stand, for a smart general. Satangkai has to think of his women and children."

"I imagine he has, sir. The women will tend to the children, before they kill themselves."

"You mean they'd kill their own kids and then themselves?"

"It's been done, sir. Josephus says the Zealots did it at Messada as the Roman legions closed in for the final attack."

"Hell, who ever heard of a Jew who knew how to soldier? Those last Zealots near the Dead Sea were fanatics!"

"I suppose you're right, sir. Sioux can get a bit fanatic, too."

The officer who'd ridden forward with the parley flag galloped back down to them and reined in, calling, "The chief wants a word with you, General. That's Zeb Macahan with him."

"It figures. Did you get a look at the disposition of Satangkai's forces up there, Lieutenant?"

"I tried to, sir. They seem to be dug in all along that line of rocks ahead. No way for a frontal assault, if you ask me."

"I didn't ask you, mister. I don't need a shavetail to tell me not to commit suicide. Did the chief or Macahan say what they wanted to jaw about?"

"No sir. They just said they was willing to parley, if you were."

"Anybody want to bet a month's pay that damned Macahan isn't offering us surrender terms? Don't anybody answer. It was a dumb joke, and I could be right. MacAllister, you know the rascal best. Ride up and see what the hell they want!"

The captain nodded and took his mount up the slope on the double. He reined in near Satangkai and

Macahan and called out, "Morning, Zeb. The general sent me to escort you in."

Macahan shook his head and said, "We don't aim to give ourselves to him on a silver platter, seeing as he's sort of careless about his word on hidden sidearms, Mac. We'll meet with him here, at the halfway mark. He can bring you or any other single officer up for a powwow. If we see guns or sabers comin' with him, he can expect us to defend our lives as best we know how."

"Wait a minute, Zeb. You and the Indian, here, are armed to the teeth!"

"You're damned right we are! You see, Mac, *we* can be trusted! And we don't mind if you put it to the bastard just that way!"

"I'll tell him, but he won't like it, Zeb!"

"That's no great shucks. We ain't out to win no popularity contests. We're in a good dug-in position to pepper him back down the mountain, though. So he'll likely want to talk it over first!"

MacAllister rode back to the army lines and a few minutes later returned with an angry, scowling Brandy Jack.

The general snapped, "All right, let's get on with the terms of the surrender!"

Zeb laughed lightly and asked. "You aim to surrender to Satangkai here, General? I reckon he'll settle for you just riding out peaceable."

"God damn it, you know that's not what I meant. Tell your friend he's got no more chance than a snow ball in hell of holding off my men and I!"

"Can't do it. It'd be a big fib, General. I know you got a passel of men and some heavy guns, but we 'uns has the mountains and more'n one long-range buffalo rifle. What's the army payin' out in widow's pensions these days, General? You're fixing to purely put the War Department in the red. Mebbe we'd better talk it over some."

"There's nothing to talk about, Macahan. My terms are unconditional surrender, and by that I mean every

weapon and every pony in Sioux hands turned over to
me at once!"

Zeb knew what Satangkai's answer would be, but
he was trying to buy time, so he translated.

Satangkai laughed harshly. "Tell the man with the
red nose he can have our guns and ponies when the
last Dakota lays dead at his feet, if he is still alive!"

Zeb nodded and said, "He ain't for them terms
much, General. Says you'll likely have to kill him and
ever'body else in his Nation afore you get weapon or
pony one!"

"That can be arranged. He's got to know he hasn't
got a chance, Macahan. I know how the man feels, but
neither side has a choice. What in the hell's this parley
about if he doesn't aim to give in to me?"

"I'll tell you, General. We want it on record that the
Dakota offered not to fight you. I wanted to have it on
record how you negotiated once again with the Indians.
When the newspapers print the casualty lists of the
American troopers who died in your fool battle, I
reckon there may be questions asked about the why of
it all."

"They can print what they like and ask what they
like, Macahan! I don't buckle under to public opinion.
I don't give a good god damn what people think of me!"

"Yup, I figured as much. What else you aim for me
to translate for the chief, here?"

"Not a thing. Not a god damned thing! You knew
what I'd say before you asked for this parley, Macahan. Why are you wasting my time? Are you just
stalling, hoping for another night alive?"

Before Zeb could answer, another rider came loping
up the slope at a dead run, waving something. Satangkai
stiffened, and Stonecipher, not wanting another repeat
of what had gone wrong with their last meeting, bellowed, "Get back! MacAllister! Keep that fool away!"

MacAllister rode to intercept the intruder. Zeb muttered to Satangkai in Dakota, "It's all right, my brother.
I think I know the words he brings!"

After a short exchange with the other officer, Mac-

Allister came back alone with the paper he'd taken
from him, calling out as he rode, "Urgent dispatch,
General! Message rider just caught up with us!"

"Well, it can wait until I settle this Sioux's hash, can't
it?"

"I don't think so, sir. It's from General Sheridan
himself!"

"Phil Sheridan! What the hell does *he* want!"

"It's a coded battlefield priority, sir."

As the confused Stonecipher took the message, Zeb
turned to Satangkai and explained quickly, "General
Sheridan is the great chief who owes me a favor. He's
in charge of all Indian-fighting west of the Mississippi
now!"

Stonecipher said, "What's it say? I don't have my
codebook *or* my specs with me, god damn it!"

MacAllister took the dispatch back and read aloud,
with a sardonic glance at Zeb: "For General John
Stonecipher, Brevet Brigadier, Army of the United
States . . . You will cease immediately all offensive
against those Sioux under Chief Satangkai. Stop. You
will adopt and hold a defensive position on receipt this
order. Stop. You will inform scout Zebulon Macahan
his presence required at your field headquarters pend-
ing my arrival in person. Stop. Signed, Philip H.
Sheridan. General, Commanding U.S. Army of the
West."

Stonecipher closed his eyes, gritted his teeth, and
said, "Son . . . of . . . a . . . bitch! He even twitted me
about my reserve status!"

Then Stonecipher turned on Zeb and snapped,
"Your presence is required, huh? So that's why you've
been pulling all those stalling tactics on me!"

Zeb smiled amiably and said, "It's an old rule in law
and war, General. The side that buys time is never the
loser for it!"

"Don't lecture *me* on military strategy, you unwashed bastard! How in thunder did you manage that
political pressure over my head?"

"Oh, me and old Phil Sheridan goes back a ways,

sir. We mebbe owes each other a few favors left over from harder times."

"All right. My hands are tied, and I'm not a man given to idle bluster. You can see this message from my superior gives you safe conduct. Let's ride down and have a drink, though I'd sooner hang you, if it was left to me. That was a rotten thing you did to Coulee John."

"I'll stay with Satangkai and mebbe keep his young men cooled down till the general gits here. What was that about Coulee John? Something happen to the skunk?"

"You know damned well your Sioux friends lifted his hair!"

"You mean he's dead? Well, I'd be a liar to say I was all that sorry, but none of us know anything about it. Last I heard of old Coulee John, he was stealing your likker and smoking your cigars."

"Your braves sent him in to us scalped and mutilated. If you didn't order it, this Indian, here, must have!"

Zeb held a short conference in Dakota with Satangkai before he shook his head at Stonecipher and said, "The chief's as mixed up 'bout it as we-uns, General. He says none of his young men have counted coup on any white man's scalp of late."

"All right, I'll concede he might have lost control of his braves. I'm still holding him responsible, but one of his bucks may have snuck out to do Coulee John in on his own."

Zeb frowned and said, "That don't make sense neither, General. What's the point of scalpin' a man if you don't aim to tell nobody?"

"What's the point? How should I know, damn it! Scalping is an *Indian* custom! It doesn't matter much to Coulee John, right now, just why they scalped him!"

"Wouldn't make much point to most Indians, neither. Let's not git into the old argument about who started scalping who. Though the records show the Pilgrim's payin' for Algonquin scalps. *My* point is that the

Dakota and other plains tribes has it down to a formal ritual. They don't just rip the hair off a cuss to be ornery. They do is so's to show their folks back home they've licked an enemy fair and square. Some Cheyenne come home with cut-off fingers 'stead of scalps. It's always for the same reason. A brave who's killed an enemy rates an eagle feather with a vermillion tip. He ain't allowed to go out and just buy one at the general store. He has to show the trophy at a formal scalp-dance and sing a song about his victory before the elders allow he likely rates that feather. You see now, what's sort of funny about Coulee John's death?"

"It wasn't funny. It was ugly as hell. Before they scalped him they worked him over with knives."

"I'll accept that, General. But it couldn't have been one of the braves up yonder in them rocks. Not 'cause they loved Coulee John for his big blue eyes, but 'cause no Dakota's likely to kill and scalp a man unless he aims to brag on it some!"

The general shrugged and said, "What's done is done. We'll let Phil Sheridan worry about it. He worries a lot about Injuns. You've won this round, Macahan. I'm pulling back a ways and digging in until Sheridan arrives. You can tell your Sioux for me that there's an open invitation to the dance should any of them come looking for another white man's hair!"

Zeb nodded, and as the meeting broke up each side rode for its own lines. Zeb explained as much as he could to Satangkai as they headed back to the dug-in Indians. But Satangkai was puzzled by it all.

He asked Zeb, "What is the matter with the chief called Stonecipher? Is he afraid to fight us, now?"

"No. He's spoiling for battle. Another great chief who outranks him is coming. Stonecipher has been told to stand his ground until the other one gets here."

"I see. Then both of them will attack us together?"

"I don't think so. The greater chief is wise, and a friend of mine."

"He sounds like a weakling. If two great white chiefs, together, are afraid of us . . ."

"Hear me, Satangkai, the chief called Sheridan is no weakling. In the war between the blue sleeves and the men in gray he was a mighty warrior who counted coup in many battles. Once, alone, he turned the tide of battle by leading his retreating men back into the enemy's gunfire with his hat upraised on the tip of his sword. Since the great war between the white soldiers, he has fought many Indians, many, and he has won every time. He is ten times the leader Stonecipher is. If Sheridan should decide to fight you, the Dakota would be scattered as the leaves of summer fly before the winter's wolf-fanged winds!"

"Then why did you send for him? Do you wish to see your brothers die?"

"No. My old friend, Sheridan, is a terrible man of war, but a man who listens with his heart to both sides. His tongue is straight, and all men can believe his words. If he says there should be peace, there will be peace."

"But what if this mighty man decides for war? Does White Eagle know all that he carries in his heart?"

"No, but I know him to be a reasonable man, albeit stern. He carries strong medicine, for peace or for war."

"Then we must listen to his words."

"Yes, and my brother must tell his people to obey them."

Satangkai thought before he answered. "I will offer him peace. I will not be humiliated. I am a reasonable man, too, but I have taken all I mean to from the blue sleeves. I shall never give in on another single point. You will tell your Sheridan this when he comes?"

Zeb nodded and, in English, muttered, "Jesus, Macahan, I purely hope you know what you've just done hereabouts!"

"What do those words mean, White Eagle? Do you compose your death song in your own tongue?"

"That is close enough, my brother."

"I too have my death song ready for the final outcome of this business. Tell me, without fear, when the great chief comes, if he and I cannot agree to terms, which side will you be fighting on, White Eagle?"

"I don't know, Satangkai."

"You don't know or you are afraid to tell what is truly in your heart?"

"I have never been afraid to speak my heart to you, old friend. But your question is a hard one to answer."

"I see. Your heart is torn between your red brothers and your white ones. This is as it should be, with a man who has a good heart. I will always be your brother, White Eagle. If you should have to fight on the other side, let us hope we do not meet in the last great battle between our people!"

"My brother's words are wise. I too wish this thing!"

CHAPTER 63

The stalemate at the Pa Sapa didn't last long, for General Phil Sheridan was not a man who believed in dawdling. The poem "Sheridan's Ride" had been occasioned by his habits of moving light and moving sudden. Phil Sheridan would never hear the word *Blitzkrieg,* but he thoroughly approved of the notion.

Stonecipher was not the only lesser light of the army who was scared skinny of the ferocious Sheridan. The junior officers and men of the Second Cav had kept a sharp eye out for his visit, and as a scout on a distant rise signaled his approach with a heliograph, the regiment shaped up to receive him properly. Every weapon freshly cleaned. Boots and saddles spit-shined. Every bit of brass burnished pale gold with elbow grease and prayer. Phil Sheridan annoyed was a terrible thing to contemplate by friend or foe.

Each troop lined up snapped to attention as the knot of hard-riding officers from army headquarters loped into Stonecipher's camp. The brigadier and his own staff awaited their commander's pleasure at the far end of a formal inspection line as Sheridan rode in ahead of his staff.

The men he passed as if on review would remember the first sight of Fighting Phil as long as they lived. For he was a sight to remember.

General Sheridan was a living embodiment of what West Point was all about. Ramrod tall in the saddle, he seemed more a god of battle than a mortal born of woman. His face was carved from gun-limber oak, and his sideburns were hammered from tempered saber-steel. An unlit stump of Havana jutted from between teeth fierce enough to grace the jaws of a ravenous wolverine. Those men unlucky enough to catch the bayonet thrust of his smoldering eyes got an electric jolt they'd long remember. It was probably untrue that Sheridan could knock a second lieutenant off his horse with a dirty look. But nobody in the Second Cav was about to test the legend if they could possibly avoid it. The great general's uniform was neat and well tailored, but faded to gunmetal blue. It seemed in fact as if he moved in an ever-present haze of gun smoke, and one felt he sweated nitroglycerine. He was said to explode as easily.

Phil Sheridan reined in, sliding his mount the last few yards of the way as he stopped in front of Stonecipher and his staff. He snapped, "At ease, Jack. Dismiss your troops and let's get down to cases! Where the hell is Zeb Macahan?"

"He just rode in, sir," the junior general began as Sheridan's keen eyes spotted Macahan lounging on his pony in the rear of the group.

Sheridan barked, "God damn it, Zeb! Front and center on the double!"

The others parted as the Red Sea had for Moses, as Macahan rode forward and nodded. "Howdy, General."

"Humph! At least you haven't gotten any uglier, Zeb."

"Wish I could say the same for you, General."

As Sheridan laughed, Stonecipher complained, "General Sheridan, I have to protest this man going over my head!"

Sheridan whipped him silent with a blazing look and snapped, "I told you you were *at ease,* god damn it! Is that your headquarters tent just over there?"

"Yes, sir. It's all set up, waiting for you."

"Good. Come on, Zeb. Let's you and me get down off these fool hosses and jaw a spell! The rest of you gentlemen go pick some daisies or something. I'll send for you when I have some idea of what the hell you've stirred up here!"

As soon as they were alone, General Sheridan motioned Zeb to a camp chair facing his own and, after relighting his stogie, growled, "By God, you've stirred things up in Washington and that's a fact! What's this I hear about you riding with the Sioux?"

"Somebody had to ride with 'em, General. Too many of your soldier boys remember what you said about the only good Indian being a dead Indian."

"Damn it, Zeb. You know I said that fool thing in jest one time, as I was powwowing with an old Comanche devil who should'a been shot in his cradle board."

"I know. Too bad that reporter was there to hear you say it. You're going down in the history books as an Indian-hater, General."

"Yeah, and you figure to go down as another Simon Girty, siding with the Indians like this. What's this I hear about you taking the scalp of a fellow scout? Have you gone clean out of your head?"

"No, sir. I'd say Stonecipher's about as crazy as they come hereabouts. I thought I explained most of it in the wire I sent you."

"I read it. You'd better be better than close to right about the situation here! You know what it took for me to override a general in the field, Zeb? I had to get the Secretary of War out of a warm bed at four in the morning to explain why a wild man named Macahan was likely to know more about the Sioux than his favorite senior officers in this territory! I don't think he believed me, but I told him I owed said wild man a favor for the time he saved my scalp from the Comanche."

"Hell, Phil, I ain't holding you to no favors, but I didn't know who else to turn to. You're about the biggest hoorah I know, and it's gonna take us both to stave off a senseless bloody war out here."

"All wars are senseless and bloody. What's so special about this one?"

"It ain't necessary!"

"Few wars are. But we don't keep an army just to look pretty. The politicians are spoiling for a final solution to the Indian problem, and this might be as good a time as any to settle the Sioux once and for all!"

"Hitting Satangkai's bands won't settle doodly-shit, Phil! Red Cloud, Yellow Hand, Crazy Horse, and lots of the others is holding back, as they wait to see what's gonna happen here. They all know Satangkai got in this fix through bad faith on the white man's part. You go and wipe out Satangkai and you'll have yourself an Indian war worth remembering! Sitting Bull's been shaking his gourds and ranting at the northern lights, dream-singing. That old Medicine Man ain't just dreaming of a strong Dakota Confederacy, these days. He's sent out messages to the Black Foot, Shoshone, Arapaho, even Kiowa and Comanche!"

"Nonsense. Quanna Parker and the Comanche have signed a treaty with us, down in Texas."

"Yup, as did Red Cloud and the Dakota. It's Sitting Bull's contention that the white man's treaties don't mean all that much. He's been stirring up the tribes all over the west, telling 'em their only chance is to form one great all-Indian army! He says we've been whittlin' down each tribe one at a time, with a little fightin' and a heap of false promises. A lot of chiefs who used to be out to lift each other's hair is starting to listen to him, too. You gotta admit he makes a heap of sense, considering."

"Come on, Zeb. The tribes have never been able to combine against us. That's the secret of our strength!"

"You mean their weakness, don't you? They tell a story, down in Taos, of a time afore us Americans moved west of the Big Muddy. They tell a story of a time when the Southwest tribes, Pueblo, Zuni, Apache, Navajo, and sech, forgot their intertribal fussings and combined, jest once, agin the Spanish in the Sangre de Cristo country. You know what happened, then? They *whupped* 'em! They drove ever' Spaniard they didn't kill south of the Rio Grande and kept 'em there for a couple of generations! Sitting Bull likes to tell that story. He's been sayin', had them southwest tribes stuck together instead of falling out agin by the time the settlers come back for a second try—"

"All right, damn it. I know about the Great Pueblo Uprising. These northern tribes are another breed. They're not as organized as the semi-civilized Pueblos were."

"You call Apache semi-civilized? They had Apache, Navajo, Zuni, Taos, all sorts of natural-born enemies killin' white men side by side, Phil! The Algonquin-talkin' Cheyenne are riding with the Dakota right now. The Arapaho are another Algonquin-talkin' tribe. The Black Foot, or Sitsika, are another, and they've never needed much urging to take a white man's hair. The Iowas to the south are related to the Dakota and . . . Hell, you can add it up, Phil. You wipe out them Dakota up the slope over a white man's mistake and, yep, you'll git your war all right. It'll be one hell of a big one too!"

"You don't paint a pretty picture, Zeb."

"Never meant to. I got you out here to see if we can call it off. Aside from my Indian friends, I got kinfolks living west of the Big Muddy. Reckon I'll have to think on movin' 'em east about the time the

Union Pacific track git tore up and the transcontinental telegraph goes down!"

"All right, you've made your point. Do you feel this Satangkai's a reasonable man?"

"Knowed him as long as I've knowed you. He's not only reasonable but honorable."

"Good. Then let's step back and take a clear look at the overall picture. Not just the rights or wrongs of it. The killing of the Count of Kiev has pushed us to the edge of a break with Russia, and we don't have enough troops in Alaska to stand off determined Eskimos. The Russian diplomats are raising holy Ned. Our State Department's apologized itself blue in the face, but the Czar wants blood. The opposition newspapers are accusing the President of weakness. We've got to see that something resembling justice rises to the surface of this boiling pot out here!"

"Hell, Phil, the Count of Kiev got his damn justice! What would you have done iffen he'd slashed you half blind across the face under a flag of truce?"

"I'd have killed him. But what I would or would not have done is not the point, Zeb. Count Sergei was a nasty little brute, but his blow was meant as an insult, not a murder. But *he* was killed. As other white men have been since the balloon went up. The government can't close its eyes to acts of murder."

Zeb nodded and said, "Nobody's asking for anyone to close their eyes, Phil. Satangkai didn't kill the count. He hasn't killed anybody I know of. I agree about justice. So do the Indians. The man who caused the whole mess was Coulee John Brinkerhoff, and he's dead, killed by a person or persons unknowed. Don't that settle the matter?"

"Maybe I could see that if the count and his Russian doxie hadn't been kidnapped and held for ransom, Zeb. It's not just homicide, you see, it's homicide, abduction, and extortion. The Sioux attempted to blackmail the U.S. Government!"

"Attempted, hell, they done it. That money was in payment for the buffalo they was robbed of!"

"Damn it, Zeb, I want this kept in perspective! I'm only a general, not the Czar of All the Russias or even the President! At any cost, we have to satisfy both the Russian court and the American public that justice has been done. The honor of the army is at stake, too. We can't have people saying their tax dollars are being wasted on an army that can't keep foreign guests of our government from being kidnapped and murdered by the Sioux!"

"Why not? It happened, didn't it? It seems no matter how we beats around this bush you keep gittin' back to punishin' innocent Dakota for simply defendin' themselves. Is that what you call justice, Phil?"

"No. I call it politics. Listen, Zeb, I want to help you. I want to keep the blood and slaughter down as much as possible, but we've got to come to an agreement that will satisfy all concerned."

"What kind of agreement, Phil?"

General Sheridan, a man who could stare unflinching into a cannon's mouth, lowered his eyes, hating his job, as he said, "We both know, Zeb, that every military leader is responsible for the conduct of the men he leads. That's an issue we simply can't get around. We've hanged *white* Confederate officers for atrocities like Andersonville prison. There has to be a trial. A fair trial in open court for the world to see."

"I dunno. Satangkai's not likely to turn over the braves you're talking about, Phil."

"I'm not talking about faceless unknown Indians, Zeb. Satangkai himself will have to face the jury."

"Satangkai on trial? What the hell for? He's the victim, damn it!"

"I won't shave words with you, Zeb. I said I'd have done the same or more in his place. But I see no other way to avoid an all-out-war."

"But if their chief stands trial like a common criminal the Dakotas will feel disgraced!"

"I don't see why, but at least they'll still be able to

feel *something,* Zeb, and it's that or feeling less than nothing as their bodies rot among the rocks!"

Zeb started to rise. Sheridan snapped, "Hear me out before you go flying off in a rage, god damn it! I can't let Satangkai off, just like that, but I can use my influence to see that he gets off with a slap on the wrist."

"How hard a slap did you have in mind, Phil?"

"I dunno. Maybe two years in a military prison, with time off for good behavior and—"

"Two years in prison? For a free-born Indian?"

"Look, I can see he's given the freedom of the post, and after a year or so, when it's all blown over, maybe we can get him a pardon."

"Hell, Phil! You know any kind of prison sentence would be the same as death by hanging! Satangkai would pine away in less than six months!"

Now it was Sheridan's turn to show anger, and he did, roaring, "God damn it, Zeb Macahan! I'm offering a ninety percent concession here and I don't seem to be getting a nickel's worth of change back from you!"

"And I'm tellin' you, the public trial in a white man's court would demean Satangkai, and a prison term would kill him! Beyond all that, like I told you, you layin' a finger on an innocent Indian would stir up more'n the Dakota!"

"It can't be helped. It's the best offer I can make. You just go to Satangkai and repeat my terms. If he surrenders, his tribesmen will be left unmolested here in these Black Hills with the treaty still in force as before."

"Or until some crooked politician changes his mind?"

" 'Crooked politician' is a redundancy, Zeb. We eat every apple one bite at a time. I can't promise anything for next year, but I can pull Stonecipher and the Second Cav off their necks for now if Satangkai agrees to come in."

"Phil, there's got to be a better way."

"There isn't." said Sheridan flatly. Then, in a gentler tone, he added, "Listen, Zeb. I owe you my life.

I consider you a friend, and I hope you know I'll always be a friend of yours. So believe me when I say I'm doing my best. I can squash the business about Coulee John. People expect scouts to get scalped occasionally in the line of duty. I've already filed a false report saying the riding you've been up to with the Sioux was on my orders. Should anyone ever ask you, remember you've been acting as a spy for me."

"Never mind my hide, I can take care of my own, but Satangkai—"

"Will come in and surrender of his own accord or else."

"Or else what?"

"You know what, Zeb. The only possible alternative is an all-out war to the death. You know the way I *make* war, too, don't you?"

Zeb nodded morosely and said, "Yeah, hit 'em with ever' thing but the kitchen sink, then throw the sink!"

"I'm sorry, Zeb, but that's about the size of it. I'm not Stonecipher. I've fought Johnny Reb. I've fought Comanche, Apache, and, yes, I've fought your Sioux. So let's have no more tricks with buffalo and grass fires. I'm not going to mess with your friends, Zeb. By this time tomorrow Satangkai will be in my hands as a prisoner or dead up on the Pa Sapa with most of his tribe"

"You figure to lose some blue bellies, too, Phil."

"Those are the fortunes of war, Zeb. You know I'm not a man who bluffs. I don't get bluffed much, either."

"How do you figure on pryin' 'em outten them rocks, Phil?"

"I'm not going to tell you till I see which side you're fighting on at the end. Suffice to say, you know I can do it, don't you?"

"Yup, you likely can, if you've a mind to."

"All right, then let me tell you something else, Zeb. Satangkai is a general, too. Like me, he knows he'll be whipped in the end. Like me, he's responsible for the lives of his people. You give him my message, Zeb. He may surprise you."

"It's his one head or the lives of all of 'em, eh?"

"You know it, Zeb. A price has to be paid here, one way or the other."

Zeb's voice was bitter as he said, "Well, he sure knows the price-payin' on his side never seems to end!"

"No matter how you and I feel, Zeb, the final say is Satangkai's. He has to decide if the price I ask is a fair exchange for the lives of all his people. Tell him, and let him think about it overnight. If he comes in voluntarily, I'll make sure he receives full military honors."

Zeb got up with a disgusted expression and said, "I'll ask him iffen he wants to wear his fanciest war bonnet!"

"You do that, and . , . Zeb?"

"Yeah, Phil?"

"If his answer is no . . . will you be coming back to ride with us?"

"Don't you already know the answer to that, Phil?"

"I'm afraid I do. I was sort of hoping I was wrong."

CHAPTER 64

It was sunset when Zeb Macahan reached the stronghold of his Dakota friends once more.

He rode his pony to the lodge of Satangkai and dismounted, ducking inside to ask the chief's young wife, "Can you tell me where my brother is, Shewelah?"

The girl looked up from the infant nursing at her breast and sighed. "He has gone to the high places to talk to the spirit, Tunkanshe, who dwells among the rocks."

Zeb nodded, "I know the place, Shewelah. I shall seek him there."

But as he was about to leave, the girl cried out, "Wait, White Eagle, is it true you have been down among the blue sleeves again?"

"Yes, little sister. I have just returned with their words."

"What do they say? Are we to have the great battle everybody fears?"

"I don't know yet. I must speak first with your husband."

"White Eagle, I am frightened. The others say this is a good time to die, but I have lived only eighteen summers, and I have this child to think of."

"He will grow to be a fine straight man, if all goes well, little sister."

"I hope so. If I have to kill him, what is the best way, White Eagle?"

"Kill him?" Zeb frowned.

"Yes, when our men are all dead and the soldiers come to dishonor us. I must die, of course, but my child must not be left behind with no mother to nurse him. Some of our women say it hurts a baby less to strangle him with a thong. Others suggest hurling him from the cliffs to the hard rocks below. What do you think, White Eagle?"

"Hear me, Shewelah, there's no need to kill the children. The blue sleeves will not hurt them. The great chief who will lead the attack won't let them dishonor any women, either. This I know to be true."

"I wish I could believe my husband's white brother. But the blue sleeves must be very cruel—why do they hunt us down like coyotes if they are not cruel? What have any of us ever done to them?"

Zeb sighed and said, "That is one of the things I have to talk to Satangkai about!"

Then he left her, leaving her to work out the details of infanticide as best she could.

As he walked through the encampment, Zeb was aware of the anxious glances cast his way. The Dakota had resigned themselves to battle without hope. Zeb wished he had some way to encourage them, but he didn't. Phil Sheridan had once chopped the Army of Virginia to a battered gray mess U.S. Grant merely had to sweep together at Appomattox Courthouse at his own convenience. What chance did these people have against him with old trade rifles and buffalo bows?

As he rounded a tipi, Zeb encountered a resplendent figure in full war paint and a handsome war bonnet. The unfamiliar Indian carried a medicine shield with what looked like a very fresh scalp sewn to its painted rawhide surface. The haughty-looking Dakota thumped his chest and announced, "Hear me, I am Little Dog, and today I stand before the world as a man! Are you the one called White Eagle?"

"Yes. Is that a new scalp you count coup on? It looks like the hair of a white man!"

"It is, White Eagle! Little Dog is your brother now, though you do not know him. The man I took this hair from was your enemy, and the enemy of Satangkai!"

"I see. Then you're the brave who killed Coulee John Brinkerhoff!"

"That was the carrion crow's name. He came to me, seeking help in murdering you by treachery."

"I see that Little Dog is not a treacherous man."

"No. Not now. Hear me, once I did a bad thing. I was driven from among the people and lived as do the coyote and the vulture. My name was no longer spoken in the lodges of the Dakota."

"I see you have been restored to manhood, Little Dog, but why are you telling me all this?"

"Because I wish to thank you! It is because of what I did for you that Satangkai praised me and restored my honor. When I told him how this man whose scalp you see intended to murder his white brother and how I saw a chance to help my people, Satangkai said I had done well. Hear me! Satangkai said I was once more Dakota!"

"My heart sings for you, Little Dog. I too say you are a Dakota."

"Thank you. When we fight the blue sleeves tomorrow, do you think we'll all be killed?"

"I hope not. My brother, Little Dog, seems not too worried about it. Does he carry good medicine into battle?"

Little Dog was cheerful as a boy with a new pony as he shook his head and said, "No. I have taken the oath of a Contrary. When I ride against the blue sleeves, I must sit my pony backwards. I must strike with my lance held blunt end first and the spear against my breast. I shall almost certainly be killed in the first charge."

"It seems a high price to pay for counting coup. Is my brother tired of living?"

"No, but hear me, I am not what you would call a strong man. My heart is good. I try to obey the laws of the Real People. But when I have been drinking firewater and a pretty squaw walks by . . ."

"I understand."

"Yes. Little Dog has lived the life of an outcast. He would die the death of a warrior, and I think tomorrow is a good day to die! Tell me, is the white chief a great warrior?"

"He is said to be the best they have."

"Heya, my heart overflows! I shall ride to meet Old Woman with a happy death-song on my lips, for, next to a brave friend, there is nothing like a brave enemy!"

Zeb wished his new friend well and excused himself to look for Satangkai.

As he continued through the encampment, he saw other braves less obviously eager to die while they were ahead in the game of honor, but no less determined to sell their lives dearly. He cursed himself again for having chanced the intervention of his old friend, Sheridan. Had Stonecipher still been in command, his Indian friends might have had at least a slim chance. If he knew Phil Sheridan, right about now some mountain artillery would be moving around to work behind their position on the Pa Sapa. Along with fiendishly clever infantry tactics, Sheridan was noted for his skill in placing his big guns for maximum effect.

Zeb left the encampment and made his way up a goat path to where Satangkai stood against the twilight on a great rock overlooking a sickening drop. The chief's arms were raised as he faced the north, where the aurora borealis flickered in the skies of winter on occasion as a message from Old Woman, goddess of death and war.

Zeb paused respectfully as Satangkai called out to the northern lights, unseen this early in the Indian summer. The chief cried, "Hear me, Old Woman! For though I do not see the rainbow flames of your tipi fire, I know you must be listening to my words! I have called on He-Who-Dwells-Among-the-Rocks, but Tunkanshe does not answer. I have asked the Great Spirit for a vision, but Wakan Tonka turns his back on me this night! I beg of you, Old Woman, make me see how I can save my people.

"The blue sleeves are all around us, for my young men have seen them as they move among the rocks like great blue lizards. There are many of them, many, and my nation is so small! Crazy Horse has not answered my messages. Red Cloud is old, and undecided about another war with the blue sleeves. Yellow Hand is hiding somewhere in the Shining Mountains. Those chiefs who have come in to join me are brave, but, like me, their bands are small bands!

"And now the greatest of the white chief comes. He has many guns, and his thoughts are red thoughts. My brother, White Eagle, goes to talk with him, but Buffalo-Bull-Who-Waits has recorded his black words. The white chief says the only good Indian is a dead Indian, and we are Indians! Tell me what to do! Send me a sign! Any sign!"

Then, slowly, Satangkai's arms lowered as he finally added, with a bitter nod, "So be it. Even the gods have turned their backs on me. But doubtless we shall soon meet face to face, Old Woman, for I feel I'll soon be coming to live with you in the lodge of death!"

He turned from the unresponsive northern sky and saw Zeb standing there. A look of hope crossed Satangkai's features, to slowly fade as he read the expression on Zeb's face.

"Heya!" He nodded. "You have spoken to the great white chief for us."

"I have spoken, Satangkai. His words were black. I bear them to you with a heavy heart."

Haltingly, trying to put as rosy an aspect on the message of doom as he could, Zeb explained the terms offered by Phil Sheridan.

When he'd finished, Satangkai asked, "How can they charge me with the death of that foolish man who slapped me? My young man killed him. I did not."

"I know. I asked them if they would let the man who did the killing stand trial for it. They said you were his chief."

"I understand. It would not be just to order another to his death. It is my life they want, in any case."

"The charge is only kidnapping and second-degree murder."

"Drives-His-Horses captured that man and his woman. But, again, I see it is me they want. Tell me, what does this thing, second degree, mean?"

"It means nobody has to hang for it. They say the killing of the one called Sergei was wrong, but they believed me when I explained it was not planned in advance."

"But it must be punished?"

"Yes. That is what they say."

"I understand. It is as I've always known. They seek the death of me and all my people."

Zeb shook his head and insisted, "Hear me. Just now you asked for advice from Old Woman. She did not answer. Will you listen to the words of a friend?"

"Of course. Tell me, White Eagle, how are we to beat so many blue sleeves?"

"We can't. There are many of them, many, and they have big guns."

"Then we shall die together as men, if my brother means to fight at my side in the last great battle!"

"There doesn't have to be a battle. At the trial, we may make them understand it was not Satangkai's fault that all those bad things happened. The trial will be open to the men who write for the newpapers. The words of my brother Satangkai will be heard across the land in the lodges of the white as well as red!"

"I do not believe this. They are clever. Always when they say one thing they trick us by meaning another. I am the heart of my people, and they only mean to cut it out with another white man's trick!"

"It is true you are your people's heart. But neither heart nor body has to die."

"How can this be possible? Listen to their words, White Eagle! They say, We give you this choice. We will attack and kill your body if you do not deliver your heart into our hands! They say to trust them to give the heart a fair trial, but how can such men be trusted? Once they hold the heart in their hands, they can simply crush it, and the body without its heart will fall dead without the risk to them of battle."

Zeb sighed regretfully and said, "Hear me, Satangkai. You may be right. It may be that the heart must die, but it may be that this time my friend the great white chief will be just. Before you answer, consider this. If you decide for war, heart and body die together in any case. On the other hand, as long as the body lives, the Dakota remain with hope. Their heart may be returned to them with justice done."

"Ah, but if it isn't?"

"The body may die. Again, it may find a new heart. Are there no other men among the Dakota? Does Satangkai so scorn his kind he thinks they would be helpless babes without him?"

The chief frowned, and for a moment Zeb though he'd pushed his old friend too far. Then the Indian nodded and said, "Drives-His-Horses is brave. Old Medicine Mark is wise. My brother, White Eagle, makes me feel ashamed. I see I have been thinking like an older wife who fears a younger and prettier one may take her place in her husband's heart."

"Will my brother then consider the offer of the great white chief?"

Satangkai nodded and said, "I have thought."

Then he straightened to his full height, proudly, and began to almost chant: "Hear me! My sun has set! My day is done! Before I lay down to rise no more from the Long Sleep, I would speak!

"Heya-heyo-ha-ya-hah! *Hear* me! Wankan Tonka made us long ago and gave us this great world to live in! He gave us buffalo, antelope, deer, and all good things to eat. The hunting grounds he gave us reached from the Great Lakes of Minni-Tonka to the Shining Mountains, with these Black Hills at the center of his universe! We roamed free as the four winds and heard no man's commands! We fought our enemies and feasted our friends with fat cow and good tobacco in the friendly sacred calumet!

"Our braves drove away all who would contest our hunting grounds! They captured horses and many women from our foes! Our children were many and fat! Our herds were too large to count!

"Our old men talked with the gods and made good medicine for war and hunting. Our young men made war and hunted and made love to the maidens, playing love songs on their nose flutes that were sweeter than the songs of birds!

"Where our tipi was set up was where we dwelled until we felt like moving on. No one said, 'Beyond this line is my land and you must keep off it,' for how can anyone own land in a sensible world?

"Then the white man came to our hunting grounds, a stranger. We took him into our lodges. We fed him fat cow and smoked with him. Sometimes as a trader, sometimes as a student of our ways, he dwelled among us in peace, for at first we thought his heart was made, as ours, from the same clay.

"Then others came. They brought us some good things and many bad. For many furs they sold us the iron sticks that shoot. They brought the firewater that makes men do weak and foolish things. With trinkets and useless toys they bought more women. Sometimes they took women pledged to one of our young men, and when the young men objected they knocked them down with their fists or even shot them!

"Listen to my words! When I was young a white man wronged my brother. I said, 'This white man is not our friend,' and so we killed him. We tried to drive them back, to hold on to the world Wakan Tonka gave us. But they were too many. Their numbers were as the blades of grass! They drove away our buffalo and shot our best young men!

"They took away our hunting grounds and surrounded us with fences. Their soldiers camped outside to shoot us if we wished to ride out after game or to hunt our enemies, the Crow.

"They have destroyed our old campgrounds and wiped our trail markers from the prairies. Where once we rode against the Crow, the Iron Horse thunders by, frightening our horses!

"Listen to my words! We fought them! We fought them under Red Wing and Little Crow. Under Red Cloud, for a time, we *beat* them! But always in the end we have been driven ever farther back. Now we are trapped with our backs to the last walls of our last stronghold.

"Now they come to say we have not given them enough. They say we must force our children to forsake the ways of their fathers. They say we must lay down our arms and live as white men. *Poor* white men!

"I have sought a sign, but even the gods have forsaken us! When I turn to the east, I see no dawn. When I turn to the west, the night hides all. The south is filled with white men who tear open our mother, the earth, with great iron claws. To my north stands only the cold dark lodge of Old Woman, who waits for all men under the northern lights. But hear me! Hear me, White Eagle! Hear me, any gods who still may listen! I am Satangkai! I am Dakota! I am not afraid!"

Then he turned wearily back to Zeb and added softly, "I have spoken."

"I have listened, with a heavy heart. What does my brother mean to do?"

"You will know soon enough, White Eagle."

"Are you going to fight the soldiers in blue sleeves?"

"No. That would mean the end of my people."

"Then does Satangkai intend to come in with me to stand trial?"

"No. That would be just as foolish. Leave me for a time, my brother. I would like to be alone for . . . Wait! Before you go, there is one more thing to be said."

"I listen, Satangkai."

The Indian walked over to the tall white man and put his hands on Zeb's shoulders. "You shall always be my brother and my friend, White Eagle. This can never change!"

Zeb swallowed and agreed. "No. It will never change. We shall always be blood brothers."

"Tell me, brother, when a white man dies, does he go to the lodge of Old Woman, or some place else?"

"I don't know. If I'm going anywhere, later on, I'd just as soon it was to the lodge of Old Woman as any other place I've heard about."

"Good. Then if we meet in the life that may come after this one, we shall roam the clouds together, hunting spirit buffalo and eating fat cow among the stars of the northern sky."

"I hope so, Satangkai. It sounds like Shining Times."

"Go now. I have many things to think about before

the sun comes up again. Are you sure the white chief gives until tomorrow for his answer?"

"Yes. Will my brother think about his offer?"

"I have thought. You will have your answer with the dawn."

Zeb Macahan went back to the encampment and hunkered down against his saddle, lying by the council fire. He knew he'd be welcome in many a lodge, but he knew he'd never get a wink of sleep this last night before Phil Sheridan's ominous deadline, and in any case the braves would likely want a private time with their womenfolk.

After a time he saw Satangkai going into his own lodge. It wasn't that all-fired hard to figure why. Shewelah was a pretty little thing, and he likely knew he wouldn't be seeing her again for a spell.

Inside the tipi, the baby was asleep. Shewelah kneeled by the small chip fire, stirring a pot of pemmican stew; her face was illuminated softly by the little flickers above the glowing coals. Satangkai sat cross-legged on a buffalo robe, staring soberly at his young wife. It seemed as if she'd never looked lovelier, and Satangkai tried to etch her beauty firmly in his mind's eye, as if to make it impossible to forget her, though he knew he could not, for as long as he lived.

The Dakota girl asked softly, "Does my husband have hunger?"

Satangkai shook his head and said, "No. My heart is brave, but my belly is filled with feathers as I think of the coming dawn."

He explained the white chief's plans to her, for even though she was young, and a woman, Satangkai loved her very much and wanted her to understand. When he had finished, Shewelah sighed and asked, "Have you decided to go with White Eagle to the blue sleeves' camp?"

"I have decided what I must do. In my vanity, for a time I thought I was our people's heart, but one great spirit-heart beats for us all. I am only a voice

There will be others as wise and brave as I to lead."

"This trial they speak of. Do you think this time they mean to treat one of our kind with justice?"

"Have they ever? White Eagle's heart is good, and he says this new leader is his friend. But one must be born with red skin to really know the white man."

"But what else can my husband do? If he leads his young men into battle against all those blue sleeves, we shall all die!"

"I know. It would be throwing away the lives of my people. I think many of the blue sleeves would enjoy that, for it would not be a good fight and they would count many coups on our bodies in the end."

"But you say you can't get a fair hearing in the white man's court. Do you mean to give yourself up to them anyway?"

"Yes. White Eagle says they won't go without me. In the morning he shall take me down to the new great chief, and maybe, for a little while, they will leave the rest of you alone. Our son sleeps quietly. Behold! He is smiling in his sleep! I hope he is dreaming of fat cow!"

"Would you like to hold him for a time, my husband? He is healthy and strong. His back grows straight. Someday he will be a warrior, like his father."

"Don't disturb him, Shewelah. Let him sleep. Let all our young ones sleep in peace this night. Hear me, in the years to come you must see he learns the ways of our people. I don't want him drinking firewater or skulking about the trading posts, begging trinkets off the white men."

"My husband's words are strange. Did not White Eagle say they meant to keep you a captive no more than two years, maybe less?"

"That is what they promised. If one could believe the promise of any of them but White Eagle, and this time I think they lie to him, too. They know his heart is with ours. He has done everything in his power to help us, but even White Eagle has a limit to his strength and bravery. I looked into his heart through his eyes when we spoke up on the rock. His eyes were filled with fear for me. He knows too well the treachery of his kind."

"I shall follow you to this prison place. Your son and I shall camp outside until they send you back to us."

He sighed, reached out a hand to stroke her hair, and said, "No. Your place is here, with our people. I have no may of knowing if we'll ever meet again. Some say one thing. Some say another. We shall have to wait and see what Wakan Tonka may decide for us, in the future."

"Do you mean we may never see you again?"

"I mean I do not know. The future, like the past, is in the hands of Wakan Tonka. Or perhaps the Great Spirit the white men call the Jesus ghost. Sometimes I wonder about such things. The white men have such strong medicine, their gods must be very strong."

"Be careful! Wakan Tonka may hear you! The old men say he is everywhere!"

"Is he, really? Sometimes I think he's gone away. If he was watching, and as strong as the old men say, why has he forsaken us to the mercy of our enemies? I have many such questions to ask the spirits when I go to join them."

"My husband's words disturb me. They are the words of one who has little hope. Come, take pleasure with my body and let me tire you enough with love to sleep until the dawn."

"I would like that, but there is no time. I must make my medicine and prepare myself for the dawn, when White Eagle shall take me to his white brothers. Will you hand me my medicine bag? It's behind you, by that basket."

The girl complied, and Satangkai opened the parfleche pouch, taking out a stick of vermillion and beginning to paint his face. He drew three red streaks down each cheek, muttering, "These marks shall show I am crying blood."

He painted a blue Maltese cross on his chest, above the scars of his sun-dance initiation ritual, and said, "This mark is to show my heart is scattered to the four winds. I shall make no coup counts for my many victories. Our victories are children's games to the blue sleeves."

As he decorated his body he began a low chant, and Shewelah's eyes widened in horror. "My husband sings his death song!"

"I know. Let me finish. For I composed my death song before I went on my first raid against the Crow, and it seems such a waste to die with it unsung. It is good medicine, and heaps shame upon one's enemies if a dying warrior gets the chance to sing his death song before they kill him."

"But why do you prepare yourself for the Old Woman so soon? Surely at the worst they don't intend to kill you before they hold your trial."

"Heya, my poor little girl! Did you really think I intended to let them humiliate me with their mockery? There shall be no trial!"

"But you said you were riding into their camp in the morning with your friend, White Eagle!"

"I said I was going to let him take me there."

Satangkai took a sharp dagger from his medicine bag and held it out to her. "You must help me, Shewelah. A warrior cannot die by his own hand with honor."

"Oh no!" Her eyes were riveted on the gleaming steel in the red glow of the fire.

"You must, Shewelah. As your husband, I command and you must obey. This is the law of our people. Are we not Dakota?"

"Please, Satangkai! Don't make me do this terrible thing! There must be another way to save your honor!"

"There is none. I shall not be mocked and punished like a thief by the white men. Our people shall remember me as I was, a warrior! They shall hold their heads up proudly as they scorn the white man's wicked lies for what they are! Heya, even our enemies will respect us. There will be no warriors prouder than Dakota!"

"Let us wait a time together, then. Let my husband hold me in his arms until this night has slipped through our mortal fingers!"

Under his paint, Satangkai's smile was tender as his young wife crawled over to him and put her arms around him, biting her lip in an attempt not to be unseemly.

Satangkai enfolded her chastely, for the dead do not make carnal love. As she fought not to cry, he murmured, "We shall let our hearts beat as one until the dawn. And then my wife must be brave. Until then, we shall talk. We shall talk of how much I have loved you, and of the son you bore me. We shall talk and perhaps dream of times to come, when our son is a man and maybe people, red and white, have learned not to hate, but to smile on one another as brothers under Wakan Tonka or the Jesus ghost, who may be one and the same in the end. Yes, we shall have a last good talk, and my little wife shall remember this as a shining night to the son who shall never know my face!"

"Satangkai, my husband, I don't think I'll be able to do it."

"Hear me, you are a Dakota! When the time comes, you will remember this. On that I have spoken. Let us now speak of happier things."

CHAPTER 65

Zeb Macahan hadn't expected to sleep, but he'd dozed off, sitting propped against his saddle, in the last few cold hours of the mountain night. The first pink-pearl streaks of dawn painted the eastern rim of the world as he awoke, stiffly, to see young Shewelah standing before him. She'd been waiting for him to open his eyes. In the dawn light, her face seemed carved from some ruddy shade of granite.

Zeb rubbed the sleep out of his eyes and smiled up at her, saying, "Good morning, little sister. Is your husband ready?"

"He is ready. He cannot speak to you. He told me to give you these things and to say he is ready to go with you now." Zeb sat up as she handed him a medicine bundle. "The bear claws were taken by him single-handed, naked, with one knife, against a grizzly. The raven's wing is to fan back the Old Woman, should there be a time you do not wish to go with her. This pebble is said to come from the lodge of Tunkanshe. He-Who-Lives-Among-the-Rocks will hide you should you ever call upon him with this talisman."

Zeb got to his feet as he accepted the gifts with a nod of thanks and said, "We'd better be going, Shewelah."

"I know. I shall take you to my husband now. He has been waiting for you since first light."

CHAPTER 66

Phil Sheridan was an early riser, too. Down on the lower flanks of the Pa Sapa he was overseeing the emplacement of a field gun in a wash as Stonecipher, polishing the apple, joined him with a sleepy yawn.

Stonecipher said, "I see, General. There's a certain hazard having the big guns in this close, but from here you'll be able to lob plunging fire into them, won't you?"

"That was my intention, Jack. If I know Macahan, he's told the Sioux to dig in. Explosive shells coming straight down out of the blue make one hell of a mess when they land in a dugout!"

"Don't you think Macahan will be able to talk Satangkai into coming in this morning, sir?"

"I hope so, Jack, but I don't win battles on hope. I plan for the worst thing that can go wrong, and if it doesn't, I just grin like a shit-eating dog! Trooper! Move those trails a little to the left. I want full elevation on that howitzer!"

Both senior officers turned to the sound of hoofbeats as Captain MacAllister joined them, calling out, "Macahan's coming in, sir."

"Thank God!" said Sheridan. "Order the men to fall out in a full dress line of revue. Let's give the poor Indian full military honors!"

"I've already given the order, sir."

"Good. We'll wait for them in the command tent."

As they went back to the tent, Sheridan asked, "Is it just the two of them, MacAllister?"

"No, sir. Hard to make out the details. But it seems Satangkai rates an honor guard. Zeb's riding at the head of a whole Sioux parade. Looks like an honor guard, on foot."

"All right, watch out for trickery, but have the men offer full honors as they pass."

He and Stonecipher went into the open-fly tent and sat behind the map table as MacAllister arranged the proper formalities of the surrender.

As Macahan passed between the end of the long double line of troopers at attention, making his way toward them slowly, Sheridan frowned and said, "I see Zeb. I see another Indian leading a painted pony. Everyone else seems to be on foot. Where's Satangkai?"

Stonecipher suggested, "Walking in as penance, sir? The old ashes-on-the-head routine?"

"Maybe. Never knew an Indian to go in for that, though." The general picked up a pair of field glasses and squinted through them. Then he muttered, "Oh, Jesus! I might have known!"

Zeb Macahan was walking his pony in ahead of a bier carried on the shoulders of six solemn warriors. Satangkai lay upon it, dead, in full regalia—his dignity beyond the reach now of any enemy.

As he reached the U.S. Army lines, Zeb reined in and held up a hand to halt the procession. He dismounted and returned to the pallbearers as they lowered their dead chief to waist level. The giant Macahan bent to take the lifeless Indian in his arms. Then he turned back once more to face the tent down the long corridor of troopers at attention and grimly walked between them.

A white-faced MacAllister called out, "Preeeeesent arms!" and a double line of bayonetted carbines snapped as one against the morning sky. As Zeb passed, ignoring him, MacAllister whipped his own saber out and touched the hilt to his chin, the shining steel blade saluting the dead chief as it glistened in the sun.

It seemed to take forever, and both generals had trouble with their breathing by the time Zeb passed between the last two troopers. As, behind him, Mac-Allister yelled, "Orderrrr harms!" and six hundred butts slammed as one to the earth, Zeb stepped into the tent and lowered the dead Indian to the chart table.

For a long moment nobody said anything.

Then Sheridan sighed. "Christ, I'm sorry, Zeb. God rest this poor man's noble soul!"

Zeb said, "You said if he came in the war was over, right?"

"Yes, Zeb. As far as I'm concerned, the matter ends right here and now."

"I only wish I could believe that, General. When will you be pulling back?"

"Right after we bury him with full military honors, Zeb. You have my word on that."

Zeb Macahan's voice dripped venom as he stared at the nervous Stonecipher and said, "Your word is likely good enough, Phil, but there's others. There'll always be others. I hear that piss-ant, Custer, just took over as head of the Seventh Cav."

"You know I'll try to keep a leash on him, Zeb."

"Yup, I know you'll *try*."

As he turned away, Stonecipher asked, "Aren't you staying for the funeral, Macahan?"

Zeb said, "Not hardly. I got chores to do as mean somethin'. Got kinfolk expectin' my help with the harvest. You reckon you can keep from havin' yourself another Indian war afore the frost is on the pumpkins, General?"

He didn't wait for an answer. He walked back to where he'd left his pony, nodded to the waiting Indians that it was over, for now, and mounted up.

As he rode over a distant rise, the soft sad sound of taps was carried to him by the gentle breeze. With a last heartsick backward glance at the brooding peak of the Black Hills, Zeb Macahan headed for home, his thoughts on the once proud free people for whom he and his blood brother, Satangkai, had done all they could, for now.

The MS READ-a-thon needs young readers!

Boys and girls between 6 and 14 can join the MS READ-a-thon and help find a cure for Multiple Sclerosis by reading books. And they get two rewards — the enjoyment of reading, and the great feeling that comes from helping others.

Parents and educators: For complete information call your local MS chapter, or call toll-free (800) 243-6000. Or mail the coupon below.

Kids can help, too!